Kay Stephens was born and brought up in Yorkshire. She spent the first seven years of her working life as a librarian, and since then has written several short stories and novels, including *West Riding* and *North Riding*, both set in the Yorkshire she knows so well.

Also by Kay Stephens

West Riding
North Riding

Pennine Vintage

Kay Stephens

HEADLINE

First published in 1991
by Random Century Group

First published in paperback in 1992
by HEADLINE BOOK PUBLISHING PLC

10 9 8 7 6 5 4 3 2 1

ISBN 0 7472 3697 6

Printed and bound in Great Britain by
Collins Manufacturing, Glasgow

HEADLINE BOOK PUBLISHING PLC
Headline House
79 Great Titchfield Street
London W1P 7FN

Bibliography

The author wishes to acknowledge that, among many books, the following have been particularly useful for researching and checking the background of PENNINE VINTAGE: *Wellington, the Years of the Sword* by Elizabeth Longford; *Sherry and the Sherry Bodegas* by Jan Read; *The Story of Port* by Sarah Bradford; and *The Factory House at Oporto* by John Delaforce.

The news which changed the entire future of the Bright family came as suddenly as the storm that had appeared, darkening the summer morning. The rain had begun sharply while they jolted across the bridge over the River Hebden. Isobel watched the coin-sized spots increasing, spattering into the dust of the turnpike road as their wagon trundled past the tithe-barn in the Calder Valley.

When her brother William steered their horses round the next curve of the hillside wind-borne hailstones smacked into their faces, making him exclaim, 'By heck – we're in for it today!'

'Bloomin' June.' Henry hauled his collar about his throat in a fruitless effort to check the trickle of icy drops.

Behind her brothers, drawing back against the cloth pieces inside the covered wagon, Isobel giggled. 'Was that lightning just now? I hope it's going to thunder.'

At twelve years old everything was an adventure, especially when she was going with Will and Henry to Halifax Piece Hall. Completed in 1779, the year after she was born, this market place for local cloth was like a glowing, stone palace to Isobel. Its triple tier of over three hundred separate rooms, built around an open courtyard and colonnaded, became in her imagination a setting for banquets and for balls, for visits from foreign monarchs.

Briefly, she coughed, tried to hold her breath against another paroxysm.

''Ere, take hold, will you.' William thrust the reins at his brother as they rattled past The Dusty Miller, its inn-sign creaking in the wind. 'I'd best get back yonder, see our Isobel's keeping dry.'

See that *you* are, more like, thought Henry. But he'd say nowt. He wasn't that bothered. Once, he'd have resented

1

this appalling weather turning a hectic day – spent visiting Halifax to sell their cloth – into an exasperating struggle. Now, though, knowing there'd not be that many more journeys of a similar nature, he could will himself to endure without overmuch complaining.

He had his plans – carefully cherished against the time early next February when he would be of age. He'd be away from Yorkshire then for much of the year, would live in a climate healthier than the one that gave half his family this persistent cough. Inwardly smiling, he glanced sideways as the road took them near the Calder which was swift-moving with water that had gushed, at intervals over several days, down wooded slopes and fields. Its surface now was darted by millions of pelting hailstones. By, but it was cold! And yet there'd been a shepherd's sunset last night, blazing its promise of fine weather over the sky beyond Blackshaw Head. Would any-body, anywhere but here in the West Riding, credit that they were into June? Aye – well, that wouldn't trouble him another summer. He'd be under blue skies beside the Douro River, or near its estuary where port was processed and shipped . . .

'I see Father's let somebody lumber us wi' getting rid of more of them poor pieces,' William called. 'Same as the last lot that were turned out near t'border with Lancashire.'

Henry snorted. 'Funny how he manages to get stuff like that on to t'wagon, isn't it? And neither of us there to help.'

'Aye – and rest of time isn't up to any heavy lifting.'

Between them, William and Henry Bright conducted their father's business, collecting finished pieces of cloth from the weavers' cottages in bleak outlying settlements bordered by Haworth, their own Heptonstall, and Cragg Vale on the far side of the valley. Since Amos B.ght had given in to the gout they'd assumed responsibility for selling the material as well, but Henry had found that he'd no desire to spend his life as a cloth merchant.

'He'll put himself out of work, if he doesn't mind what he's doing,' William stated, from inside the dry wagon. 'He only needs to slip in a few more low grade pieces like this to suit his cronies and he'll have lost Brights' reputation. And good clothiers aren't that easily established.'

'That's right,' Henry agreed. Amos was too readily influenced by his drinking friends. 'Happen it's time you had a word with him again, about handing over to you afore he runs the business down.'

'Nay, I'll not do that.'

Isobel felt panic quicken her heartbeat. She couldn't bear anything to change. 'What will Father do all day, if you take over?'

Same as now, try to look busy, to appear that he carries us lot and the business, an' all, thought Henry. He said nothing.

His brother's anouncement began while Henry was trying to hold the horses on the road as their hooves slithered on a surface treacherous with rain and the unseasonal hailstones. Even if he hadn't been so occupied, he'd still have found it a potent shock.

'You needn't worry, Isobel,' he heard William assure her, but loudly so that the words wouldn't fall snort of their real target. 'Father's not going to be handing over to me. I've got a new position waiting for me.'

You've kept that quiet, thought Henry, half admiring William's containment, then bided his time until he was told more detail.

'Is it in Halifax Piece Hall?' Isobel asked breathlessly. She had noticed how both her brothers had grown well respected there.

'It's a lot further afield than that, lass. I'm off to Portugal.'

Henry swallowed at the news, freed a hand to drag it across his eyes and clear off some of the rain. Not that it helped him to see anything clearly. Portugal! That was to be *his* territory . . . 'What are you intending to do there?' he asked, his voice strained because all the muscles in his throat and neck were taut.

William laughed. 'Is there anything else there? Ship port, of course.'

'Have the Fortescues offered you the job?' He was compelled to ask, even though he sensed that he knew the answer. The Fortescue cousins were old friends, the people who'd fired *him* with the longing to join their port shipping

3

company, as soon as he came of age. They'd as good as promised him work.

'In a manner of speaking, aye. They need somebody willing to learn the trade, someone who'll not shirk responsibility.'

Henry swallowed, set his lips in a grim line. His grip on the reins tightened. The horses set up a swifter pace. He couldn't feel sorry when he suddenly heard Isobel's laugh as his brother lurched sideways when they hurtled round another bend.

William would be laughing as well, if privately, on account of having scored over him. Will had known his younger brother cherished the ambition of working with the Fortescues. Even of one day taking charge of their company – weren't both cousins in their sixties now, and neither with any offspring . . .

'Didn't they tell you *I* intended to work with them?'

'You're not old enough yet, lad, are you? There's no chance you'll be free to pick and choose yet awhile.'

'It's only a matter of months now,' Henry protested.

'Happen they'll take on both of us.'

And happen they won't! He'd spent enough time listening to Matthew and Luke Fortescue to understand that they retained a highly efficient Portuguese gentleman, and were only seeking one Englishman to assist out there. It should have been him! For long enough now he'd counted the months towards his next birthday. And even if the Fortescues should think to take him as well as his brother, he'd turn that idea down. William and he didn't get along badly; but nor did they work well together.

As Henry saw it, William had more than a share of their father in him. He relished dodging an unpleasant job, and never missed an opportunity that was to his own benefit. Now, certain that William had deliberately forestalled him, there'd be no tolerating the situation. Forgiving would be difficult; forgetting impossible.

'I'll take over t' reins again, give you a break,' he heard William offer. The downpour had ceased as abruptly as it had begun.

'There's no need,' Henry answered firmly. He was darned if he'd have his brother taking charge, just when the sun was appearing through a break in the clouds over the distant Sowerby hillside.

The animals between the shafts were steaming before long, and his own clothing as well, also the road itself, together with piles of muck dropped by other horses heading the same way.

Some while later, driving down the hill into Halifax, the buildings of millstone grit glowed golden, warm and welcoming. As they neared the magnificent Piece Hall, Isobel was hugging herself, but no longer with undiluted delight. Her brothers had spoiled it all. Henry by turning so quiet with his face so stern that he alarmed her, William by shattering everything that was familiar and by gloating.

The ungainly wagon had lumbered down to the Piece Hall itself. Gazing about her to all sides of the square and its rows and rows of rooms where cloth was traded, Isobel felt better. She wouldn't let it matter who looked after the family clothier's business, she'd still come here, nobody would stop her, one day she'd convince Father of her capability. She saw that William and Henry were busy already, greeting men who'd been dealing with the Bright family for years, showing samples of the cloth they carried, discussing prices.

She'd been told to be good, to mind she didn't lose herself. As if she could – hadn't she explored every foot of these galleries, run up and down the steps here since she was barely able to toddle? She would do so again today, climb right to the top storey for a splendid view of all the merchants and of the amazing assortment of coloured cloths being bought and sold here. She would let all the sounds envelope her: the voices of traders and their occasional laughter, the neighing and restless clomping of horses.

And first she would see the horses. She had saved them some carrots. They were rather squishy now, tied in her kerchief. She'd only managed to collect carrots that had been cooked, Mrs Robinson had been kneading dough and

5

watching her when she slipped into the kitchen. Isobel loved the patient packhorses best, hated to see them weighted down, as they generally were when they approached Halifax over the steep tracks leading from the moors. She headed straight for them now. She remembered the days before Father had become one of the first cloth merchants in the area to invest in a wagon.

She was still thinking about horses when she reached the upper level of the Piece Hall and paused to gaze. But the horses she pictured now were fine steeds, beautifully groomed for drawing the elegant carriages which, she believed, should grace so magnificent a building. They would discharge silk-gowned ladies and velvet-coated gentlemen, who would be here to enjoy themselves.

'Enjoying yourself, love?'

It was their Henry just behind her, smiling, concerned that trouble between Will and himself had hurt her. She didn't know it but he frequently read her rapt expression, sympathised with her dreams. She reassured him and watched as he hurried along to the room where he'd left a regular client examining some of their cloth.

Several hours later, their business concluded, Henry announced he was staying in Halifax for a while. And he didn't explain.

They'd sold most pieces brought to market, even eventually the ones considered inferior, although their price had been no better than the material. Henry didn't like Bright's handling poor stuff. Whatever line he chose, he'd make sure he was proud of what he was selling.

Except for Mrs Sutcliffe, their middle-aged housekeeper, Matthew and Luke Fortescue lived on their own, in a roomy stone house built last century with innumerable mullioned windows which stared out across a steep-sided valley on the outskirts of Halifax. They were better-class folk, although orginally sheep farmers. It was their common interest in wool which had forged the initial bond between Brights and Fortescues.

The cousins were at home now, Henry concluded, smoke drifted from both chimneys. Exposed as they were to winds tearing over beautiful open countryside for as far as the eye could see, there weren't many days when they could manage without a fire. But their housekeeper was a careful Yorkshire body who wouldn't think to start a blaze in more than the one grate if her masters were abroad.

It was Matthew who greeted Henry after he was admitted, and this made him feel uncomfortable. Wasn't Matthew his own godfather – the elder of the cousins, the one who'd encouraged him with long conversations about Portugal and its wine?

'Henry, glad to see you – come on in. Sit down, lad . . .'

Matthew asked after his old friend Amos, and after Henry's mother, Eleanor. While he was replying Henry tried to still his agitating pulse, even tried to toughen himself to dislike the man and render complaining easier. But there was nothing to dislike in Matthew Fortescue. Keen in business, he was genial in everything else. And, left a widower at an early age, he'd always shown particular affection towards his godson.

Henry cleared his throat, smoothed suddenly sticky palms down the sides of his second best buckskin breeches. 'I'll be straight with you about the reason for my visit. Our William's spoken up about the job he's getting . . .'

'I was afraid that was it, I'd hoped to have a word with you first. There's something I want you to know about the situation, Henry.'

'Is there?' He couldn't be gracious about it, even if he'd wished to. And he was too hurt to be concerned for anything but expressing his own feelings. Nothing in his previous experience had taught him how to conceal his reaction to so grave an injustice. 'I thought that position were as good as promised to me.'

'We couldn't wait, lad. It was that simple.'

Henry was compelled to battle for the job. 'It's nobbut a few months till I'll be of age. I was sure you were going to hang on.'

'For someone to begin being groomed for following on

after us, yes. Unfortunately, there's more to it than that. To put it bluntly, we urgently needed to lay hands on more capital.'

'Grandmother Bright's money! That's it, isn't it? Our Will got his share when he were twenty-one. And you – took it.' Henry was so appalled, he couldn't believe what his own lips were stating.

'He made us an offer which my cousin and I were agreed was too good to be ignored.'

'You did it for the money . . .' He didn't enjoy hearing that his own brother would all but bribe them, and discovering that the Fortescues had no qualms about such a situation shook him even more.

'If you've a mind to be in business, Henry, the first thing you learn to accept is that you've a need to look to the financial side above all else.'

'But I'm your godson.' He was struggling to contain the disappointment welling inside him.

'There'll be a place out there for you as well, when the time comes. If port's what you want to work in . . .'

'Not with our Will there ahead of me. I'll not work under him.'

Matthew Fortescue sighed, dragged a veined hand across his plentiful white hair. 'Happen it'll turn out for the best, lad.'

'I'll be frank with you again,' Henry continued. 'I've no desire to spend my life as a clothier, there's too much that's changing . . .'

'I thought a change was what you were after,' his godfather interrupted, settling more comfortably in his oval-backed armchair.

'Aye – a complete one, to get me out before weaving alters out of all recognition. All they talk of now is new sources of power. There's mills going up for spinning, it'll be for weaving next, there'll soon be no cottages with looms in their top storeys.'

'There's no saying that'll come in your lifetime, Henry. Development's slow. It's near enough a hundred years since Thomas Savery patented an engine for raising water as they put it – "by the impellent force of fire".'

8

'I don't know about him, it's folk like James Watt and Matthew Boulton that I've been keeping my eye on.'

'Aye, but don't you see – it's taken this long from the time Savery had his workshop in London. I'd an uncle went there once, you know, in Salisbury Court off Fleet Street, right near St Bride's church.'

'I don't care how long it takes, it'll come; and I'll not be comfortable selling cloth produced in some big mill. That's if the mill masters themselves don't start selling direct.'

Matthew smiled slightly. Light appeared in his blue eyes. He'd done his best to discourage this second of Amos Bright's sons from throwing everything up to start afresh with Fortescues'. He'd be justified now in looking to the company's interests. 'I can see you've thought things out for some while, lad.'

'And you've floored me – I'd set my heart on making a new life over yonder.' Henry ran a finger round the inside of his collar.

'Does it have to be i' Portugal?'

'It's all I've ever thought of. You know that.'

'We shall need a man with a good head on him in Spain before long.'

'Spain?' Henry repeated. 'I didn't know you'd interests there . . .'

'You've forgotten then, I dare say. It was in Spain that Luke and I first became involved in shipping wines.' Smiling to himself, the elderly man chuckled. 'I'd gone to Cadiz for an altogether different purpose. To purchase Merino rams, with a mind to producing better wool from our flock. While I was out there I became acquainted with several sherry merchants. I was much like you, Henry, eager to see fresh horizons.'

'You're saying you want somebody in Spain – to learn the sherry trade?'

'If you could begin, say, next year you'd have a good grasp of the business by the time Luke and I are past all the travelling.'

'You're not thinking you'll retire in the near future?'

His godfather laughed. 'Some days, I'm determined I'll

settle for a warm hearth for the rest of my life. And then again I see the orders coming in when word gets round that we've a good vintage . . . There's times I believe I'll die in my boots, with my hand on a full glass.'

Henry grinned at him across the elegant room. 'You've taken a load off my mind, I hope you know that! I've never been more put out than when our William announced what he intended.'

'I only hope your parents will forgive us in time,' said Matthew seriously, 'for taking both of you out of the business. Luke and I would be sorry to lose their friendship.'

'I think Father has a good idea that I'm for getting out. I've not tried to hide my interest in the company you run.' Not like some, he thought.

Henry felt uneasy, nevertheless, as he strode off across Midgley Moor on the way home to Heptonstall after staying to dine with Matthew. Aching for a new life hadn't taught him a good way of relinquishing the old. He didn't like hurting folk. There was a difference between recognising that his own father preferred yarning over a good bottle to a day's hard graft, and showing his mistrust of Brights' future by leaving. He only hoped he'd arrive back before William had announced his own departure at home.

Since that morning's storm the day had been glorious. The evening sky was cloudless. The strange clarity which often followed rain brought the surrounding hills into crisp focus. Distance became misleading. It looked as if he might just step from the springy heathland here across to Heptonstall church over yonder. A part of him wished that were possible; he'd always been one for getting trouble over. On the other hand, his father's disappointment would be sure to quell his own enthusiasm for the new life that he needed. There was his mother, as well – she'd not say a great deal; Eleanor Bright was economical with words, but her brown eyes were always expressive.

Young Isobel had brown eyes also, and she'd not be able to conceal her emotions. The lass had already been alarmed to learn that one of her brothers was leaving. Dread weighted his boots when he considered what he was about to tell his family. The last stretch of the way, down the steep slope of the valley to Hebden Water and up the other wooded hill to Heptonstall, revealed how exhausted he was, and that was without the anticipated conflict.

'Hallo, love,' he began when Isobel met him at the track to their stout home. He tried to lighten his voice, but felt it thicken with emotion.

Her dark eyes were wide with distress, her face beneath the bonnet was ashen. She'd been coughing as he approached. 'I came out here when our Will went,' she told him breathily, 'I couldn't bide in there, Father was ranting that much.'

'Went?' Henry echoed, appalled. 'Will's not left home already?'

Isobel shook her head. 'Nay, he'd not do that. He's gone to see Phillida, I suppose. He set off in that direction.'

'But he has told them?' Henry checked, with a nod of his head towards the stone house they were approaching.

'Aye, he has that! To hear Father talk, you'd think t'world were coming to an end. I tried to tell 'em that you'll see we're all right, but nobody listens to me.'

And they know well enough that I'm after different work, he thought, but couldn't steel himself to distress her further as he went in and found his father sitting at the solid oak table. The port bottle was at his elbow, an empty glass before it. As Henry closed the door, Amos raised the bottle and filled the glass almost to its rim.

'Beaten you to it, hasn't he, your brother? Did you have to let him see you were hankering after turning into a merchant of wines? I dare bet he'd have stayed content with t'clothing trade but for your prompting.'

Henry inhaled, steadying himself. 'I'm sorry he's going, Father. But it wasn't my doing that he got the idea into his head.'

Amos shrugged, disconsolately. 'Be that as it may. I'm still the loser, aren't I? What am I left wi'? You – to run the business with a bad grace, because Will's taken t'job you were after!'

Henry swallowed. He would have to tell them, risk his

11

father's increased wrath, add to his mother's grief. If he kept his plans to himself tonight, he'd be justly accused of compounding their troubles by his secrecy; or, worse, would never make the break.

His father gave him the lead. 'Made you abandon your schemes, hasn't he? By being able to buy himself in, and by getting in afore you.'

'It's not quite like that,' Henry began, wishing he dared sink on to the nearest chair but knowing that he would risk a berating for showing disrespect. 'I've come from Matthew Fortescue just now. You'll have to know some time. Him and his cousin are offering me work in Spain – learning the sherry business.'

His father's anger erupted. Spluttering, Amos banged down his glass on the table. 'Wasn't it enough that our Will's deserting! Couldn't you be content that he was set on ruining us?'

Isobel gave a little cry and then, weeping, turned and dashed outside again. Henry willed himself not to escape with her.

'I do regret that this is the way things are, you know. But I've always dreamed of making my own life out yonder . . .'

'*Yours*? Or Luke and Matthew Fortescue's – seems to me like you're selling yourself to them. Or are *you* putting hard-earned Bright brass into their company, an' all?'

'That aspect hasn't been settled yet,' Henry announced, trying to keep his voice even.

'Happen it will, soon enough, the day you inherit,' his mother suggested sharply.

'You're against me bettering myself as well then,' Henry said, and realised how slight his hope had been that she might even be proud that he'd not simply wait in line for his father's boots. That he'd not stay here to let all the changes in the cloth trade overwhelm him.

'I'm again' owt that'll take my lads away from here. That's all. What you do with your brass is your concern, love. What you do with your life hurts me if it hurts your father. But I'm saying nowt more now. You're nobbut a few month short

12

of being of age, if you don't know by now whether you're doing right or not, we'll never learn you.'

'Happen you'll find you've an urgent appointment some-where now, like your brother, eh?' Amos baited him. 'Take yourself out of here now, will you, while I cool down a bit? Not that I'll ever get over such rank ingratitude!'

William's escape hadn't exactly proved to be the relief from disapproval that he'd hoped. Phillida was waiting in the yard behind the cottage where her father, John Walshaw, wove a large amount of the cloth sold by Bright's. She'd stood there for the best part of an hour, wasting time that she could have spent at her spinning wheel, and made guilty by the clattering of her father's loom as he utilised the last glimmer of the dying day.

'I expected you long afore this.'

'I know, love, I'm sorry. I've had a bit of bother at home.'

'You could have let me know, I'd have been working then.' She was the fastest spinner in all Heptonstall, a lot quicker than her mother, Hilda. If her father was kept waiting for yarn tomorrow, there'd be more than a bit of bother here. Too irritated to ask what was wrong, she half turned from him. 'Let's go for that walk while we can still see a hand in front of us.'

William silently commanded himself not to protest that he was already exhausted. Phillie, wearing her best pale silky gown with lace at the neck and billowing out below the elbows of its tight sleeves, appeared fragile because of her exquisite features contrasting so vividly with auburn hair. In fact, she was toughened by her upbringing. To his mind, she seemed as unrelenting as the message preached by John Wesley on these hills and reiterated, with a regularity that William found depressing, in Heptonstall's octagonal chapel. Being the loveliest girl that he'd ever clapped eyes on ensured her the freedom to exercise her beliefs and still hold his interest. Even annoyed, as she so patently was tonight, she made him want to hold her. First, though, he would need to comply with her determination that they would take the walk which he'd promised earlier.

13

She was ahead of him now, striding in a manner that belied her elegant dress, along the track towards Blackshaw Head. Inwardly, he groaned. He was tired out, couldn't she tell? Didn't she care?

'You want t'cobwebs blowing off you!' she exclaimed, pausing and facing him as he caught her up. And then she smiled. Phillida Walshaw's smile was what had enchanted him ever since he was a lad attending the local grammar school. Tonight, it made him smile back, and forget instantly that he'd wished her any different.

'It was about my future that we had trouble at home,' he announced abruptly. She might smile, but while she remained on her dignity he'd wait for ever for her to inquire what had occurred. Will could never abide waiting. 'I'll tell you as much as I've told them. It's only right that I should – you must know by now that I intend you'll have a share in it.'

Phillie was delighted, at last, and not slow to show her pleasure. Her arm slid through his and she accommodated her pace to his more contemplative stride. 'Go on, Will – let's be hearing.' She'd waited a long time to have William Bright confirm that his eloquent eyes and their covert kisses had not intended to mislead.

'I've studied for many a year how some folk have set themselves up as merchants in more than one line, as you might say,' he began, and congratulated himself on a good opening. 'Folk like Peter Stubs of Warrington; and Abraham Dent. Now *he* dealt in knitted stockings, was a shopkeeper, and a wine merchant . . .'

'You're thinking we should take to knitting stockings then, eh? I don't quite know when we'd find the time, but . . .'

'Not that, no.' Abruptly, he stopped. He'd have to go carefully, putting this to her. Phillida and her family were too strict to hold with drinking alcohol. 'But I know you'll be glad I'm thinking of our future, determined to make it successful.'

'I thought Bright's was doing very nicely, any road. It's not going downhill, I hope?'

'No, no – nothing like that. You've got to understand,

14

Phillie; I need to – try myself with something that hasn't been bred in me.'

Phillida's green eyes narrowed. She didn't know where she was with him. One minute he'd had her believing this was turning into a proposal of marriage, the next – well, she didn't like this uncomfortable premonition that he was about to shatter her.

'I've always admired a bit of spirit,' she said, wondering why she felt so uneasy because he hadn't come straight out with his intention.

'With all the trouble between us and the French, and then their Revolution last year, lots of folk are looking elsewhere for good wines. It's the perfect time to snap up the offer I've had to join a business engaged in shipping port.'

'A wine merchant?' Phillida cried, appalled. '*Wine*! Oh, William – how could you? Haven't you any idea what bother it causes, the lives it ruins? Nay, lad – haven't you watched your own father?'

'I know he likes a drop, but . . .'

'A drop? Folk like him don't stop at a drop, nor at one glass either. And you're seeking to encourage them. I never thought I'd hear you say you were tackling owt so disgusting.'

'If I weren't going to be bringing it over to England, there's plenty more as would. It's a way of earning a living, Phillie. A good living, an' all, that'll provide for our future.'

'Don't talk to me about a future of that sort. Founded on *evil*, that's what it'd be. Bought with the lives of folk that's daft enough to turn to drink!'

'Oh, come on, love.' He couldn't bear that she should be so angry with him. Couldn't endure her failure to understand, when he'd needed her to be the one person here who didn't condemn his judgement. 'Don't you see – it's only a means of earning enough to set us up.'

Gradually, she was calmed by the prospect of having a home with this attractive man, who for so many months now she had pictured as her husband. Although shaking her head in regret over his suggested career, she couldn't stiffen herself to hold William at arm's length. Once his hands slid

15

about the narrow span of her waist then went to her spine as he drew her against him, Phillie's annoyance yielded. Whenever in the past he had contrived their being alone she'd thrilled to the masculine strength of him, to the pressure of his firm chest and the thrust of a taut thigh against her skirts. Tonight, the shock of his announcement and her resultant alarm had sharpened her emotions. To remain unresponsive she would have needed to adopt the chill grandeur of the surrounding moors. And there was nothing cool about Phillida Walshaw.

His lips were more assertive than ever, moulding her mouth to his. The arms crushing her close seemed to promise eternal protection along with the passion stirring between them. She'd been so afraid that she'd never get William to declare his intention.

'We'll marry soon, Phillie, have a home of our own.' And if that got him away from his father's hearth he'd avoid a deal of discomfort.

The half-understood urgency within her was screaming that she must consent. She was reminded that she'd always loved William Bright for his habit of surprising folk, and for the courage to go his own way.

'There'll be a lot of planning to do,' she said, smiling into his grey eyes which were uncharacteristically anxious. 'Happen we'd better begin talking things over.' She didn't entirely trust even her rigid upbringing while his kisses were growing more intense, and she had never needed more to be reassured that their love wasn't about to change as well. She was growing alarmingly aware that the rough turf surrounding them would serve for a bed. And darkness was falling.

William was in no condition for further discussion; he felt he'd been savaged enough by the dissent at home and Phillie's initial appalled reaction. But she never seemed perturbed if she did most of the talking. Tonight, as they walked on, she indicated how she visualised their home life.

'There's a nice little house empty, just across t'road from the chapel,' she ventured.

William contained a groan; he would have to explain more

16

thoroughly. 'I can't think I'll be living in Heptonstall much longer. When I'm not out in Portugal—'

'Portugal?' Phillida interrupted sharply.

'Aye, surely you know where port comes from.' He couldn't help feeling impatient with her for making everything so difficult.

'I'm not interested in the stuff, I've said.'

'Any road, when I'm not out there, I shall need to be in one of the larger towns, with better communications.' If not in London, he added, to himself.

'Well, that's it then,' Phillida said flatly. 'You'll bide there without me, unless you can come up with something more practical. Haven't you thought of my work? Haven't you realised how much my father depends on me? It might not look much to you as businesses go, but we turn out some of t'best cloth in t'West Riding, and my spinning's an important part of the process.'

'I know, love, I know. I agree with every word you've said.'

'What's to be done then, eh? What hope is there for us married, for I'll not stir from Heptonstall!'

2

William Bright had never felt so perturbed. Normally easy-going and of a cheerful nature, he hadn't previously experienced the disapproval of so many people who mattered to him. And Phillida, especially, did matter – more than anyone he knew.

They stood for a while, both too stunned for saying any more, while the sky darkened around them. They were right on the edge of the escarpment. Below them the road from Lancashire accompanied the Calder, scarcely visible now, seeming to him like the barely perceptible path through the unfamiliar life that he'd chosen. And the precipice on which they were standing appeared so insecure that one more sharp word from her and he'd be plunged into a void.

'We'd best be getting home.' His tone was more decisive than he felt, a fact which made him thankful. No one must ever even guess how alarmed he was by the consequences of his choice of livelihood. He left Phillida at the Walshaws' stone cottage, and hurried ever more uneasily towards his home.

His father was standing, back to the hearth, a strangely assertive look in the grey eyes which his own so closely resembled. 'You can go, lad, and good luck to you,' he informed William swiftly. 'I've told Henry t'same. I'll not let it be said I've held either of you back. As from now on, I alone will run Bright's and, by heck, I'll run it better nor you or anybody else might have done!'

'Good,' William responded carefully. 'I'm sure you will, Father.' But what was it his father had said – that Henry was going an' all? He'd guessed his brother had been to see the Fortescues, but didn't want to believe he'd be going out to Portugal with him. He noticed the others: Henry standing in the shadows of the far corner, behind the straight-backed

18

chair on which young Isobel was sitting, and their mother motionless in the doorway that led to the kitchen. No one smiled, and nor did they looked relieved that Amos Bright was asserting his determination to continue as a clothier.

'There's summat else,' his father added now, staring hard straight at William. 'We shall set up house nearer Halifax.'

'Oh, Amos – are you sure?' Eleanor protested, as she had earlier when her husband first mentioned his intention.

'I am that! I've just told you all, haven't I? I need to be nearer yon Piece Hall when I've got to manage on my own.'

'But you'll still have just as far to travel, picking up cloth from weavers out here in Heptonstall and beyond,' his wife observed.

'Aye, I know, but that'll be when I choose. I'll not be obliged to put up with t'long journey back here at end of a day down yonder. And I shall be better able to keep up to date with what's going on in t'trade in Halifax, and in Bradford an' all.'

'Your father's promised there'll always be a bed provided for you and Henry, no matter where we're living,' Eleanor told William.

He read in the set of her lips and the sadness in her dark eyes that it was only her persuading had ensured their being considered.

'Thank you, Father,' William responded, but his gaze was turned towards their mother.

Eleanor swallowed her sigh, nodded, and mouthed an inaudible 'Goodnight.'

Her feet and legs numbed with misery, she plodded across the room and slowly up the curving staircase. No matter where Amos found them a home, she'd not take to it the same. She had loved this house ever since he'd bought it, when he began showing he could prosper as a cloth merchant after taking over from his father. Isobel and Charles had been born in the half tester bed in the largest chamber here, as had the two little ones whom she'd lost so quickly. She'd feel she was deserting them when she was compelled to leave.

They had a lot to be thankful for, she supposed, four of their children had survived, even if two of them now were contemplating work that would take them away so much. She'd always vowed that she'd keep the family together. Her own parents were dead now and her brothers and sisters were scattered from Kendal right down as far as Derby. Still, you couldn't hold folk against their will, you could only do your best. At least she hadn't let Amos show them the door; for the present, she must let that content her.

Her furniture was serviceable rather than handsome. The press cupboard was severely fashioned in oak, although Eleanor had given her toilet table a petticoat of tammy cloth. The whitewashed walls were clean if plain, but there were good thick covers and draperies on the bed, sufficient to keep out the cold of even a Yorkshire winter. The windows were mullioned in stone, she treasured the outlook which was enough to lift anyone's heart of a morning. Facing away from the cluster of houses embracing the thirteenth century church and the chapel, the view was over tree tops and fields, the densely wooded slopes that concealed the river. Hebden Water – she'd lived near its banks as a lass; until Amos Bright came asking the price of a fleece off the sheep farmed by her father.

They'd been drawn together at once, had taken to walking for miles over the neighbouring moors, in much the same way that now William and Phillie Walshaw did. Looking back, she supposed she and Amos had also imagined that nobody knew what was going on.

These hills were good for the soul, untamed as they were for many a mile, spaced from the rest of the world – aye, and beautiful. She never ceased to be amazed by the variety of different greens, the earth tones as well, and the purpling of distant heather. Perhaps best of all, though, was the aspect which the eye couldn't see – the skylark tossing his song to the air, and the wind that seemed not to pause and freshened the spirit within you. Out here you had the closest to freedom that you'd find in this life.

'You'll not tie them to you, no matter how hard you try, Eleanor.'

Amos was behind her in the darkened room, she'd not heard his progress up the stair.

'Do you think I don't know that? Any road, I'm not trying anything of the kind.'

'What're you sulking for up here then, with no light in the room?'

'I was thinking, love, not sulking.' And maybe wondering how I'll tear mysen away. But she'd not mention that. Amos had enough to contend with if he was going to manage the business on his own. She'd been astonished when he'd asserted that he'd do just that; she'd been suited, an' all – it would be like old times to have him on the go all the day, and no time for sitting with a bottle and a glass. 'What do you really reckon to t'pair of them going in for trading in wines?' she asked him, finding tinder to light the candles.

Her husband chuckled, warming her with his unexpected delight just as his laugh had always warmed her. 'If it weren't so regrettable that neither on 'em wants to work alongside me, I'd say it were champion. We know Luke and Matthew Fortescue well enough to be certain they've framed very well at shipping wines.'

'I think I'd feel easier in my mind if our lads were both going to t'same place. They'd be company for each other, like.'

'Nay, they aren't a couple of lasses! Do 'em a power of good to strike off independent of each other. And Henry wouldn't have wanted to follow Will out to Portugal, not the way he stole a march on him.'

'Aye. I wish William hadn't done that.'

'He's always gone after what he wanted, that one. It might stand him in good stead.'

Below them in the parlour William had watched Isobel going upstairs in the wake of their parents before turning to his brother. Poor lass, she was taking the news badly. And while young Charles was confined to his bed with an appalling cough, there was nobody able to distract her.

'Is it right what Father said, are you bound to go, an' all?' William inquired.

'When I'm of age. I shan't turn up at your heels though.'

'Where're you off to then?'

'Spain – Jerez, where sherry comes from.'

21

'I do know where it's made. So you went to see the Fortescues?'

'I saw my godfather, aye.' Although he felt better about the situation he couldn't avoid mentioning the aspect that hurt most.

'I wish you luck – as much as I wish myself. It's all to try for.'

'Aye. When are you thinking of leaving, Will?'

'Not for a day or two yet, there's things I've got to settle.'

'Fancy Father deciding to get rid of the house!'

'Staggered me, did that. I know it's made from two places knocked into one, but it's not all that big for 'em.'

William sailed for Oporto two weeks later, less elated than he'd hoped. Leaving Yorkshire had been a wrench; the hills and wooded slopes were so glorious, urging him to remain. But it was his folk who were more a part of him than he'd understood. Henry had seen him on to the mail coach and young Isobel also, her brown eyes resolutely dry, yet her hug had nearly throttled him. 'Look after yourself, let us know how you're getting on out there,' she'd said huskily, echoing Henry's sentiments. The parting with Phillida had been far worse.

All the way on the laborious journey through the English countryside he'd been haunted by her disapproval, had seen nothing of the softening landscape. Even the busy towns where they changed horses were obscured by Phillie's face before his eyes, her disapproving voice had dulled the sound of horses, wheels and post-horn.

'You chose your way of life, William, you'll not deny me the right to choose mine,' she'd told him, standing at the door of her father's cottage, steeling herself to resist his embrace.

He wasn't so soft that he'd let her decision mar his ability to tackle the job, but he was shaken by her cool dismissal of him. His excitement had dwindled, he needed the voyage to restore anticipation. Yet William quickly learned that he was not a good sailor. He didn't adapt easily to the movement of the vessel, and cramped conditions with dubious arrangements for sanitation added to the stench and completed his misery. By the time he was at last met at the quay by Luke Fortescue, he would be grateful for anything that guaranteed him space on dry land.

Luke grasped him firmly by the hand as they greeted each other, and William felt keen blue eyes assessing his condition.

'How was the voyage?' Luke inquired wryly, and smiled. Both he and his cousin were appreciated for the humour which tempered their business acumen.

William grinned. 'Happen I'll soon get used to travelling.'

'I hope so, lad, or you're not going to relish these next few years.'

It had been explained already that, in addition to learning every stage of port production, William would need to acquire a thorough knowledge of its shipping. This would entail working for Fortescue's in London as well as in Oporto. There would be innumerable voyages.

'I shall be all right when I've had a decent night's sleep,' William assured him very quickly.

'So, you're not hoping for a round of introductions tonight then?'

'Do you mind if we postpone them until tomorrow?'

Luke Fortescue laughed, and shook his head. 'Not in the least. As always, I've a mountain of papers needing my attention. And you'll be meeting Fernando Trancoso who insisted on driving Fortescue's landau the short distance along the quayside. So few streets here are suitable for carriages that our driver isn't employed full-time. Trancoso has taught me all I know about port and I believe he's looking forward to teaching you, too.'

'He's not going to be afraid I'll eventually usurp his position, then?' William asked rather anxiously as he tried to coordinate legs reduced to pulp by too many days at sea.

Luke shook his head. 'Don't go moithering on that score, William. Fernando Trancoso is even nearer than I am to the age when he'll be glad to sit back with a pipe of tobacco and let you youngsters do the work!'

23

They turned away from the vessel and William took a closer look at the numerous tiers of buildings which he had noticed as they were entering the river mouth from the Atlantic. As they were walking past the ship's stern, Luke grasped him by the arm and pointed further along the waterside. 'This is Vila Nova de Gaia where most of the port lodges are; Fortescue's is just in sight there.'

'Lodges?' William inquired.

'Where the port is blended and matured. In this context, lodge comes from the Portuguese word *loja* – translated as shop or warehouse on the ground floor. Ours is the one with the imposing white frontage.'

'And it's right on the waterfront.'

'Aye, it is, an' all!' Luke exclaimed.

They both smiled at his use of Yorkshire, and continued on towards the landau which now moved away from the shade where it had waited and headed towards them.

Trancoso himself was at the reins, and offered a thin hand as he greeted William in immaculate English when introduced by Luke. 'Good afternoon, Mr Bright. I hope you had a good journey?'

When William looked uncomfortable Luke answered for him. 'I understand that our friend, here, prefers other modes of transport to ships.'

Fernando Trancoso's smile remained cool and formal. 'I trust that you will soon recover.'

'Thank you,' William replied equally gravely, as he and Luke clambered up into the carriage. He began to wonder if all Portuguese appeared so solemn, or if Fernando Trancoso disapproved of him.

But he seemed to have given consideration to William's introduction to the business. 'You will remain in Oporto and Vila Nova de Gaia for a week at least. That way you will learn something of the processes involved before we go up the Douro and you are expected to concentrate on culture of the vines, and the working within our press houses.'

'And the language – ought I to learn to speak Portuguese?' asked William, eager to prove a good student, but wondering how he would find time to include so much that was new.

24

Luke smiled. 'You will discover that most of the men with any authority in our wine lodge have an adequate command of English. You'll win them as friends, of course, if you attempt to speak their language. And you'll do well to remember that I learned the hard way that they can't cope with our Yorkshire dialect.'

The jolting of the landau was too unsteady for William to be other than disturbed by its effect, which was all too reminiscent of the motion created by the sea. Despite the courtesy of the dapper, white-haired Portuguese gentleman, he couldn't feel sorry when he and Luke were deposited at the arched entrance to the port lodge. He thanked Fernando Trancoso for meeting him and agreed that it would be pleasant to get to know each other better.

Luke was about to conduct him inside, but William was gazing curiously towards the gracefully curved boat from which casks were being offloaded. 'Is that the wine coming in?'

'Aye, it is that, partially prepared. The boats are *barcos rabelos* – you'll see them all over the River Douro. They all have that rather square sail, and many bear their company insignia. You see ours is a stylised ram's head. You heard tell, I hope, how we set up after seeking Merino rams introduced us to Spain?'

'Your cousin's often reminding folk that was how you first came to be introduced to port and sherry.'

Still intrigued by the boat, William was crossing towards the edge of the quay.

'In our business, all the casks contain a quantity referred to as a pipe,' Luke told him, pleased by his curiosity.

'Which is 115 gallons – and a bit more in the lodges, to allow for evaporation.'

Fortescue chuckled. 'You're learned something already then!'

'These boats fascinate me, though. They have a very high poop, haven't they?'

Luke nodded. 'That's where the helmsman stands, he steers with that long oar for a rudder. Look over yonder, there's one just about to put in to the side.'

25

'They have quite a team of oarsmen.'

'You'll see, when you go upriver, why they're needed. Every one of the *barcos rabelos* can carry sixty pipes of wine, and it's a journey that demands skill; there are rapids to negotiate as they come down the Douro.'

Although interested in the river traffic, as well as the view across to Oporto itself on the opposite bank, William was growing extremely conscious of the heat which was making him feel lethargic. He asked if they might retreat to the shade, commenting, 'It's certainly a good coat warmer here, you'll not be needing such thick walls as we have in the West Riding for protection.'

'Except from the sun, just you wait till next summer, you'll wonder what to do with yourself.'

William nodded, thinking it was fortunate that he'd chosen to come out here for the first time in the autumn. 'Do you get any rain at all?'

'We do that – and it's just what we need upriver where the vines are cultivated – tremendous rainstorms, sometimes with massive hailstones. So long as they don't come out of season we're all right. We couldn't do without the scorching hot summers for which the Douro is well known.'

'I'm looking forward to seeing the vineyards.'

'You'll like the region, I believe. But I'm not going to tell you so much about the Douro, lad. Most of the thrill of the scenery is in that first surprise impact. And you've come at the best time of all: the vintage, or harvest, which begins towards the backend, just before the end of September as a rule.'

William's introduction to Fortescue's large port lodge was brief, a cursory inspection of the area where what appeared to be thousands of casks were stored, followed by an equally hasty visit to Luke's office.

The evening was agreeable, eating food selected by Teresa, Luke's elderly housekeeper, to allow for English tastes. With only his host for company, William began to relax after the days spent travelling and to find everything less of an effort. Luke had insisted that he should stay in the Fortescue home, a stout granite house on the slopes of

Oporto, until finding himself accommodation either here or across in Vila Nova de Gaia. In his room, deeply exhausted, he slowly removed coat and waistcoat, his cream breeches and stockings, and his stock and shirt. He'd never been more thankful since leaving England for the declining fashion in wigs. The thought alone of wearing one here made him sweat.

Although keenly interested in all that he'd seen since his arrival, William could not help longing for the bracing air of the hills surrounding Heptonstall and Halifax. He'd never realised until away from them quite how stimulating they were to the vitality. And had not known, until away from Phillida, how a man could ache in spirit as well as body for a woman's understanding.

He hadn't seriously questioned his own decision to join Fortescue's, so he only hoped this longing for her wouldn't erode his confidence. And that his coming away would somehow convince Phillida to follow him.

William's absence had triggered in Amos Bright the determination to show his other adult son that there would be no undue hardship suffered as a consequence of *his* eventual departure. On the morning after his brother had left, Henry rose early as was his custom. He found his father had already had breakfast and was out in the yard preparing the wagon.

'Good morning, Father. How's the gout?' he asked carefully from the doorway, hoping to pacify Amos who normally relished any consideration of his affliction.

Amos grunted, glanced briefly over his shoulder. 'It'll mend, it'll have to! I'll not be hampered wi' a bit of pain while there's a business to run.'

'Here, let's give you a hand,' Henry volunteered, blinking the sleep from his eyes as he strode across to assist with the harness. But he saw then that his father had almost completed the task, and saw also that he wasn't alone.

'Hallo, Henry,' young Isobel called from the far side of the wagon. 'Father says I can go with him to collect t'pieces.'

Isn't she too young, and have you overlooked that she's a girl? wondered Henry, but checked both questions. There'd only be more bother if he began commenting on everything that Amos did. He didn't like being made to feel that he was dispensable, but he reminded himself that he had wanted some assurance that the business wouldn't decline without him. The months would pass swiftly, any road, he'd not be working here much longer.

'We're going up Cragg Vale first,' Isobel announced. 'And I'm to keep the records of each piece we load. You can come with us, of course, if you want. Happen we'll be glad of another pair of hands to put stuff on to t'wagon.'

Henry experienced a strange conglomeration of emotions. In a way, he was delighted by his twelve-year-old sister's newfound confidence and her enthusiasm for work which a girl of her age might have thought dull. He wasn't certain, though, that he entirely approved of her assuming a serious role so early; and he most certainly didn't relish this impression that he, like William, was unnecessary.

He looked towards their father who grinned and jerked his head in Isobel's direction. 'You hear what t'lass says – you'd better get a move on if you're coming with us.'

It had been scarcely daylight when he emerged from the house. By the time they were heading down the steep-sided valley from Heptonstall, the sky was a mass of small scudding clouds against a promising blue.

Passing the Walshaws' cottage, Henry noticed the open door and Phillie already spinning yarn as if her life depended upon it.

'You're up early, Phillida!' Amos shouted cheerily.

Although she nodded and smiled her lovely face didn't light. Henry winced for her, reading in the shadows beneath her eyes the restless night from which she'd been glad to rise. He didn't know what had gone amiss between Phillida and their William, but he'd have been a fool not to guess that it had more than a little to do with his working to import more of the wines that she'd been taught to abominate. He couldn't help feeling for them both. It's a good job I'm not putting anybody out by choosing a similar occupation, he reflected. Leaving family and the business they ran was bad enough without antagonising a lass who regarded you highly.

Some way further down the hill they stopped beside another long stone cottage with the extensive row of windows in its upper storey which proclaimed it a weaver's home.

'Just see if Samson has owt ready, will you, Henry? Molly Gaukroger sent a message wi' their Susan to say that he was over the ague and should have summat for us by now.'

It was Susan who answered the door. A pretty enough lass, with pale curling hair and eyes as blue as Hebden Water, she'd have delighted many young fellows with a glance or a smile. Henry wasn't particularly smitten; he'd always thought her young for her age, which now was seventeen. She never had much to say for herself. He'd not suspected for one moment that the reason was her overwhelming interest in him.

She shyly asked him in then ran upstairs to the room from which the rattle of the loom was coming. When Susan returned it was in Samson Gaukroger's wake, and she hovered nervously in the background while Henry inspected the cloth he was given.

'It's a grand piece, Mr Gaukroger, up to your usual standard. And are you over the ague, then?'

'Aye, I am that, thank you. Can't abide feeling off colour, much rather keep going.'

Henry knew this to be true, as well as the fact that tending his loom meant escape from his wife Molly's eternal domineering.

'I hear your brother's left us,' Samson remarked. 'There's a rumour, an' all, that you'll not stay round here much longer neither.'

'Is there indeed?' said Henry lightly, not wishing to perturb anyone about too many changes in the future of Bright's.

Samson grinned, shook his head, and turned away. 'Best get back to my work. I can tell you're not bound to let on what's happening.'

His daughter, however, was disturbed by her father's words. She hadn't heard that Henry Bright might be going away, but both parents tended to keep things from her and her brother. She didn't know how in the world to extract the

29

truth from Henry himself, so bidding him a hushed 'good morning' she rushed to open the outer door. Seeing Isobel on the wagon, Susan smiled and waved. When she managed to catch the girl on her own she would ask her what Henry's plans were.

Isobel was getting over the sadness of William's departure. Nothing would fetch him back, she might as well enjoy what she was doing. At least she wasn't incarcerated indoors with one of the curates from Heptonstall church who acted as her tutor; and she hoped she'd done with school work. She was better than her father, and as good as either of her older brothers, at arithmetic. She could read any page placed before her, and her handwriting was so clear and even that no one could fault it. Her younger brother Charles was welcome to the Reverend Peter Horsfield's attentions, though he only received additional tuition from him. Charles attended the local grammar school. For the first time in many a year, Isobel had stopped resenting being the one girl in the family and denied the education she might have had there. While she was little, she'd gathered that Heptonstall folk were fortunate in having such a school and that those who attended school stood more chance of becoming important. And the knowledge had perturbed her. Isobel had known for a long time that she wanted to do something worthwhile.

The first shock of hearing that not only William was choosing to leave, but also Henry, had been replaced by a secret elation. She would miss her brothers, of course. And so would their parents. But she could be useful much sooner than she'd expected – by being the one that Father could always rely on. As long as she could remember Bright's had been one of the best local clothiers. She would see to it that it stayed that way despite her brothers' absence. There had been no time to find other help, and their Charles was even younger than she and so beyond consideration. Poor children and orphans were often compelled to work at twelve years old, if not younger, she reflected, and their labour was far harder than any that she would experience learning to be a clothier. She knew they'd all say that she was far too young and she was determined to prove them wrong.

She had a space ready now for the piece that Henry brought out to the wagon. Rapidly she noted down details of the length and width of the cloth, entering them against Mr Gaukroger's name before the horses took to the road again. She was proud of her neatness, didn't mean to have it spoiled by any jarring of her hand. She was also determined to be free to enjoy the journey ahead of them.

In Mytholmroyd she smiled at the first glimpse of The Dusty Miller. Before they turned away to the right into the Cragg Vale road she was thinking of the excitement there must have been in that inn during the time up to about 1768, only ten years or so before she was born, when the gang of coiners had converged there. Henry had told her frequently how the men had clipped the edges from gold coinage and melted down the clippings to forge new coins. She'd heard that at one time at least eighty people from all over the area were involved in coining, but then a band of them had killed an Excise Man. Several of those involved were caught, tried and hanged – one of them, David Hartley, was buried in Heptonstall.

Almost as interesting as the coiners themselves, were the homes where they had carried out their illicit craft. Although she loved this particular valley for its woods and the brook, for its majestic slopes leading up to Blackstone Edge, she loved these reminders of exciting times even more. 'I can see Keelham House now,' she exclaimed, as her father slowed the horses approaching yet another weaver's dwelling. 'Can't you just picture John Wilcock standing at its door!'

'Nay, lass,' her father observed dryly. 'He'd have kept out o' sight, would yon – if he'd any sense, he'd make sure nobody but his cronies ever saw him.'

'Well, you know what I mean,' said Isobel, then became efficiency personified, finding the correct page in their book ready for entering the pieces her father would collect from the cottage.

'Are we going right up near Bell House today?' she asked her brother while they waited with the wagon. She sometimes thought Bell House the most romantic of all, the last house before the moor and exquisitely positioned for secret coining activities.

'Ay, I don't know, love. I thought it was you as had all the details to hand today . . .' he teased.

Isobel gave him a look from beneath long brown lashes, saw the amusement in his hazel eyes, and shrugged. 'One day, Henry Bright, you'll not talk to me in that tone of voice – you'll see! You think I'm nobbut playing at this, but there'll come a time when I'm well known throughout t'West Riding.'

'You'd best mind out that it's famous you become, not notorious like these coiners you're so fond of!'

'You've got to admit they were brave, though, and clever an' all, some of 'em.'

'Clever's all right, so long as it's a good use it's put to,' Henry reminded her.

Isobel experienced a familiar feeling that her own cleverness was being exceeded again; she couldn't find an answer for him. But then he did have nearly nine years' advantage over her.

'Thomas Spencer managed to avoid being captured after he'd been involved in defeating that Excise man, didn't he?' she persisted. Whatever anybody said, she'd continue to be impressed.

'Didn't do him much good, though, he was hanged on Beacon Hill at Halifax a few year since.'

'Aye,' Amos agreed, joining them again to add several pieces of new cloth to those already stacked aboard. 'And that were for leading Corn Riots there, it'd take a wiser man nor me to argue the justice or otherwise of that trial.'

By the time Isobel had entered the details of the latest additions to their stock, her father had turned the wagon and was heading back. She was disappointed that they weren't continuing towards the moors, but when they turned right once they'd arrived back in Mytholmroyd her spirits soared. 'I didn't know we were going to t'Piece Hall today.'

'Well, we're not,' Amos informed her. 'Although I hope as you'll not be too disappointed. I've a mind to see a house that I'm after. And I'll thank you to keep quiet about it to your mother, an' all, until I'm sure I'm going to buy and then I'll tell her mysen.'

★

Even though he wouldn't be spending much time in the new home, Henry was unable to quell the small tremors that seemed to be rising from his stomach. The whole of his life that he could recall had been lived in that same house in Heptonstall. Moving right away from the locality seemed like the marking of a new era.

Where was this new house? He and Isobel alike scoured the hills to left and right all the way along the Calder valley as far as the junction with the road up through Luddenden. Here, their father turned aside up the steep track to their left, with neither a word nor a smile to indicate how close they might be to their destination.

'You're thinking to settle somewhere near the Fortescues, are you then?' said Henry some while later, recognising the direction they were taking when they eventually left Luddenden village.

Amos smiled to himself at last. 'Have I said so? Happen I'm taking you a roundabout way . . .'

You'll still not confuse me for long, thought Henry. He had roamed these hills since he was a young lad, thinking nothing of walking ten miles or more with his friends or to visit Luke and Matthew. He had lain in the springy heather, listening to the cries of curlews, watching bees drone by, or idly gathering bilberries. He had walked them in winter with snow around so deep that it obliterated all the fields and their tracery of drystone walls, until only the contours of the hills remained.

The terrain they reached today, though, became less familiar. They had passed the Fortescue place and still continued on, climbing, the wind catching at the tarpaulin of their wagon. Henry had been this way but once or twice, and saw from Isobel's widening eyes that the ground was alarmingly new to her. 'Happen these folk, whoever they are, won't want to sell,' he whispered reassuringly to her.

Amos heard him. 'Do you think I'm wrong in my head? I'd none come this far out of my road if there weren't summat to our advantage at t'end of it!'

The house might be very much to their advantage, Henry

33

recognised at once when their father tugged on the reins to halt the horses, then pointed towards the crest of the rise. 'You'll not better that for position, eh? We'll not be overlooked. And it's nobbut a short ride down yonder into Halifax.'

Henry would have disputed that, he reckoned they were six miles at least out of the town, but he'd not spoil his father's evident satisfaction. And besides, why should he care – wouldn't he be spending most of his time in and around Jerez, in London, or travelling Britain to set up orders for the sherry that he'd be shipping?

They left the wagon to inspect the view of ranged moorland hills. In some of the valleys woods were visible, others seemed as though their slopes might be as stark as the heath which surmounted them.

'I've not arranged for you to see inside the house,' Amos stated. 'That's done on purpose – I'll not have you inspecting it afore your mother.'

He'd had a mind to win their approval of the place, but had reconsidered; Eleanor's approval was what counted, and he'd value that less if she were coerced.

'It's a grand bit of scenery,' Henry conceded, impressed despite his personal preference for a few more trees in sight.

Isobel, too, was gazing at the house. Constructed of a similar stone to the Piece Hall, she couldn't fail to love the exterior; and it was large, there seemed to be several more rooms than their present home. She could picture herself entertaining here when she was grown up – when she was 'somebody'. If they were nearer to Halifax, they could well become involved with better class folk . . .

'Well, you've had a look,' Amos abruptly interrupted their reflections. 'Don't forget what I've told you – you're not to trouble your mother with information about yon place, not till I've brought her here. So, think on!'

He would choose his time for showing Eleanor their new home, and would choose as well the most propitious circumstances for revealing his plans for the old one.

3

The smell of maturing port which already seemed to be growing permanent in William's nostrils was declining now as he walked with Luke away from the side door of the wine lodge.

'What do you make of what you've seen so far?' Luke inquired with a glance towards the lean, but broad-shouldered young man at his side.

'It's interesting, of course, though I'd like to have studied each process in more detail.'

'Time enough for that. I want to ensure you've a grasp of the layout of the place, and I've an idea you'll not be sorry to inspect what I'll be showing you next.'

They had crossed a narrow unmade road, little more than an alley, and Luke unlocked a gate in the surrounding wall. 'This is ours as well,' he announced. 'As a matter of fact, much of it is *yours* – this being how we're spending your investment.'

Tall and elegant, Luke led the way in through the door of the long, low building which was enhanced by chestnut beams and white archways, then he paused just inside, awaiting William's reaction.

Following the unearthly quiet of the lodge, the noise here could hardly be endured: William's ears were battered by hammering, the screech of saws, and the hissing of heat on moist wood.

'The cooperage,' Luke told him, shouting to be heard.

Smiling, William nodded. 'Where the casks are made.'

'Until we purchased this place, we bought in all our casks, but we reckon we'll save in the long run by making our own, they'll be better, an' all, now we can control quality.'

'So it wasn't entirely to get you over a bad time that you needed the brass?'

'More in the way of making certain we're not held to ransom again by them as makes the casks.'

'And what kind of wood do you use?' William began, determined to learn as much as he could about every aspect of the trade to which he was committed.

'Oak – it's by far the best for ageing wine. But come on over here and have a look . . .' Through warm air fragrant with new wood, the smell of sawdust, and woodsmoke from the chippings tossed into the flames, he led the way through the flagged workshop to where planks of timber were stacked. 'This was bought seasoned, it's been left for close on eighteen months to dry out,' Luke explained. 'Next the planks are cut into staves, then they're hollowed out and planed. It's after that that it becomes interesting.'

He took William across to a brazier where men were holding wet staves over the blaze. 'That's to make them sufficiently pliable so's they'll curve into shape before the iron hoops are slipped over them.'

William watched for a while until, glad to escape the heat, he followed Luke to where a group of coopers were wielding large mallets to ram the hoops into position. He was shown how the cask tops were fitted, and rushes forced into every tiny gap between the staves.

'To test them, they're filled with a water solution and rocked about to make certain there are no leaks,' he was told. 'And even after that they're not ready for use. Every cask has to be seasoned with either a cheap port or wine for at least a year.'

'It's a long process!'

'Aye – you can say the same about owt to do with wine making,' Luke remarked. 'I hope you're a patient fellow?'

William shrugged, gave a short laugh, and his grey eyes lit. 'Happen I haven't been properly tested yet as regards patience.'

The answering smile was rather wry. 'You will be, lad, you will that!' Luke smoothed down the white hair which made the Fortescue cousins resemble each other as closely as brothers.

There was no patience required that day, however, nor

during any of those first weeks in Oporto. From the cooperage they returned to the lodge itself and in the stillness began William's introduction to the creating of port.

'You'll see the vines for yourself afore long,' said Luke. 'And how grapes are gathered, then the actual treading. We'll assume, therefore, that you can accept that we begin here in Vila Nova de Gaia with the partly prepared wine from the previous year's vintage being delivered, which is usually round about February.'

'In *barcos rabelos* like those we saw yesterday.'

'And many a dozen of 'em at that time of year, all loaded to capacity, and seeming to jostle for moorings at the quay. As you will imagine, every available man is required to offload the boats and begin shifting the casks into the lodge. You'll love it, William.'

As he was speaking they arrived at the entrance to one of the great cathedral-like buildings, and were met by its own peculiar incense of wine maturing in wood. Gazing upwards beyond the rows of casks stacked three or four high, William saw dust motes drifting in the sunlight filtering between twisted chestnut beams, and above those glimpsed tiles that were darkened through aeons exposed to wine fumes.

The quiet struck him again and he revelled in the atmosphere which seemed near-reverent. Eager though he was to understand more about port, he would have been content simply to absorb this ambience without listening to Luke Fortescue. He'd never dreamed anywhere like this existed, couldn't have visualised so many of his senses being assailed at once. He felt exhilarated.

'Blending and tasting, then blending again are the secrets of making this wine of ours,' William was told. 'I believe you already know that there are various kinds of port, we're going to show you what contributes to those differences. You'll need an understanding of what makes one pipe sweeter than the next, and what bestows a deeper colour.'

'How do you begin blending?' William asked, already enthralled by the introduction to this fascinating new life in Portugal.

*

Amos Bright was no less happy to be familiarising himself again with the cloth trade. Now that he'd been jolted into resuming his role as head of the business, he readily forsook the hours spent sitting idle. With clean air in his lungs from driving the wagon over one hillside to the next, and less alcohol in his bloodstream, he felt healthier already, and infinitely more cheerful.

'I thought I were done for, you know,' he confided to Eleanor one afternoon. 'It's not always for the best to train your childer to follow on in what you're doing. I saw our Will and Henry taking over more and more of t'work until eventually I thought, "Well, let 'em get on with it." But it's no sort of a carry on, sitting in t'front of t'fire with nowt but your thoughts for company.'

'You certainly seem much better now, love,' his wife said mildly, though she'd never forget how troubled she'd been that he'd appeared an old man at forty-five; and content to be so.

'I'm taking you to look at a house I've my eye on,' he continued. 'It's not far from Luke and Matthew Fortescue's – so there'd be some folk in the neighbourhood that aren't strangers to you.'

'I see,' said Eleanor, only she didn't see – how could she ever understand Amos for wanting to live near the two who'd encouraged half her family to work so far from home?

'It's a beautiful house, inside and out,' Amos perisisted.

'So's this,' said Eleanor sharply, her lips compressing.

'I've explained, haven't I, that it'll be a lot better to live nearer to Halifax.'

For you, perhaps, thought his wife, but contained her thoughts. Amos was a good husband, a good provider when kept off the drink, and men had a way of expecting everyone else to fall in with their wishes.

'We'll go there tomorrow,' he promised. 'Our Henry can manage to pick up any cloth that's ready for collection, and the roads won't be as busy, it's not a big day for t'Piece Hall.'

Eleanor would have liked more notice of the outing. They would be using the carriage and she wanted to look her best

38

for the present owners of this house which was becoming her husband's obsession. Out here they lived simply and, although their status justified her having Mrs Robinson to help in the house, they employed no living-in servants. She would have to prepare her one good gown herself and, with only young Isobel to assist, would have to dress her own hair.

By the following morning Eleanor had worked herself up into quite a state. No matter how hard she tried, she couldn't make her fingers form her glossy brown hair into the ringlets that she visualised. And instead of staying to help her, Isobel had ridden off in the wagon with Henry.

When Eleanor finally emerged, Amos beamed his approval of the cascade of dark curls, glinting with golden lights in the sun, and with a wide-brimmed hat anchored above them. The hat was blue, echoing the colour of her gown, a wide-skirted creation acquired two years ago for a family wedding.

'By, but you look grand!' he exclaimed, but smiling to himself as he noticed how Eleanor never failed to fix quantities of fine white lace over the square décolletage of her few elaborate garments. Personally, he'd have settled for somewhat less concealment, but the lace contrasted nicely with the blue of the silk, and matched the drapery falling from elbow to wrist.

Eleanor's smile was taut as he assisted her into the carriage. No amount of compliments would compensate for his rushing them into buying another home when she was happy in their old one. 'I've told Mrs Robinson we might not be back when our Charles is out of school. She says she'll stay behind after she's done t'cleaning. She won't be wasting her time, there's plenty of mending she can be getting on with.'

'That's good, love,' said Amos absently. His mind was already on their destination, and how to present its best features so that his wife would feel compelled to live there.

He took the same route from the Calder valley as he had with his son and daughter, talking all the while of the splendour of the scenery, of the healthy air.

In time, Eleanor decided she'd heard enough. 'Anybody'd think you were selling the place, not buying it, the way you're going on! There's nowt wrong wi' the air or the view where we're living now. If you have to carry on like this, preparing me, I'll think there's summat up with yon house long before I clap eyes on it!'

Amos choked down a snort. He tended to forget that Eleanor was no fool. Happen it was because she'd spent all these years devoted to bringing up children, and schooling herself to see through all their little schemes, that she hadn't lost the knack of seeing through *his*! He spoke hardly at all during the rest of the journey over the green hump of the hill, and took little note of the occasional dwellings standing amid windblown fields and woods.

They both glanced sideways when he slowed the carriage in front of the loveliest stone building of them all. In spite of her reluctance, Eleanor felt a surge of delight spiralling from deep inside her. No woman could fail to be impressed. And this place would get him away from his worst drinking cronies. 'You're a clever fellow, Amos Bright, I'll say that for you. You've gone and picked out the grandest house anybody could wish for. I daresay you'll tell me, an' all, that they're eager to sell . . .'

Her husband grinned. 'I'd not have fetched you all this way, if they weren't. As a matter of fact, it's a young lady lives here on her own just now. She lost her mother last backend, then her father took sick after Christmas and he died as well a few week sin'.'

'The poor girl! It's certainly too remote out here for a lass on her own. Has she got an eye on another place?'

'She's getting wed, soon as she decently can after her bereavement. I gather he's a farmer, so she has a home ready-made, not that anything she takes with her will come amiss.'

The interior of the house was no less pleasing than what Eleanor had seen from the road. The rooms were large, and every bit as clean as her own home. The windows looked out on three sides to countryside quite as open as she was accustomed to at Heptonstall. 'Are we really fairly close to Halifax?' she asked Miss Wilson, an agreeable young lady and sensible enough to win Eleanor's approval.

'A few miles down the road, that's all.'

Until today, Eleanor hadn't considered that she might find advantages in having access to a town. Suddenly, she was picturing herself with local aquaintances in Halifax – people who might have interests wider than the clothing business and rural occupations. Didn't every woman long to better herself? Slowly, considering how the move might also change her husband for the better, she turned to Amos. 'I know you've set your heart on this house. *Providing you mean us to have a fresh start*, I'll not stand in your way. I've said my say about Heptonstall, I'll not harp on about stopping there.'

Many of the particulars regarding the purchase were discussed there and then. When they had agreed as much as they could pending legal assistance, Miss Wilson insisted that they take tea with her. Her service was of silver, looking splendid indeed on the highly polished walnut table set before the window.

I'll have a silver teapot like that, Eleanor resolved, and everything to match. She wouldn't mind a similar table either, and she loved the idea of placing it near the window so you could absorb the quiet landscape instead of sitting up to the hearth. The only things Eleanor wasn't sure about were the armchairs. In the style of Chippendale, if not originals, they were from his oriental phase and, though their lime-yellow upholstery and gilded frames were bright enough, she thought them rather too intricate.

'You've surprised me today,' Amos told her as they eventually set out on the homeward journey. 'I was afraid you were determined nowt would shift you from where we are.'

'I've been content there, as well you know, but I reckon that in time I shall settle just as well in t'new house.' She would have Isobel and Charles about her, after all, and the other two whenever they came back to England.

Amos smiled and squeezed her arm. He couldn't have been more relieved. He'd never wanted anything more than this move to fresh surroundings. Normally, Eleanor proved intractable once she had her mind fixed on something. Today, she was all he'd ever wished her to be – so amenable that he experienced a strong urge to go out of his way to please her.

He had turned the carriage down a short stretch of uneven road and then along the line of the hill. A few moments later, he slowed the horses again. 'Does owt look familiar to you from here?'

Eleanor emerged from contemplation of the imminent changes, and saw the Fortescues' home a little way ahead of them. 'Oh,' she said warily. 'We're not going to be so far away from them, are we?' Her eyes narrowed. Amos might think he was doing her a service bringing her to live near their old friends, she wasn't at all certain that *friendly* was the way she felt towards them, these days.

This afternoon, no one, not even Mrs Sutcliffe, the Fortescue cousins' housekeeper, was at home.

'It's a shame, is that,' said Amos when there was no answer at the door.

Eleanor considered her acquiescence regarding the new house entitled her to be forthright now. 'I can't say I'm bothered,' she enlightened him. 'I'll be right with 'em when we do meet, I don't believe in being otherwise, but I'm not going to put myself out to see them two again.'

Nearing Heptonstall once more, with all the fields and woods which were etched into her daily life, Eleanor felt every one of her original misgivings returning. Panic surged up inside her. It was here that she belonged, where every lane and field corner would have been recognisable if she were blindfolded. She knew and loved every sound of all the four seasons: spring birdsong, summer harvesting, autumn gales, the eerie quiet bestowed by a snow covering. But she'd made her vows, all those years ago: she'd not give Amos cause now to doubt her willingness to move with him.

'You'll have to be looking for somebody a bit sharpish to buy our house then, won't you?' she said briskly, pressing back deep down inside her the immense tug of emotion which she'd experience when the time came for leaving.

'I'll do nowt of t'sort,' her husband announced.

Astonished, Eleanor wondered for one moment if the outing today had only been to test her readiness to go

42

wherever he wished. Happen now she'd given the right responses Amos was going to relent and let them stay in their old home. And despite her earlier resolve to concur, she felt some relief for she'd grown acutely conscious as they approached Heptonstall that by moving she'd sacrifice a lot. 'Ay, love . . .' she began, delighted to have her wishes considered.

Amos interrupted. 'I'm none selling. I said our William, Henry as well, would be given a home whenever they were in England, didn't I? This place'll be theirs as soon as we move out, theirs as long as they live. It were made out of two houses for us, it'll be plenty big enough for them and their families to live there.'

As well as disappointed, Eleanor was uneasy, compelled to question him. 'Haven't you thought, love, that they mightn't allus get on wi' each other, living so close?'

Amos chuckled. 'I'm not daft, you know! 'Course I've thought of that. They mun learn to get on, else lose t'place. I'll see they're tied down to getting on together here.'

Eleanor knew at once that her husband's decision had been contrived to punish their sons for quitting both home and business. A part of her longed to argue that he should temper his conclusion with love, but she desisted. The other half of her own heart was already heavy with William's absence and with the pending departure of his brother. Maybe there was some justification for this action; and at least it would prevent friction in her own home on occasions in the future when William and Henry's visits to England coincided.

Henry was told about the idea that same evening. His immediate response was dread of living alongside the brother who'd pre-empted the position he'd sought with Fortescue's. He was angered, as well, by his father's blatant reprisal for the decision to work elsewhere. Only the knowledge that he need spend little time in Yorkshire enabled him to reply quite calmly. 'That's generous of you, Father, I've always loved living here.' He was becoming adept at concealing his emotions and managed now to make his smile bland, even appreciative. Behind each word he uttered, he was framing plans that would keep him absent for longer periods.

He would need an extended visit to the bodega in Jerez and to the vineyards in the area. He knew less about sherry than he'd gathered already in conversations with the Fortescues about the production of port. Following his initial training he would expect a through grounding in the trading of wine, some of which was continued in the coffee houses of London. Matthew Fortescue had spoken of their opening a branch office, perhaps in Leeds or Bradford. At the time when this was first mentioned he'd imagined that living in the new house near Halifax and travelling there each day might be feasible. Now, he would never even try to reside anywhere but wherever he happened to be working: the last thing he wanted was living on his own with their William.

'You'll be glad to see each other when you've been apart for a while,' said Eleanor, willing Henry to believe something that was no more than an over-optimistic hope on her own part.

'Aye, I daresay we shall,' he concurred, and resolved the more firmly to avoid such a situation. Soon he had had enough of pretending enthusiasm for his father's schemes. When it became evident that Amos, if no one else, had already accepted that his idea would work, Henry made the most of the improvement in the atmosphere and excused himself to take a walk.

The fact that he'd had a tiring day, humping lengths of cloth out of cottages and hoisting them up on to the wagon didn't encourage him to go very far, and he was in no mood for cheerful reflection. He moved briskly through the cluster of houses that was Heptonstall itself, and paused only when out of sight of the family's windows. For a while, scarcely noticing exactly where he was, he leaned his aching back against a drystone wall, and inhaled deeply. Below him in the field that sloped down from the track, cloth was stretched to dry on the hooks of tenter frames. A familiar enough sight in this part of the West Riding, but one that always made him consider the clothier's trade. He might be eager to enter a different business, that didn't mean he'd no concern for

Bright's and that they should continue to thrive. His own discontent had been aroused, in part, by the signs of change along the Calder valley and anywhere, in fact, that spinning and weaving took place.

The search for sources of power which had resulted in water being used to work factories where cloth was produced was surging on, driving men to explore more advanced methods. Since the day in 1784 when a cotton mill opened at Styal over in Cheshire it had become inevitable that the days of cottage weaving were on the wane. Only the other day he'd heard tell at the Piece Hall that the owner of that same Styal mill had built an apprentice house for pauper children, whom he'd exploit as cheap labour. Henry had always known that the youngsters of poor parents were put to work, had watched them in weavers' cottages doing their share. What he couldn't stomach was the little beggars being compelled to sweat out the day in regrettable conditions, with no one to question it.

Happen he was selfish to want a different way of life for himself while there were Isobel and Charles still at home, and both of them, according to what they said, set to work in the family business. But then, he was only their brother, and not responsible for them. He was young enough to experience the tug of ambition, maybe sufficiently mature as well to ensure his dreams materialised. It might even prove, in the long run, to be the saving of them all. For instance, by the time young Charles had completed a thorough education, and was capable of tackling a job, he himself ought to be in a good position with Fortescue's. Who could guess what he might be able to do for his young brother?

'Thank goodness you're looking a bit more cheerful than you were!' a voice exclaimed behind him, startling him, for he'd remained unaware that he was observed.

'Hallo, Phillida,' he replied, glancing around as she came down the narrow path at the side of the field then over the stile to join him. 'I was just thinking . . .'

'Aye, I noticed it looked painful!'

Her smile removed any acidity in her words, though, and compelled him to smile back. Phillida Walshaw was a bonnie

45

lass. If he didn't understand better than most their Will's motives for leaving home, he'd have doubted his brother's sanity.

'How are you getting on?' he inquired, and saw her green eyes shadow.

'Not so bad, I suppose. We're kept busy, as well you know, that helps.' She paused, considering. 'You've not had any news get through as yet?'

'Nay, there's been no word so far. It'll take time, you know. He'd be two weeks or more sailing out to Portugal, then there'd be a similar period for news of him to get back. That's if anyone from Fortescue's or any acquaintances of theirs were bound for Yorkshire.'

'There's the mail, isn't there?'

'Aye, but even that requires somebody to travel from Oporto to London first off. I don't expect William will have found out if mail is being sent direct from there.'

Phillida's expression was rueful. 'If he even thinks to send me a letter, any road.'

'He didn't promise to write then?'

'I know him too well to even ask. He'll do his own way, he allus has, nowt's going to change him now.'

Yet you still remain interested in him, Henry thought, I wonder why? There couldn't be many more differences between any pair. There was Phillida's family adherence to John Wesley's teachings for a start, while if their Will managed to look in at Heptonstall church twice a year it was as much. There was the Walshaws' intolerance regarding all alcoholic drink, what must she have thought of William's determination to make his career in bringing greater supplies into the country?

'I don't know why I bother,' she announced. She might have been reading his thoughts. 'Him and me seem to have less and less in common. I've made it clear I'm not leaving home for him, not now.'

The sadness in those expressive green eyes, though, was telling him differently, making him ache on behalf of the beautiful lass who cared too much. Aye, and to ache as well for the man out there in a strange land, who'd wonder if he'd

46

ever keep the affection of this girl who had been his first love while they were growing up together.

'Happen he'll realise how much you mean to him now that he can't see you just when the fancy takes him.'

Phillida sniffed. 'And happen I'll start noticing there's more folk than William Bright were born on this hillside!'

But the frozen look in her expression revealed how unlikely that was. Henry had often thought when other folk called her Phillie that it sounded like the foolish young creature which she most certainly was *not*. Today he began to wonder if the diminutive was well-judged!

The Douro took William's breath, left him close to gasping with its magnificence. They'd come most of the way upriver by *barco rabelo* before transferring to mules which plodded their way up a track far more hazardous than any packhorse trails in Yorkshire. On the water, he'd been too entranced by the view ahead and to both sides of them to heed either his own discomfort or his dread of their overturning. Here, with the terraced slopes dropping away to their left and soaring in further terracing above them, he again had no room for any emotion but wonder.

The river itself looked as blue as the cloudless sky over their heads, curving between steep-sided hills where trees fringed the vineyards. Containing the terraces were stone walls, and the earth itself appeared almost as rocky.

'Aye, the soil is stony,' Luke confirmed. 'But it suits the port-wine grape, as do the hot, dry summers.'

'I hadn't realised it was such an awe-inspiring area.'

Luke smiled. 'Don't tell me it beats owt we have i' Yorkshire!'

William laughed. 'It comes a close second,' he admitted, then corrected himself. 'Actually, it does seem more impressive.'

'They're mountains rather than hills, aren't they, and almost canyon-like in places where the Douro has sliced a way through.'

Approaching the Fortescue *quinta*, the cluster of buildings where the company accommodated the workers they brought in, as well as the *adega* for the initial stages of producing wine, Luke called over his shoulder to William, and pointed along the hillside. 'See that – they've begun gathering the grapes. We bring in folk from villages throughout the region, you know, and they stay with us until every last grape is picked.'

Narrowing his eyes against the sun, William could just discern a row of men, slowed by the immense baskets carried on their backs, as they strode steadily in line along the precipitous ridge.

'Each one is carrying well over a hundred pounds of fruit which has been transferred from smaller baskets by the women who do the actual picking.'

'It's to be hoped the men don't trek very far in this heat!'

'Here, it's quite some distance. Most of our vineyards, though, are so far away from the *quinta* that the grapes come in by bullock cart. Then we buy in from other growers as well. You'll see all that while we're up here.'

Drawing nearer to the *quinta*, William heard the singing. The men surprised him by still having breath for song but the sound thrilled him as it soared about the surrounding hills.

He was exhausted and sore when they eventually dismounted from the weary mules. Luke led him across the courtyard and into the nearest building. A large granite tank, raised above the floor, was being filled with grapes by sweat-soaked men who touched their hats to Luke, and greeted him in Portuguese before staring curiously at William.

'That's the *lagar* they're filling,' Luke told him. 'As you can see, it's almost ready for the cut.'

'The cut?'

'The Portuguese word is *corte* – the first treading. Should be this evening.'

Although eager to see every process in the making of port, William was so tired that he couldn't believe he'd remain awake to watch. Later, however, after washing, shaving and donning a fresh shirt and breeches, he felt more inclined to pay heed to what was going on.

48

Luke took him back into the *adega* and introduced him to Eduardo Leite, their manager in the Douro region.

'I hope you will enjoy this process,' the darkly-tanned man with black hair and glittering eyes said.

William hadn't been prepared for it to prove entertaining, but as soon as the team of bare-legged men appeared, clambered into the massive tank, and began singing, he smiled to himself.

'We've none of us out here found owt to beat bare feet,' Luke confided as the men stretched arms across one another's shoulders, and marched to the commands of their leader. In no time at all they were wet to the thighs with the dark red juice.

Drawn by the singing, several people had drifted in to watch. It was Luke who eventually took William away. 'It continues like this for two hours, then afterwards they dance in the *lagar*, and follow that with a more measured treading –each man walking in the "must" which by then is growing easier to work.'

'What does the must look like at that stage?'

'It has virtually reduced to liquid, purplish in colour.'

After they had eaten Luke insisted that they return to see this last stage of the treading. Quite a crowd had gathered to join in the singing, but William could scarcely hold his eyes open while he was shown samples of the dark sticky mass.

'This will be left until fermentation commences,' Luke explained and laughed as William tried to disguise a yawn. 'I must let you get to your bed, we've an early start tomorrow, touring the vineyards.'

The vineyard manager was Antonio Vasques, a man not much more than William's age who impressed him immediately with his knowledge of wines and a reasonable command of English.

Half the time, though, as he and Luke inspected the terraced slopes around the Fortescue *quinta*, William's attention was drawn away towards the surrounding mountains and the river that carved its way through them. Although so different from the hills about his home, their beauty seemed to induce nostalgia, and made him long for

49

Phillida. Much of the time since his arrival in Portugal had been so crammed with information which he must retain, and with processes and regulations to learn, that he'd spared no more than the occasional brief thought for her. Those thoughts had been loving, nevertheless, and in no way tempered by the differences on which they had parted.

Today, the splendour of the scene made him ache to share it all with Phillie, to bring her to experience for herself the wonder that it generated. If only he were able to stand here with her at his side, it might lessen the yearning which now was gnawing into the heart of him.

—4—

Isobel had never been more delighted. Her father had promised to pay her for the hours she put in working with him. She felt more grown-up already. Today, she was determined she'd really show how sensible she could be. She had prayed and prayed that she would be given a chance to prove that she could be so useful that Bright's would never manage without her.

Henry was visiting London with Mr Fortescue to meet someone connected with the shipping of sherry. As soon as he heard about this Father had arranged that Eddie Gaukroger, the son of one of their best weavers, should accompany them to Halifax. Eddie was to help with any heavy lifting, but she knew well enough he'd not be fit for much more. The bit that Eddie understood about cloth was what he'd learned during the part of his eighteen years when he'd assisted in his father's weaver's cottage. Eddie could use teasels to raise the nap, could hold the woven cloth taut to hook it on to its tenter frame, and in his early days he'd no doubt learned how to comb out the wool ready for spinning, but he'd never make a clothier. He wasn't particularly bright either. His speech was laboured, and he laughed a lot, when things weren't really funny. Isobel often heard her mother saying it was a pity for him.

She had decided that, somehow, she would encourage her father to take Eddie on permanently when their Henry finally left. For weeks now she had worried about how she'd ever grow strong enough for humping all that cloth, not only when hauling it up on to the wagon, but down at the Piece Hall when the material had to be handled while it was being appraised.

Isobel was determined to become her father's real assistant herself. Not that she'd announce her intention yet – folk would only tell her not to talk daft. If she was going to become the one person that Father could rely on, she would have to ease herself gradually into the way of it, and that was beginning today. She wasn't particularly concerned about being barely thirteen years old; and she didn't understand that the youth generating all this eagerness was responsible also for her inability to foresee potential difficulties. What Isobel did fully understand was that other youngsters of her age were being employed, so who could stop her working for Father? Even he admitted she was quicker than he was at doing sums. She'd try that hard, he'd soon be glad to have her to hand whenever he went to the cloth market. He had praised her for her neat writing more than once, said it was better than either William's or Henry's.

Eddie seemed to be good with horses, even though he said he'd not had dealings with them in the past. He was sitting up front now, grinning away to himself while Amos Bright let him take the reins.

'There'll be ale for thee, lad, and a good dinner,' Amos told him.

Eddie nodded, his grin widening in the placid round face. He stiffened his rather loosely hung body, and his head of straight golden hair shot upwards. 'Thanks, Mr Bright, I'll try and be good.'

Isobel had visited the Gaukrogers often enough to be aware of the regularity with which his mother instructed Eddie to behave. Of all the times that Isobel had chatted with his sister Susan, whom she greatly admired, there'd never been one when Eddie became naughty. Today, he was resolved to please, following like a shadow – a misshapen shadow on account of all the finished cloth he carried – while Amos did business at the Piece Hall.

After the briefest visit to the rows of waiting packhorses, Isobel joined the pair, still confident that her father would grow accustomed to having her around him here. There was no time now for gazing all about her as before. Ever since her older brothers had shaken them all with their intentions, she'd been willing herself to grow up swiftly. She wakened every day wishing there were some means of hastening the

52

process. She must find a way of being ready to replace Henry next year in 1791.

As they went about the cloth market, she noticed thankfully that her father was so busy explaining everything to Eddie that he was relying on her to record each transaction. She learned swiftly to note all the details, and after the first sale was writing down names, lengths of cloth and the selling price even before her father turned to instruct her.

Their transactions for the day were concluded more swiftly then Amos had expected and he smiled as he led the way through the crowds to the yard of The Union Cross inn. 'We mun sit out here,' he told them. 'Yon's no place for a little lass.' He felt massively protective towards Isobel. He'd been deeply touched by her eagerness to help him, and she'd amazed him with her practical common sense which he hadn't been able to fault.

Isobel was elated to be dining out in Halifax and noted that the girl who served them looked hardly any older than herself. She ate as delicately as she knew how, sitting upright, and trying not to notice Eddie's wolfish manners. She might have developed beyond imagining the Piece Hall a palace, but she'd not deny herself pretending the inn was a fashionable eating house. Gazing beyond the roofs of Halifax, she tried to locate the general direction of their new home where she hoped to grow up to become somebody important. Behind her was Beacon Hill, long and steep, and grass covered, with occasional trees and glimpses of a packhorse route.

The tollroad used today was roughly ahead of her now, climbing up from the town before it followed the valley of the Calder. Their future home, therefore, must be somewhere to the right of that, the way to it obscured by the town's houses and shops.

'Aye, 'course I'll see she behaves hersen.'

It was Eddie Gaukroger's promise which alerted Isobel to the fact that her father was rising, about to walk away from the table with a man whom she recognised as a clothier from Luddenden. She gave Eddie a look. *He'd* see she behaved indeed! Her morning's decision that Father must be encouraged to engage Gaukroger's son took an abrupt lurch. But she was bound to acknowledge, however privately, that it must look to everyone else as though she needed supervision. She couldn't expect them to understand yet how swiftly she was maturing. Not till she'd proved how much she could tackle.

Walking away towards the door of the inn, Amos glanced back, checking that Isobel was all right. He could leave her, couldn't he, just while he had one drink? Being greeted by Septimus Hallewell here had reminded him that he wanted somebody to talk to. The day so far had been a strain, he was entitled now to a small recognition of its passing without catastrophe. He had been compelled to tell their Henry and Will that he'd carry on in t'future without them; he'd not have either of them thinking they were indispensable. But he'd lain awake into many a night since then wondering if he was still physically capable of managing everything himself.

'Have you finished for t'day down at t'Piece Hall?' his fellow clothier asked.

Amos nodded. 'Aye, but I can't stay long in here, Septimus, I've plenty to do.' And this was the day when he would prove he could take just one drink without making a fool of himself.

To demonstrate her new maturity Isobel began discussing the people around them, gentry walking towards their carriages, the ladies in elaborate gowns, some of them very wide-skirted to accommodate quantities of petticoats. 'Just see her,' she exclaimed to Eddie. 'You know of course that it's a sign of wealth to wear layer upon layer of clothing.'

Eddie grunted, shook his head. 'Don't know as it bothers me.'

'It's good for trade, though,' Isobel observed, although she didn't think these materials were the kind made in the West Riding. Briefly, she wished that they were – some of the cloths handled by Bright's were as dreary as they were good. She'd love to trade in brilliant silks or gleaming velvets and satins.

'I like that one's hair,' Eddie declared firmly, so loudly that the lady whose intricate head was being noticed heard him and was unsure whether to feel gratified.

The hair was arranged in massive swirls on top of her skull, and lavishly spread with white powder. Isobel hated it. 'I think it's horrible, and powder's going out fashion, any road. Just as well too – they use some sort of lard, you know, to keep that lot in place, then it gets all caked with powder.' Her voice lowered in horror: 'Mice can creep into it at night, isn't that dreadful?'

If she were a lad, she'd choose to grow into the man she'd had her eye on for some considerable time. Tall, he was exquisitely dressed in new buckskin breeches, boots with splendid silver buckles, an embroidered coat the green of the woods near home, and a magnificent tricorn hat. It was the hat, she decided, which she most envied him – or the angle at which he'd contrived to place it. He looked so stylish and assured, infinitely more in command than men like her father and brothers who wore the plainer round-brimmed hat, so countrified in appearance. Since no amount of wishing could make her mature into a man, she must tailor her longings while she planned her future appearance. Happen she'd settle, after all, for looking like the young lady who this moment was descending from a sedan chair to greet that splendid fellow.

Attired in a pale gown that drifted out so daintily around her, with a broad-brimmed hat trimmed with ribbons – and didn't a *hat* look far more positive than a mere bonnet – she clearly had the man enraptured. He was gazing so fondly when he grasped her gloved hand as it gracefully emerged from the cascade of lace at her wrist. Isobel longed to be so elegant that somebody would admire her. 'The trouble is all that lace and them wide skirts will only be in t'way when I'm clambering on and off the wagon,' she reflected.

Eddie only grunted; he was enjoying a nap.

Isobel hadn't realised previously how much she loved people. Maybe that was why she'd relished her early visits to the Piece Hall so much. She always liked to observe the crowds of merchants there, listening to their urgent voices, and greeting everybody who knew her father. No matter if she was to remain sensibly dressed for the rest of her life, she would enjoy that life, so long as she was involved in all this activity, selling great quantities of nicely woven cloth.

Easing herself into a different position on the hard bench, Isobel shivered a little as a cool autumn breeze rattled the inn sign, and blew dust about them. But suddenly she felt not quite thirteen years old again and rather alarmed. Where was Father? What time was it? She couldn't have been asleep? She shook Eddie's arm until, with a splutter and a muttered oath, he ceased snoring and opened dull blue eyes.

'It must be time we were making our way home,' she announced. 'Will you please go inside and find my father?'

'Aye, I think I better had.'

Slowly, he prised himself off the bench and away from the rough table. Rubbing sleep out of his eyes like a massive baby, he lumbered towards the entrance of the inn. When he emerged, he was supporting Amos with one arm beneath his arm and around his back, the other hand was steadying his chest.

'Father!' Isobel exclaimed, anxiously. Bounding to her feet, she sent the bench rocking behind her and ran towards them. 'Whatever's wrong?' she demanded and then, because Eddie was slow to answer, tugged at her father's arm. 'Father, what's happened?'

With immense difficulty, Amos focused on his daughter. ' 'Lo, Isobel,' he said, and chuckled.

She realised then the full significance of days when he had seemed similarly indisposed, recalled innumerable occasions when she'd been hustled out of a room, or maybe sent to play elsewhere.

'He were drinking wine or summat, I don't think it's gone so well wi' the ale he'd supped,' Eddie announced.

'It went down a treat,' Amos contradicted.

His voice sounded peculiar, but not so strange that Isobel couldn't recognise his condition. 'We'll have to get him to the wagon. I'll go to t'other side of him, give you a hand, Eddie.'

Struggling with her father towards the wagon took a lot of effort and, what seemed worse to Isobel, attracted the attention of every passerby as well as all the people lingering outside the Union Cross. Once they had heaved Amos up on to the wagon she was thankful to see Eddie taking up the reins.

'Good job I learnt how to handle this on t'way here,' he remarked, pride in his newfound status making him sit more erect.

'Are you sure you can manage?'

'I'll frame better nor a little lass like you.'

'Well, just get us home quickly then.'

'There's no rush,' Eddie told her, with unaccustomed sagacity. 'The longer we take, the better he'll be when we get there.'

Twice they stopped while Amos vomited at the roadside, horrifying Isobel because his colour was drained along with his stomach, leaving him looking so waxy that she was afraid he really was ill. But by the time the wagon was slowly tackling the steep incline up to Heptonstall, Amos was beginning to regain command of himself. As they approached Gaukroger's cottage, he straightened his clothing and put on the hat which he'd earlier abandoned.

'I'm stopping 'ere for a while with you, lad. Have a bit of a rest.' He turned towards Isobel. 'You can go on home. Tell your mother I've got to have a look at a bit of a problem Eddie's father's having with t'cloth he's on wi' . . .'

'But father,' Isobel began, not knowing how to convince her mother that nothing was amiss.

'Do as I say – go on. Off this wagon with you, and over yonder as fast as you can! And if you don't do as I say this is t'last time you'll go to Halifax wi' us.'

That threat was more than sufficient. Nearly tripping over her skirts in her haste, Isobel vaulted down from the wagon and began running.

Watching her, Amos laughed, nudged Eddie. 'See that, don't you – that's how a lass should be. Now, are you takin' me inside. . . ?'

'We'll go straight up to t'weaving,' Eddie declared. He wasn't so silly that he'd risk his mother seeing them just now.

At the Brights' house Isobel's explanation received less acute attention than she'd feared. When she hurtled in through the kitchen door and blurted out the words she'd repeated all the way home, Eleanor nodded, hardly looking at her.

'We've got company,' she told her daughter. 'Best wash your hands and face and go through. Our Henry's back, and Mr Fortescue with him.'

Eleanor busied herself with the bread she was spreading with good farm butter, hoping that her task concealed from Isobel the fact that she'd only just dried her eyes. The reason that Mr Fortescue had come here with Henry was to ask that he be free immediately to go to Spain.

'If Amos can spare him earlier than we'd agreed, we'd be immensely grateful,' Matthew had told her. 'One of our most reliable men out there has taken to his bed, the doctor is concerned for his heart. It wouldn't be so bad if it wasn't at our busiest time . . .'

Eleanor had said that she supposed Amos would agree to Henry's setting out immediately. But it wasn't Amos who'd feel this most, even though he'd be losing such a good worker, she was the one who was close to breaking at the prospect of losing another son so soon. To make matters worse, Henry was all smiles, he seemed thrilled because he was getting away from home so quickly.

Willing herself to wipe all emotion off her face, Eleanor picked up the tea things, straightened her shoulders and walked through to the parlour.

Isobel had settled close beside her brother, her arm through his and her glossy brown head against his sleeve. She was listening while he described the crowded London coffee houses where they had done business.

'It's a whole world different from round here, you know. You'd like it, love – there's that many exciting folk.'

Isobel grinned up at her brother. 'This'll be all right for me for a year or two,' she revealed, in words she'd picked up from some grown-up somewhere. 'There's exciting folk, an' all, in Halifax. I had a right good look at 'em today.' Her heartbeat quickened. If Henry was going away soon, she'd be needed more to help with the wagon.

Her father had different plans though; sobered and walking in to the news from Matthew Fortescue that he wanted Henry immediately, Amos shrugged. 'There's a promising young man I've heard of not long since – lives over

58

in Luddenden, near Septimus Hallewell. He's been helping his father with t'farm, but his heart isn't in it. His family were asking Septimus if he would set him on, but you know what he's like – won't be bothered learning folk.'

'Can you get word to him that you'd like him to start wi' you?' asked Henry while Matthew Fortescue looked on in concern.

'I don't want to leave you with problems,' Matthew told Amos.

'You won't,' he said sharply, glanced across the room to his son. 'You needn't give him the idea there's nob'dy can take his place.'

It was only some time after Mr Fortescue had set out for home that Isobel at last was able to make sure of speaking with her father alone. 'Do you have to set this new man on?' she asked earnestly. 'I thought I'd be able to help you when our Henry goes.'

'Ay, love, and so you will. But you're nobbut a bit of a lass yet, you can't go seeing to stuff that a grown man can.'

'Happen not, but we could manage like we did today, with Eddie Gaukroger to carry t'pieces about. And he was good with the horses.'

'Never! I'd have to pay him nearly as much to do half a job as I'd give the other fellow for being a lot more use to me.'

There seemed to Isobel no way that she could persuade her father otherwise. Even she acknowledged that reasoning with him was beyond her. She went to bed that night bitterly depressed. She was saddened by Henry's imminent departure, but most of all she felt sickened by her father's refusal to give serious consideration to her suggestion of working with him.

The following day Eleanor Bright rose early, thinking to walk to Cartwrights' farm and purchase meat. She'd heard they'd slaughtered a pig, and if their Henry had to go to Spain, she'd see he had a right good send-off.

Amos was downstairs ahead of her, sitting before the empty fireplace.

'You could have lit the fire while you've been sat there,' she reproved him, nothing galled her more than having too much to do while other folk were idle. 'I'm off to get some meat for our dinners. I'll be needing flour, an' all, so I'll be wanting a shilling or two.'

Amos felt in his pocket, and handed across a few coins.

'Nay, that'll not be enough,' his wife exclaimed contemptuously. 'We're going to give our Henry a dinner to remember. It isn't as if we were short, it was only yesterday you were at t'Piece Hall.'

Amos tried not to let his discomforture show. Money was tight, these days, with a new house to pay for. And drinking yesterday with Septimus he'd somehow got drawn into conversation with a couple of other acquaintances from Luddenden. Septimus had paid for one lot of drinks, then *he'd* paid for another round, and then one more . . .

'Come on, love, please,' Eleanor persisted. 'If I don't get that meat and have it in the oven by half past, it'll none be ready afore the lad goes.'

'I'm afraid that's all I can let you have.'

'Oh. . . ?' Eleanor got no further. Suddenly, looking past her husband, she saw on the back of the door where he had tossed it, the good coat that he'd worn yesterday. The stains down the front were of a nature already too familiar. 'You were drinking again, weren't you?' she flared. 'Despite all your fine promises of how you'd keep the business going, you've succumbed again. And while our Isobel was with you.'

'She was all right, young Gaukroger were looking after her.'

'You surely don't think he's a fit person – though I daresay he's more sense than you seem to muster, these days.' Exasperated, she looked at the coins. 'Are you sure this is all you can let me have?'

'I've told you once, haven't I?' Amos snapped. He didn't enjoy this feeling that, by drinking, he had let them down. His self-esteem had fallen dispiritingly yesterday when he realised that he'd so readily forgotten his resolve. He wished he knew what was wrong with him, other folk were able to have just one glass in company. It was no fault of his that all those years ago he'd needed something to boost his courage. Establishing Brights' had taken his father some considerable time, and the young Amos had been of an anxious disposition. His father had stiffened him with a drop of port when he found confronting competitors and even their own clients trying. And if there was less need now of alcohol as a prop he'd developed a liking for the warm confidence it induced.

Eleanor sniffed. 'Maybe this'll get us a bit of that pork. We'll have to make that do with a few vegetables from out at the back.'

Amos hadn't been brought up to apologise. He was a Bright, wasn't he, had been trained by a father whose determination had eventually created a lively business and a manner that dared folk to question his attitude. Amos himself wasn't quite of that mould, the inherent nervousness had never really dispersed, though he'd learned how to disguise it. But this morning he felt disappointed and still rather ill, and he was irritated by his wife for noseying into what he'd been about.

Walking faster than any runner, Eleanor tore up the hill to Cartwright's farm. In the big homely kitchen, Jessie was setting dough to prove in front of the fire. When Eleanor appeared in the open doorway, she smiled at her. 'Hallo, love, is there summat you're wanting?'

'I'd like a nice cut of pork if you've a joint you can spare, please. Our Henry's off sooner nor we thought —' The lump in Eleanor's throat threatened to choke her.

'Here . . .' Jessie Cartwright wiped floury hands down her apron, and drew up a ladder-backed chair.

'It's just all got on top of me,' said Eleanor presently. 'First our Henry getting ready to go straightaway, then Amos . . .'

'What's to do wi' him? Not taken poorly, has he?'

'That was yesterday, with the drink he'd supped. Ay, Jess – I fair believed he'd given that up.'

Her friend shook a greying head. 'But they don't, love, do they, not once it's got a proper hold on 'em.'

'I wouldn't care, but I've done my level best to be accommodating. I said hardly owt at all, did I, when he came

61

up wi' this idea of going to live over near Halifax. I didn't say as much as I could have either when he didn't try to stop my lads from leaving home. He could have thought on those things, couldn't he, and kept to his word!'

'Nay, men don't think – only of their bellies and their work.'

'But Amos isn't thinking of his work, is he? And there's nobody else to mind the business while he's hardly got the wit to know what's going on.'

Witnessing her friend's distress, Jessie wondered if she had suggested too readily that Amos would never overcome his fondness for alcohol. 'Well, happen we shouldn't look on the black side so much. I daresay your Amos will take himself in hand now young Henry's off an' all.'

Talking with Jessie while a good joint of pork was prepared for her made Eleanor feel slightly more optimistic. What she *didn't* feel any more was so amenable to the proposed move. Walking back down the hill, she realised that once they moved to Halifax she'd be denied Jess Cartwright's company. She was going to suggest this one last time that they remain where they were.

When she arrived back at the house Isobel was alone in the parlour, and looking no more cheerful than Eleanor felt.

'Father said to tell you him and Henry've gone to see that fellow we're thinking to set on.' She was praying the lad wouldn't accept.

'They have, have they?' her mother responded and sniffed. She just hoped that the folk Amos was seeing today didn't offer to open up a bottle. And it'd be like this every time her husband was out of the house now – with no lad of their own old enough to keep an eye on him, he'd take advantage every blessed day.

Isobel was studying Eleanor's expression, watched how she ran her hand through her hair. She hated her mother being upset. 'We'll find a way to stop him drinking so much, don't worry, we'll find a way.'

'Disgusting, I call it,' Eleanor snapped. 'It's not right a little lass like you should be involved in the way he goes on!'

The pork was cooking nicely in the oven and vegetables

simmering on the fire when Amos and Henry returned. But the fact that they hadn't touched more than a glass of ale while they were out was almost outweighed by the gloomy humour they were in.

'Whatever do you think,' Amos began heatedly as he strode into the room. 'Yon lad weren't seeking a decent job, not to my way of thinking. He's been set on to comb wool for one o' Hallewell's weavers. A bit of a bairn could do that job!'

'Happen t'weaver hasn't any bairns,' Eleanor observed.

'That's just it,' her husband confirmed. 'Up to now, their little nephews have helped, now their mother wants 'em to go to school.'

Tending the pot of vegetables, Isobel had been listening, feeling the giant surge of excitement growing inside her. She would be needed after all!

Later, though, while sitting at the table Henry spoke up. 'If you can't manage, I'll stay on in Heptonstall till next year.'

Isobel wondered then if this might be best for everybody. She didn't wish Henry to go so far away just yet, and she could watch how he did everything, she'd be learning, growing older all the time. 'And I could help you, Father,' she insisted. 'Like yesterday.'

'If your father takes you on it won't all be roses,' her mother snapped. 'When the thorns prick remember nobody forced you into it.'

Amos carefully avoided his wife's keen gaze. But taking Isobel with him, and Eddie Gaukroger for the rough work would be one way of keeping Bright's going until their Charles was old enough to come in with him. And it would ensure him the freedom to please himself about what he did. He was aware now of the temptation to overindulge. This was the opportunity to be convivial without upsetting anybody. He'd mind he never had too much. Eleanor would be none the wiser.

'We'll see, we'll see,' he promised airily, without answering Henry, and keeping his smile as well as his motives to himself.

But his wife knew him too well for his plans to be anything

but transparent. 'If you set our Isobel on then come back once more the worse for drink, you'll not get me to leave this house for any other, so think on.'

'I have thought,' said Amos blandly. Until they made the move to Halifax he'd be extremely abstemious. Eleanor just didn't understand, that was it – being good company was part of a clothier's job.

Henry was more uneasy than ever about taking up his new position. How could he go off to Spain, knowing that his father would never resist a bottle that was put in front of him? How could he leave when young Isobel might have to bear the brunt of Father's excesses? That evening, despite heavy rain, he trudged off over the tops to see Matthew Fortescue again. 'I have a problem,' he began as soon as his coat was taken from him and he was led through to the welcoming fire in the exquisitely furnished parlour. He explained his father's failure to acquire the assistant he wanted, and his own reluctance to depart.

'It's a great pity, is that. You've looked forward so long to a new life, Henry. Your brother's settling well in Portugal. There's a letter for your family here, it's just arrived with news from Luke.'

William's evident delight only irritated Henry. He experienced afresh the intense annoyance he'd felt when first learning his brother had taken the job which should have been his own. On top of which making him into the second one to leave had turned *him* into the one with heaviest responsibility for the family's fate. Grimly, Henry steeled himself. 'Supposing I postponed going till into next year – after all, it was the original plan to join Fortescue's in the spring.'

Reluctantly, Matthew shook his head. 'I'm sorry, Henry, we're in trouble, like I said. I'll have to get somebody to replace our man who's ill. Once I've done that and if, as we hope, he recovers there'll be no possibility of setting on anyone additional.'

'Oh, I wish I knew what to do.'

'Sit down, lad, we'll have a bit of a talk.' Matthew was fond of his godson, and not too friendly with Amos Bright not to recognise his shortcomings. He rang for Mrs Sutcliffe and asked her to bring in a pot of tea then leaned forward, speaking gently but firmly. 'I've known your father for many a year, Henry. There's a lot that's likeable about him but, as wi' most of us, there's a selfish streak an' all. You know he said as he was going to make Bright's prosper on his own, I still reckon that could be the saving of him.'

'You don't think I'm being selfish wanting to choose my own life?'

'It's every young fellow's right. As I see it, it's only a pity that there's more families don't think that way, instead of assuming their sons will follow their father.'

'How – how would it be if I do as you suggest, and go out to Spain, learn as fast as I can so's I'll be some use to you. But if it becomes obvious that my father isn't managing to run the family business, ask you then to release me?'

His words dropped into a disturbing silence which extended into an alarming pause. 'Aye – go on,' his godfather agreed at last, though his smile was grim, 'I'll tell you now, though, I'd be sorry if it came to letting you go.'

Henry chuckled, glad the decision was made, and to have someone believe in him. 'How do you know that? You've not had me working for you yet!'

'I know you, though, don't I?'

Henry was given details of his passage, and promised that arrangements would be made for him to be met on his arrival in Cadiz.

'I can't believe this is happening at last,' he exclaimed later as he bade Matthew goodnight. 'It doesn't seem real.'

Cadiz was real enough, however, when his ship sailed in across the bay and Henry gazed at the port which had developed on its isthmus. In the intense sunlight all the buildings gleamed white, so startling that he used a hand to shield his eyes.

While they docked, shouts in the strange Spanish tongue reached him, combining with smells equally foreign and the fierce heat, exciting him. He'd been told to wait on the quayside where he'd be met by a carriage in the Fortescue livery of dark green with the ram's head outlined in gold. Despite wondering how he would be identified among so many disembarking passengers, to say nothing of men beginning to unload the vessel, Henry was in no mood for worrying. He had made friends during the voyage, three fellows of roughly his own age who were also engaged as sherry merchants. Saying goodbye to them now, promising to meet again, he was preoccupied and did not see the carriage approaching.

Turning from a final word to his new friends, his eye was caught by the insignia for which he should have watched and intuition cautioned that the person at the reins was impatient. Striding across and swiftly removing his smart new tricorn hat, Henry gave a sharp little bow. 'Henry Bright,' he announced, 'I believe it's me you've come to meet . . .'

'Yes, that is correct,' the driver responded with good English in a voice that sounded soft. When the person alighted to assist with his bags, the swirl of skirts confirmed his growing realisation that she was female.

'No, it's all right, thank you,' Henry said very quickly, stowing the bags rapidly to prevent her helping.

The dark brown eyes meeting his gaze were amused. 'I really am quite strong,' Catalina Escutia told him. 'But how are you, Señor Bright, I trust that you are not too fatigued by the voyage?'

'A little tired, thank you, but I enjoyed the time spent on board.'

She introduced herself, then asked: 'You travelled with friends?'

'Met them on the way. They're trading in sherry, an' all.'

He noticed a slight twitching of her firm lips and remembered what he'd understood from both Fortescues. 'I mean "as well",' he explained. 'You must tell me if my local speech sounds wrong.'

'I am sure you will be too careful for that,' she said smoothly, although her eyes were serious again.

'How is your father – er – Señor Escutia?' Henry inquired.

'It's him that's indisposed, isn't it? I hope he's showing signs of recovering.'

Catalina sighed. 'He is still very weak, and has been advised to rest indefinitely. But Ignacio Escutia has always had a strong constituence – er, *constitution*. He will not be forever incapacitated,' she added, motioning Henry to get into the carriage. 'This night we spend in Cadiz, in the morning we go to Jerez,' she told him.

Watching Catalina while she steered the carriage away from the busy harbour and on through narrow streets, Henry saw how he had first believed she might be male. Her black gloss of hair was drawn back tightly into a knot beneath the round brim of her severely plain hat. Her features were quite sharply chiselled with a large nose and a wide mouth which in repose had a tendency to turn down. Over her red silk gown she wore a dark jacket which could have been tailored for a man.

'You did not expect a woman to meet you?' she asked now over her shoulder.

Henry laughed ruefully. 'You don't miss much!'

Catalina glanced back at him. Her sudden smile illuminated her entire person. He sensed, though, that it could be rare and wondered what might be the cause of her habitual seriousness.

'I am the eldest in our family, Señor Bright,' she explained. 'My brother Carlos is only eighteen, a student in Seville. When my father is unwell and neither of the Fortescues in Spain, I try to become a substitute for them.'

'You work for the company then?'

'Normally, I keep the ledgers, that kind of thing. In an emergency – who knows?'

'My young sister would wholeheartedly approve, she's made up her mind to assist my father.'

'He is a cloth merchant, yes?'

'Aye. So, Matthew's been explaining my background?'

'It was Luke Fortescue who told me. Since we were without my father for the vintage, Señor Luke came to us for a day, to ensure that all was well, you understand. It was quicker that he should travel from Portugal than that his cousin come out from England.'

'They don't each keep to one line then?'

'I am sorry – you were saying. . . ?'

'I should be the one apologising. Your English is so good I'm forgetting it's not your native language. All I meant was to ask if Luke doesn't keep to working with port, and his cousin with sherry?'

'Now, most of the time they do specialise, but it was not always so. When I was small we saw them in turn, or so it seemed, in order that both might be totally familiar with both processes.'

'Very wise,' said Henry, wondering how he would frame when it came to learning *one* process.

Conversation settled on the Fortescue cousins, how they had been introduced first to Spain and then to Portugal, and to their wines. Later that evening, over dinner, Henry described to Catalina the Fortescue home in Yorkshire, the contrasting greens of the surrounding valleys and hills, the wildness of the moors.

They were staying in an old house in the heart of Cadiz, with an elderly housekeeper and manservant who spoke scarcely a word of English, and yet had succeeded for years to maintain a comfortable home there for anyone connected with Fortescue's who had business in the port.

'Are you driving me into Jerez in the morning?' Henry inquired, as Catalina bade him 'Buenas noches', and was pleased when she nodded.

He pondered on what she'd told him of how most sherry producers still worked in Cadiz, some had set up bodegas in nearby Puerto de Santa Maria and others in Sanlucar de Barrameda. Fortescue's were among the few to choose Jerez itself, but they were very close to their vineyards there, and received the grapes more swiftly and in better condition.

According to Catalina's prophesy, most sherry shippers would one day centre their production on Jerez. Tranferring the casks of finished wine to a port would be relatively simple, she maintained.

After leaving Cadiz behind the following morning and gazing out at the scenery, Henry noted that the low hills surrounding Jerez seemed to be covered in vineyards. As they approached, the many spires of the city's churches and cathedrals drew the eye onwards and up towards a fortification.

'See the *Alcazar*?' Catalina called him. 'The fortress . . .'

'You'd have a job to miss it, but then that's the idea, isn't it!'

'It may not quite compare with the Alcazar in Seville, but it is important to us.' Adroitly steering the carriage, Catalina turned a corner past a competitor's bodega. 'Fortescue's is across the city, towards its northern edge.'

Henry smiled and nodded, scarcely able to believe, despite the foreign feel of the place, that his new life really was beginning.

Leaving behind the ancient streets of Jerez with what had seemed to Henry an extraordinary number of churches, the exterior of the Fortescue bodega looked pleasingly uncluttered and cool. After passing through its gates Catalina sprang down from the carriage and turned to check that Henry was alighting.

'You may leave your baggage there, it will be safe until we go from here this evening,' she told him.

He waited while she handed the reins to a grave-faced young man who had appeared to open the gates. When Catalina turned towards him again she was smiling at Henry's interest in the expanse of grapes, spread out on round esparto grass mats. 'We are sunning them,' she explained, 'to bring out the sweetness.'

Carefully, she led the way around the edge of the mats which were so numerous that they seemed to Henry to fill the entire area between where they were standing and the arched white frontage of the bodega itself.

They were heading towards the main entrance when Catalina suddenly turned aside to their left. Walking close to the white walls, Henry felt the heat coming off them, increasing the discomfort he'd experienced since arriving in Spain. 'It's still hot, isn't it, even though we're well into September,' he observed.

Catalina nodded, her dark eyes glittering. 'You should be thankful you did not first come here in the middle of summer. We are only a relatively short distance away from Seville – the city that is considered the hottest in the whole of Spain.'

'I certainly think it'll take me some while to acclimatise.'

'Well, now for a while you are escaping the sun,' Catalina told him, opening a door and entering a stark room housing several large square wooden troughs. 'Oh, they have finished treading for today,' she exclaimed. 'I thought perhaps to show you.'

'I didn't know that went on at the bodega itself.'

'Only because some of our vines are close at hand here. You are quite right that the process is carried out beside the vineyard.' She glanced up at a large clock hanging on the wall. 'The men have stopped early today, or perhaps they did not work – there are not many more grapes remaining now from these particular vines.'

They were about to move on when Catalina went over to one corner. 'I show you, though, the *zapatos de pisar* worn by the men.'

Henry glanced down at the leather boots which were studded with nails. 'I always thought they used their bare feet.'

She shook her head quite fiercely. 'No, that is the Portuguese method, ours is more effective,' she informed him, her manner suggesting that the differences between the races included far more than the making of wine. This surprised Henry as well; he'd always considered the Portuguese were akin to Spaniards. He would have to be careful what he said.

He was being conducted through into the main section of the massive bodega. The heady sherry fragrance which had gradually increased with their approach now seemed intense, and was tempered only with the scent of the wine butts themselves.

'I am going to introduce you to our capataz,' Catalina explained. 'He can tell you far more than I about the making of the sherry.'

The capataz, or head cellar man, was younger than Henry had anticipated, not more than ten years at most older than himself. When they located him between two of the many rows of stacked butts, Catalina introduced him to Henry, then immediately began speaking in her own tongue and the capataz nodded.

'This is the venencia,' Alberto Martinez the capataz explained, indicating his silver sampling cup on a long

71

whalebone handle. 'I show you how we use . . .' Whereupon he went to the nearest barrel, dexterously immersed the venencia, and prepared to pour into one of three glasses held in his left hand.

Instinctively, Henry stepped well back when he noticed the venencia being raised higher and higher until it was above Alberto's head. But not one drop was lost as the thin stream of pale brown liquid descended into one of the glasses. The process was repeated until each glass contained sherry; and then Alberto offered the venencia to Henry. He was reluctant to take it. He'd no intention of showing himself as incompetent.

'Nay, you've fair capped me!' he exclaimed, shaking his head.

Alberto smiled, having understood the gesture but not the words. 'I show you how – you try now, *si*?'

'I'm sure that would prove very wasteful. How long did it take you to learn to do that?'

Alberto merely shrugged, shaking his head whilst an amused Catalina turned and walked briskly away from them.

'The butts are oak,' Alberto explained when Henry inquired. 'Made in our own coopery. I will ask someone to demonstrate, we must choose a time when they are charring the new butts.'

Henry grinned. 'You'll not catch me out with that; Mr Fortescue has described how the butts are made ready by firing the inside.'

'Then it is not so exciting! You know what you are expecting.' The capataz, brown eyes sparkling, took him aside instead and showed him one cask where the entire surface of the wine was covered with a thick layer of what, at first sight, looked like a pale crust.

'That is the flor,' Alberto told him. 'It grows on the surface of the sherry quite spontaneously. Flor means "flower" and we consider it distinctive, as it appears hardly anywhere else besides Jerez. It is, in fact, a yeast – you will learn in time the significance of its presence at different stages of maturing of the wine. Today, I wish that you simply familiarise yourself with its nature. You see here how thick and white it is.'

Turning away, the capataz found another sample butt. 'In this one, however, note please how the flor is thinner and of a yellowy hue.'

'What's the reason for that?'

'You cannot guess? I was going to ask you.'

'I'm sorry, I haven't any idea.'

'We were obliged to replace just one stave of that barrel with fresh wood, that was sufficient to affect the process once it again was used for wine.'

'The sherry won't be spoilt?'

'No – different, that is all. All is good, the changes taking place when the flor is present determine the character of the sherry that emerges finally. As you will know already, some is less sweet, some seems lighter, and so on . . .'

'There's a lot to learn.'

'*Si* – but do not be forgetting that we are here all the time. We can advise or inform always if difficulties arise.'

'Thank goodness for that!'

'You will learn much whilst you are at the bodega and when you examine the vineyards, but you are the merchant – so long as you absorb sufficient to be able to speak with confidence of the wine you are handling, more will not be expected of you.'

'I feel as though I'll need to be here day and night to learn all that goes on.'

'Night, hardly at all, unless you wish to see the treading. The men commence at midnight normally and work until noon. But the interesting part is what happens afterwards to the juices we extract.'

'I'm sure it is.'

Again, Alberto smiled. 'You must not look so anxious, and especially today. Did Catalina not tell you that she plans for you to visit Sevilla before work really begins for you?'

Not having suspected that he would be seeing Seville already, Henry felt guilty about avoiding work and also that he was unprepared with any reading on the history of the city. As they rode towards the centre of Seville, however, and the splendid Giralda became visible ahead of them, he felt his spirits soaring.

'What an elegant tower!' he exclaimed, noting the carved arabesques and mullioned windows. 'Is it very old?'

Catalina nodded. 'But yes – originally a minaret, the main part is twelfth century. You will see later that there are bells in the upper structure. That was added much later, after it became Christian.'

'I've never seen anything so lovely. And is this the cathedral?' he asked as they entered the square.

'*La catedral, sí*. An easy word for you to remember, that is why I tell you in Spanish.'

Henry repeated the word, and won a small smile from her. He'd observed already that Catalina didn't smile very readily, but the way her dark eyes lit when she did so was worth a long wait.

He glanced at the cathedral again before they drove past towards another corner of the square.

'See the Alcazar,' Catalina said, nodding towards ancient walls, and then they too were out of sight for she had turned the horses away between houses with wrought-iron balustrades complementing flower-laden balconies. 'We have a house here,' she continued. 'My father was at the university, like my brother whom you will be meeting. Father fell in love with the city and always is happy to return here.'

'I'm not surprised.' Henry had sensed that the Escutia family might be anxious to get him away from Jerez for a few days. The original arrangement that he should stay with them until he found somewhere suitable for himself couldn't be very convenient for them while Señor Escutia was ill. But Catalina had explained during their journey from Jerez that they were here to inspect some fine new wine bottles. An English friend of her father, too old now to travel, had acquired a new supply, marked with his crest. And suddenly Henry's conscience was cleared. There was time enough to learn his new job and all he experienced now was an intense feeling of being completely captivated by Seville.

'This area is the Barrio de Santa Cruz, it is renowned for its picturesque narrow streets, and for the people who have lived here . . .'

'The Escutias maybe?' Henry suggested.

Catalina laughed, shaking her head. 'No, no – we are very ordinary family. But close by our home is the house where the artist Murillo lived. And Velazquez also just around the corner.'

They were hardly more than names to Henry. Briefly, he wished he'd had a university education, though perhaps such a longing was foolish: hitherto he'd been proud of his grammar school, and at least it had prepared him sufficiently to make possible this new career.

His surroundings would not permit any regrets. Each corner their carriage turned presented new aspects enhanced by the rows of balconies spilling foliage and flowers over white walls. And when they reached a square where buildings surrounded orange trees, and above nearby roofs the Giralda and La Catedral were visible, Catalina announced, 'We are arrived.'

There was no time for hesitation. She led him through double doors that gave onto a courtyard, its tiled walls multicoloured, the central fountain and surrounding greenery exquisitely cool after the blaze of Andalusian sunshine.

Their approach had drawn out an elderly housekeeper to welcome them, and running footsteps brought Carlos Escutia down a staircase.

He and Catalina embraced, then his grasp was firm over Henry's outstretched hand. 'How do you do?' Carlos said with a sharp little bow of his head of dark, curling hair. His voice was more deeply accented than his sister's, and Henry wondered if this might be the extent of his English. 'Did you have a good journey?' Carlos inquired, proving the supposition incorrect.

'It was champion,' Henry began, remembered, and grinned. 'I mean it was very good indeed, thank you.'

'We must show you your room,' Catalina insisted, her hand light on Henry's arm. 'You will be given everything you need by Señora Leal, here. She has no English, if there is anything you require and you cannot make yourself under-stood, please ask either Carlos or myself.' They would eat as soon as he had unpacked, she also explained, and then perhaps he would wish to see something of the city?

In common with other Spanish families, they ate *la comida* later than any good Yorkshire wife would serve midday dinner. The quantity and variety of the food amazed Henry. They began with innumerable small dishes to be sampled; *calamares* which he loved until told they were squid, serrano ham which was delightfully cured, and pieces of *tortilla*. When it came to time for the main dish of meats cooked in sherry he almost felt too full, but the aroma was too wonderful to resist and its flavour was anything but a disappointment.

At first they had given attention to the meal with either Carlos or his sister explaining the traditional recipes, as well as relating how Señora Leal had cooked for them since the day their father bought this house. All at once, though, Carlos glanced over the table to Henry, his brown eyes glittering with excitement. 'I take you to the Maestranza, *la plaza de toros, si?*' he suggested.

When Catalina translated this as, 'the bull-ring', Henry did not know how to reply. They couldn't have done more for him ever since he'd disembarked in Cadiz, how could he be so churlish as to refuse to fall in with everything they had in mind for his entertainment? Yet he could summon no interest at all in watching a bull-fight.

'I think perhaps not today,' said Catalina, rescuing him.

His answering smile expressed his gratitude. 'If you don't mind, there's so much else to see . . .'

'And Carlos is obsessed with the bull-ring.'

'And why not?' her brother challenged. 'The matador is to be greatly respected.' He added, to Henry: 'I make that my career, you know.'

'I fear that our parents do not approve of the plans Carlos cherishes for becoming a matador,' Catalina observed later when she and Henry were ambling towards the cathedral. 'Father maintains that he did not send Carlos to university for that. But we Escutias are strong-willed, I suspect that there is going to be quite a battle.'

'I can't say owt against that, can I?' said Henry ruefully. 'Look how I decided to cut loose from t'family trade.'

'And your father also was displeased?'

'You might say that. What made it worse was our William beginning to ship port. Did you hear about that?' he asked, looking sideways at her.

'I understood that you were not the first in your family to join Fortescue's.'

'It was me that should have gone into port shipping. I'd been offered work out there long since.'

'*Que lastima!* I hope you are not too disappointed.' Her expression which tended so often to be enigmatic gave nothing away.

'Not now, I'm right enjoying myself. Even though I feel as if I ought to be working instead.'

'But you will be learning when we examine those new bottles. And the harvest is in, are we not entitled to come away from Jerez?'

'Happen you are!'

'Your turn will come, have no fear. Although Father is recovering he will need to lean on you for some long while. We mean to use you to the limit. The moment we return, we shall keep you so occupied that the days will run into each other.'

Remembering to remove his new tricorn hat, Henry followed Catalina inside the cathedral where she explained, 'Only St Peter's in Rome and your own St Paul's are larger than our *catedral* here. We were living in Seville when I was confirmed, therefore it is especially important to me.'

Henry nodded, suddenly overwhelmed. He had admired St Paul's during his recent visit to London, but only from the distance as it dominated the city skyline. 'It's a heck of a lot bigger than Heptonstall church!' he exclaimed, smiling.

'Are you Catholic, Henry?'

'No, Church of England.' He hadn't thought very deeply about differences other than those between his own Church and the Methodists which had sprung up through the Wesleys' teaching. For the first time ever, he wondered how it might be to belong to a worldwide faith such as this. It

77

must be grand to enter a church in any country you visited and experience the feeling that you were at home.

'This way, I think, first . . .' Catalina whispered.

Gazing repeatedly to left and right, amazed by the size and the splendour of the chapels they were passing, astonished by the quality as well as the quantity of their statues and carvings, Henry was unprepared for standing before the tremendous altarpiece. He'd never seen so much gold, had never even contemplated that men could create such magnificence. Moved, he stood rapt. He sensed Catalina's gaze upon him.

'There are thousands of carved figures,' she murmured.

There were colours other than gold, he noticed now, reds and blues, touches of white, bringing the figures to life. 'By, but it's grand!'

The mood of wonder persisted, drawing them together while they explored further treasures, holding them in companionable near silence when they emerged and began climbing up inside the Giralda. The swift-grown affinity altered Henry's opinion of Catalina's apparent self-containment, it became instinctive to extend a hand for hers when the slope of the continuous ramp seemed to grow steeper.

Catalina smiled up at him. 'Whenever I come here, I envy King Ferdinand who – so legend says – rode up the inside of the Giralda on horseback.'

'Do you ride?' he asked her, recalling how well she handled the carriage horses.

'But naturally! I am Andalusian.'

The next minute they stepped out on to the open section of the tower where others were pausing to gaze out over the city. There seemed no limit to their view. Over the conglomeration of rooftops and the generous breadth of the Guadalquivir river, the eye was magnetised by the hills that ranged outwards until distance hazed them. 'You'd think you'd be able to see the vineyards surrounding Jerez!' said Henry, feeling how strange it was to have this expansive view and not be atop the moors or the steep, wooded hills of Yorkshire.

'I am afraid that is being rather fanciful,' Catalina began with another smile.

The bells striking the hour interrupted her. Right beside them as they were, their clangour was deafening. They were both greatly startled as they felt the entire edifice vibrate. Instinctively, Henry reached out, then steadied Catalina against him. Her former self-possession no longer appeared a barrier between them. Even though she still impressed him as out of the ordinary.

She seemed to scorn the presence of a *duenna*, and he could imagine there had been family arguments about her driving the carriage herself.

The man they were to visit lived but a short distance from the Escutia home in the Barrio de Santa Cruz. As soon as they were admitted Henry recognised that his great age must indeed prevent Mr Ashton from leaving home.

There was a youthful eagerness, nonetheless, in his enthusiasm for his newly-purchased wine bottles. Obviously carefully made, there was a pleasing uniformity to their shape, and this was of the latest more slender style which was gradually being perfected. 'These are far more elegant than what we were getting round about 1750,' their host told them, fingering the imprint of his seal as he turned one bottle for their inspection.

'And they stand very steadily with the pontil-mark pressed upwards into this sort of cone shape, don't they?' Catalina remarked, scrutinising the base. She and her father wouldn't hesitate to recommend the manufacturer to other clients who insisted their sherry was deserving of a pleasing bottle. What was more, she could now tell her father that he'd be justified in investing a little capital in such a fine producer of glassware.

'I didn't know you were interested in bottles,' Henry remarked after he and Catalina had said farewell to Mr Ashton. 'I thought all the wine was sent out of Jerez in butts.'

'And so it is, but we like to keep up with developments connected with the trade; and some of our wealthier clients care sufficiently about their sherry to have bottles designed especially.'

Glad that he had learned something more associated with his new work, Henry was well content. Strolling through the early evening towards the Escutia home, he felt easier than he had for some weeks now, almost as though he might have found somewhere to be himself.

Not for the first time, Eleanor Bright was vexed with her husband. Amos had somehow urged on the move to their new home, convincing Miss Wilson that he must occupy the house sooner than anticipated.

'There's no need to sell our old place, after all, Eleanor love. And since the lads will be living there whenever they're in England, we can leave owt there that we want to. We'll have new furniture as befits our new beginning, won't that suit you a treat?'

Eleanor had hardly found words to reply. She loved her old home, loved all the possessions which Amos relinquished so carelessly. Leaving everything to the lads who'd let her down by going to work for them two Fortescues would never compensate for anything.

The day they left Heptonstall, Isobel resolved not to cry, even if liking their new home didn't outweigh attachment to this one. Since their Henry went away, she'd determined even more fiercely than before that she'd replace both him and William in the family business. If she wished to be accepted as mature enough to help, she felt she must now show perfect composure. While her parents were gathering together the things which they were taking to the new house, she slipped out of the door. Her own belongings had long since been accumulated in the living room, where nothing could be missed. Unable to sleep, she'd been out of bed at half past three, silently moving about on cold bare feet that seemed in their discomfort appropriate to her new life.

The only good thing about leaving Heptonstall was the difficulty Father was experiencing in finding her a new tutor. What need had she of someone to direct her learning? She could read well enough to tackle John Bunyan's *Pilgrim's Progress*, works by Daniel Defoe and recently *The Diary of Samuel Pepys*. Without being immodest, she knew that she was as bright as her family name, and possessed the capacity to use the intelligence she'd been given.

The thin light of the autumn dawn was spreading up into the sky from behind the rough moors purple with heather as she ran along the familiar track to say farewell to Susan Gaukroger. They would meet, of course, quite frequently when cloth was to be collected from Susan's father, but it wouldn't be quite the same, nothing ever would be.

Eddie, who had been washing at the pump in the yard, grinned when Isobel approached and stood shivering, head and shoulders dripping, while he slowly asked if Amos wanted him today.

'No, it's not today, Eddie,' she explained, trying not to be impatient with his forgetfulness. 'We told you there'll be two days, at least, while we're settling in over yonder. It's your Susan I'm here to see, is she up yet?'

'I don't know,' Eddie replied ponderously, lumbering off towards the house, and never thinking to invite her inside.

The older girl appeared in the doorway, beckoned Isobel and whisked her away up the narrow staircase to her own chamber. It wasn't the first time that Isobel experienced the longing to reassure this lass nearly six years her senior, yet who seemed to have so little backbone.

'Have you had news from your Henry yet?' Susan inquired now, her lip quivering slightly as she made no attempt to disguise her feelings.

Nay, Susan, thought Isobel, where's your spirit? What's happened to your pride that you don't even think to conceal your affection for a man who's hardly noticed you? Smiling kindly, Isobel shook her head. 'It's too soon yet, love. And now we're off an' all, but only a few mile away, and you know we'll be calling often enough for t'cloth. Happen you'll be able to come and stay with us, if your mother can spare you.'

She doubted that Mrs Gaukroger would agree to anything that relieved her of the unpaid servant which Susan appeared to be becoming. It seemed scarcely credible, now, that until quite recently she had actually admired Susan Gaukroger. Maybe it was since becoming more resolved herself that she'd come to see the other girl as ineffectual.

Awkwardly, Isobel jolted herself out of her reflections, and realised that the desire to talk with her old friend had shrivelled. Giving her a hug and kissing the cool cheek, she told Susan that she'd be wanted at the house now and hastily departed.

With the exception of Amos, they were strangely silent all the way to their splendid new home in the hills outside Halifax. Isobel appreciated her mother's reservations about deserting Heptonstall and their Charles' mistrust of change. She resolved the more firmly that her own outward acceptance would demonstrate how adult she'd become.

Her changed manner didn't go unnoticed. When eventually, by nightfall, some kind of order had been given to the new house and Amos and his wife were in bed Eleanor sighed, weightily. 'I'm afraid our Isobel's sickening for summat. She's been that quiet lately, and she's stopped playing with her dolls – with all her toys, for that matter.'

'She seems right enough to me.'

Aye, thought Eleanor, you only see what you want to know is there. 'If she hasn't got her nose stuck in a book, she's poring over your old ledgers.'

'You don't want her illiterate, do you, nor ignorant?'

Eleanor pressed her lips tightly together. He'd wounded her again; as if he didn't know full well that her own education had wanted for a great deal.

'It's most likely nowt no more than t'age of the lass,' Amos added.

'She's nobbut just gone thirteen,' Eleanor reminded him. 'There's not been any sign of owt like that yet.'

'Is that all she is?' Isobel was growing so useful to him, he really was beginning to think of her as older.

You don't know your only daughter's age now, thought his wife, wondering again about the true nature of this man she'd married. She never knew what went on his head; but then what woman did truly comprehend her husband? It wasn't for the want of trying either, but she supposed that was considerably influenced by every man's love of appearing inscrutable.

Amos was snoring regularly now, beside her. He

surrendered to sleep under their new roof as though he had infinite trust in the arrival of the morning, and that it would herald a day no less agreeable to him than the last. Even when provoked, as he had been by both William and Henry announcing their decision to leave Bright's, he'd not let rancour disturb his slumber. And when he'd claimed the other week that concern for Bright's had kept him awake at night, she'd known how he exaggerated, because she knew what sleepless nights were really like. Still, but for the one occasion, Amos had remained sober enough to keep the business running, she'd not cease being grateful for that. Losing her eldest lads might, in time, seem a fit price for a situation that encouraged her husband's sobriety.

One person who soon made no secret of his delight to have left Heptonstall was their youngest, Charles. Following his brothers in attending the local grammar school hadn't achieved all his parents might have hoped. Even the extra coaching from their curate hadn't sparked in Charles the incentive to learn. Eleanor could only hope that the new school Amos vowed to find for him would somehow inspire the lad to make more effort.

Charles was much like his father in temperament, she feared; an extrovert who relished company and was easily deflected from work. Happen she shouldn't be so concerned that their Isobel showed signs of being too serious.

Eleanor's disturbed night became the template for subsequent nights in her new home. No sooner did she undress than her mind began its anxious journeyings. If she wasn't worrying about some aspect of their new life here, she was pondering on what might be occurring in those lands across the sea where her sons had chosen to make their living. Even when news brought by Luke Fortescue assured her that William, at least, was settling well, she felt in no way relieved. With distances what they were and travel so slow, news was old before it arrived, and often too insubstantial to remove anxiety.

What Eleanor lacked most of all, though, was the will to adjust to living in a house which, however beautiful, did not feel 'hers'. Aware that her wishes had been overruled in its selection, she'd need an amount of time to learn to let herself like the place.

Their daughter, however, found their new home much more to her liking than she'd first expected. Despite being uprooted, Isobel felt almost at once that she belonged in the lovely big house which stared out through tall sash windows over the range of heather-clad hills.

By the time of their next visit to the Piece Hall she was excitedly anticipating the new journey into the town. The way was downhill, quite steep in several places, and she began to relish the pace made by the horses drawing their wagon.

Eddie Gaukroger was with them to help with the heavy pieces. When calling to pick up Samson's cloth yesterday, Amos had told the lad's parents that he could stay the night with them. 'There'll be somebody coming back to Heptonstall after we've done selling t'cloth, I'll arrange for Eddie to ride with them.'

The young fellow had been delighted with the Brights' new home, even after he'd been dispatched to his bed in the room over the stables, he was found wandering the house, exclaiming to himself on the comfort of first one room then another. Eleanor hadn't liked the way in which he seemed to creep about the place, but both Amos and young Isobel had assured her that he was harmless. Her youngest son, Charles, had shamed her into concurring by exclaiming: 'I think it's nice that we can so easily make somebody like him happy.'

Eddie had grown more useful with each time that they went to market the pieces; unloading swiftly, without a word of complaint, then seeing to the horses, and carrying bolts of cloth for them. He also seemed to know instinctively the right moment to appear with the wagon afterwards. This reminded Amos that somehow, he couldn't have told when it had come about, Isobel had adopted the habit of remaining adhered to her father's side all the time that they were at the Piece Hall. No matter whether he was selling to old acquaintances or new clients, she would be there, a pen at the ready for signatures, books to hand for noting details of each sale.

Inexorably, Christmas was approaching. Young Charles, who'd persuaded his mother that some of the friends he'd left behind at Heptonstall Grammar School might come to stay, was reckoning the days. Isobel, who'd been promised a more adult gown, was planning to spend some of the money she'd earned on a necklace which she believed befitted her status as assistant to her father. Whilst Eleanor was bemoaning the absence of reliable help, and yearning for Mrs Robinson, left at the cottage near their old home from which nothing would entice her.

'Our Isobel will have to turn her hand to cooking now we're living in such a remote place,' Amos heard his wife complain one evening. 'There's nobbut a couple of lasses prepared to work here, an' neither of them capable of doing more than cobble together a bit of a pie or a plain stew, and then only under supervision.' And they hadn't wanted to live in, even though there was room without placing a servant's bed in the kitchen, something Eleanor would never tolerate.

'Have you had a word with Mrs Sutcliffe, the Fortescues' housekeeper, mightn't she recommend a good woman?'

Eleanor gave him a look. Was he deliberately provoking her? As if she'd go admitting to any of that lot that life here was far from ideal.

'Happen you'll think on to ask her over Christmas,' Amos persisted. 'I daresay we'll be seeing quite a lot of Matthew and Luke.'

'If they're at home,' his wife retorted, and prayed that she wouldn't encounter them.

—6—

The sudden deterioration from warm days, when the sun hardly faltered, to alternating storms and a dismal drizzle in no way lessened William Bright's enthusiasm for Portugal. Through Fernando Trancoso's instruction and the continuing concern of Luke Fortescue, he was not only assimilating a great deal of knowledge about the making of port but was also enjoying an extensive social life.

The fraternity of port shippers was extraordinary: as in any line of business, competition was taken very seriously – but there was as well an agreeable affinity between one company and another. William felt that the interest he had in the wine was no greater than the interest held for him by a gathering of fellow shippers. One thing that surprised him was Luke's revelation that there was hardly any intermarrying between Portuguese and British engaged in the trade. A certain constraint remained between the two races.

'Old allies, we may be,' Luke had added, 'and prepared to overlook rivalry at times, for the common good, but we're not given to total surrender of innate differences.'

Luke had been grinning, his blue eyes beneath the white eyebrows glittering with amusement. He'd inquired then if William had perhaps found some encounter with a local girl intriguing.

'Nay, it's not that. There's a lass at home I long to wed; if she'll not consent, I'll take no other.'

'You're young to be so certain, aren't you, Will?'

'I wasn't too young to come out to a new life here, was I?'

William's swift adoption of a different trade, in a foreign country, was being mirrored in Spain by his brother Henry. In this instance, though, the situation *was* influenced by a native of that country. Henry would be the first to admit that his indoctrination had been greatly enhanced by Catalina

Escutia, the young lady whom no one would call beautiful but who nevertheless was enchanting him.

The visit to Seville had continued as delightfully as it had begun, culminating in a leisurely walk through a succession of streets, colourful with strolling Sevillanos. When they'd reached the river Guadalquivir, the darkness was only relieved by lights which shone on board vessels and the candles flickering from windows of the city behind them.

Scarcely visible, but suddenly acknowledged by all his senses, Catalina had seemed ethereal that night. Her gown gleaming silver in the light from passing boats, her Latin skin and black hair were its perfect complement. It was she who had paused beside the Torre del Oro – the golden tower, bidding him feel the heat retained by its stones. Their fingers had touched on the rough textured building in a momentary contact too potent to dismiss. Quietly, Henry had drawn her to him, and when Catalina didn't resist had traced her lips with his own. They had walked arm-in-arm back to the house and her brother Carlos that night, for all the world like lovers in a city which seemed built for exotic beauty.

Back in Jerez Henry could scarcely believe he had ever kissed her. Catalina was so in command here, of herself as well as the practicalities of running this part of Fortescue's. She appeared aloof once more, though he understood by now that arrogance was no portion of her nature. Henry was torn, longing for the excitement of their closeness, yet well aware that he needed to concentrate on work.

Here in Spain, the year was waning in rainstorms and a cooling of the temperature which suited Henry in one way, restoring his natural energy; and in another made him regret the loss of the brilliant sunlight which he'd grown to love.

Ignacio Escutia was gradually recovering his health, although he was weak still and the day that he'd attempted to return to work had turned to disaster when an onrush of chest pains had resulted in his abrupt departure from the bodega.

When Catalina and Henry arrived anxiously at the Casa Escutia that evening they were relieved to find him apparently no worse, sitting at the head of the table, and declaring himself quite well. But Catalina watched him as concernedly as her worried mother, while Ignacio himself discoursed on his favourite topic – the making of sherry – with a vitality belied by his blue-tinged lips and gaunt face.

Afterwards Catalina confided in Henry, making him wish he was the one who could help her. The attraction drawing them close was deepening, making him protective. 'I am afraid my father might not ever work again. We have to let him believe he will soon be his normal self, but I shall be relieved to discuss this when Señor Fortescue arrives.'

Matthew's visit, despite the cloud of Ignacio Escutia's illness, made Henry's introduction to the sherry business all the more interesting. His godfather and the Escutia family spent many an evening enlarging on its history whilst sipping a favourite blend, and he even learned that a considerable amount of wine which may have been a forebear of sherry was exported to Rome from Andalusia as long ago as the first century AD.

Catalina's mother was something of a connoisseur. '*Naturalmente* I do not deny my appreciation of the product to which my husband has devoted his life!'

'If Carmen had less to occupy her in running the household, I would find her every day entirely overcome with our sherry,' Ignacio declared.

They all laughed, but Henry, who still felt that he might be imposing on his hosts, expressed a little of this anxiety. 'And now you have me staying here, an' all – I hope it isn't making too much extra work in the house.'

Still smiling, Carmen dismissed this with a gesture of one long-fingered hand. 'We would not think of having you stay elsewhere in the city. Fortescue's is so much a part of our life that anyone concerned with the company increases our enjoyment.'

'And we have staff here, you must remember,' Ignacio put in. 'Carmen herself is concerned only with household organisation.'

Matthew told Henry afterwards that both Ignacio and his wife had always treated Luke and himself as though they were family. 'Carmen only has one sister, and Ignacio was the only child, I like to think that happen their involvement with Fortescue's has made up for 'em not having any brothers or sisters.'

'That's nice,' said Henry. But it also emphasised the pain Ignacio would feel if he were unable to continue working.

'Aye,' Matthew agreed when this was put to him. 'It's a good thing their Catalina is so interested in the company, that'll make it easier for him to maintain the contact.'

'She's an amazing young woman.' He told Matthew how much he'd loved the visit to Seville, if not how he'd been enchanted by the guide who took him there.

'You seem to have settled well in Spain, lad.'

'Aye, I have that! Far better than ever I expected.'

'. . .When it isn't *Portugal*?' Matthew inquired ruefully, with a tilt of one white eyebrow.

Henry nodded. 'I'll not deny that did create reservations, but I've thought nowt more on them lines since I got here.'

'Good, excellent. You will need to assimilate knowledge of the business pretty rapidly, I'm afraid. I don't like the look of Ignacio, these days.'

'And you are sure, aren't you, that I'll not be treading on anyone's feet by assuming more responsibility?'

'Whose? I ask you, lad, who is there?'

'What about the head cellarman, Alberto Martinez?'

'A fine capataz, and that's all. I believe it's all he wants to be, as well. His only interest in the shipping of the wine is in matters like what quantity of brandy need be added to best preserve sherry for the journey overseas.'

'And what about Catalina?'

Matthew snorted. 'Nay, there's no woman'd think of being a shipper. The sherry business itself is really a man's world. She mightn't frame so badly, sticking to what she knows, but she'd never master dealing with shipping companies, learning all there is to know about stowage.'

Despite Matthew Fortescue's predictions, however, it was Catalina's privately cherished ambition to widen her role within the company which sparked the first contention between herself and Henry.

Matthew was to depart eventually for Portugal to meet up with his cousin Luke. During his stay in Spain, he personally had supervised his godson through every process of preparing the grape juice, or 'must' as Henry had learned to call it. They had thoroughly examined the qualities of the flor to which he'd been introduced by the capataz. And so it had been with each stage until Matthew acquainted him with the solera system by which the nature of the finished wine was established.

'The oldest wine is in barrels stored here on the floor – hence *solera* from the Latin word *solum*,' Matthew began, pointing out rows of barrels stacked in tiers.

'The younger sherries are marked by their years and stacked accordingly above them,' Alberto Martinez elucidated.

Nodding, Matthew continued explaining while the capataz demonstrated the process. 'These are the *criaderas* . . .'

'Our word for nursery,' the capataz put in, smiling.

'When we are blending the wine ready for shipping, we take the required amount by withdrawing from each of the oldest butts. This sherry is replaced by a like quantity from each of the next oldest, and so on until the newest butts which are topped up by the *anada* – wine of a single, more recent vintage.'

Watching while this was done, Henry nodded to himself, fascinated. 'And so none of the wine we ship is so new as to be undrinkable.'

'Quite,' said his godfather. 'Presently, I'll show you more of how we control its quality and so on. But you'll be gathering that we try to eliminate problems by being painstaking in our methods.'

Henry turned to Alberto. 'How often do you taste a bad sherry, one that you can't approve?'

'*Nunca*, never. I use this, always.' He tapped the side of his considerable nose. 'Never once has a poor wine reached my lips.'

'He's right, you know,' Matthew confirmed. 'We couldn't better Alberto to look after every drop we're going to offer for sale.'

Henry's quick thinking facilitated learning and his god-father's delighted approval became so evident it could be missed by no one; since they both were staying with the Escutias Catalina couldn't avoid noticing.

She'd seen at the bodega that Henry never needed twice telling, and if a process was thoroughly demonstrated he frequently grasped all salient points before the end of any explanation. She felt perturbed. And annoyed with herself for wanting them to remain close. Since the day she had met Henry Bright down at the quay in Cadiz, she'd recognised that this personable young man with dark hair and flecked hazel eyes was as attractive as anyone she knew.

She liked his concern for her father, his reluctance to be a nuisance in their family home, most of all the readiness of his smile. Never easy with new people, she'd been glad of their time in Seville, and had responded when he kissed her. Now, however, she was beginning to realise that being magnetised by Henry was a situation which, for the sake of her own future, she must resist.

Outwardly composed almost to the point of severity, frequently it was only Catalina herself who was aware of the ultra-feminine core which still continued responding to Henry, until she ached to give and receive affection. This part of her nature, all warmth, tenderness and passion, could provoke her own downfall. For that reason she determined not to permit any such excitement to overwhelm her.

Her reaction to Henry's arrival at the bodega had been complex. On one hand, she was relieved to know that while her father was unwell, and if neither of the Fortescue cousins were present, she would have someone to share responsibility; on the other, she felt threatened. Her work within the company, which was expanding to cover many aspects of the business and therefore suited her eagerness to master every challenge presented, was the most pleasing facet of her life. She'd grown to love the sherry, as much for the intricacies of its production as for all the satisfying features of colour, bouquet and taste appreciated by connoisseurs. She liked the majority of their workforce, and between herself and their capataz, Alberto Martinez, there had matured an excellent rapport, founded on mutual respect.

And now here was Henry Bright, charismatic in his dealings with her family and at the bodega, clever enough to impress Matthew Fortescue already, charming Catalina herself with his sheer Englishness, to say nothing of the excitement aroused when he was near. If she for one moment succumbed to her own senses and softened towards him, she'd soon be letting him take over all that she held dear within Fortescue's – surrendering her interests. Instead she found that once she steeled herself against admiring his judgement in each tasting he undertook, it wasn't all that difficult to consider him an upstart: a newcomer too inexperienced to assess good wine.

She considered that Henry Bright had been fortunate in his godfather. It was because of this connection that he'd been faced with little opposition from either skilled men like Martinez or from unskilled workers whose job was moving the hefty butts. Catalina had also learned recently that he'd secured his position by investing an inheritance. The morning when she encountered him in the coopery, wearing tattered clothing and charring the inside of a new butt, she smiled, recognising that Henry Bright wasn't above sweating like a labourer and didn't shirk physical work. And yet, even while delighted by this new side of him, didn't it show how powerful he might become? As he smiled at her across the fire in the barrel, was he intent on proving this was something that *she* couldn't attempt?

Later that same day, after witnessing his muscle-power and capacity to endure discomfort, Catalina could remain silent no longer. When Henry grinned and observed that he'd seen her admiring his mastery of yet another aspect of the job she retorted, 'I'm not sure coopering is a necessary part of shipping wine. Or have you come here simply to prove your versatility?'

Henry only laughed. 'Do you never experience the urge to tackle more facets of the work?'

His apparent obliviousness of her ambitions riled her. 'I've taken on as much as possible; no doubt now that you're here you'll show me where I've fallen short.'

The trouble was that she did mind about the fact that there were some physical aspects of the sherry trade which were beyond her. She was determined, though, not to let him realise this. Never in all her working life had she been made to feel inadequate, or that someone else might be better able to satisfy Luke and Matthew Fortescue. What would become of her if they eventually deemed Henry equipped for running the place without her? Fear tightened her throat and every muscle, hardening the already strong features. He's making me a shrew, sensed Catalina, without reflecting that the transformation sprang from her own insecurity. Instead of enjoying Henry's company, she grew increasingly watchful for further signs that he might one day usurp her own position.

Alarm bristled when she walked into the office and found Henry sitting at her desk discussing with Alberto the next wines for shipment. Although they both rose as she entered and Henry hastily surrendered the chair, it was too late.

'Come on, I'd just as soon stand.' He smiled, glad to see her.

Catalina shook her head dismissively. 'No – do continue. I can see I'm not needed here.' Gathering her shredded dignity as swiftly as her long voluminous skirts, she hurried off with a rush of shimmering emerald green silk.

For the first time that she could recall, she went home early that afternoon, saddled her fine white Andalusian mare, and rode away from Jerez's jostling streets, churches and cathedrals, past familiar vineyards into the free expanse of rolling hills.

The springy heather dusty beneath her feet and trailing skirts, Eleanor Bright was striding swiftly across the rim of the moor. Over to her left lay Midgley Moor, beyond that wooded valleys, and hilltop Heptonstall, her natural home. Ahead of her was Oxenhope, somewhere over yonder the Worth Valley – they were names, that was all to her. Eleanor had no desire to find them.

She was walking off her annoyance. Amos was abed. It was Sunday, he wasn't neglecting work, but he was sleeping off an evening's drinking. Worst of all, he'd been with the Fortescue cousins. As near alike as brothers, with their easy smiles, the pair had charmed her an' all, years ago. But that was before they'd taken two of her lads, she'd not pay heed again to Matthew or Luke. Real friends wouldn't have worked on her eldest sons, instilling in them both the longing to spend their lives across the sea!

She'd discovered that during last evening Amos had invited Matthew and Luke to join them after Christmas dinner. Yet nobody had even told her if Henry would come home. Those two said they didn't know, that they'd just returned together from Portugal. Spain or Portugal, they were all the same to her. Isobel had shown her on the map and all she'd seen were two countries clutching each other. They were coloured differently maybe, otherwise indistinguishable. She only knew they were both so far away that it wrung her heart.

In his more lucid moments before going to bed, Amos had assured her William was returning for Christmas, but he'd been too confused to furnish details. And Eleanor needed the date of her son's return so that she might anchor her all too uncertain hope. More and more nowadays she needed to look forward to something beyond this existence. Her own company was growing unsatisfactory, she despaired of her husband relinquishing drink, and her daughter was turning into such an efficient creature that Eleanor herself daily felt more ineffectual.

She had been less anguished straight after the move from Heptonstall. She'd busied herself at first with putting the new house to rights and afterwards had baked cakes, pies and puddings ready for the festive season. Since then the new furniture which Amos had promised her hadn't materialised. He had purchased four new chairs and then, evidently shaken by the price, had gradually fetched across bits and pieces from their old home. That lovely best parlour looked ridiculous with their old heavy table, exquisite mahogany chairs, and nothing else to speak of. The pictures which should have been ranged in orderly fashion along the colourwashed walls were absent still, exposing to anyone who called the patchy evidence that her predecessor had taken with her a good collection of paintings. Not that she had many callers now! And that was another disappointment. Life hadn't prepared Eleanor Bright for more than caring for husband and family. The thin education she'd received left her ill-equipped for the absence of friends, and long hours alone. During the first weeks here, seeking company, she had more than once gone with Amos into the town.

Although she had visited Halifax in the past, she didn't know it well, and had felt intimidated by streets crowded with strangers. From elegant ladies in sedan chairs to ragged women begging for scraps at the market. Among them Eleanor hadn't seen one familiar face, nor anybody that she'd wish to call a friend. By now she suspected she never would.

Despite having no help in the house, she found little to keep her busy in the half-empty rooms. She'd less self-sufficiency than even their youngest, Charles. When not at school, he occupied himself for many an hour, drawing and sketching.

Some sound behind her amid the ceaseless buffeting of the wind made Eleanor swing round. Staggering on uneven tussocks of heather, she steadied herself, pushed beneath her broad-brimmed hat strands of the hair that seemed to grey more swiftly since moving house.

Here was young Charles now, gladdening her heart as he ran uphill. 'I didn't hear you go out, Mama – but I saw you from the window. Aren't you cold?'

'Aye, love, a bit.' But the worst chill was inside her, the icy premonition that life's present unease could worsen.

'I finished those sketches of the house, can't do any more till there's some snow. That will make it all magnificent, won't it?'

Snow. Eleanor shuddered. There had been flurries of flakes already, driven by the north wind down upon the house. Real snow, though, in the quantity customary in the West Riding come January, would pile into great drifts, severing them from the world. But wasn't she severed already – torn by circumstances from folk that were her kin, and from places established as roots?

'I wish I could stop you looking so sad.'

'Ay, Charles love . . .'

Tears pricked behind eyes forbidden to shed them, and when Charles took her arm in the manner that, aeons ago, her husband had taken it, Eleanor fiercely willed herself not to gulp. 'We'd better be getting back else t'dinner'll be spoiled,' she managed.

Clinging to domestic tasks again, Eleanor tolerated where she could not see a way to improve, and was rewarded at last one evening when the urgent clatter of the knocker sent her rushing to the door.

William stood there. He had ridden into Halifax on the mail coach and then had walked the rest, struggling uphill with all his belongings. He looked well, nevertheless, bronzed so deeply by Portugal's autumn sunlight that the subsequent rains and the days when mist clung to the River Douro hadn't erased his tan.

Later that evening he confided that he was back in England for more than Christmas, would remain for several weeks; some of the time in London but the rest investigating the viability of Fortescue's opening an office in Bradford. 'Luke believes there are so many merchants in other lines doing good business there that we might profit from such a venture.'

Eleanor would not permit herself to hope that might become a reality. But she was cheered just the same by this reminder that things might be worse. Neither of her eldest sons were in work which entailed their living permanently, without a break, in a foreign country.

Another person who experienced similar relief was Phillida Walshaw. The uneasy terms on which she and William had parted had rendered the months of his absence doubly painful. She had heard from him, but only rarely in stilted letters which initially made her yearn for the personal contact that the words lacked, but then induced the dismal conclusion that too much between them had become flawed.

The instant Phillida saw William, however, filling the doorway of their weaver's cottage, she was reassured. He looked splendid in a new outer coat and matching breeches of plum-coloured cloth, between the coat and his good white shirt was the gleam of a waistcoat's gold edging. Best of all, his grey eyes were warm with affection, his arms outstretching to hug her. With only the briefest glance over her shoulder to her parents, Phillida went to him.

They talked all together for a while, but only long enough to satisfy John and Hilda Walshaw. Will had always found their strait ways inhibited: now he'd experienced living his own life abroad he'd not be stifled. The walk he suggested to Phillie was only as far as the now empty Bright home which he was to share with Henry. Once over the threshold, he drew her to him again, this time searing her lips with starving kisses.

'You know why this place hasn't been sold, do you?' he asked at last, his voice breathy with longing.

Phillida stepped back a couple of paces to look him in the eyes. 'I don't *know* – but I did hear tell that it's yours now.'

'Half on it, aye.' The grey eyes were gleaming, the sense of power he'd acquired by following his urge to strike out in a new world intensified with the prospects generated by possessing a home. 'I'll show you round; since I'm the eldest I think it's only right we should choose which part'll be ours.'

'Ours?' echoed Phillida, confused. 'Will, have you forgotten what I said – I can't condone the work you're doing.'

'Your chief objection, as I remember, was being expected to live away from Heptonstall. Because you were needed to work with your family.'

'But . . .'

'And now we'd be living here, nobbut a few minutes' walk from them.'

'We? Or would it be me left here most of the time on my own, while you went off to Portugal again?'

'There will be occasions I'm needed out there, aye, but not continuously. And Fortescue's might open up a Bradford office.'

'Or you'd be stuck i' London,' Phillida interrupted.

'That's where most wine merchants have their British headquarters.'

'You're sufficiently concerned then to have found that out?'

Phillida swallowed. Hadn't he known? Did he really have so little idea of the extent to which she'd yearned for him? But wasn't she only making her own future difficult if she yielded to his enticements? Slowly she nodded, trying behind an impassive glance to contain the desire in her which he generated. 'Naturally, I was interested. That doesn't mean I'd contemplate what you're suggesting. I need a real husband, one that'd be living wi' me all the time.' There had been no means of holding on to the sob that emerged when she uttered the last sentence.

From standing in that dank parlour, motionless, staring at her, Will was galvanised. Seizing her again, crushing her against his chest, he murmured into the auburn hair where the scent of spun fleece lingered. 'I'd look after you, lass. You'd not be on your own that much, I can promise.' Hadn't he been desperate to share the splendid scenery of the Douro valley with her, hadn't he been constantly plagued by the need to make her his in the one way that was certain? There'd scarcely been a day, and surely had not been a single night, when he'd been free from this immensely powerful desire.

The chill of the house was seeping through towards Phillida's bones, winning her attention away from Will and his promises, awakening her to what it would be like to live here isolated, and him away for months. Men were that selfish! It'd be all right for Will, travelling the globe, excited by his new life, forgetting her. She'd never be warm in this place, would never feel at home.

'I'm better as I am.'

He overcame the force willing him to seal the future now, released her abruptly and turned towards the stairs. 'I'd better check that everything's all right here, if *you* want nowt to do with either my home or me.'

William was absent so long, first striding from chamber to chamber somewhere over her head and then alarmingly silent, that Phillida eventually was compelled to go and look for him.

He was at the frost-patterned window of his old room, gazing out through the one pane he'd cleared, across once-familiar woods to the moors. The warmth, briefly generated by his return to the land that was his, had evaporated in the pain of Phillie's renewed rejected. He was sure of nothing now. She'd killed all enthusiasm for his new work, had doused his eagerness to live here with her.

Her touch on his shoulder startled him, and seared through every layer of his clothing. He wished to God she'd finish this repeated screaming of his senses.

'I'm sorry, Will love . . .'

'Sorry?' Rage and desire mingled as he swung round, and both forced him to take her by the arms. I'll show you what you mean to me, some strange fierce creature inhabiting his head decided; show what need means! The cloth of her sleeves was cool, but deliciously smooth, alerting nerve endings in his fingers as if to echo the pulsing deeper within. Sharply, he jerked her closer towards him, slid one hand from her arm to pass over her waist and down to press her roughly against the root of his discomfort.

Her startled lips parted further beneath his kiss, but the groan she expressed confirmed the existence of her own need. Moulding her to his body, he felt her skirts flattening against him, warming. Her mouth was fully surrendered, inciting him to probe with his tongue.

Her arms were about him now, her delicate fingers tracing his spine through the silk of his shirt, making him sigh for release by their journeying which aroused him unbearably. Despite her winter-weight gown, her breasts were relaying their own message of enticement. Thrusting and firm as the pressure he exerted was, it was matched in strength by Phillida's.

Barely conscious of his own intent, desperate with love, he caressed the curve of her breast, kissing her deeply while he leaned sharply into her. Again, her kisses intensified, he felt her body stir with him.

'William, no . . .' she said, at last and pressed with firm

hands at his shoulders. Her voice, though, was laden with regret so sincere he could not doubt that it equalled his own.

'What are we to do?' he groaned, despairing. 'What do you expect, if you deny that we'll marry?'

Against the white of the horse, her wide emerald skirts and short black jacket were magnificent, the angle of her dark head beneath the broad-brimmed green hat seemed to reveal her attunement with the rolling hills surrounding them. Henry had wondered previously if he could be learning to love Catalina and suspected tonight that his freedom was surrendered.

He cantered to within hailing distance of her, his own mount slowing to manage the loose stones of the gradient. She made no move to meet him.

'Catalina . . .' Henry began. If only he knew how to save her pain, how to find words to deliver the news. . .

She turned and faced him. They could have been the only people alive amid the miles of vineyards. And Catalina still remained where she was, silhouetted against the grey winter sky. Her strong chin was raised, her long nose tilted and yet, however splendid, she seemed strangely vulnerable.

'You had no need to follow me,' she said, her English sounding cold instead of charming as it could do. 'Shouldn't you be with someone who'll advance your business interests?' Out here, isolated with her thoughts, she'd begun to fear that his original affinity with her had merely been calculated to further his plans for taking over.

Henry walked his stallion the last few paces until both horses were side by side. Miserably, he watched them nuzzle each other. 'There's no easy way to put this,' he said in a rush. 'It's bad news, I'm afraid. Your father's been taken ill again . . .'

She swallowed. 'Is he – alive still?'

'He was when I left the house. Your mother's with him.'

Catalina took off sharply, spurring her mare to thunder down the slope. They were up and over the crest of the next rise before Henry prepared to follow.

In all the days since his arrival in Jerez he'd never felt so much the outsider. He returned to the Escutia home, dismounted and waited uncertainly near the centre of the immense tiled courtyard. He noticed the fountains were stilled and wondered if that was a sign of death. Distantly, he heard voices from the servants' quarters to the rear. They appeared subdued, drained of the normal Spanish volubility. Other voices, from somewhere beyond the gallery above him, sounded yet more hushed, more ominous than silence. Although wounded by Catalina's recent change of attitude towards him, Henry sensed that he must remain for her sake.

A heavy door opened somewhere in the shadows upstairs, an angular priest emerged with Catalina, looking even more angular, at his side. As they descended the stairs into the light, Henry saw her face, strained with emotion, and the colour of sherry flor.

Approaching him, she nodded wearily. '*Muchas gracias,*' she said, 'for searching for me.'

He stilled the urge to hold her. 'Your father is. . . ?'

'Barely alive. *El padre* has adminstered the last rites.'

Gravely, Henry nodded. Without understanding fully, he could recognise its significance to Catholics. Inside, he wept for her.

The effort visible, Catalina gathered herself. 'There are cold meats in the dining room, we must eat . . .'

'No, no – really. I don't want owt.' All at once, though, he realised that if he managed to force something down, so might Catalina. It was the wrong time to sustain her by holding her, but this could fortify her for the night.

The servants hovered unobtrusively, uncannily quiet, offering wine and the crisp bread he'd grown to love. The table was spread with dishes of *tapas*: alongside the cold meats, were squid, grilled sardines, shrimps, and portions of *tortilla*. Suddenly ashamedly hungry, Henry took a selection on his plate and began slowly to eat.

Catalina toyed with a few strips of serrrano ham, sipped at a pale sherry. 'If – if nothing has occurred by then, Father would like to see you before you retire.'

'I'd like to see him an' all.' He'd always regret that

circumstances hadn't allowed him to benefit more fully from Ignacio Escutia's experience by being schooled by him at the bodega.

'He has taken to you,' Catalina admitted, too exhausted and distressed to care now that Henry might usurp her. The threat of bereavement also made her realise this man could mean much to her.

'I'm glad to hear it. I've liked him from the start. I've always admired men that put their backs into their work, wished my own father . . .' He stopped, aware that this was hardly the occasion to expect her to wish to listen.

'No – por favor, tell me, Henry.' Listening to anything would be preferable to anticipating the outcome of her father's latest relapse. Despite all reservations and uncertainties, she needed to know more about Henry, had been warmed just now when told by her mother how he'd offered to ride out and find her.

'Ay, I suppose he's feckless, at times – hopeless, really. He's allus – *always* mixed with folk, though in his younger days he found that difficult. I believe a drink used to help, now he's rather too fond of it, lets it get the better of him. Then he has the gout . . .' He glanced up.

Catalina nodded. 'Is a similar word in Spanish.'

'When me and our Will worked with him, he made the most of that. Every little twinge was an excuse to leave everything to us.'

'Is that the reason you had to get away?'

Henry shrugged. 'Happen the way things were started it off. But the clothier's trade as we know it is on its way out. And I'd always looked up to both Matthew and Luke Fortescue. In some ways, they were everything my father wasn't. And they possessed the guts to make a go of dealing in wine. When I was a lad it was like a tale by Daniel Defoe, listening to them talking. It was many a year before it even occurred to me that it could be possible for me to join them.'

'And your father now – is he working more effectively again?' Catalina asked, not wishing to dwell on Henry's eagerness to succeed in Jerez.

'He seemed to be buckling to when I left. He's got our Isobel, my young sister, helping him – of all things.'

'Are there many young women in the cloth trade?'

'Eeh, no! Not as merchants, any road. But Isobel's only just gone thirteen. T'young lass is suited to death about the work, which is more than I can say for my father. His one hope now is that our Charles will show a bit of interest, though you can never tell with him. In the meantime Isobel's a bright 'un, happen she'll do all right. As long as it lasts.'

Catalina gave him a questioning look.

'Like I just said, clothiers are doomed. As they work nowadays, that is. It's all the factories setting up, you see. Machines.'

'Perhaps the business will survive long enough for your father. And your sister will, no doubt, marry.'

'That's some way off, though, isn't it? Meanwhile she's given up all thought of any more schooling. Spends all her time trying to convince folk that she's growing up fast. I know there's younger ones that have to work, but it doesn't seem right, not when it's your own kin. And she doesn't have to earn.'

'Still, if she's happy . . .'

Henry grinned. 'You should see her – sitting up on t'wagon, pen in hand, ink set carefully to one side so's it can't spill on to the cloth.'

The heavy wooden door opened and simultaneously they glanced towards it. Ignacio Escutia's old manservant nodded gravely, then reeled off a string of urgent words in his native tongue.

Her eyes troubled, Catalina translated. 'The doctor says he's nearing the end. Come with me, Henry – even if he doesn't recognise you.'

There was no way he would have refused, so he followed slowly as she led the way up the elegant staircase to their meeting with grief.

Her mother Carmen was seated near the head of the carved wooden bed, her fingers still entwined in her husband's, even though it was all too evident that Ignacio was past responding.

Watching the uneven rise and fall of the sick man's chest, the only signal that he lingered, Henry was aware of Catalina moving towards her father's other side and laying a hand on his shoulder. At that Ignacio's eyelids moved fractionally, then settled. His lower lip stiffened slightly as though he might even speak. He sighed, deeply, and then they all shuddered, hearing his last breath catch as it failed to reach his lungs.

The women wept immediately, closing in to embrace their loved one as they needed no telling that he was lost to them in this life. More moved than he'd expected, Henry cleared his throat. The sound appeared disproportionately loud in the solemn stillness of the darkly panelled room, and only increased Henry's feeling of being out of place here among family and fellow-onlookers.

When Catalina moved, however, making way for the doctor to attend her father's body, it was to Henry's side that she crossed. 'He is at peace,' she stated, dry-eyed now, composed. 'Jesus Lopez, Mother's brother-in-law, will ensure that she is all right here. There are things we must do. The Fortescue cousins must be informed, naturally, also Alberto Martinez or someone concerned with running the bodega.'

'And your brother Carlos, and the rest of the family?'

'A messenger has ridden off already to Seville, to bring Carlos here. The little ones will be brought in to pay their respects, then they are going home with my uncle, Mother also is to stay with them. She and her sister Eva Maria are very close.'

'So you'll be on your own here, except for Carlos . . .'

'It is not really alone, in a house full of servants. And there is yourself.'

Her smile was wan, but a smile nevertheless. Henry marvelled that their differences hadn't prevented her acknowledging that he might now fulfil some purpose.

'I'll do owt I can to help, you've only to say.'

'*Gracias*.'

*

105

The ensuing days seemed unreal to Henry though they passed swiftly enough, with messages to be delivered both within Fortescue's and the wider circle of sherry shippers, and a watch to be kept on the way the business was running. Catalina was, naturally, preoccupied. From the first she had assumed control of all arrangements, allowing her mother to sink into the grief which had divested her of so much strength.

'She will recover once Father is laid to rest, you will see,' Catalina prophesied. 'But do not forget there are long traditions here of womenfolk existing solely through their men.'

And not only here, thought Henry, recalling his own mother's unselfishness and wondering how she was faring in the new home that she'd been obliged to accept. For the only occasion in weeks, he felt homesick, experiencing a physical ache for family, and for the Yorkshire hills.

Catalina had discovered a surprising calm, not only within herself but in the Englishman's presence, that was to sustain her throughout the funeral. She'd already appraised his Yorkshire common sense, these days it became a staff beside her; just knowing he was somewhere about the house or in the bodega strengthened her to carry on. By contrast Carlos had disappointed her, arriving with an emotional outburst of filial sorrow then failing to collect himself sufficiently to be of more than fleeting use. Finally exasperated, she'd suggested he might help care for their mother. The alacrity with which he'd departed for their uncle's household near Cadiz had confirmed her opinion of him.

Henry was appalled. He couldn't leave her here, on her own, with her father recently buried; did no one care about her sorrow? 'You want to get away for a bit, Catalina,' he said. 'Tell you what – come home wi' me – just till after the Christmas season.'

Neither of them fully understood how grief was affecting Catalina's brother, even after the funeral when he'd returned to Seville.

It was his private place; the one room where Carlos knew no one would find him. He'd grown to feel at home here, despite the absence of furniture and notwithstanding everyone else's assertion that some 'presence' rendered the atmosphere uneasy.

If there was a ghost here, he was too troubled by more recent events to pay it any heed. And the physical exertion for which he'd set the place aside would, he hoped, blunt the sharpest edge of the anguish which made him seem weaker than his older sister.

He'd begun exercising long ago in this ill-lit room to the rear of the house in Seville, tuning his body for the day when he would at last be author of his own future. The bull-ring was no arena for ill-prepared fools, and Carlos Escutia was determined to prove his mastery there. And equally determined today to master emotion.

He had made an excuse to miss this morning's tutorial; but his bereavement was no secret in the university, they were showing him a certain lenience. And his father's death was indeed the cause of this need to be alone; this grief was shattering.

Commencing the stretching designed to loosen up his spine and induce flexibility in his limbs, he still couldn't close his mind over too many distressing memories. That message had been such a shock, shaking him out of the assumption that his father was tough enough to survive his illness.

In those few moments Carlos had grown out of the youth who considered little beyond his ambitions and his associates here. He'd seen before his inner eye his own neglect of family, and searching had provided no reasons to extenuate his behaviour. And this time his cheerful, cocky approach would seem even less acceptable than in the past. He envied Catalina her coolness which, though it conveyed a false impression of being dour, did at least prevent public disintegration.

Strengthening his exercise to power every muscle, Carlos willed himself to face the knowledge that he had run from the mourning in Jerez, much as a child would run from a ferocious dog. And he thought to tackle bulls. . . !

Had he been justified in rushing back to Seville, towards the comfort that hadn't seemed available within his own family? Did this indicate a softness as vulnerable as a body ill-protected from a bull's horn?

There had been a girl. He was no less human than his fellow students, no less male. He'd relished her company these past several months, had laughed with her and talked, kissed and held, most of all had savoured her admiration of his chosen career.

She had been there on his return, had come back here to sit as they had so often in the past, sipping wine in the cool courtyard. But she had been different. The awkwardness had been in her shifting eyes, and in the way she'd resisted when he attempted to confide. Hadn't she seen that, for the first time for him, talking hadn't come readily?

Certainly she herself had admitted that she didn't know what to say. 'I haven't been this close before to what happens when someone dies,' she'd told him before she departed. Nor had he, though, nor had he.

His entire body was better attuned already, co-ordinated, responding. Time for the next vital stage. Falling without injury and coming straight up again was imperative. He practised repeatedly, tossing himself to the matting then bounding up as though to avoid being gored.

Today, there was a fresh force to the impact, and more immediacy in scrambling to arise. But, hitting the ground for the fourth time, it seemed something snapped – *not* in limbs or torso, he'd have borne that more easily.

Panting generated by exertion turned into an extended gasp. Sobs tore at his throat, and humiliating tears leaked from eyes tightly closed. Time and again he beat the matting. *I haven't been this close before to what happens when someone dies.* Why devote so many years to confronting dread on my own when I need one other person?

Catalina had resisted for long enough, protesting that she would get along very well where she was, with their housekeeper Señora Trujillo to keep the house warm as even the Spanish nights grew chill, and maids enough to make eating no problem. But she did not convince Henry who saw that every little thing seemed to press her down: momentary injustice, anger on the part of one of their workers, even remembered portents. 'I should have known we were in for a bad time,' she remarked gloomily one evening as they left the bodega together. 'The storks didn't return here to nest last season.'

In any other circumstances, he would have laughed at such a grave consequence being attributed to the absence of a pair of birds, but her manner made him more determined that she should accompany him to Yorkshire.

And so here they were now, tired by the voyage and the long drive by mail coach up to the West Riding, but still able to appreciate the high sweep of moorland ahead of them.

It had snowed for days, by the appearance of the hills. Deep drifts concealed black drystone walls, merged distant fields with roads, softened the contours of crags.

'I'll bet it's fair grand up Heptonstall i' this,' Henry told her, smiling. 'I'll take you there, for sure, afore we have to get back.'

Catalina, who had thrilled to the sight of ranges of hills, snow-blanketed and some as steep as the escarpments in the *sierras* of her native land, could imagine nothing more wonderful than the scene before her.

'I've still got a sort of home in Heptonstall, any road,' Henry continued. 'When my father bought the new house, he left the old one to be shared between me and our Will.'

'I hope you can live agreeably together,' Catalina remarked, smiling as she remembered differences between herself and Carlos.

'We'll manage. If we have to. Can't tell if it'll come to that yet – with both of us away so much.'

'You would perhaps arrange that you inhabited the *casa* on separate occasions, no?' she suggested, warming him with the humour which daily was superseding her grief and apprehension about the future.

'That wouldn't be a bad idea.' He explained how he and William viewed life differently. 'He's always looked after himself first. I daresay he'd be no less glad to have my room rather than my company!'

Catalina laughed and he rejoiced that he'd taken some part in restoring her.

'You'll like my mother – I hope. She's plain in her ways, but the best you'll find this side of the Pennines. I wish my father treated her right, but it's only thoughtlessness on his part. He's always distressed when he doesn't do right by folk.'

Catalina gave him a look; she wondered how it would be to have this man's consideration permanently. Entertaining the prospect was foolishness, of course, just a brief escape from gnawing grief – and maybe an attempt by her subconscious to find some substitute for her respected father.

The carriage they had hired in Halifax stopped at Henry's command before the pleasing house whose gold-toned stone glowed in the sunlight patterning the snow with blue shadows. Catalina gazed up at its tall sash windows while their baggage was placed around them on the path and Henry settled with the driver for this last stage of their journey.

'I thought somebody'd have been out by now to see what were going on,' he exclaimed. 'Our Isobel, if nobody else, would want to know who was arriving.'

'Perhaps they're remaining inside because of the cold,' suggested his companion.

Collecting together their belongings, Henry grinned at her. 'You'll feel it cool, I suppose, a bit different from Jerez.'

The bitter wind did seem intense to Catalina, icing her cheeks already, sharp as a mosquito sting about her eyes. Gamely, though, she shook her head. 'It is no worse than I expected. Both Fortescues have told me often about your harsh climate. I feel sure the welcome will banish any chill. . .'

There was, however, no welcome. Henry dragged on the iron bell-pull and they both cringed at the resultant clamour; he rattled the brass knocker, hammered with the side of his gloved fist on the thick wood of the door. When no one came he left Catalina by the front entrance and went striding, through snow that reached his boot tops, away to the rear.

110

He returned, shaking his head. 'There's nobody at home.' He felt slighted, on his own account for receiving no greeting on his appearance after a long absence, but mostly on behalf of Catalina. He'd never thought of such a thing as there being no one here to draw her into his family.

'Happen they've gone round to Matthew's. I can't think they'd go much further nor that i' this stuff. If it hadn't been for storms delaying the ship, we'd have been home for Christmas, they'd never have been out then.'

They stowed their baggage in an outhouse and set out to tramp across to the Fortescue home.

Her contentment surprised Catalina herself, and she had felt this way since the morning they put out from Cadiz harbour. Their days had seemed ordered, quietly enjoyable, even Christmas Day which she had been dreading. Dining with the Captain and the scattering of fellow-passengers who hadn't suffered sea-sickness had held nothing to remind her of Escutia family Christmases. There had been a young priest aboard as well, he'd given her Communion and thus removed one source of yearning.

Smoke drifted up from the Fortescue chimneys and a narrow pathway, freshly-swept, led through a drift to the door. 'Thank goodness for that! There's somebody at home here, any road.'

Catalina smiled up at him, curiously warmed by his anxiety that things should be just right for her. If he did but know, this was so infinitely preferable to remaining in Jerez that she'd have been content to have no other company. If that had been proper, she reminded herself silently with thoughts of the duenna who would accompany less obstinately determined young women. But she trusted Henry so completely she'd ceased to view him in the same light as other men. Maybe he'd not be flattered by that knowledge, though it existed alongside the excitement of the attraction which he generated. Ever since he'd kissed her she'd felt they both experienced this amalgam of affection and desire. Only in the bodega had she watched him warily, allowing their working lives to become dominated by the threat that Henry's growing mastery of the job would displace her.

'Somebody's coming,' Henry announced as footsteps approached on the other side of the door.

'Well, I don't know!' exclaimed Mrs Sutcliffe, her normally neat hair awry beneath her crisp white cap, and sleep clouding her eyes. 'What're you doing here, instead of at your brother's wedding? That's where they've all gone, Mr Fortescue an' all.'

'Wedding?' Henry echoed. 'To Phillida Walshaw?' Was it distance alone had prevented his knowing their William's intentions?

'Aye, this afternoon. Over i' Heptonstall, in t'Methodist chapel, if I bethink me right . . .'

They were asked in and invited to take tea. Mrs Sutcliffe was interested to meet Catalina and chatted readily with her as soon as she learned of her involvement with Fortescue's. Eventually, however, Henry became restless and rose stiffly to his feet.

'We've done more than enough sitting about in yon mail coach, time I were doing summat.'

'You're not bound for Heptonstall, are you, not i' this?' Mrs Sutcliffe inquired.

'No, I don't think we better had set off, it'll be dark in another hour or so.' The sky was heavy with snow, as well, grey as far as the eye could see, clouds like grimy swansdown sitting on the surrounding moors.

He was concerned for Catalina, as well; he had observed how she occasionally shivered. The black gown she wore for her father was full-skirted, exquisitely styled where it was caught in to her firm waist, but its square neckline was wide; she must be feeling every draught. And there'd not be a bit of warmth in that cloth; he'd like to provide her with a good length of fine Yorkshire woollen . . .

Darkness was increasing when they arrived back at the Bright family home, and it was no longer unoccupied. The housekeeper his mother had found just before Christmas was stoking up fires, and had a pot boiling in the kitchen. She seemed sceptical, at first, when Henry told her who he was, maddening him because all he wanted was to make Catalina feel she belonged here with him.

Suddenly, though, the wrinkled face relaxed in a smile and she straightened her pale apron as though to acknowledge his status. 'Aye – I can see your mother in you now. Well, you'll have a wait afore they gets back. I got a ride home on a cart as were passing t'lane end, so's I could see to t'fires. The master hired a carriage, said he weren't risking his own i' this depth of snow, but from what I know of him he'll be hanging on wi' t'company over yonder as long as there's a full bottle.' She appeared to recollect who Henry was, and gave a small shrug. 'Not that it's for me to say . . .'

After she had left them alone Henry found Catalina a comfortable seat. He remarked, 'You must think we're a funny lot over here,' and ignored her disclaimer. He often longed to hold her again, to reassure them both of their real feelings. But *did* she feel as he did? It would help if he learned Spanish. If they travelled back together he'd get her to begin teaching him during the voyage. He wasn't sure yet if he might stay for a bit in England. There was all this talk of maybe setting up further offices over here for distributing the wine. He'd heard William would be involved and didn't like to think of his brother excluding him. . .William. What a discreet beggar he was becoming, with his sudden changes of occupation, this sudden marriage.

'Did you not know of your brother's wedding?'

He looked at her. 'I knew nowt definite. He were seeing her regular afore we left home, t'last time I bumped into her she'd heard nowt from him. Not that that surprised me, our Will doesn't put himself out for anybody.'

Whereas *you* do, thought Catalina, so very pleased to be here even if Henry was perturbed by the circumstances so far.

'If they're not here soon, I'll find you a room, see to a fire in it, and a warming-pan.'

'Warming-pan?' she inquired lightly.

'For t'bed. You've not been needing owt of t'sort in Spain.'

She smiled, her smile as warm as her home town because Henry was so concerned for her. 'Certainly nowhere away from the mountains.'

'There are mountains over there, are there then?'

'But yes. One day I will show you. Not far away from Jerez, is Arcos, a very old town built on a precipice.'

'I'd like to see it.' He'd love to explore the whole of her country with her, if only there were sufficient time.

'So far, you have been occupied learning the basics of sherry production. Without – without my father, there will be adjustments to make in the way our work is allocated. But that will not take forever. Some day we will have everything organised to our satisfaction.' And time then to get to know each other more fully.

'I hope so. I'm wanting a word with Matthew Fortescue while we're over here.' He hadn't considered that Catalina should be present at their meetings, but understood now that he couldn't exclude her.

The cloud that had hazed her dark eyes on mentioning her father had remained shadowing them. He couldn't harden his heart to wish away her absorption with the company, yet it still seemed all wrong that he was obliged to take account of a woman's interests there.

Hooves and wheels masked by the snow-covering, it was only the creaking of the carriage as it halted which alerted them. Henry was merely half-way to the door when it opened.

Isobel was the first person indoors, rushing into his arms with a yelp of joy the instant she saw him.

'Hallo, young puppy,' he exclaimed, hugging her.

She reprimanded him with a grimace.

'It's how you behave,' he reminded her, grinning. 'You'll have to learn not to launch yourself at other young fellows that way . . .'

'You are daft! It's good to have you home, though, even if you are too late for our Will's wedding.'

'Was it a great occasion?'

'Hardly – not with all Phillie's family staring down their noses every time Father touched a glass. She looked nice, though – not a bit like herself.' Phillida's beauty had never appealed to Isobel.

A small laugh from Catalina made Henry turn. 'You're

114

making me forget my manners already,' he told his sister. 'Come over here, and meet the Señorita Escutia.'

Before introductions were completed his parents were in the room as well, shaking snowflakes from their cloaks then gazing in amazement to find Henry at home.

'And to think we were all out, what a day to arrive. You couldn't have timed it worse if you'd been trying,' Eleanor observed. 'And you with a young lady, an' all. What must she think of us?'

'I think you have been supporting your older son on a very special day, Mrs Bright,' said Catalina, coming towards her with both hands outstretched.

'Special?' came a snort from Henry's young brother Charles. 'Boring would be my description. Hello, Henry – have a good voyage? What have you brought me?'

'Nay, lad, let him get in t'house before you're asking for summat.' This was from Amos, moving slowly, leaning on his stick. His gout had not benefited from the day's celebrations. When, following Catalina's introduction to the old man, father and son greeted each other Henry was relieved to find Amos no worse than a little merry. And every member of his family had been unstinting in their welcome of his Spanish friend, this seemed to confirm the wisdom of persuading her to visit Yorkshire.

'So, how come our Will decided to wed then?' he asked them. 'What made Phillida Walshaw change her mind?'

115

·——8——·

Will drew her away from the window long before the lights of his parents' carriage had ceased to reflect upon the snow of the hill.

'Phillie, lass,' he began affectionately and read in her green eyes emotions that mirrored his own. Further words stuck in his throat, but she spoke for them both, coming to his arms.

'I thought they'd never leave, I know it's wrong of me, but I couldn't help wishing they'd have the tact to go.' Ever since William's return to England she'd been seared by this urgent need of him. Whatever common sense had insisted, there could have been no ignoring her own sensuality. Marrying him hadn't come a day too soon, and her body was granting her no peace since the vows that made him her husband.

Together, they went to secure the door, pausing only to kiss before taking up the candle and starting up the stair.

In the doorway of their chamber, Will hauled her against him again, his mouth covering hers, bruising her lips while his touch on her breast sent her passion soaring.

'You looked more beautiful nor ever today,' he murmured. 'Thank God you agreed to wed me.'

Phillida smiled ruefully. 'I couldn't go on denying you . . .' The words ended in a sigh. His lips were at her throat now, creating yet more tumult deep within her. Against her he felt hard, but there was love along with desire in the fervour of his kisses. Tomorrow, she'd be glad of the caring and concern. Tonight, passion's flare was demanding full attention.

Will was swift steering her towards the bed, he had her layers of skirts aside while she was beginning to unfasten her bodice.

'Later, lass, we'll undress,' he asserted.

He was caressing the cool flesh above her fine stockings,

firing the whole of her and intensifying the great pulse storming inside her. He loosened the fastening of his breeches and came close again, pressing on top of her then smiling against her lips when her legs parted for him.

'Oh, Will . . .'

She hadn't been scared of what he would do, but she had dreaded the newness of it all, the embarrassment. And now here they were only concerned with putting an end to the waiting, too much in need to heed aught but their coupling. Eager as she was, there was but one moment of pain and then she could feel him, moving in rhythm, inciting with each renewal of pressure until they stirred as one. She surrendered to the sensation of being loved.

He was peeling away her stained skirts when Phillida awakened from the sleep into which she'd drifted. Naked himself, Will was anxious to make them comfortable for the night. Smiling to herself, she helped by unfastening the bodice of her gown, wriggling free of the layers of petticoats.

Will shivered against the cold sheets on his side of the bed. The arm that stretched out to pull him towards her aroused him again. When Phillida responded as he stirred, William kissed her deeply, began again to make love with her.

'It's as well my family live a few mile away,' he remarked afterwards. 'We'll want no visitors here.'

The only guests they entertained were Henry and Catalina, invited by Phillie's message when word travelled through the weaving community that William's brother was home and a Spanish lady with him.

Phillida had thought to demonstrate what an effective homemaker she was, having swiftly grown proud of the difference she'd wrought in a house which had begun to look neglected as well as empty. She had polished the good old furniture which remained there, all the doors also. The flagged floor she'd washed repeatedly, and she had cleaned the tiny panes of each mullioned window.

Briefly, when Henry walked in and, after introducing

117

Catalina to them, had gazed about him, Phillie had been delighted. But then, nodding to himself, he was smiling.

'I'm glad you two are looking after t'place. Can't do with it getting run down even before we work out the living arrangements here.'

William hesitated midway to finding himself a chair, shifted uneasily from one foot to the other. Did Henry intend moving in with them in the near future?

Phillie couldn't find one word, she was so shaken. Never for a moment since marrying Will had she thought of this house as being anything but their own. *Hers*, in fact, with the prospect of Will's departure heavy upon their days now. Her home – which would console her during her husband's long absences.

Henry said nothing more, but he did go up and inspect his old room. The damage had occurred, though, hardening Phillida towards him. And she couldn't tell where Catalina fitted in.

'You're a friend of Henry's then. . . ?' she asked the elegant woman who looked so foreign and whose gleaming gown, for all its being black, outshone her own best blue outfit.

'Yes, that is right,' Catalina confirmed, but giving nothing away.

'It were a pity you just missed our wedding,' William remarked kindly. He thought Catalina seemed uncomfortable with his wife.

'Yes, indeed,' she agreed.

Phillida felt there was no real regret in the señorita's voice. 'It was a nice simple ceremony. Are you chapel, an' all?'

Catalina shook her head. 'No, all my family are Catholic.'

Phillie checked a disapproving sniff. No wonder Catalina seemed so different. Long before she was ready to serve their dinner she was hard put to it to find something to talk about. But William appeared to be unperturbed by this Spanish woman. He began discussing with his brother the possibility of opening a Fortescue office in the West Riding. They were soon comparing what they'd learned about making port and sherry. And Catalina was joining in, talking about the cost of

118

having an office here, as if she understood such matters. And she actually corrected Henry when he quoted the quantity of sherry they'd shipped last month. Before Phillida had the meat on the table she felt excluded. She hadn't wanted any part of Will's working life, but she was confounded by this woman who fancied herself in a man's world.

Henry was aware that his new sister-in-law hadn't taken to Catalina. He tried to prevent things worsening, and couldn't help wishing Catalina didn't appear so self-contained today. She'd responded to his parents and Isobel, and young Charles. But then, happen he shouldn't be surprised that it was with William and his bride that there was this awkwardness.

Their wish to leave early wasn't just an excuse to get away. Earlier, setting out from the outskirts of Halifax, Henry had planned that he'd walk with Catalina along the line of the hill here. He'd show her a bit of the splendour that was his part of Yorkshire.

Catalina flourished again once they were alone, exclaiming delightedly as they strolled through his favourite wood, and listening, her dark eyes glinting, while he recounted some of his boyhood adventures here. When they reached the escarpment with a sheer drop from their feet to the road that led along the valley beneath them towards Lancashire, she gasped and turned to smile at him.

'I did not know you had such scenery here. Thank you for bringing me to Yorkshire. And thank you, *caro*, for not permitting me to remain in Jerez.' She had needed Henry to prove how much he cared about her.

'You look so much better, I can't help but know it was t'right thing to do.'

She kissed him full on the lips, leaning a little away at first then all at once sliding her hands around his shoulders.

'Do not allow me to place our situation at work between us, Henry, will you?' she said, dreading the loss of their mutual affection.

He frowned, recalling how readily she'd behaved as if he was trying to displace her there, and aware as well of his own need to succeed in this new job. Regardless of other folk.

'You're different altogether now you've had a while away from the bodega, you'll not be perturbed like that again,' he said. But words were easy. And his intuition was asserting that her ambitions and his own might never be compatible.

The day that Henry and Catalina left the West Riding Isobel chewed solemnly on her lips, determined not to weep. She'd always loved their Henry but if anything she loved Catalina more. She was all that Isobel longed to be in a few more years: elegant, employed in a successful business – an interesting person.

Isobel had loved hearing about the city of Jerez, about Catalina's young siblings and her brother Carlos who was so determined to be a bull-fighter. As they said goodbye the only thing that consoled her was being invited to visit Jerez.

'You would enjoy exploring with my family, Isobel. And the sight of Carlos in the costume he has in readiness for becoming a matador would make you laugh,' said Catalina, hugging her.

'I'll come one day, I'd love to. When we're employing someone else as well to help Father.'

Amos snorted. 'Nay, lass, you're not indispensable, you could go now as far as I'm concerned.'

Pain shot right through her. Couldn't he, just this once, let on that she was useful to him? But she'd not go, allowing somebody else to take over her father's books. Since moving here Charles had started attending a new school which seemed more to his liking. He was learning quickly and talking of prolonging his education. But her father would much prefer Charles at his side rather than Isobel herself, and wasn't above snatching at any chance of bringing that about. And besides, even though Catalina did smile and laugh a lot more now, her family were in mourning. This was no time to visit, they'd not be able to let themselves go and have a bit of fun.

'Some time soon, I hope, Catalina,' she responded, in her best grown-up manner. 'Thank you ever so much for asking me, I'll right look forward to coming.'

Henry had said goodbye to his mother reluctantly, wishing she seemed happier. She was standing impassively at the outer door, even her normally expressive brown eyes revealing no emotion.

'I will try to get up to Halifax again afore I sail,' he assured her. He was remaining in London to learn more of this end of the business before following to Spain on a later vessel.

When he saw Catalina aboard at London docks a few days afterwards, Henry's emotions were mixed. They had grown closer than ever during her stay in his home, and yet he wasn't sorry to be having a short while away from her. Matthew Fortescue was in London. Henry welcomed the opportunity to go into further intricacies of shipping wine without eternally wondering if his grasp of the work might be troubling Catalina.

I wish you'd give your heart to being more womanly, he thought, embracing her as they stood on deck. It was abnormal that she should measure her worth against a man's efficiency. He was much happier with her when they were away from business matters and could enjoy a more traditional relationship.

Henry met Matthew Fortescue at Tom's Coffee House in Cornhill. The crowded interior still excited him. He had to remind himself not to listen in to the keen conversations generated at nearby tables as business was conducted by the merchants congregating there. He was quite disappointed when Matthew led him out to his carriage.

'We've acquired premises of our own,' he told Henry, 'in Queenhithe.'

When Matthew eventually stopped the carriage and stepped down, he checked Henry with a hand before he entered the tall building. 'This here's Queenhithe Dock, you'd best have a look. It's ancient, you know.'

Fresh from seeing Catalina aboard her ship at one of the great London docks, Henry was unimpressed. The dock here was but a trifling area of still water overshadowed by what looked like warehouses.

Seeing his expression, Matthew laughed. 'You mightn't think much of t'place, but it was first mentioned in 899, in Alfred the Great's charter. There was a time when it ranked in importance with Billingsgate as a dock.'

Already more interested, Henry followed him through a narrow doorway and up a steep stair. He was excited by the aroma of foreign spices, evidently imported by other merchants sharing the building. Although already nicely appointed with good solid furniture, Fortescue's office was far from grand but, as Matthew explained, it would serve to contain this end of the business. And would, he thought, be better than sending out circulars from a coffee house address.

'And what about this office we're setting up in t'West Riding?' Henry inquired.

Matthew sighed. 'I'm afraid that notion has been laid aside, for the time being. With taking on this place our recent outlay has been more than sufficient. Setting up yet another office is out of the question before we're all convinced it'll pay for itself.'

'I see.' Henry, recalling his conversations with his brother, wondered if Will had fully understood that the scheme was in no way definite. He couldn't avoid thinking that Phillida mightn't have been in such a hurry to get wed if she'd known the nearest William might be working was London.

'Travelling about the country grows increasingly easy,' Matthew assured him, smiling. 'With mail coaches and turnpike roads, as well as companies who specialise in transporting goods. And besides, with you learning so quickly in Spain and your brother in Portugal, we'll keep a better eye on shipments.'

'Even without Ignacio Escutia?'

'His loss will be felt, naturally, but I'm confident you'll soon cover for him. Now what I want to discuss today is the condition of the wine when it arrives in England.'

Matthew settled himself more comfortably on his large leather chair, and gazed approvingly through the small window at the view of St Paul's cathedral whilst considering a report on the desk before him. Glancing across towards Henry, he announced, 'We're still experiencing some problems which haven't quite been eliminated by adding brandy to the sherry. Luke was to look into this with Alberto Martinez during his stay there. I want your opinion of the quality of the resultant wine.'

Henry was flattered, but surprised as well. Surely, few people knew more about sherry than their capataz?

'You have a fresh palate,' Matthew reminded him, 'that could well be useful as a guide to how new clients would react to wine that has more brandy added. We value customers who know and love sherry, but we always need to look to extending our market.'

'I'll bear that in mind and report back to you.'

'Martinez will be instructed to collaborate with you over any adjustments made to the amounts of brandy used. We are finding that its addition arrests fermentation, thus creating a rather different wine. We need to understand more about this aspect, in order to hold onto clients who are faithful to the original product. Records must be accurately maintained – see that Señorita Escutia understands this, and complies with our requirements. Luke seems to think she has neglected the clerical side of late.'

'She has taken a lot on since her father became ill.'

Matthew nodded, then smiled again, blandly. 'Agreed, and now you're becoming well-grounded in the production side, there's no reason she shouldn't concentrate solely on documentation again.'

That won't suit, thought Henry. He only hoped he wasn't the person who'd be required to tell her.

'You'll explain, of course, if she doubts what her role is to be,' Matthew added, making Henry's spirits sink.

The older man read his expression. 'Nay, you're not a bit of a lad now, you'll have to cope with situations that don't always make you popular. In this case, Señorita Escutia's a reasonable young lady, she'll realise the arrangement's for the best. And it'll do you no harm to have a bit of experience of the dislike that bosses sometimes are obliged to earn.'

That's all very well, Henry reflected, if you aren't already close to loving the person concerned. How would he bear it if the recent good terms established between himself and Catalina were destroyed? Only this morning he'd been thinking that he'd be glad of a short break from always considering her reactions; that didn't mean he wished to contemplate a situation where the strain between them was so great that they no longer communicated.

'She's a woman, isn't she?' Matthew persisted. 'I'll bet it's not so long before she marries some *caballero* and forgets all about Fortescue's.'

Henry was appalled. From wishing that Catalina would think of more homely matters he was now driven to consider that she might do that very thing – with some man other than himself.

Long before he left on the voyage to join her in Jerez, he'd grown unnaturally perturbed. Between ensuring that she kept to the boring jobs which she felt did not occupy her to capacity, and the dread that she would up and marry some local young man, he was in for a terrible time.

The news that the company was not to open a Yorkshire office shook William very gravely. He'd grown so dependent upon energetic love-making with Phillida that he was horrified by the prospect of spending months away from her, if not in Portugal in London.

Phillida was no less disturbed, but she consoled herself that soon they would have the family for which she longed. Caring for a child and continuing to spin wool for her father to weave should help her to endure Will's absences.

As winter progressed, however, with their part of the West Riding frozen in one of the coldest for years and no sign of the baby she yearned for, she couldn't avoid being depressed. William wasn't fond of writing letters, and in any case mail from Oporto took over two weeks in each direction. Messages from him came whenever either Luke or Matthew Fortescue returned from Portugal. But they were received only second or third hand from one or other of the Brights and merely made her ache all the more to be with her husband.

Phillida continued to blame the wines imported by Fortescue's for keeping them apart and, whenever word reached her that her father-in-law had imbibed too well, reflected that maybe this was no more than the family deserved. This view was regularly endorsed by her own mother and father who were hardly reconciled to her marrying outside the close community of their hillside chapel.

Her young sister-in-law Isobel was growing accustomed to her father's lapses into drunkenness, and his earnest contrition. He had scared her last week, though, by disappearing from the Piece Hall. After scouring the crowds there, she'd eventually set out with Eddie for The Union Cross. Horrified, she had seen Amos staggering towards them, reeling into the wall by which he was feeling his way. They had rushed to help him and arrived as he was slithering to the ground. Eddie had succeeded in hauling her father into a sitting position, but they'd been obliged to remain there with him, and all Halifax looking on, until he was fit to reach the wagon.

Isobel was recovering from the experience when she was shaken by her father's announcement a few days later about Eddie Gaukroger.

She and Charles were sitting at the tea table with their parents. They had been discussing her younger brother's growing reluctance to do as he'd first intended and eventually become a clothier. For some time now Charles had insisted that he wanted to study law. Isobel was secretly delighted. Although it was understood that Charles must extend his education, she'd known that if he did come into the business she'd have to be careful she wasn't pushed out. But suddenly it was Eddie, of all people, creating a threat that she would be replaced.

'Eddie's framed far better nor ever I expected,' Amos said. 'I think he's justified in hoping I'll give him more responsibility. I'm pleased to say he feels he can tackle keeping our records now.'

When Isobel didn't speak, her father beamed across the table. 'That'll give you more time to enjoy yourself, won't it, love? See more of your young friends. I've never been happy that a lass your age should have to work so hard.'

How on earth could she stop this happening? 'I've liked what I were doing, I've never grumbled, have I?' she managed at last, her face and neck going hot, then just as swiftly icy. 'I've allus wanted to work wi' you, Father.'

'You'll not put a stop to that now, Amos?' Eleanor asked.

'No – if Isobel wants to come along wi' us, where's the harm?'

She gulped, swallowed, willed herself not even to blink on the tears stabbing at her eyes. But if she was only allowed to ride back and forth on the wagon, what use was that? Writing up the books was her job. Nobody could take more care, there wasn't once she'd made a mistake. And the folk they met down at the Piece Hall had taken to her. These days, hardly any of them talked to her as to a child. If they'd accepted that she was capable and not to be patronised, why couldn't her own father see her that way? What had she done wrong?

'It's nowt you've done wrong,' Amos told her now, as if her attempt to disguise what she was feeling was fruitless, and he saw beyond her set little face. 'It's different for a fellow, Eddie must be given a chance.'

Or is it that *he* won't let slip, here, that you've been drinking some of t'brass you've taken? wondered Isobel with sudden insight. But understanding one possible reason for her father's support of Eddie didn't alter the danger of her losing everything. She couldn't swallow another mouthful. The lump in her throat was so immense that she couldn't speak either. But she'd not cry in front of anybody. And she wouldn't leave this table while by sitting and enduring she might learn what her father really intended. Whatever could she do to stop him getting rid of her?

The matter was dropped, though, and Amos didn't refer to it again before their next visit to the Piece Hall. Having Eddie with them, appearing no different and saying nothing about his ambitions, confused Isobel. He had been a great help since they'd set him on, especially when Amos was tempted to drink. Eddie was adept at getting him back on to the wagon, and at listening to how sorry he was. He also watched that Amos didn't part with the entire proceeds of their sales.

'He's not so bad today, you know,' Isobel assured Eddie that afternoon while her father dozed in the back of the wagon as they drove up the hill out of the town. 'I don't believe he has drunk so much.'

Eddie said nothing. He liked Isobel who didn't treat him as if he was dense, even while she did the work he wanted. He'd not upset her with the truth. If Amos was always sober he'd maybe not listen to Eddie Gaukroger's ideas for bettering himself. And maybe not need his help so much.

Arriving at the house, Eddie clambered down from the wagon while Isobel collected together all their records of cloth sold. She felt abnormally tired after anxiously waiting to be told that she must hand over to Eddie. But that suggestion hadn't come, so it seemed only a small worry that Father had drunk himself to sleep. They both went to rouse him.

'We'll take him in the back way,' Isobel announced and they struggled to haul Amos out and help him down on to the ground.

From an upstairs chamber, Eleanor was watching. She'd heard the wagon and, as always, was beside one of the curtained windows, anxious to learn how her husband was. Inwardly she groaned, her stomach heaved, a now-familiar pain commenced beneath her ribs. Both Eddie and young Isobel looked unperturbed getting Amos on to his feet. Was there no one in this world who cared that this was her husband, the man she'd fallen in love with when he was ambitious and enthusiastic, when he'd enjoyed being with her?

Seeing how he'd changed was breaking her heart. Between one bout and the next he always recovered sufficiently to eat the substantial meals she produced and to sate his other appetites with her body. Never once did he seem to imagine that she might need to feel loved or to have her own desire satisfied. Couldn't he understand how she hated his intoxication? He was ready enough with his sorrowful grey eyes and his careful sentences which might convince some folk he genuinely would control his drinking. She wished she could go back to the time when she'd had faith in him. He'd sat on their bed here only the other day, promising her the world; she could hardly bear to remind herself.

'I'll show you, Eleanor love, I will. It hasn't really got a hold on me. I'll limit myself to one glass, I only have to be sociable. And I need summat to make me feel as good as the folk I'm meeting.'

She would not condone his determination to destroy himself, Eleanor had decided. Her mind made up, she waited, listening, until she heard Isobel and Eddie returning down the back stair. Inwardly shaking but visibly imbued with a terrible calm, she strode along to the room where Amos was drowsing.

'You've done it again, haven't you,' she said. 'It doesn't matter how many times I've begged you not to do this to yourself. Well, if you can't see that you should get a grasp on your self-respect, somebody's got to teach you. This is t'last time, Amos.'

'Aye, lass, aye – I'll not have too much again. But I'm not drunk, you know, not today. It were only that I met up wi'. . .'

'I don't give a hang who you met! You've always had an excuse and you allus will have. It's bad enough letting your wife see you in this state, but our young daughter knows and that disgusts me.'

' 'T won't happen again, love, I promise you that.'

Eleanor closed her eyes, praying for some hint that she could believe him. But then she looked at him, a dishevelled, sickly mockery of the man she'd married. If she didn't act now, he'd only become worse. 'I'm not having our Isobel brought up to live wi' this. I'm clearing out and I'm taking her with me. You'll not set eyes on us again unless you come to your senses.'

'Nay, lass, you don't mean that. You *can't* . . .' He was so sure she'd not do anything so drastic he didn't even get off the bed.

Eleanor hadn't made a hasty decision, and it had been

confirmed by learning Eddie Gaukroger would be more useful. If Amos pulled himself together the two of them could keep the business going. And Mrs Darwin their housekeeper had promised he'd eat regular meals.

As for herself, she was so set on shaking Amos into changing his ways that she'd had a bag ready and waiting since his last drunken return from the cloth market. The intervening days had strengthened her intention, if not her desire to leave him.

Her sudden impulse to kiss him goodbye was checked along with her sigh. All her feelings were for the man Amos used to be, she'd not get him back if she softened now. Walking briskly into the room they had shared, Eleanor picked up her belongings and the bag she'd packed for Isobel. She hurried down the front staircase, out of the door and around the stone building towards the rear. She'd have to steel herself for tackling Isobel, especially since she'd made different arrangements for Charles whose schooling mustn't be interrupted.

Isobel was coming towards her, carrying all her papers and books.

'We're going away for a bit,' Eleanor announced sharply. If she took her time over this she would weep. 'Just you an' me.'

Her daughter gawped at her, shaking her head in disbelief and then total horror. She blinked twice, her brown eyes glossing with tears. 'Mother, we *can't* go away, we *can't*. What about Father, and our Charles?'

'I've arranged all that – Charles is going to bide with one of his schoolfriends, I've told them it's only temporary.'

Eleanor turned towards Eddie Gaukroger who had been standing with his jaw agape since her first sentence to Isobel. 'I'll have you take us into the town please, Eddie.'

Isobel was as still as a puppet, except for her mouth which was silently forming words she hardly dared say.

'Come on, love,' Eleanor persisted. 'I've got your things here.'

'No,' Isobel said at last, 'I work for Bright's, I can't go anywhere.' She thrust everything she was holding under one arm, reached out a hand. 'Can I have my stuff, please?'

Their hands overlapped on the bag, her mother's felt strange, clammy. 'You don't really want to go . . .' Isobel ventured.

'It'll be for the best,' Eleanor asserted, but was she assuring herself? Isobel had rebelled, and insisting that the girl obeyed would achieve nothing. 'You could meet up with your father, regular like, while he's out with the wagon.'

'That's not enough.' Isobel felt a tug as she took the weight when her mother released the bag. 'I'm sorry . . .' she said huskily.

Eleanor would break if she listened. 'The wagon'll do, Eddie, I'll not wait while you hitch the horses up to t'carriage.'

She couldn't direct Eddie to take her all the way to her destination; she'd not have him revealing where she was. Leaving Amos was to make him sweat. Not knowing where to find her would aggravate him and might shake him into curbing his drink.

The mail coach was preparing to depart as Eddie set her down, but Eleanor delayed hurrying towards it until she was satisfied that their wagon was heading away from the centre of Halifax. He'd not see her.

Waiting to cross the road and board the coach, she felt terrible. Would she ever see Amos or her family again? Could she exist if she'd nowt more to do with them? She hadn't spared one glance over her shoulder at the house, but when had it ever been her home?

The walk was long from the point where the mail coach dropped her to the house in Heptonstall. Phillida looked utterly confounded.

'Can I come in, love?' Eleanor asked. 'I never intended intruding, but I've nowhere else to go. Can you give me a room for a bit?'

Still too taken aback to manage words, Phillida nodded. Her poor mother-in-law looked totally distracted. 'Let's have your cloak,' she said to her eventually and placed it on the hook behind the door. She sensed Eleanor observing her slow movements, but who could blame her for needing time to collect her wits?

'Sit yoursen down, I'll make a pot of tea,' she continued at last. But when Eleanor followed her to the kitchen instead, she caught herself wondering if Will's mother was here to check there'd not been too many changes.

'You've got it looking lovely, Phillida,' Eleanor remarked with an effort about what had been her home. Hadn't she felt all the way here that she *was* coming home? 'I can't put up wi' his drinking a day longer,' she added abruptly. 'If this doesn't stop him, nowt will.'

'Aye. Well, you know I'm again' it. Even though Will makes his living in t'wine trade. Folk aren't meant to be that immoderate.'

Eleanor hadn't known what to expect here. When Phillida continued sermonising day after day, she didn't know where to turn next. Before long, she'd be convinced that Amos' condition was *her* fault for permitting strong drink in the house. Her daughter-in-law seemed to think that any laxity should have been curbed when Amos first showed the tendency.

'He's never listened to me, except when it suited him, you know,' she explained one afternoon when Phillida's lips were set in a disapproving line as she sat spinning. The day after Eleanor's arrival, the spinning wheel had been fetched from the other side of the village and Phillida had intimated that it was so she wouldn't waste so much time going back and forth to her father's cottage. Eleanor, who was aching to have the house to herself, felt deprived of privacy. Yet knew she didn't belong here.

Isobel appeared at the door three weeks after Eleanor's return to Heptonstall, and her brother Charles with her. Brought by Eddie Gaukroger, they came with their father's plea that Eleanor would come back with them.

'He'll not touch another drop o' drink, we're to tell you,' Isobel announced, brown eyes round and earnest in her pale face.

'We miss you such a lot, Mother,' Charles insisted. His fair hair looked dull and in need of a good brushing. Dark circles ringed the grey eyes so like his father's.

131

'I thought you were staying with yon Cecil's folk . . .'

'I didn't like it there. Father said I could come home.'

Eleanor's gaze anchored on her youngest son. His hair was that matted, all its beautiful pale sheen vanished. She swallowed, willed herself to think only of stopping Amos becoming a permanent drunkard.

Phillida gave the children cake which even Isobel devoured as if it was the first decent food in days. Charles had wolfed his portion before Eleanor had taken her first bite. Unable to force the crumbs past the lump in her throat, she coughed, close to choking. Abruptly, she left the table and went out to the pump to draw water.

Isobel followed. 'Are you all right, Mother?'

Nobody had sounded so concerned for her in many a day. Phillida only accepted her because there seemed no alternative, the lovely features never quite disguised her reluctance.

'Aye, love. Aye.'

She was positive Isobel had grown, just in these few weeks. She was tall for her age, and far too scraggy.

'Now you're here, you'd better stop,' she said. 'I'll talk to Phillida. You'd be able to see Susan Gaukroger again, all your old friends.'

Isobel was shaking her head; looking all of twenty, disturbed but resolute. For the second time Eleanor felt whipped by her sad brown eyes and compressed lips.

'I'll not leave Father. I told you. You do understand, Mother? If we come to live here, he'll have nobody. He'll never manage on his own – he'll drink more nor ever, and t'business'll go downhill.'

'Serve him right,' muttered his wife severely.

'It isn't only him cares about t'cloth trade now. I've worked with him for ages, I'm not chucking t'lot down the drain.'

'You're thirteen years old, Isobel,' her mother reminded her. How could the lass want so much responsibility?

Isobel smiled wryly. The look in her eyes could have been an adult's, their depths were tinged with so much awareness. 'I don't feel it, Mother. I've set out to show I could step in like a grown woman, and I haven't made that many mistakes.

Leastways, not as a clothier. Running the house doesn't take my fancy, happen that's why we could be better organised.'

'I'd never have come away if you hadn't had a housekeeper over yonder. Don't tell me Mrs Darwin's useless?'

'She's right enough,' Isobel mumbled. They didn't get on; what woman that age would take comments from a lass so much younger? 'But you always kept a good table, and had the house bright and clean.'

Is that all I exist for? thought Eleanor.

'We'll try and make it easier for you if you'll only come back.' That was young Charles in the doorway, his face screwed up as he contained unmanly emotions.

Aye, thought Eleanor, I daresay you two would. But in some moods, your father'd step round me if I collapsed on t'kitchen floor. After her youngest children had left, she felt she had to escape Phillida's suddenly sympathetic green eyes and bolt upstairs. If only she could get her husband to change *and* still take care of her family!

Will learned of his mother's action when Matthew Fortescue next arrived in Oporto. Hearing that Amos was teetering on the brink of dousing his problems to obliteration with the bottle again, he longed to get a message to his family. He'd like to warn his father not to be so daft – it was only by mending his ways that he'd a hope of getting Eleanor to return to Halifax. He'd urge their Isobel to carry on as well, keeping her eye on both the household and t'cloth business. And he'd ask their mother if she was wrong in the head. Who would keep her? Away from Amos, she'd no brass of her own, she couldn't expect Phillida to provide for her indefinitely.

They only had Phillida's earnings from spinning to eke out what he sent home to Yorkshire. And what would it be like when he did manage to get home, if his mother was still living with them and no privacy?

'It's a great pity that idea of an office in t'West Riding fell through,' he said to Matthew Fortescue. 'If I'd been at hand my mother wouldn't have come seeking a bed then. Phillie's far too soft.'

Matthew, whose opinion of Phillida was rather different, sighed. 'Happen it'll all blow over soon. Any road, when Luke and I do retire it'll be up to you and Henry to decide where you'll have offices.'

Although thankful for reassurance that they were being groomed for taking charge, it didn't help at present. It was now that they needed some means of bringing both parents to their senses.

Henry was no less disturbed when Matthew conveyed the news to him. 'I can't say as I blame her, but I wish to goodness she'd not behaved so drastically. Father's not always drunk, you know that, don't you? And he doesn't do it on purpose.'

'That's right,' Matthew agreed. 'I'll try and talk to both of them when I get back home, maybe they'll listen to me.'

'Your mother will not listen, I fear,' said Catalina sadly when Henry confided in her. 'She cannot forgive either of the Fortescues for taking you and your brother from her.'

'If only it hadn't had to happen just now,' Henry exclaimed. Since returning to Jerez he was working with renewed vigour on getting to know their wine, and on improving the means of its shipment. It seemed also that Catalina had accepted her position of providing figure work and records rather than becoming involved in the actual wine-making or storage and transportation. Having thus lost some reasons for awkwardness between them, Henry felt able to enjoy the occasions that they were together.

Much of the time at the Escutia *casa* they were the only ones, other than servants, in residence. Although recovering slowly from the shock of her husband's death, Carmen was adopting widowhood as a reason for avoiding responsibility. Retiring frequently to her sister's home and despite having her youngest children, Marcos and Maruja, with her, she seemed to exist in a half-life from which she roused herself only when her son Carlos repeatedly emphasised his determination to make his career in the bull-ring.

'If only your father were alive,' she observed to Catalina, 'there'd have been some means of preventing such a course.'

When Catalina only sighed whilst containing her own

knowledge that Ignacio had been no more successful than they were in influencing Carlos, her mother turned to Henry.

'Do you not consider it only proper that a son should respect his parents' wishes for him?'

A sharp laugh was surprised out of Catalina. '*Madre*, have you not thought? Henry would not be here if it were not for disregarding his father's business interests.'

The fact that they each had family difficulties drew Henry and Catalina more closely together. He frequently mounted the horse he'd previously borrowed on the day he'd summoned her to her father's bedside, and they rode out over the undulating hills surrounding Jerez, relishing each other's company in the cool of early morning.

Because of the long delays involved in communicating with England it was to Henry that his brother William wrote, expressing his disapproval of their mother's leaving home.

I fear it has been too easy for her, with a bed being available over in Heptonstall. If Father doesn't fetch her back afore long, we shall be obliged to intervene. That house belongs to us now, after all, you'll stand by me I trust in opposing Mother's remaining there.

'I'll do no such thing,' Henry confided to Catalina. 'She's our mother, when all's said and done, and happen we should be ensuring she does keep away from Father – it could be t'only way he sobers up for good.'

'And she may become very useful where she is when Phillida begins having children.'

Henry snorted ruefully. 'I doubt that'll be the case, not with Phillie – all she wants is our Will coming home to her and peace to get on with minding a house full of childer in her own way.'

9

'It's time you and me had a talk.'

Her father's words sounded like a command, put to her as they finished supper after a long day at the Piece Hall. But when she looked across the table Amos had unusual concern in his grey eyes. She'd been certain he was going to stress his determination that Eddie be given the chance he expected. This concern made her less sure.

'We can't keep on stopping young Gaukroger trying to improve himself,' Amos announced. 'I know you're again' the idea, but I'm afraid you'll have to put up wi' it. It's not only for his sake, tha knows. I need you as more than my second-in-command for Bright's.'

And whose fault is that, thought Isobel, resolved that she'd say nothing to help him. If he'd behaved reasonably, in the first place, her mother would never have left, and Isobel would never have been obliged to deputise for her here, trying to see that Mrs Darwin kept on top of running the house.

When his opening sentence received no response, Amos stifled a sigh. He needed to win his daughter's cooperation. The complete straightforwardness which would guarantee her assistance came hard, and required willpower which was some minutes in being marshalled.

'I'm determined to win your mother back,' he told her solemnly. 'That's why I'll have to count on you more to look after things.'

'How do you mean?' She'd learned enough, these past few years, to refuse to contemplate any of her father's plans without first being acquainted with all the details.

'For a start, I'm going to have this house looking less neglected. Don't get me wrong, love, I'm not blaming you for the way it's kept. I only want you to promise you'll see it's improved. If I'm ever to get your mother to come back, it's got to be to a better home.'

'It isn't me and our Charles that makes a mess here,' Isobel ventured. If there were to be enough changes they must spring from her father's altered behaviour. The only way that they had persuaded their housekeeper to remain was by Isobel herself cleaning up after Amos when drinking made him ill. Mrs Darwin wasn't being difficult, she simply was not accustomed to anything so unpleasant.

Isobel saw his greying eyebrows shoot towards his thinning hair. Once, she'd have been too terrified to stand her ground. Tonight she was too determined on change to be perturbed about the means.

'I fully realise that I'll have to lay off the bottle,' he stated, surprising her into lowering her guard. 'That's really what I want to talk about. I don't like drinking too much, you know.'

Isobel's glance was far more sceptical than a girl of her years should have produced. And she said nothing.

Amos swallowed. 'I never believe I'm going to end up in that state. I just need summat to make me feel at ease with folk.'

His daughter was astonished that he ever felt less than at ease with other men. He gave every impression of being convivial.

'Ours weren't much of a business, when I began working with my own father. I hated the shabby clothes I wore to market when all the time I was handling beautiful materials. A glass or two made me confident enough to forget how I looked, helped me approach better-class folk.'

Isobel could see how the dependence upon alcohol might have developed. And she sympathised with the young man who had been Amos Bright before success had provided some standing. His honesty induced her to hear him out.

'I want you to keep an eye on me, lass – to watch I don't go having too much, not only when we're at home but while we're out.'

'I could only do that if you didn't slope off to drink with your cronies,' Isobel protested, past experience stronger than his fine resolve.

Amos nodded gravely. 'I agree, lass. That's why we've got to free you to be with me. By giving Gaukroger some of t'work.'

If her mother could be persuaded to return home, life would be altogether different. It would be a proper home again, for their Charles as well as Father and herself. She mustn't let her own feelings about the work she did for Bright's stand in the way.

'We'd better give 'im a try then,' she said, and wished fervently that she could rid herself of feeling that she was being compelled to toss away everything for which she'd struggled.

When Eddie next accompanied them to Halifax Piece Hall he was told by Amos to sit in the wagon with Isobel. 'She'll explain us way o' recording stuff,' he said, smiling to himself as he took up the reins.

'There's a page for every weaver in the front of the ledger,' Isobel began, showing Eddie. 'And at t'back we note down who buys each bolt of cloth, and for how much. That's all you need to know really.'

'You'd better show him how we list the cloth as it's collected,' Amos called back to her.

Isobel felt colour rush to her face. She'd known her explanation was sketchy, but couldn't help loathing Eddie taking over her work.

'Oh aye, have a look,' she said swiftly, she didn't want him to feel awful about her reluctance. 'We picked these up t'other day.' Gazing down at her own neat handwriting made her itch to enter in more figures. Eddie's writing would look different, would spoil the whole book. But there was no way of averting her father's plans.

'We have to keep records like this,' she continued, forcing herself to explain. 'To find out how much profit we're making, but also so we know where each length of cloth is from and where it's gone to.'

'Looks easy to me,' said Eddie, grinning. He'd show 'em all!

'It's not too difficult, so long as you're careful. I hope you've washed your hands afore you came out.'

Eddie tried hard that day, writing down each sale laboriously while Isobel instructed, and entering figures in the columns indicated. When there were words to write, she had to spell them, letter by letter, and even then they were often scarcely recognisable. Secretly, Isobel stifled the first stirrings of satisfaction. Happen Eddie would prove himself incapable.

Amos, however, was adamant. Young Gaukroger would be trained, and if he failed she would be held responsible.

Isobel began to understand more a month later. She tackled him about Eddie, whilst on their round collecting up finished cloth. 'You're not saving time by giving him the records to do, it takes far longer wi' me telling him every letter than doing it on my own.'

'Be patient, lass. He can't help being slow.'

'But maybe we're doing him anything but a kindness by making him work so hard. He can't enjoy it, it's too much of a struggle. All he's proved so far is that he's very little use with a pen.'

Amos scratched his grey head, thinking. The lass could be right; certainly Eddie was less cheerful, and he got upset when he made mistakes or scattered blots over the ledger. There were, though, his own plans to have Isobel out of the business and at home by the time he'd persuaded her mother to return. If she had the lass about the house every day, Eleanor wouldn't have cause to be miserable.

'Give him a while longer, Isobel. He's willing enough.'

And why wouldn't he be, she thought, when he's got the chance of taking over my work! Not that she'd give up without a battle; but she wished she knew how to deal with both Eddie and her father. She was breaking her heart over the way all the pleasure was taken out of everything.

Eddie moved awkwardly as he scrambled up on to the wagon that morning. He'd got a very stiff neck which started in the roots of his hair and ran right down into his shoulder. He had sat last night, over by the candle that stood on his bedroom window sill where it couldn't set fire to the room. The draught had been cold, but he'd stayed there just the same. Hour after hour, he'd laboured over copying the letters which he'd found in one of their Susan's old books. He had tried to read what the words said, an' all, but only a few of the more simple ones had made any sense to him. He didn't want to be a failure, but if he didn't find some clue to how letters should be strung together, he'd be bound to admit that he had taken on more than he could manage.

'You'd better take notice today,' Amos told him. 'T'next time we go to market our Isobel's stopping at home.'

Isobel had to put a hand up to her mouth to stifle her cry. But when she glanced at Eddie she saw he was no less perturbed.

'Don't worry,' she said gently. 'Just do your best, only try to be a bit quicker.'

It was when he reached for the book to enter details of the second piece of cloth which he'd collected that he turned too suddenly and wrenched his painful neck. 'Oh, heck. . . !' he exclaimed and put up a hand to the sore muscle.

His elbow caught the ink bottle and overturned it across a bolt of cream coloured material.

'Look what you've done,' Isobel shrieked.

Amos checked the horses before they travelled more than another pace or two, and clambered into the back to inspect.

'Accidents will happen,' he began, but then he saw the extent of the damage.

Instead of quickly setting aside the inky cloth, Eddie had glanced about in agitation for an old rag with which to mop up, and had inadvertently let surplus ink drip on to a second bolt of material.

'Just leave it, I'll see to it,' Isobel began impatiently.

There's no need,' Eddie argued. 'It's up to me to put it right.'

He'd spotted some waste at the side of the wagon. Stretching across her, though, he again overturned the ink. This time it splattered on to the open ledger.

'Nay, what're you doing?' Amos snapped. 'Between you, the pair of you will ruin me.'

Already distressed by the damage to the cloth and to the ledger as well, Isobel sank her teeth into her lip. She'd not say owt. If she opened her mouth she'd either bawl like a

140

bairn or would tell both Eddie and her father what she thought of this experiment.

There was worse to follow on the occasion when Amos and Eddie went to the Piece Hall without her. Isobel spent a miserable day trying to occupy herself with household chores while all the time her mind painted pictures of the cloth market. If this was the way her life was going to progress now, she'd need to find something to get her away from here.

By the time her father returned several hours late she was desperate with the anxiety that he would have been drinking himself senseless.

Amos was icily sober. He was also rigid with anger. Stalking into the room, he threw the ledger on to the table. 'You'd best see what you can do with that. Made a proper muddle of it, he has! Then he'd the rank audacity to tell me it's all my fault for asking too much of him.'

'Nay, Father, what can I do – I weren't there . . .' Isobel began.

His helpless glance stopped her. She'd never seen Amos Bright switch so quickly from fury to complete dejection.

'You'll happen make summat of his writin', I'm danged if I can. He just seems to string all his letters together all anyhow. And I can't make head nor tail o' them figures.'

Isobel wasn't surprised. Disregarding columns, Eddie had jotted down numbers all over the place, with no indication of which were quantities or measurements, and nothing to differentiate between pounds, shillings and pence.

'Made me look a right fool, he did, an' all,' Amos concluded, sinking on to a high-backed chair. 'Couldn't tell one of our best clients where t'cloth I were offering were woven. *If* Gaukroger had noted it down, even he couldn't read what he'd written. And he has no memory for what he's done.'

'He can't help it, it's a pity for him,' his daughter murmured. Any relief that she would be regaining her job was balanced out by the need to restore some kind of order to their books. She was astonished when Amos sat up with her after supper, attempting to coordinate what he remembered about the pieces handled that day.

'Some good staying sober has done me,' he remarked wryly when at last they had completed sufficient to ensure they would rest easy in their beds. 'I've ended up worse off nor I were weeks ago, and no nearer freeing you to be a companion to your mother.'

'That's why you wanted me to stay at home today, is it? Not because you've found I'm no good to you?'

'Ay, lass, you shouldn't take on so. You ought to know by now that I'm only too aware I'd find nobody better. It's just a pity that you weren't born a lad. A lad could have come into t'business without any trouble.'

You'll never be satisfied with me, no matter what I do or how clever I become, Isobel thought. It was something she could do nothing about, and it was ruining every day for her, and threatened to ruin her life. But Amos couldn't help the way he'd been conditioned; it wasn't really his fault that his latest experiment had distressed her and caused him anger.

She rose, went round to his chair and hugged him. His cheek was rough against hers and when she glanced at it she noticed the gathering wrinkles. There was something more disturbing, as well; the tired grey eyes were clouded with tears.

At the door on her way upstairs to her chamber, Isobel paused. 'Don't be so long now, you need a good night's sleep,' she said, sounding exactly like her mother.

Glancing around the room in the light flickering from the one remaining candle, Amos let the weighty sigh emerge. He would go up to bed immediately. The master bedchamber was the one room with no place for secreting ale or bottles of wine. This day seemed to have destroyed all his latest ideas for making Eleanor come back to him; his only hope now was to offer his abstinence as a desperate plea to the Almighty.

If he could only summon enough willpower and maintain it, he could manage. He wouldn't stop feeling as if just one drink would make him much better, but he could school himself to accept that life had shown that it only ever made everything far worse.

Phillida awakened in the night, the flow of blood and pains dragging at her inside alerting her to her condition. Yet again, she'd failed to conceive. This time she was a day or so late, had come to bed only last evening with hope beginning to stir in her heart. She reached for the candle, found tinder and flint. She would have to go downstairs and outside to draw water in order to cleanse and put herself to rights.

Half-way down the staircase, she halted, listening. Her mother-in-law was moving about the kitchen. If she weren't driven by necessity, Phillida would have gone back to bed.

'What's wrong? What do you want?' asked Eleanor, swinging round, startled by Phillie's sudden appearance.

'I might ask you that,' her daughter-in-law replied. 'Creeping about our house when folk are asleep.'

Eleanor's dark eyes narrowed. Phillida was always implying that she was up to no good here. 'I couldn't sleep, that's all. Looks like I'm not the only one either. Unless I wakened you.' She'd tried not to. She often tiptoed around her old home as though she dreaded even the mice behind the dado being reminded that she was here.

Wearily, Phillida shook her head. She'd no wish to make Eleanor feel any worse, poor woman. 'It's nowt to do with you. I had to get up, that's all.'

This time in the month she often felt unbearably hot; as a consequence the night air struck the more coldly and Phillida was shuddering when she picked up the pail and returned indoors. She'd been praying that her mother-in-law would have gone to her bed, but Eleanor was standing by the hearth, watching for her to come in.

'What ails you, Phillida?' she asked gently. She'd ensure that they'd get on better together. 'You're not a bit well, are you?'

'I'm right enough, thanks,' Phillie answered.

'Is there a bairn on the way, love?'

'No, there isn't.' Please don't sympathise and have me crying.

Eleanor read in Phillida's sorrowful green eyes that the absence of children was making her miserable.

'So, that's the way of it,' she said quietly. 'Ay, dear. But you shouldn't let it make you unhappy, not by now. You've not been wed all that long.'

143

'Seems like forever,' William's wife muttered. She closed her eyes, willing Eleanor to leave her on her own.

'Happen it'll not be long before Will's home again. I'll do my best to make things easier for you. There's plenty of jobs I can do while he's here so's you'll have more time together.'

Phillida swallowed back a gasp of horror. Did Eleanor think she'd still be living here by then? All she could anticipate was being made to feel awkward with him in their own home, as if they were on show.

'No, it's all right, thanks. I'll manage,' she said grimly.

'I only want to help. Happen if you'd less to do during the day . . .'

'And happen if we'd less folk round us all t' time . . .' Phillida began tautly, then regretted it but her mother-in-law was hurrying towards the stairs and the sentence went unfinished.

Eleanor willed herself not to weep as, stumbling over the hem of her nightgown, she scuttled towards her room. Why did Phillida blame her for the inability to conceive? If she'd been slapped she couldn't feel more hurt. And all she wanted was to make things easier for the lass, to be some use to anybody.

Phillida leaned heavily against the cold kitchen wall, ashamed of her outburst and wishing there was some way that she could bring herself to explain how this great yearning inside her made every aspect of life so intolerable. She knew Eleanor meant her no harm, and she did genuinely feel for her since she'd been driven to leave home. Expressing all this was beyond her, she knew, but unless someone found some way of improving the present situation, she couldn't envisage any means of avoiding further conflict.

If only Will were here . . . she thought, and realised immediately that she'd been correct a minute ago when considering his visits would be spoiled if they could no longer be alone here.

She felt the blood trickling down her legs, took off her nightgown and began sponging away the mess. Tears were running down her cheeks, splashing on to her bare feet, but she was too blinded to be able to manage anything but rubbing away at herself, as though that could eliminate the evidence that she was barren.

Why did she want children so much? She'd had no such craving before she married William, had she? All she'd thought then was that it would be nice to have a family. Everything had changed since the day she'd got wed; and there wasn't one change that she could call an improvement.

Eddie Gaukroger reverted to his original role, seeming quite content again as he fetched and carried for Amos and his daughter. Outwardly, they appeared to have returned to normality. Isobel could have told anybody that this didn't apply to her.

She'd always remained acutely conscious that she lacked both the years and the long experience which might have made her feel secure at her father's right hand. Since Amos had demonstrated how readily he could replace her she'd become unnerved. So far as she could tell, she disguised this from everyone else, but that did not prevent her constant apprehension.

The one good thing about the weeks that followed was her father's determination to stay sober. He so consistently abstained that eventually she felt quite proud of him. Their housekeeper, Mrs Darwin, enjoyed cooking for them while the master was in a state to relish their meals, and Isobel began to look forward to the evenings when she and Charles sat down with their father.

All the while now, in everything he did, Amos was looking to a future when Eleanor would somehow be convinced she should come home. He admitted privately that he had been selfish in the past, and knew that he'd never truly appreciated his wife. He swore that if ever she should return he'd make up to her for all that had gone before.

The severest problem keeping them apart was Eleanor's adamant refusal to see him. He had called at the old house many times in the early days of her absence from home. Only once had she relented and agreed to speak with him, and her manner had been so unlike her usual self that he'd come away believing he was better off without her.

Every time he thought about Eleanor now, he could still see the parlour over in Heptonstall as it had been that day after Phillida had admitted him and then excused herself.

He'd expected his wife would look gaunt and troubled, and instead had found her plump of body and face, sitting ramrod straight on one of the high-backed chairs while she confronted him.

'Hallo, love, you're looking well,' he'd begun, suddenly feeling further words draining from his mind now that he finally faced her.

Eleanor did not speak.

Amos wasn't to know that she'd been confounded by his being that blind he could think that she was well. Hadn't she despaired whilst tugging at the fastenings of her gown, struggling to confine the disgusting wodges of flesh which resulted from over-eating. And her brain felt as dull as the body that she had crammed with food in her fruitless efforts to fill her empty life. How could she respond to him?

Baffled by her silence, Amos had stood there, feverish with the need to break the impasse and alarmed by his sticky palms and the trickle of sweat down his back.

'Our Isobel and Charles miss you,' he'd announced, then cursed his inability to tell her something she didn't already know. For didn't the youngsters visit quite regularly, making him feel the more keenly the reproach in Eleanor's reluctance to see him. He'd swallowed. 'And I miss you an' all, a very great deal.'

He'd approached her chair, leaned towards her, because it was only by coming close that he'd be able to begin to re-establish the easy familiarity between them which had been insidiously destroyed.

Eleanor had looked up at him, for one glorious moment he'd felt certain those brown eyes were warming. And then she had sniffed. 'You've been at the wine now, haven't you?'

'One glass, that's all.' And that was the truth, but he'd needed something to stiffen him to endure the encounter.

'Hadn't you sense to keep off it, just for today? Can't you get through one day now without alcohol?'

'It's not like that, love. I hadn't touched a drop for t'best part of a month.'

Eleanor scrutinised him as he drew away from her. She longed to believe him, to accept that he could control his drinking, that they would be able to live together again. But even now he was shifting from one foot to the other, appearing so awkward that he conveyed anything but the impression that he had steadied.

'What have you come to say?' she asked. 'If you're thinking to get me to go back yonder, you'll have to do better nor this. I want convincing that you're mending your ways.'

His throat was dry again, as it had been all day with the prospect of this ordeal. He'd swallowed pints of water before leaving Halifax, trying to slake his thirst and to drown the wine's odour. Now his kidneys were responding to its cleansing action, causing him such discomfort that he could think of nowt but the urgency of relieving himself.

'I'll just have to go out the back,' he announced abruptly, and all but ran for the door.

Has he made himself poorly again? wondered his wife, more certain of how to cope with that than with their present situation. But then she realised that he was sober after all. His colour when he returned confirmed this, and although she was experiencing the clamour of her pulse which had always been her reaction to his drinking, she gradually felt her heartbeat steadying. Happen Amos really was trying at last, maybe they only needed a bit more time apart. Didn't his uneasiness now prove how much her going back mattered to him?

Amos had been afraid the promises made on that occasion had failed to move her. He'd taken a long time gathering courage to try again. He had told no one of his intention, this time, wanted none of the cross-questioning from his children that had followed his previous attempt. Making the excuse that he was visiting a sick friend in Hebden Bridge, he'd set out in the rarely used carriage, and couldn't help but feel relieved when the first person he saw was Eleanor, taking in washing from the garden.

'No, don't go rushing off inside, *please*,' he began. 'I'd rather we talked out here.'

'It's going to rain afore long, that's why I . . .' She glanced down at the clothes which already she was pleating with restless fingers.

'All right, but until it does I'd rather we stopped out here.'

'Phillida isn't in, she's taken some yarn over to her father's.'

'Are you happy here?' Amos inquired, and for the first time in what felt like many a year Eleanor recognised in his grey eyes genuine concern. Did he really still care whether she was happy or not?

Her chin stiffened and then, amazingly, began to tremble. A film of tears hazed the brown of her eyes. 'What do you think? I'm not wanted here. It's not Phillida's fault, she needs to look after t'place in her own way.'

'But you *are* wanted at home. Ay, lass, can't you see that's what's fetched me here again? And I am different, these days, I can understand how selfish I were in the past.'

Eleanor weighed the prospect of returning. She'd had months of being barely tolerated, of annoying her daughter-in-law no matter how hard she tried not to. Going back to Amos couldn't be much worse.

He was strangely quiet during the drive over the moorland track, a fact that Eleanor couldn't regret. She had left Heptonstall in haste, without pausing to collect her belongings, for hadn't even she been afraid that one moment's consideration might cause her to question what she was doing. What she needed now was time in which to compose herself, to try and banish the lump rising in her throat.

The children came rushing out to greet her. Charles reached the carriage in time to help her step down. He'd been reading beside the window to catch the last of the daylight, and had scarcely dared to credit the evidence of his eyes. Isobel seized her mother's arm as soon as Charles released her from his hug, and Eleanor felt thin but achingly familiar arms being wrapped about her.

'We'll make everything nice for you from now on,' Isobel

said fervently. 'There won't be anything to make you unhappy ever again.'

That night Amos tried to draw her to him in their bed. Eleanor resisted. It would take weeks for her to grow accustomed to the intimacy of simply sleeping with him again, she was too much on edge even to contemplate making love. And such commitment could only come when she was completely reassured that there would be no more upheavals.

After a few weeks Henry visited them and some weeks later William called while he was staying in Heptonstall. Both sons appeared so well and so satisfied by their work that Eleanor decided there could be reason to be pleased with their family. Happen her dissatisfaction had been partly due to them growing up and needing her less.

Isobel flourished in her mother's company, even beginning to take an interest in simple homemaking matters, she was so thankful to have another woman in their family circle again.

It was indeed as a woman that Isobel now thought of herself. It was of no consequence to her that the calendar pronounced her little more than fifteen. She had read Mary Wollstonecraft's recently published book *A Vindication of the Rights of Women* and whilst not fully understanding it all, had nevertheless been greatly influenced.

The one thing that still caused Isobel despair was her immature figure, although she had rounded out a little, a fact of which she was conscious on her numerous outings selling cloth. But what she longed for was the femininity which might introduce more excitement. She was afraid that most young men she met had watched her helping Amos since she was twelve, and must think of her as just a little lass.

Her father, however, was giving her more than enough responsibility to remove her own lingering doubts on the permanency of her position with Bright's. That side of her life couldn't have been happier.

'You make up for t' rest of 'em not being interested,' he told her one day. The disappointment over the decision Charles had made no longer soured him. Since Eleanor's return, Amos had begun numbering his blessings. And if his wife remained less enthusiastic than he had hoped he couldn't fault his daughter.

With the agony of her mother's absence removed, Isobel had learned to laugh again, to enjoy the Piece Hall and journeys around the West Riding collecting finished cloth. Now that Eddie Gaukroger was no threat to her future with the company, she joked with him, teasing him out of any sluggishness of mind until only those aware of his history suspected that he wasn't over-endowed with wit and wisdom.

And suddenly there was a newcomer among their fellow clothiers: tall, dark-haired Roger Wheatley who'd begun working for his uncle, and always looked out for Isobel. Noticing how he paid her attention, other young men also began to admire this graceful girl, who seemed to brim with vitality and possessed the intelligence to assist her father.

Isobel privately savoured their responsive smiles and their greetings, but still concentrated on her job. She was young enough yet to have no anxiety regarding her own future. Naturally, she would marry, one day. And in the meantime she'd seen enough of the differences between her parents to be conscious that taking care was essential before choosing a life partner. With the renewed security concerning her work, and added sparkle because of the growing admiration she attracted at the Piece Hall, she sensed that life was going to be good again, she would savour it.

Returning to Jerez following the visit to Yorkshire which had confirmed for him that his mother was permanently established in the family home, Henry felt immensely relieved. And for the first time in many a month he was no longer too preoccupied to be truly aware of what was happening in the wider world.

France had been proclaimed a republic. Along with everyone whose business involved international trading, he wondered what the effect would be upon his own concerns. During his two week voyage in that September of 1792, word reached their ship that Louis XVI had been deposed.

150

Henry was, however, coming back at the height of their grape harvest. His thoughts might no longer be so engaged with his parents' difficulties, but that didn't mean he was free to dwell for long on the changes in France. There was work aplenty awaiting him in Spain, and there was his own conundrum. Catalina.

Whilst away from her, he had been acutely aware of how greatly he had come to rely on her presence. Whenever they were in daily contact he could live with only a rare kiss to express the physical need of her. Wasn't she a part of every other aspect of his life at Fortescue's – and of his home life in the Escutia *casa*?

Each time they were apart, though, his yearning grew more intense, until he might have surrendered even his position with the company for the chance to be with her. Despite the fact that mail services were improving, between England and Spain letters were so often delayed that he'd be aboard ship again before they could exchange greetings.

This time he arrived back in Jerez convinced in his own mind that immediately the grapes were in and being processed, he would propose marriage. And he had no reason to suppose that Catalina would refuse him. The affinity developing between them over the years was too strong for him to have been mistaken about her feelings for him.

Compelling himself to wait until the hectic activity of this busiest period of the year was over wouldn't be easy, but he would endure. Only then would they have a few hours to themselves.

He went straight to the bodega and was pleased at once, seeing the grapes set out on their round mats for sunning. How reminiscent it was of his introduction to the sherry business, and how he revelled in all the work involved. He might have come into Fortescue's relatively easily, but he had paid towards the opportunity as soon as he came into his inheritance.

After the early months of his introduction here, he'd met unexpected conflict from some of the Spanish workers. There had been uneasy days when he'd been plagued by black looks and outright discourtesy, and then it had been explained to him that some of the men had resented a newcomer like himself assuming authority. It was Alberto Martinez who had told of their feelings and assured him that his own were totally different. But then, Alberto was content with his role of capataz.

'What'll I do?' Henry had asked him, anxious to be accepted by everyone within the company.

'I would think that you should do nothing, they need time, that is all. Perhaps it will only be when the Señores Fortescue retire that the men will come to understand you are not a threat to them.'

Waiting for that eventuality had seemed a painful prospect, but time was passing more swiftly now. And, as Alberto had assured him, it was not yet necessary for him to get to know all their workers and to win their loyalty.

Henry supposed that was true. Certainly, there was sufficient to occupy him ensuring the good quality of their wines, selling, and organising their shipment. Today, he felt optimistic that they might be entering an era when he and the men were in greater accord.

Catalina was part-way along one of the gangways between the rows of casks. She half-turned and nodded towards him, but her concentration was focused on the venencia she was extracting through the bung hole of a butt. As Henry approached, he could see that she was pouring wine into each of two glasses which she was holding. Although surprised that she was completing the sampling herself, he wasn't particularly taken aback until noticing that her companion was not Alberto Martinez. The man at her side was her own brother, Carlos.

The three of them exchanged greetings, and Henry raised a questioning eyebrow prompting an explanation.

'Alberto succumbed to a sudden illness almost immediately that you had left for England,' Catalina said quickly. 'He's improving now, but we could not manage without someone in his place. As you see, I am trying to keep watch over what is happening within the bodega, and Carlos here is helping in every way he can.'

She went on to explain that, between them, they were supervising the harvest as well as the treatment of the grapes once they arrived here. And, as he saw, they were controlling the maturing wines.

Henry merely acknowledged her words with a nod. What was wrong with using some of the men who assisted Alberto Martinez; why had Catalina felt personally obliged to take a hand? And why involve Carlos who simply helped out here occasionally when his bull-fighting commitments permitted? A condition which had eventually encouraged Carmen Escutia to agree that her eldest son should become a matador. But Carlos surely couldn't know anywhere near so much about sherry production as the men who'd worked for years under Martinez.

His withholding of approval must have been evident in Henry's troubled hazel eyes. The moment Catalina joined him in his office her chin tightened and was raised, while she challenged him with a steady gaze which travelled the length of her forbidding nose.

'I did what I thought best,' she informed him. 'So far as I am aware it has caused no crises.' And she had enjoyed applying herself to a variety of tasks.

The precise quality always present in her English sounded over-formal and arrogant. Henry might have flinched. Instead of that he squared his shoulders and continued to return her glare.

He'd never felt more disturbed, but equally he'd never let that show, and most certainly not with this woman.

From somewhere he unearthed a bland smile. 'I trust that'll remain so. And I hope you've not been neglecting your own figure work and documentation.'

'I'm as well aware as you are of the necessity for keeping it all up to date,' Catalina retorted, dark eyes glittering. She'd been hoping he'd be pleased she'd had the sense to keep things running.

'To which you may now address your attention,' he told her. 'Since I am returned and able to take over . . .'

'That's just what you always want, isn't it? You've never hesitated to show me my place.' She turned abruptly, with the flair she had for revealing annoyance in every muscle of her slender form. At the door she glanced back, glowering. 'I would have thought that good manners, if nothing else, might have ensured that you spared me a brief *gracias* for coping while you were away in England.'

The door was closed so quietly that it seemed more ominous than a good slam. Henry was left with conflicting emotions battling throughout his head, around his heart as well. He could admire her spirit and her determination never to give in without a fight when he steered her away from a stronger role. Angry, Catalina looked splendid, exciting. But she did also generate dread. And so long as she refused to accept a more mundane function here, she was fortifying the growth of barriers between them. No matter what he'd intended only so recently, she could prevent his ever asking her to marry him. Was there no hope for them? The prospect of their future plagued him anew.

10

The freedom Eleanor gained by returning to her own home sustained her for a few weeks. The house had been neglected, but even if Isobel was maturing as each year passed you couldn't blame a girl her age for not overseeing Mrs Darwin.

'I'm sorry the place isn't looking better, madam,' the housekeeper had said sincerely on the morning after her mistress's arrival. She was a conscientious body who'd spent the past fifteen years in service since being bereaved, at the age of forty-four, of her invalid husband.

Although meticulously clean, Mrs Darwin lacked imagination and, even when Eleanor was at home, didn't always show the best room with its plasterwork festoons to advantage. Not, thought Eleanor now, that there was much nice furniture to arrange to good effect.

And there was a long list of things required for the kitchen. As Mrs Darwin said, 'We've hardly got one decent pot or pan, and yon carving knife's been ground away to nothing.' There was a dearth of good crockery as well, though she'd not trouble the mistress yet while they could manage with stuff that didn't match. What they ought to have really was some of that lovely Worcester ware. Her previous employer had owned a set of chocolate cups and saucers, greatly admired for their painted decoration of fruits, and their cheerful green border.

Mrs Darwin had warmed to Eleanor Bright from the day she'd arrived to work for her, but had often been disgusted with the way the master appeared so indifferent to everything.

Although professing to be keen to refurnish their home, Amos was exasperating Eleanor. He was ready with promises of pattern books from which a new table and sideboard might be copied, but she was still waiting to see even one such pattern. And even when designs were eventually agreed upon, she dreaded the further wait which she supposed would follow. Amos knew 'just the man' to fashion the things that she wanted; she could guess the delay that would entail. All in all, the novelty of being back with her family was beginning to grow thinner with each day, and there weren't sufficient differences here to convince her that her life was improved.

Phillida went more earnestly than ever in the past to her chapel in Heptonstall, giving fervent thanks that Will's mother had come to her senses and gone back to her own home. She sang Charles Wesley's hymns and listened to the minister who had been so deeply influenced by his brother, and she believed for a while in John Wesley's concept. For wasn't it true that it was here alone that she might find forgiveness? Phillie knew she'd been less than kind to Eleanor Bright, but John Wesley himself had said of Christ and salvation, 'He has taken *my* sins, even *mine*, and saved me from the law of sin and death.' Phillida had never been more willing to believe the assertion.

Alone again in the old Bright home, she began to feel a renewal of hope. She'd received a rare letter from William who said once they'd taken in this year's grapes, he was setting out for England. He would be spending the first few days after his arrival in London. For the first time ever, Phillida wished he would suggest that she might board the mail coach and meet him there. Perhaps, subconsciously, she had coupled the eagerness to see her husband with her reluctance to have their reunion in the house where she had behaved badly towards his mother. All she really understood was that she genuinely wanted to meet Will in one of the places that had become an important part of his life.

By the time he sailed from Oporto, however, Phillida had received no such suggestion from him. This wouldn't have surprised anyone who had recorded the occasions during the past three years when she had refused to accompany him anywhere outside Yorkshire.

It certainly didn't surprise Isobel who called in one morning while Amos was collecting cloth from Phillie's father.

'You could always suggest going back to Portugal with him, that'd do you both good,' the girl remarked.

'Not there. That'd be different,' Phillida began, but Isobel interrupted.

' 'Course it would, different entirely than what we're used to round here. Just think of all the places you'd see on your way to join the ship, as well as once you got over t'other side.'

Phillida hastily changed the topic. 'Has your mother settled in now?' she asked. Her conscience needed assurance that Eleanor was all right.

'I think so,' Isobel replied. Her own interest in the household was now fleeting, she'd been glad to give her whole mind to their clothier's business. 'If you had a hand in getting her to come back to us, we'll always be grateful.'

Her words were just what Phillida required to prove that she'd done her mother-in-law no harm. Once William arrived she would be her old self again. Maybe that would ensure that their love-making gave her the child for which she yearned.

William's homecoming began optimistically. He was in good health, the sea voyage had rested him from the additional work in recent weeks, and he'd long since adapted so that sea-sickness no longer troubled him.

He was in fine spirits also, relieved as anyone in the family that his mother had returned home. 'I'm glad it was you she turned to, though, lass,' he told Phillida. 'Just goes to show she thinks on you as a daughter.'

His wife said nothing to that. Thank goodness no whisper of her impatience had emerged.

They made love that night with all their original ardour, and sought each other again towards dawn, relishing the luxury of lying close in the privacy of their own chamber.

'It's that good to be with you, love,' William sighed. 'I do wish we'd more time together. If only you'd come back with me to Portugal. There's so much I want to show you.'

And he would feel so different with Phillida at his side

when he met other shippers. He couldn't forget the latest of the many occasions when he'd been invited to dine with one of the families long established in the port trade.

He'd sat at table with Ernest Parker, deeply conscious that his daughter Rosalind had been instructed to ensure that William Bright should not feel embarrassed about lacking a partner. Then there had been the moment when he'd bade them goodnight. How could thanking them be sufficient, when all he ached to do was to invite them in turn to sit at his table. With Phillida as hostess, her splendid auburn hair glorious above some flowing silken gown, he'd have been proud to welcome the entire port shipping fraternity. Without her it was not possible.

'You'd enjoy getting to know the folk out there, it's like belonging to one big club. We have a grand time, dining at each other's houses.'

'And drinking?' she asked, willing him to assure her that it was for the food and the company that they met. That way, she might have begun to believe such occasions acceptable.

'Naturally. We all relish surprising our competitors with a good bottle.' He was so accustomed to the way things were out there that it was several moments before he understood the reason for Phillie's sudden quietness. Then he said, 'You don't have to drink wine just because there's plenty of it being offered.'

Phillida turned her head towards him on the pillow. 'Wouldn't they think I were peculiar not wanting any?'

'We only need say you don't like wine.'

'I'll have to think about it.'

Because of Phillie's promised flexibility the rest of Will's stay in Heptonstall was agreeable. He went with her several times to her parents' home. Never having felt easy with John and Hilda Walshaw's abstemious ways, he hadn't experienced in the past anything approaching filial affection for them. Now, however, the atmosphere between them was improving.

He'd always respected John Walshaw's capacity for hard work, and the two women's contribution of providing ample supplies of yarn for John's loom. Today, distanced from the cloth trade, William happily examined the latest bolts of finely woven material, or listened while they told of recent developments within the industry.

'Your father were wondering if I'd work any faster wi' one of them new "flying shuttles" that's supposed to be so marvellous.'

'And have you tried one?'

John Walshaw shook his head. 'Nay, I told him, straight. There's nobody round here weaves any faster nor me. That's been good enough for thirty year or more. T'old ways'll see me out.'

The conversation frequently turned to William's sister Isobel and her remarkable progress within the trade.

'I can remember her a few years ago, when you left home.' Hilda remarked, as she set the table for tea. 'I thought then that she were too tiny to scramble up on to yon wagon, never mind do any good when she were sat up there. She's confounded us all, an' no mistake – taking to the work as if she'd learned t'cloth trade when she were in her cradle.'

'It's being born to it as does it, I suppose,' said Phillida, smiling. She felt genial towards everybody, so long as Will was at her side.

Her father nodded. 'Aye, aye. Though it's taken more nor that, I'll be bound, to make her persevere.'

Hilda Walshaw smiled. 'I was having a word wi' Mrs Gaukroger t'other day when their Eddie come home from Halifax. He certainly had plenty to say about how Isobel takes over, though I'm not sure as all of it were meant complimentary.'

They all laughed over that, but Phillida had heard rumours about Eddie's attempts to better his position with Bright's and had wondered at the time if Isobel wasn't rather too bossy for a bit of a lass. She wasn't certain she held with girls taking so much upon themselves.

On the Sunday during his stay, William let himself be talked into accompanying Phillida and her parents to chapel. Despite being in a good humour, he didn't enjoy the occasion. Give him a proper church service any time, with hymns he'd known since he were a little lad, and less of this

Methodist severity. Next time he was home, he'd see that Phillie attended his church, not that it had ever been the same there since Mother and Father moved away from Heptonstall.

His parents had changed considerably, as well, William discovered when he called on them. His father was beginning to look old, though he wasn't fifty yet, and his mother's face wore evidence that life still wasn't as she wished. Her leaving home and eventually deciding to return had done more to her than ever it had to Father. The good face with kind brown eyes which had been his childhood source of approval had hardened beneath a tracery of lines etched by distress. It was her eyes which most disturbed him. Only when they narrowed while she watched her husband did they lose the guarded look beyond which she appeared to be retreating.

Eleanor watched her husband a great deal, unaware that her expression revealed her dread that at any moment he would produce a bottle and glass. Although perhaps understandable, this seemed to Amos totally unjustified. Well aware that their marriage remained precarious, he hadn't once succumbed to his longing for the drink which might have taken the edge off the strain between them.

He couldn't do owt right, no matter what he promised her. If she wasn't creating a fuss about patterns for furniture, she was moithering on about all manner of objects required for the kitchen. She ought to know by now that she'd have them all, in time. Trade was going downhill, though, now there was so much competition from the mills being built all over the West Riding. He wasn't of a mind to throw away good brass till he was more certain of their future. He'd got to keep Bright's going until Isobel was married, and young Charles earning at last. Being proud to have a son determined to study law hadn't prevented him feeling burdened by the continuing responsibility.

Charles wasn't at home, he'd made new friends in the course of his studies and spent less and less time there now, but William was disappointed to find him absent. Even as long ago as when he himself had gone his own way, he'd sensed that Charles was different from them all, a lad who wasn't so integrated with the rest of the family.

This could have been just the time to get to know him better, and happen to encourage the lad to confide in him. Will surely didn't suppose that Charles confided overmuch in either Father or Mother.

Isobel was the only one who didn't cause him anxiety. Sitting with a ledger before her, she was engaged in adding up columns of figures, but that didn't prevent her from joining in the general conversation.

After inquiring how Fortescue's was faring and listening carefully to assurances that they were doing well, Amos had begun bringing him up to date with his own trade. William noticed at once that his mother seemed to retreat into her own thoughts, but Isobel contributed all kinds of information. She knew exactly who was selling what down at the Piece Hall and to whom, which clothiers were doing badly and those who were managing rather better. She also knew every detail of the factories which were starting up.

'I see you're keeping a finger on everything that's happening,' he congratulated her, proud of his young sister.

Although she smiled, Isobel said nothing.

Their father also was smiling. 'Our Isobel's all right,' he said evenly. From Amos Bright, that was enthusiastic praise.

Trying to draw his mother into the conversation, William asked if she was aware her old friend had moved from the farm in Heptonstall. 'You know – Auntie Jessie, we all called her.'

'Aye, I know, all right.' Hadn't she thought to spend many an hour with Jessie, so that she could get from under Phillida's feet? And had found their farm deserted.

She didn't dwell on all the changes. Nor on things like her husband's attitude which hadn't changed enough. Still, she could be glad for their Will now Phillida had finally consented to visit Portugal. Maybe things would work out for them.

Neither Phillida nor Will had felt so elated since the day that

161

they were married. The sun blazed down on autumn-bronzed trees and purple moors as they rode in the mail coach taking them south from the West Riding. Her promise to accompany him had surprised them both, making his smile as expansive as the surrounding hills, and Phillida remarkably excited.

She'd not admit it, but she was escaping the restraints of her upbringing and, although she'd never give in to any kind of overindulgence, she was expecting to enjoy herself. Even when the inn where they halted for the night proved to be even more spartan than her own background, Phillie didn't once complain, choosing instead to relish the plain fare, which was at least hot. And, though their bed was hard, their ardent love-making resulted in deep sleep and Will's arms about her.

The day that they sailed at last for Portugal, William was recalling his own introduction to the sea, afraid his wife's happiness might wane. But Phillida's determination to relish the experience astonished him yet again. And when another couple who were aboard proved to be followers of the Wesley tradition, she settled contentedly to forgetting any short-comings of the voyage in their descriptions of the country they were approaching.

'We've never had so much time on our hands and nowt but each other demanding attention, I'm sure it's done us good,' she declared to William on the day that the vessel eventually headed towards the quay.

He smiled then nodded pensively. No doubt Phillida's years of working at home, producing yarn, had created an attitude opposed to doing nothing. She had, indeed, startled him when setting out by inquiring if they could manage to take her spinning wheel. He was thankful that its being impossible had taught her to relax.

Their arrival in Oporto was in the early hours of the morning, even before anyone belonging to the port lodges would be hurrying to work. After their possessions were off-loaded, Will located one of the carriages rarely seen in the area to take them to his home.

Phillida seemed pleased with the house, though it was

sparsely furnished, and she appeared happy to go up to their bedchamber. Last night she'd hardly slept, her mind was so busy anticipating what she might find here.

The sun was pouring in through the window when she awakened, and William, fully dressed, was looking into the room. 'I'm just off, love,' he began, smiling.

'Off? Where to?'

'To the lodge, that's all. I've been away for weeks, got to get over there and see how things are.'

'Can't I come with you? I'll only take a minute getting dressed.'

William stifled a sigh. He'd visualised a few hours undisturbed, catching up on some of the accumulated paper work.

They had almost reached the bridge of boats by which they would cross to Vila Nova de Gaia when the clouds which had gathered over the sun released a harsh shower. Phillida was indignant. 'I'll be soaked to t'skin afore we get there! I thought rain at home were bad enough for catching you unawares.'

William grinned as she tried to tuck strands of red-gold hair beneath her hat, and then moved her hands to cover the wide bare neckline of her gown.

'We'll take no harm,' he assured her. 'It's warm enough, any road.'

Phillie was more concerned that she would be introduced to folk at the lodge while her hair was plastered to the sides of her head and her gown clung wetly all about her. But she was determined not to grumble while she was here and made herself smile. The smile faded somewhat when she saw the boat bridge, and a frown of concentration appeared as she discovered how insecure it felt beneath her saturated shoes. Grimly, she plodded forward, glad of Will's hand on her elbow, without which she'd have felt even more nervous. She was totally unable to heed him when he indicated one of the many buildings on the far side of the river. Being told it was Fortescue's couldn't interest her while she still had three-parts of this so-called bridge to negotiate.

The rain had slackened a little, though, when they reached

the lodge, and the patent approval in her husband's grey eyes cheered her. 'There don't seem so many folk here for such a big place,' she exclaimed, entering and gazing around her at all the rows of barrels.

'We don't need a lot – so long as it's blended right, and stored properly, the wine has to be left to mature on its own.'

'Aye, I suppose so,' said Phillida. She hadn't been interested in wine-making in the past, and still wasn't. She also hadn't anticipated that the place would reek so, but she'd not say owt.

'I'll find Fernando Trancoso, see if he's got time to show you round while I learn what's been happening. Come on, love . . .'

Phillie hesitated, she was drenched and she was disappointed. She'd pictured Will sitting in big offices, surrounded by staff, not the bit of a place she could see now at the far end of this massive building.

'Is that where you work?' she demanded.

'When I'm not out here somewhere, examining the pipes of port.'

She was not impressed. When they entered the office, it seemed no bigger than the room accommodating her father's loom. Again, though, she thought of her resolve not to criticise. William couldn't have been more delighted to have her accompanying him, and she wasn't going to spoil anything.

Phillida tried hard to like the Fortescues' wine lodge, it wasn't her fault that she hated the pervading smell and could only understand one word in half a dozen when Fernando Trancoso began explaining everything in his accented English.

'Don't they talk funny here,' she remarked to Will that evening. 'Even their English doesn't sound right.' She had been humiliated, an' all, when the old Portuguese taster had to keep asking her to repeat what *she* had said.

The difficulty of communicating was perhaps the chief factor marring her stay in Oporto. Even with the English people who'd become such an important part of her husband's life, Phillida felt uneasy. Most of the conversation was of the state of the port trade, and conducted in phrases and dialects which she'd never before encountered. Trying to keep up was a strain, and the effort of not complaining of this to William was exhausting.

The evening that they entertained a group of his fellow shippers and their wives started off more promisingly. Phillie had grown to like the house, high on the hill that was Oporto, and felt more at ease than at the lodge. Her gown was new, purchased in London on their way here, an exquisite creation of green silk which complemented her eyes and was a good foil for her brilliant hair.

The meal which the housekeeper had prepared was approved by all their guests, and Phillida would be a long time before she forgot the delight the occasion was bringing to her Will's eyes. Talking with the women present was less of a strain than she'd found any conversation since arriving in Portugal. But then as the meal ended, Will indicated that the ladies were expected to withdraw, leaving the men to enjoy their port.

The other wives seemed unconcerned by this, it was only Phillie who felt slighted. What was so special about men, that they had to be on their own? And what was she going to talk about in here now that they were penned like a fold of ewes? Phillida did try to hold on to the earlier pleasant atmosphere, she tried as hard as she could to haul up something to discuss, but she soon sensed all too keenly that as a hostess she was beginning to fail.

'What's wrong?' her husband hissed when the men eventually drifted in, in twos and threes, and found their wives now stony-faced, and virtually silent.

'I didn't know what to talk about, not once we'd been banished.'

Firmly, she swallowed, bit into her lower lip to prevent the tears now pricking at her lids from falling. And although the men's return soon restored a measure of geniality, Phillida still felt that she had failed.

This growing sense of being inadequate dogged her stay in Oporto. No matter what she did, she couldn't like the port lodges and the overpowering smell of wine any more than she could bring herself to taste the product itself. She couldn't decipher the street names, and hated shopping for the most ordinary household items when explaining her requirements was as difficult as making some of Will's colleagues understand her properly.

Worst of all, perhaps, she hadn't fully realised how much time he put in across the Douro in Vila Nova de Gaia. The days seemed interminable with her scarcely daring to venture out for fear of getting lost, and no spinning to occupy her fingers. She had been in Portugal a little over a week when she was overcome by the longing for familiar Yorkshire woods and moors, for hills that lay ridge after ridge as far as the sky reached, and for sunlight on their stone house.

William came in earlier than expected that night, found her in tears, and tried to cheer her with the prospect of travelling upriver.

'It's all so beautiful, love. You've never seen the like of such high mountains, and terraced vineyards.'

But his wife didn't want such strange sights, she was eating her heart out for her own dear surroundings. Being marooned here had gnawed right through all her resolve. She felt the struggle to prove that she could fit in with his life abroad slipping away.

'I think I'd better be getting back,' she said, her voice breaking.

The day her husband saw her aboard for the hastily arranged passage home to England, Phillida summoned a few scattered particles of determination, and remained dry-eyed so as not to upset them both. Inside her, though, she was weeping, inconsolable because her strongest efforts had resulted only in the dread that she'd ruined everything between them.

Isobel met her when the mail coach arrived in Halifax. Phillie had never been more relieved to see her young sister-in-law. And it was Isobel who eventually convinced her that maybe she hadn't done their marriage irreparable harm.

'Our William will be glad you've been there and tried to like it, he'll not be measuring how successful it turned out. Just you see, the next time he comes home you'll get on better nor ever.'

166

There were times, though, during the next year or so when Isobel wondered if any married couples got on together. She grew sorely disappointed with the situation at home where her mother seemed to have too little to occupy her. And Father, unable to discover how to please her, began to drink again.

Eleanor suffered some kind of nervous collapse on the day that Amos arrived from the cloth market with his aching head supported between hands that tremored, his clothes messed up with vomit, and only able to stand when their Isobel helped him.

The fragile new foundations of her life swept from beneath her, Eleanor steadily sank into hopeless disinterest. In turn, both Henry and William came home again to Yorkshire. Young Charles took time away from his studies and spent hours with his beloved mother. Isobel spared what time she could from helping to organise the home again and assisting with the business, and Amos made a massive effort to remain sober once more. They all might have been actors in a play which Eleanor found infinitely boring and unworthy of her notice.

Individually and collectively, the family talked with her and about her, and gradually admitted that they were making no difference to her state of mind. Inexorably, with no will to prevent her, Eleanor slipped further into this world of her own which made no sense to the rest of them.

For years afterwards the family rarely brought themselves to mention that distressing winter of 1794.

Amos and Isobel returned as usual late one afternoon from Halifax Piece Hall, found no one at home and were immediately alarmed. Snow lay thickly across the moors, whipped by a north wind into drifts that reached the first floor windows. Neither could believe that even in her disturbed state Eleanor would set out.

Charles came in from school, a tall lad of fourteen now with a man's concern for his womenfolk. He and his father went out with lanterns, searched until they could stand against the wind no longer, then dejectedly came home. The night hours inched by, weighted with anxiety, then the following day's with them. Again, father and son set out, and Isobel beside them, remaining indoors was intolerable.

A week passed in the unreal tempo of distress, and left them tortured by knowing nothing. Amos took to searching the wild countryside alone and came home certain that he'd seen his wife on a distant horizon. They took the carriage then, forcing the horses through the snow that made each pace a hazard. Remaining out as long as daylight lasted, they returned only when mist swirled in to merge darkening sky into snowscape. Every inhabitant of each wayside cottage or house had been approached, they'd searched neglected barns and other outbuildings, and had found no sign of Eleanor.

Amos, compelled to return to some kind of routine of collecting cloth and selling it, told Isobel to remain at home, to be there if . . .

The north wind had shifted to the west, bringing an icy rain that lashed the house windows and moaned like some tormented spirit as it struck the gable end. During the late afternoon Isobel thought she heard the wagon in the lane and was puzzled when her father didn't turn into the yard. Going to the door, she noticed that snow had slithered from the roof and must have caused the sound.

About to go indoors again, she changed her mind. She could shovel off that snow and more with it to clear a pathway around to the side of the house.

It was away to the side that she found her, where the thaw was exposing the grass. Emaciated, her face the grey of the wet stone path that led to the moors, her mother was as lifeless as the slabs themselves.

Sobbing, Isobel first knelt beside her, then began struggling to drag the body around towards the nearest door. Eleanor's clothing was torn; frozen rigid, her face and limbs were lacerated following some struggle, if only against the elements. Unable to move her as far as she wanted, Isobel knelt in the melting snow, and began meticulously scraping grimy particles of ice from her mother's poor face.

Amos found them like that, wept over them both, and sighed when told where Eleanor had been lying. 'She weren't

168

there long, that I do know. I prodded and poked into every drift deep enough to conceal somebody.'

Eventually, the doctors concluded that Eleanor had wandered the moors, disturbed, and then had been trying to reach her home when starvation and the cold finally took her.

Her loss when she was within reach of safety was doubly traumatic, a miserable circumstance from which none of them felt exonerated. In his heart, Amos blamed himself for neglecting Eleanor's needs. Shattered, he grew silent while his troubled mind scoured the past for someone to share the responsibility.

He found his tongue and lashed both William and Henry while they stood at the graveside. 'There'd have been none of this if you two hadn't been determined to get away. I hope you're ashamed on yourselves! Your mother broke her heart over t'pair on you going, nothing t'rest of us did could ever appease her.'

'Father,' Isobel began, alarmed, a gentle hand going to his arm.

Tension gripped family and friends alike. Henry's face turned as white as the snow capped hills. It was William who swung round on Amos, 'She was your wife,' he reminded him in a taut voice. 'It wasn't the way we'd behaved that sent her back to Heptonstall. Have you never thought she must have been at her wits' end?' And would they ever know what had driven her to wander out across the moors?

'Please . . .' Isobel said, not knowing who to side with. Couldn't they see they only had one another now, they'd have to pull together.

Will turned on her then. 'You could have been more of the companion that Mother needed, made life better for her.'

'Happen I could. If other folk had been helping with Bright's.' Isobel was struggling to appear composed. She had wept for her mother when she found her, there'd be tears again in private. Behaving older than her years had become instinctive, but she'd had to steel herself to organise Father into arranging the funeral properly. And now they'd all ruined everything by quarrelling.

Phillida and Will departed swiftly for Heptonstall, leaving

Luke and Matthew Fortescue attempting to comfort the rest of the family.

Charles seemed broken since that eternity of anxiety had ended so tragically. Isobel was afraid he would never get over losing the mother who had meant more than anyone to him. Henry was doing his best to console him, though his own face was gaunt with grief.

But Henry had someone to stand by him. Catalina had insisted on travelling with him for the funeral, which had been delayed for over two weeks to allow the brothers to come home. Isobel wished they were staying longer; Henry hadn't hurled any home truths. Still, despite differences, all her family had been together. She wondered with increasing dread if they ever would be again.

Henry was battling with his father's accusations. On the morning they were leaving Halifax he went back to his mother's grave. Catalina couldn't bear to have him go there alone. Feeling rather embarrassed by her company, he made his step brisk walking through the churchyard.

Snow had fallen again, not in such quantity as earlier in the year, but sufficient to renew the covering on the surrounding hills. The sky itself was white with further snow in prospect, only isolated houses and dormant trees broke the monotony of the pale landscape. Inwardly, he felt just as cold and equally desolate. Struggling to contain his sadness seemed as bad as this awful emptiness. And now there were these doubts about his own responsibility for his mother's death.

His constraint wasn't strong enough to endure until he got away from the cemetery. Standing, staring down at the newly disturbed ground that so recently had received his mother's coffin, Henry felt the tears he'd dreaded slipping beneath his eyelids.

Aching for him, Catalina drew him away, speaking all the while of the journey ahead of them, then hastening to the carriage that would carry them to pick up the mail coach for London.

When they stopped to change horses during the long hours travelling south, she knew the time had come to stop concealing her own feelings. She had worked for years at convincing herself that Henry Bright was a rival for her importance within Fortescue's. These past few days she'd come to understand that he was the man whom she loved unreservedly.

'You have to grieve, I know,' she told him. 'But don't let that be alone. When my father died I didn't exclude you; I've been a fool ever since for refusing to believe you mean all the world to me.'

The first night aboard ship he slept in her arms, and even smiled the next day over the unnatural absence of their mutual attraction. But there would be time for passion in the future, when this pain had eased enough to permit them to think solely for each other.

In the months after his wife's funeral Amos took even more frequently to the bottle, exasperating Isobel even though she shared his grief and knew of his unspoken regrets. During one of Henry's subsequent visits home she confided her despair.

Henry felt for the girl who even yet was too young for handling so much responsibility. But they were into late summer now and he was busier than ever. The previous vintage had been hit by freak storms damaging the ripening grapes; this year should bring a magnificent crop, he must coordinate everyone to ensure full yield from the harvest.

'Just cope for a while longer with him, love, and I'll see what I can do once the grapes are being processed.'

Aware that no one else could spare the time for coping with her father, Isobel struggled on. During his sober days, he was amenable, eager to please, still determined to remain a good clothier. But then he'd stagger home or to the wagon, vomiting and incontinent, until her hands were cracked and raw with cleaning Amos himself and his clothes.

Haunted by her mother's fate, Isobel grew to doubt her own ability to continue in this way. Someone would have to speak up. Their last visit to the cloth market had been distinguished by Amos, inebriated, getting into a ferocious argument with an old friend.

'About tomorrow . . .' Isobel began, as she was clearing the table after their meal on the eve of their next journey to the Piece Hall. Amos looked at her, his grey eyes clouded with misery. He looked much older than his forty-nine years, his face seemed sallow and sagging.

'It's a sort of illness,' he stated pensively, staring away from her now towards the curtained window. 'I've never admitted to mysen before that there was owt wrong. Now, I'm going to fight it.'

Isobel nodded without believing there'd be any great alteration.

'To my dying day, I'll know I killed your mother,' Amos continued. 'It's got to stop afore I drive you away an' all.'

Although her father did seem determined to keep his word, nothing else about their existence improved. Trade was being decimated by the introduction of more modern methods, and Amos was reluctant to spend on the home. Isobel would look around ruefully at the badly furnished rooms, recalling how she'd visualised a future entertaining here. The house itself was lovely but, as her mother had known, wasted by the way they used it. The place was cold, as well. None of the windows faced south to let in a bit of warmth, folk had once believed that it was the south wind that carried the plague which must be excluded.

In 1795 Isobel received news that really cheered her. The day the letter arrived telling her that Henry was to marry Catalina she was ecstatic. Her father didn't enthuse. Although pleased for the pair, his opinion of matrimony was soured, he declined his invitation.

'I'm none stopping you going, mind,' he told Isobel in the voice which he used when he considered he was being magnanimous.

It was as well those were his sentiments, nothing would prevent Isobel attending! Even when Phillida declared she'd not visit foreign places again, and Charles scoffed at the suggestion of dressing up to attend a wedding, she wasn't deterred by travelling alone.

She'd heard plenty over the years from Henry and Will to prepare her for any discomfort during the sea crossing, but

Isobel enjoyed the voyage. And she was too well grounded in looking after herself in difficult situations to let the absence of refinements worry her.

William had travelled from Oporto and met her in Cadiz, delighting her with his genuine surprise because she was maturing swiftly in appearance. They laughed and talked all the way to the Escutia home in Jerez.

As soon as they arrived they were drawn into the excitement. Tomorrow everyone would travel to Seville. The marriage would take place in the cathedral near the Escutia family's second home there, delighting Catalina's mother with a ceremony permitted as a result of Henry's instruction in their faith.

Coming so far on her own, Isobel impressed both Catalina and her mother, and Maruja and Marcos Escutia also, ensuring her all the attention a seventeen-year-old girl might wish. When she slipped on her splendid silken gown to follow the elegant Spanish lady she was attending slowly through the great cathedral, Isobel was thrilled. Henry, always her favourite brother, was touched by her being there, by her affection for his bride, and her youthful enthusiasm.

Impressive herself in the assurance brought by years developing into a competent clothier, Isobel stunned those she met for the first time. Still so lean that only the fashionable wide skirts and softly draped sleeves disguised her boniness, she possessed the delicate little face and expressive brown eyes that always had belied her strong Yorkshire determination. The instant she'd met Carlos Escutia, on whose arm Catalina was to enter the cathedral, it had been Isobel's turn to have her senses struck. The visit became a mass of exhilarating impressions.

No one resembling Carlos had approached the vicinity of Isobel's life amid moors and woods, and towns where houses and factories existed for folk who only survived by hard work. On the first evening she saw him, magnificent in the richly embroidered gold cloth he wore for his contest in the Plaza de Toros, she was overwhelmed. He might have stepped from her childish dreams, suitably garbed to stroll in

173

the palace she'd once imagined Halifax Piece Hall to be. Only Carlos was *real*, he was a matador! Genuinely brave, he was here beside her, and often laughing.

For too long there had been seriousness in Isobel's life, especially due to worry about her father. Even during his abstemious spells she was compelled to acknowledge that the habit could return. If it did not finish the business that was their livelihood, it could well finish him.

Visiting Spain for Henry's marriage and meeting Catalina's brother changed Isobel. And, for the first time aware that it wasn't only cloth merchants who needed to know their goods in order to sell effectively, she found she'd a keen interest in everything she was shown about producing sherry.

After the cathedral ceremony and the reception which followed, she became integrated into the Escutia family. Already well-liked by Carmen Escutia, she was urged to return frequently to Jerez where all the people who'd grown to love her brother would happily welcome her. But would she be able to get away from Bright's even once more?

11

Finding a new interest in Spain, and discovering her own liking for travelling, Isobel decided her first visit must be followed by others. When she would ask again to be taken to the bodega and, depending upon the season, into the vineyards. Jerez had seemed such a magical place, she loved the Spanish people with their excitable way of speaking; so different from solid Yorkshire folk. She enjoyed the way they ate leisurely meals in the early afternoon, and the fun of dining late at night and frequently out of doors.

In order to visit the Escutia family, though, she'd have to find some means of ensuring that Bright's was run satisfactorily in her absence. It was to be several years before she could go away with an easy mind. Returning home that first time, she'd found her father crotchety, and the books in such a state that righting them took days.

For a time the extra work had seemed a just price for the excitement she'd had in Spain. She held such vivid memories, and mostly of Carlos. He'd teased about her seriousness in the bodega while she inspected barrels and questioned the capataz about samples extracted with his long-handled venencia. Wherever they had been, in fact, Carlos was fun.

Although she was still glad to meet old friends like Roger Wheatley down at the Piece Hall nobody else attracted her as much as the carefree matador. She couldn't forget his black glossy hair, and gleaming eyes as brown as her own. He had alerted all her senses, making her feel quite different from her ordinary self when he was near. She clung to thoughts of how he came into a room and his smile made her pulses surge; how he said her name and even his accent made her feel special.

When a year had passed and there seemed no prospect of

175

leaving Amos to manage without her, Isobel couldn't help feeling resentful of the ceaseless work tying her to Yorkshire. The fact that this was the job she'd always wanted only made her feel worse. Spain was so far away, and the yearning often overwhelming. If she'd cared less for Bright's, she would have been more certain that she deserved a break. As it was, she needed persuading when help was offered to relieve her.

Phillida surprised her with the suggestion when Isobel was collecting cloth.

'I know you're wanting to get away to Spain again and even if them foreign places don't appeal to me, I can understand. If you like, I'll keep an eye on things, help Amos.'

Isobel was staggered. And torn between accepting without further thought and wondering how on earth Phillie would get on with Father. 'Oh, I don't know . . .' she began.

Her sister-in-law interrupted. 'I expect you'll want to leave a long list of instructions. I promise I'll bite my tongue with your father. And I'll guarantee he'll not do so much drinking!'

Isobel was forced to smile. 'But what about your spinning?' she asked.

'There's enough yarn ready for t'loom for many a week, you needn't let that bother you.' John Walshaw had slowed down a lot of late.

Isobel couldn't resist the offer, and endured her father's disapproval until it was time for her to sail.

She arrived in Jerez as the vines were being stripped, but was too elated to care that Henry was very busy. All the Escutia family accepted that Isobel and Carlos would spend as much time together as his career permitted. And they were just as delighted with each other as during their first encounter.

The only dissension came the evening he invited her to the bull-ring, and she hated the occasion. And even then any awkwardness was dispersed by laughter. 'You looked fair grand,' she'd assured him quickly. 'I just didn't like what were happening.'

'I thought you Yorkshire folk were tough,' he teased, hugging her.

Although too elated in Spain to give much thought to Bright's, she was keeping her visit shorter than she'd have liked. The days seemed to hurtle by with scarcely time for anyone but Carlos. And then one evening Henry tackled her, concerned that his young sister might be vulnerable.

'He's said he'll not marry, or not so long as he's a matador. I don't want you hurt, love, I know you're getting fond of him.'

Isobel surprised him by smiling reassuringly. 'You're a lovely brother for worrying about me, but you don't have to. I know Carlos won't be wanting to get wed, and that suits me an' all.'

He had told her quite solemnly, 'No one who enters the bull-ring should take responsibility for a wife.'

He'd made it seem acceptable to her that they were drawn to each other, yet neither would question her own resolve that she'd never be free to leave her father. While she was here in Jerez, though, they might have been created for each other.

Arriving back in the West Riding on a blustery autumn day produced conflicting emotions. Even though she'd had to leave Carlos all those miles away, her heart soared as soon as the mail coach crested a familiar ridge and she saw the expanse of hills again. During the last hour of the journey she was itching to see her father and learn how Bright's was faring.

She was met at the door by Mrs Darwin. 'Mr Bright has taken to his bed, I'm afraid. Says his gout's bothering him.'

Isobel's immediate alarm waned as soon as she ran upstairs to his chamber. Amos was leaning back against his pillows, reading.

'You're back then,' he said. 'About time, an' all.'

Her inquiry as to how he was received a grunt. He proved more eloquent on what ailed Phillida.

'She had no idea, of course, didn't frame at all. She can reckon up, I'll say that for her, but she couldn't get the hang of the job.'

It emerged later, from Phillie herself, that Amos had given her no chance. She wasn't Isobel, therefore she'd never suit.

If Isobel hadn't known how compelled she'd been to visit Jerez, she'd have felt nothing but regrets about the arrangement. But at least she'd returned with news that Amos soon would be a grandfather. And in a few weeks' time she was charmed by the tiny painting she received of Catalina's first-born, young Ignacio. She'd never seen a happier family than Henry's, and admired the tolerance with which all their differences were always accepted. The religion which might have created contention simply demonstrated that compromises could be made.

Henry had undergone sufficient schooling in the Roman Catholic faith to enable him to share Catalina's love of her Church's ceremonial. He'd also agreed that their offspring be raised according to Catholic doctrine. Catalina, meanwhile, considered his concern for their safety. She promised that she would continue rearing their family over in Yorkshire during any of the all-too-frequent periods when conflict between their two countries might put them at risk.

Isobel saw during the next few years that her sister-in-law's coming to Yorkshire was proving the greater sacrifice. Catalina might have grown to love the rugged West Riding scenery, but she loathed the cold and the rain which so contrasted with the sun-baked climate around Jerez. And there were other greater problems here.

William came striding up the hill one summer afternoon in 1804, smiling despite the drizzle which drifted in the wind across the valley to Heptonstall. Another turn of the rough lane and the house would be in sight.

Even before he reached that bend, the lad came running, delighting Will as he hurled himself into powerful arms. Laughing, the pair jogged the rest of the way between drystone walls to be met at the door by a dark-haired scrap of a girl scarcely able to stand.

Watching, Phillida gnawed into lips progressively narrowed by disappointment. Those children, with their brown Spanish eyes, seemed to exist to torment her. It was over thirteen years since she and Will had wed, and despite her yearning their marriage was childless.

William strode in, tossing his baggage aside to draw her to him, no less loving than ever in the past. And concerned because of the massive hurt which he couldn't assuage. 'It's been a long time,' he sighed into her hair. No matter if his absence had been a few days in London rather than a long stay abroad, his emotions were always the same. Being apart was a strain. But he still reminded himself how Phillida once had tried visiting Portugal.

Catalina had quietly collected the children, taking them up to her room to permit husband and wife some privacy. She liked William, if not his wife, and would deny neither of them anything to make life easier.

Phillida, though, needed some power greater than Catalina's intervention to make her contented. Even Will's return, these days, could be soured by her distress expressed in grumbling.

'She can't keep them from under t'feet, you know.' she complained now, dulling her husband's desire before he'd the opportunity to begin to express it. 'Young Ignacio's impudent, an' all – called me old to me face t'other day. T'little lass'll be as bad, as soon as she can talk. Stares you out already, she does, whenever you say owt to her.'

'All right, all right,' Will said slowly, gentling her. 'Forget them now, love. I'm home again, don't let them matter.'

'Oh, Will . . .' Before she pressed her head wearily against him the moisture in her green eyes revealed the abyss that only children could heal. He felt in the stiffening of her slender body the anguish that prevented her relaxing. Even with him. Later, there'd be their true reunion, in the seclusion of the master bed; but would it be dominated by her anguish?

Beneath his fingers her once-glorious auburn hair seemed to be coarsened, just as her originally exquisite features were becoming distorted in bitterness. In his arms her body felt angular, resistant to him now as though rebelling against fate made her rigid.

'You're my lovely lass,' he murmured, and willed her to become so.

Phillida quelled another sigh. She'd had evidence that

179

their last union was fruitless. She felt wretched and knew she looked no better. 'How long are you home for this time?' she asked, and loathed in her own tone the carping that would hardly be satisfied whatever the answer. Did Will no longer understand her? Couldn't he comprehend that she ached so much for children, it wasn't enough to delight in having the need of each other sated!

'Here in England, for several weeks.'

'And in Yorkshire?'

'Until Monday.'

Phillida groaned. 'And is there still nowt no more about opening up a place i' Bradford?'

'Nothing definite, I'm afraid.'

'It's your Henry's holding out against it, you know that, don't you? I told you years since it's all down to him.'

'He's not entirely wrong, you know, we can't tell how trade'll be affected. Don't forget we are at war with Spain again, that makes it exceedingly difficult to arrange each shipment of sherry.'

'You don't need to tell me we're at war with them, not when she's here all the time. Not when she's nobbut spent a few weeks in her own country since t'last war with them started, back in 1795.'

'All right, my dear . . .'

'It's not all right. It were nine year since, Will.'

'You can't blame Henry for wanting his wife and children here, away from danger and from problems of their being on opposing sides.'

'He should have thought of trouble wi' Spain afore he wed her.'

Despite himself, William grinned. 'Nay, love, you can't say they were the ones that married in any haste. It wasn't them that couldn't wait a day longer.'

'Aye, I know, I know.' But where were the ecstatic lovers who once had been Will and herself, where the couple who drowned everything in each other, and couldn't wait to press close again? Their rapture had gone, and awareness that she was responsible made existence now all the harder.

*

The entire family was deeply conscious of Phillida's distress, and this was one of the reasons Isobel visited her old home that evening when William was newly arrived. But it was for Catalina's sake that she had ridden over, she'd always enjoyed her company and for a very long time had secretly needed this link with Carlos.

Laughing over the children's antics, they prepared Ignacio and his sister Yolanda for bed. Their conversation was normally of Spain or some aspect of Fortescue's; tonight, however, Catalina could think of nothing but the news startling all Heptonstall.

'I saw Susan this morning,' she began. Susan Gaukroger had grown from the naïve lass who'd idolised Henry Bright into a sensible young lady, married to a local farmer, and happy to befriend Henry's wife.

Isobel gave her a look. 'She's told you an' all, judging by your expression!'

Catalina nodded gravely. 'Yes, she seems proud of what her father is doing, justly so, perhaps, if you do not consider how it will affect all the cottage weavers and clothiers around here.'

'Aye, you can't blame Samson Gaukroger for investing the brass he's come into in such a way that he makes a lot more out of it.'

'But a factory for mechanised spinning . . .'

'And plans to go into weaving an' all, as that develops. It's time he were giving up working, never mind going into summat different.'

'It will hit your father very badly, *si?*'

'And others like him. He's taken it hard, always being a friend of Gaukroger's. And having their Eddie work with us that long an' all.'

'Is he still employed by you?'

'Eddie telling us he'd got a fresh job made us think there was summat in the wind. Neither me nor my father could see who'd take him on. Mind you, fair's fair – Eddie's always been very useful.'

'I understand they're not the first to set up in the West Riding.'

181

'Far from it, and there'll be more. I only hope Bright's keeps going long enough to bring Father a living. He's too old to change.'

'And what about yourself?'

Isobel didn't reply immediately, smiled instead at her thoughts. 'Oh, I shan't lie down under this lot – you won't see me resigning myself to all these new ways, not without a bit of a fight.'

'But what can you do to prevent mechanisation?'

'There's plenty of folk think nowt can be done. But there's a few won't relinquish ways that's tried by time without demonstrating what they believe's right.'

Catalina nodded gravely. With further conflict in her own country, her only relief from anxiety for her husband and her people was in young Ignacio and Yolanda. Until now she'd envied Yorkshire folk their peace. But now a more alarming threat emerged of neighbours who might oppose people reared in the next house, and kinship guaranteeing nothing.

'Phillida appears to have a great deal of work, despite any changes,' she remarked, as she finally placed the heavy-eyed Yolanda between the covers, drawing blankets well up around her gleaming dark head. None of them ever seemed sufficiently warm here.

'Aye, she'll not lack for work. John Walshaw's our best weaver. He'll make a living as long as cloth is sold in Halifax Piece Hall.'

'That is good. Phillida needs some means of occupying herself.'

'Aye – it's a bad do, her not having childer.'

'She makes me feel so – embarrassed,' Catalina admitted.

Isobel hugged Ignacio to her before coaxing him into the bed across the room from his sister's. 'You mustn't let her spoil your happiness, love. She's takin' it out on you three, I can see.'

'I would not mind too much for myself, one cannot like people to order. Is with my little ones that I wish her more agreeable.'

Knowing what was causing Phillida's attitude, Catalina refused to question it. But during his last stay here, Henry

182

had been indignant because his sister-in-law was doing her utmost to ignore Yolanda.

'Can't you respond to t'little lass, all she wants is for you to notice her,' he'd demanded. 'What have you got against my children?'

Catalina would never forget the sorrow in Phillida's green eyes, nor her pallor when she'd faced Henry.

'Nothing,' she murmured, then her voice had grown savage. 'I've nowt again' any children. I have to be careful, haven't I? I mustn't let myself get over fond of youngsters that aren't my own. I scare myself sometimes if you must know. I get such an urge to grab any lovable bairn I see playing by t'wayside.'

'When's Henry coming home again?' Isobel inquired now.

'I cannot be sure. Because of the situation between our countries, he often attends to matters himself which normally he would delegate.'

His sister nodded. No one had proved more conscientious. What kind of danger is he in? Isobel wondered, but could hardly ask his wife.

Riding back over Midgley Moor to her father, her concern for Henry was overshadowed by anxiety about Carlos whose rare letters, which never indicated if he was in any danger, had lapsed yet again. And although Catalina had whispered he was due on a visit very soon the rest of her news about him tempered Isobel's delight. Their long partings gnawed into her, as they had for many a year, filling her with yearning for Spain. It was an old conflict, but she still had to remind herself that she was the one who'd done everything in her power to begin working for Father. She shouldn't feel resentful that her success meant she'd become shackled to Bright's.

Amos had Luke Fortescue with him and a bottle between them, but Isobel's swift checking glance confirmed they had drunk only enough to be convivial. And she was always content to see either Fortescue here.

Both cousins missed the company that they had relished before retiring, but Matthew was often ailing now and it seemed increasingly that Luke alone was able to visit friends. He remained for a while, discussing the war with Spain and how it was disrupting life for Henry's family. 'I've never been glad to come out of shipping wine, it's summat I'll always miss, but there's many a time when I wonder if things aren't going to become even more uneasy out in the Peninsula.'

'And not only there,' Amos remarked. 'I've heard as the French are so determined they'll end up over here, they've illustrated a plan for fetching their forces across by *tunnel* as well as ships and balloons.'

'Never!' Luke exclaimed. 'Somebody's been having you on, Amos.'

'Nay, they haven't – t'fellow I were talking to is half-French, a clothier like myself. He saw a print of this invasion plan t'last time he were across t'Channel visiting his mother.'

'They couldn't tunnel under the sea, could they?' asked Isobel.

'Not and live to tell the tale,' said Luke.

Isobel was too unsure of the feasibility of such a scheme to let it worry her, and was disciplining herself to catch up on some paperwork despite concern for Carlos. Most days she was fully occupied training the strong young lad who was to replace Eddie Gaukroger.

Alfred Hanson was an orphan who'd arrived with his twin sister Meg to labour in one of the new mills in the bottom end of Halifax. But Alfred had swiftly put himself out of a job by complaining about having to crawl in and around the machines, collecting up the waste wool that gathered there. His only home the room behind the mill in which the orphan children dossed, he'd wandered hopelessly through the streets until drawn towards the Union Cross by the prospect of scrounging food. If he hadn't begged the crust from the pie Amos was eating, he could still be wandering the Halifax streets. As it was, his wiry strength was noted, and he was invited to prove he could work.

And Alfred was willing, he followed both Amos and Isobel with the devotion of a youngster who knew he was fortunate to be in their employ. When at the end of the first week they allowed him to sleep in the stark room over the stables, he became their liegeman for life.

At first, Isobel had felt awkward about receiving such overt gratitude but, as well as being strong, Alfred Hanson possessed gleaming dark hair and brown eyes which reminded her of a young Carlos Escutia. Before very long, she was as happy to spend time coaching young Fred as he was eager to learn what was required of him.

No one knew his age, both Alfred and his sister had endured so rough an existence that, whether out of the desire to forget the past or simply through ignorance, they took no account of the years. He must be about twelve or so, Amos reckoned, but if so he was a big lad. Isobel thought he could be older than that, she also considered he should receive some form of education.

Her attempt to enlist her brother Charles's assistance was unsuccessful. But then, Charles wasn't an easy person to approach. Their mother's decline and tragic death had greatly affected him, turning him from the boy who'd possessed charm enough to thaw a Heptonstall winter into an introverted man of twenty-four.

Amos would watch him covertly, looking for some sign that the gregarious lad still existed. All he found was the chill solemnity of a man applying himself to lengthy training as a lawyer.

Both Isobel and Amos had long since accepted that Charles would never join the family business. He hadn't been too young to identify the cause of his mother's unhappiness at home, and he didn't dismiss resentment. These days, Isobel wondered why ever she'd once been glad about her brother's decision. She enjoyed the work no less, still relishing the company it brought her within the cloth trade. But if Charles had been willing to participate she wouldn't have to spend most of her life separated from the person who mattered most to her.

It seemed so long since she'd done more in the way of social pleasures than dine with clients or fellow clothiers. And she could hardly believe that tonight she was at long last anticipating a visit from Carlos. He might not have guessed, but she'd been so deeply affected by him that she'd never taken any other young men at all seriously. Since most of those were people she saw at the Piece Hall who'd watched her growing up, friendship without romance had always seemed mutual.

Catalina had been alarmed when she heard that her brother had been gored in Seville's Plaza de Toros. Only on learning that it wasn't some grave internal injury, but damage to his leg, had she been somewhat reassured. Señora Escutia, however, had written of the impatience Carlos was displaying because his wounds were slow to heal. Catalina's invitation to stay with her had been as much to relieve her mother as out of concern for Carlos himself, and she knew Isobel would help her to occupy him.

Her sister-in-law had been more delighted to agree than Catalina could have realised. Everyone seemed to assume that she'd outgrown the admiration she'd felt for Carlos when she was seventeen. Since then she'd tended increasingly to keep her feelings to herself, while she got on with her work. Hoping that she might help him to recover gave the prospect of meeting him again additional warmth. She could understand how frustrated he must be feeling without his bull-fighting.

Believing she understood hadn't prepared Isobel for the shock of seeing Carlos so changed by his accident. He was due into Halifax on the mail coach arriving on one of their days for trading at the Piece Hall. She had insisted that she would meet him in the town, and accommodate him for the night before driving him over to Heptonstall.

Although wearing an elegant coat, cut-away in front and with revers, and pantaloons instead of out-moded breeches, Carlos was still scarcely recognisable as the dashing matador she remembered. The way he greeted her soon revealed a sombre mood that couldn't be less characteristic. The smile that flickered over well-defined lips did not approach his eyes, and seemed to conceal rather than convey any pleasure in seeing her.

Disappointment surged through her. But concern for his state of mind, as much as for the injured leg supported on crutches, generated a fierce surge of sympathy. She was very quickly to learn – sharply, through a succession of failed

186

attempts at helping him – that such sympathy was scorned. It seemed that bitterness threatened to sour the once-dynamic young Spaniard.

Later that night, following an uneasy meal where Carlos had hurt her again by appearing more attuned to her brother Charles and to her father than to herself, Isobel went upstairs to her chamber.

Carlos was standing on the unlighted landing, leaning awkwardly into an angle of the wall, and staring out over the wild landscape. Hearing the murmur of her silken skirts, he glanced towards her as she approached. '*Perdone*,' he said. 'Forgive me – you are being so kind, and I am discourteous. It is not the pain, you understand; that is nothing beside the dread of never challenging bulls again.'

Isobel swallowed, seeing Carlos as she'd first known him, so splendid and so proud. How could she ask him if he mightn't one day be restored sufficiently to return to the Plaza de Toros? He disturbed her so much she hesitated and eventually discarded all of the things she might have said. But her concern hadn't altered; she cared too much to do nothing, to leave him standing here, so alone.

'Ay, Carlos love . . .' she murmured, and hugged him.

Carlos drew her closer, feverishly, burying his troubled face in the white lace cap covering her hair. When he kissed her his lips were hard, not with passion but with his anger against the injury.

'I cannot tolerate weakness,' he said at last.

No, thought Isobel, and how long will it be before you permit anyone even this close again, in case they suspect you're admitting to human emotions of distress?

By the following morning Carlos had recovered his composure. She wasn't certain his icy comments as she drove the carriage across the moors were an improvement. For the first time ever, she could find no means of getting near him. It was years since she'd felt so upset. At the house in Heptonstall she remained only long enough to see Catalina welcome him, accompanied by boisterous greetings from Ignacio and Yolanda which threatened to destroy his precarious balance.

Having Carlos out of sight didn't prevent his problems invading Isobel's mind. No matter how occupied she was writing up ledgers, going out with her father and Alfred to pick up cloth, or working to obtain a good price in the market, he was with her. Images taunted her – of his flair for dressing for the bull-ring, his old easy conversation and the glint that once shone in brilliant dark eyes.

No matter how perplexed she was by his attitude, Isobel couldn't keep away. And Carlos did smile when she visited her former home; he rose with difficulty while his niece and nephew darted across in Catalina's wake to hug her. The look in his eyes was rueful but he wasn't disguising the pleasure that warmed his tanned cheeks.

'You have not decided then to keep away whilst Catalina's sour brother is staying here?' Against his innate independence, he was willing her to reiterate her concern for him. He'd been freed, now, of needing to appear in command of himself as he had in his mother's home. It wasn't a freedom that he relished, but it had stopped him denying his longing for Isobel's company.

She grinned at him, ignoring his question, asking how he was.

Carlos snorted. 'Very well – as you see. I have two legs still, no matter if one of them is incomplete. I have my health, I can walk; so long as no one removes either of these wooden props.'

'You ought to be out of here then,' she said, not entirely seriously. 'Don't you know there's no finer air anywhere than up on t'tops here?'

'You cannot expect me to venture beyond that door,' he responded, his tone no more weighty than her own. 'The wind that tears across these *sierras* of yours would soon have me off my feet.'

'You're too scared to try, that's your trouble,' Isobel goaded. She wanted to be alone with him, unobserved by familiar eyes.

Their progress was appallingly slow, up the rough track towards a farm Isobel remembered as once belonging to her mother's friends. It was deserted now, its cowshed derelict, likewise the stable where she'd once shoved more hay than she could comfortably hold in her tiny fingers towards the horses that she adored.

'I suppose I was told Auntie Jessie had left,' she remarked, half to herself. 'I've not come this way for many a year. Since my mother died I've . . . well, I've not dwelt too much on how things used to be.'

'You were deeply hurt by the circumstances of her passing,' said Carlos quietly, stirred out of his own dread by Isobel's gravity.

'Aye, I was, naturally. But there wasn't any point in going on about it forever. And there wasn't time, not with Father –well . . .'

'Needing you to prevent his killing himself with drink?'

'I daresay you know all about us, don't you?'

'Would that be a bad thing. Isobel?' She had been wrong to believe him concerned solely with one person and the career he had chosen. He had thought of her countless times, had ached for her more than he'd ever admit. And today he wanted to know the whole of her past, to hear her present longings . . . all her future desires.

Isobel smiled. 'I don't suppose it'd be at all bad, love. You're nearly one of t'family, and it's grand to have somebody to talk to who isn't going to react to owt I say about either Mother or my father.'

Carlos nodded, recognising another person who normally survived alone, making something of life purely by persisting. He felt a massive urge to ally himself with her, to face together the world and what it had done to them separately. His kiss was on her lips and strong, willing her to need no explanation of his feelings. This strangely sensitive creature he'd become could no longer be trusted not to indulge in unmanly distress.

Isobel's need to express the warmth she felt for him combined with the sudden igniting of attraction. Her mouth softened, moistened, lips parted to admit his tongue. Her ages-old longing for understanding blended with the pressure of desire, then merged with his need to admit her to his life.

189

They pressed closer until, all too soon, his unsteady limbs made Carlos shake his head regretfully. 'What use am I, Isobel?' he demanded furiously. 'And not even able to hold you steady in my arms?'

She walked unhesitatingly to the warped door of the farmhouse, Carlos pushed with a shoulder until the lock shattered. The flagged rooms were chill, damp from years of neglect. Against the far wall of the kitchen there was an old wooden bed, the kind used by a servant.

In wordless agreement, their glances travelled from the bed to each other. Carlos set aside one wooden crutch, took her arm, and limped across to sit there. 'At home in Seville,' he told her frankly, 'I feel unable to raise my head. Who has time for a matador who lets the bull gore him?'

'Ridiculous nonsense! Any road, I don't know how anyone can muster the courage to face them, they're such massive creatures. Just because you were unfortunate it doesn't mean you're a coward.'

Didn't he understand his bravery was, to her, undiminished? He'd always generated excitement; it seemed enhanced by this new sensitivity. And he was miles away from Seville; from that artificial splendour which could have been a barrier between them.

If any other circumstance than injury had brought me here, Carlos was thinking, I'd be pursuing this young woman whose life has kept her a virgin. I'd have her for my bride and defy life to defeat us.

'Isobel . . .' His voice was hushed.

She gazed at him, waited for him to continue.

'You're so young, too young, to be worn down by responsibilities.'

With him at last, Isobel did feel younger again, relieved of some cares. She chuckled, surprising him. 'I wish you'd tell that to my father. I know I brought it on myself, I were that determined I'd become a clothier. But what's it all for?' Sighing, she answered herself. 'If we don't take good cloth to market, there's others as will. Specially now they're starting to make it in factories.'

It seemed to her that a hundred years had elapsed since she

was the girl who'd thought Bright's must never be allowed to diminish. Since she'd wanted nothing more than being a part of the family business.

'How can you speak this way?' Carlos protested, concerned. From the beginning, he'd most admired Isobel's enthusiasm for Bright's. 'Oh, perhaps it is not the kind of work that we choose which matters, but the way that we carry it out is vital. You will only live with yourself, surely, by giving of your utmost, unceasingly . . .'

'That's your nice way of putting it,' Isobel exclaimed, smiling as she thought of William and Henry determined to succeed as wine shippers, and as she thought of herself. 'I've always liked you, you know. And not only for your dashing ways and your handsome clothes.'

Carlos smiled. There hadn't been much space in his ambitions for getting to know young women equipped for more than a night's easing of his intense nature. But despite his obsession with an occupation that couldn't be called beneficial, he liked to be considered thoughtful. He longed for a better command of English; his own didn't extend to expressing all the feelings Isobel generated. And gradually these finer emotions were diverging, besieged by his own body's messages.

Featherweight kisses on her ears and hair dissolved Isobel's remaining reservations. The instant that his mouth returned to her own, she felt the surge renewing within her.

Surrendering her parted lips at last, Carlos gravely questioned her: 'Is there anyone, Isobel, will you ever marry?'

'Who'd take on the business an' all, with trade declining in favour of mechanisation?'

And who would take on your father? he thought, but kept silent.

The ache was strong within him, and not only of passion. He'd spoken scores of times of love, to glossy creatures who'd traded themselves because of his fame. Today, with the body that had paraded before crowds imperfectly healed, he was closer to the meaning of love than he'd ever expected to be. It was years since he'd been tentative, yet his touch was gentle on the curve of her bosom before his tongue probed between her teeth.

He needed her, Isobel could not doubt. And hadn't she, over the years, felt this deep affection for Carlos increasing? Neither of them was committed to anyone else. She yearned to make up for all the anguish of his injury. And for herself ached to belong to him.

'With my leg shattered and my place in the bull-ring so uncertain, I'll not marry,' Carlos whispered, wanting no illusions between them.

Against his lips, she smiled. Each sentence he spoke made him all the dearer. She hadn't supposed they would marry, that needn't mean they would deny love. They weren't uncaring about the future, but caring more what they might be to each other.

'Carlos – I had to grow up long since.'

His lips were hard, trapping her own against the sharpness of her teeth, while his hands continued caressing through the stuff of her gown. She might have been dormant until that day, existing for Bright's and for her family. The unfamiliar Isobel, responding by pressing nearer, was fiercely alive. Each tiny tremor of her pulse, of veins and muscles, nerve-endings, was screaming for him.

Carlos was holding her to him now, alerting all her senses with the kisses that stormed her mouth, and the energy that filled him. He groaned in passion so intense that the experience he would savour could not be delayed. Hampered by the damaged leg, he shifted awkwardly and sighed in exasperation when pain prevented his swift move to undress her. To aid him Isobel loosened the fastening of her bodice and of her skirt, then rid herself of petticoats.

Silently cursing the injuries removing refinement from their loving, Carlos again kissed her lips and slid a hand between their bodies to his buttons. Curbing the ferocity of his need, he traced the line of her hip, caressed her skin, silkier to his touch than the stockings she wore.

Her sigh was the stifling of a moan, inciting him to urge her to accept him. Willing himself not to hurt her, Carlos let the massive stirrings of his need carry him home.

Isobel gasped, surprised by the violence of their desire, thrilled more than alarmed by the strength of each successive thrust. If there'd been time for anticipation, she'd have expected Carlos to be powerful but couldn't have imagined her own response this fervent. I don't want this to end, she thought, yet couldn't restrain the inward clamour demanding her release.

Slowly, when peace overtook them, she felt him easing away and despite the hardness of the bed, they slumbered. It was dusk when they awakened, stiff from their contact with bare wood.

Overwhelmed by the fullness of his love for her, Carlos felt desire surging again and Isobel, pressed close, responded. Briefly, he grew serious. 'We cannot deny each other, *querida*, but I will take care of you. I will not let you fall with child.' Letting passion have him take that risk a second time would be unforgivable. In a million years, perhaps, when his life had purpose again, when he was whole, he might contemplate giving her the little ones which he longed to rear with her.

12

If anyone guessed that love had drawn Carlos and Isobel together no whisper reached them of the news having spread. Several times during his stay in Heptonstall they revisited the deserted farm and once, when caring for Catalina's children so that she might call on Susan Gaukroger, they spent an evening in the room Carlos was using.

His injured leg was healing, but unsatisfactorily, still causing intense pain and a debilitating limp.

'Without your love, *querida*,' he told Isobel, 'I would be desolate. There can be no returning now to *los toros*.'

Carlos did nevertheless eventually return to Jerez. Despite the frequency of their meetings, neither of them could pretend that his staying in that house was congenial. Phillida, who already greatly resented the presence of Henry's wife and children, certainly did not take any more readily to Catalina's brother.

And both Carlos and his sister were concerned for Señora Escutia and the younger members of their family. Word, when it came through from Henry, wasn't alarming, but nor was it of signs of peace. The past several years had brought so much conflict: war between Spain and Britain interspersed with repeated battles against the French.

Isobel, who'd schooled herself for years to ignore many of her own wishes, was already conditioned to the need to submerge any longing for a different life and get on with her everyday existence. Attention must be given to the increasing development of factories challenging Bright's existence. And her father, visibly, was ageing. By the time there was victory at Trafalgar, she was compelled to accept that her work would permit only rare visits to Spain.

Henry had at last been home to England, looking exhausted, but making little of the dread he'd had that the business he and Will had taken over from the Forescues might be forced into a decline. At times, getting sherry to the quayside and on board ship had demanded ingenuity bordering on intrigue. Only by relying on those with an intimate knowledge of the locality between Jerez and the sea had they succeeded in exporting.

In common with many sherry merchants, Fortescue's normally used ox carts to carry their butts as far as the river Guadalete at El Portal, to be conveyed down river for transfer on to sea-going vessels. When war made this means too hazardous, Henry organised his workers into assembling every local pack-horse and mule. More than once, he travelled with them along tracks between vine-yards, over undulating hills to rendezvous with the ship which would take to the Atlantic. On one such occasion they reached a headland to find enemy warships as far as the horizon and a blockade of British ships outside Cadiz. He and his men had been obliged to wait, concealed, witness-ing the gunfire and willing the French to depart for another battle area.

He had thought then of how eagerly he had come out here years ago. He'd been almost as guilty as William of considering this way of life more agreeable than a clothier's. Not that he'd choose differently, had he his time over. He only wished that there were fewer separations from Catalina and the children, and a more settled life in which to plan ahead for Fortescue's and for young Ignacio's education.

And if all this worry had drained Henry, the news he'd brought home of Carlos had been no less disturbing. Against advice from his doctors, he had gone into the bull-ring to try himself. The leg, though, had troubled him greatly, in-capacitating him so much that he'd been compelled to retire from the arena.

Isobel couldn't bear not being with him, absence had in no way diminished the intensity of her love. In so many ways, the Carlos who was struggling to survive the loss of his career was more appealing than the matador whose flamboyance had first charmed her. When Henry went back to Spain she would find some means of accompanying him. Meanwhile she spent her days teaching young Alfred Hanson as much as he could absorb, and her nights planning details of her visit.

Three days before she and her brother were due to leave, Amos became ill. Even while he was drinking less his gout still disabled him. Now it flared into a particularly vicious attack. Not only were the joints of his lower limbs afflicted, but wrists and fingers as well. He often called out, wakening her in the night to stumble wearily along to his room – where she found him biting his lips against pain which seemed to paralyse his hands. How could she leave him? 'I'll have to stay,' she told Henry. 'There isn't any way that I can go out to Spain with you.'

'I can see that.' Although concerned for his sister he was too elated with his own news to be greatly perturbed. Catalina had conceived again and she spoke of returning to Jerez before the baby was born, by which time it was hoped that peace would be lasting.

'Tell Carlos how disappointed I am that I shan't be seeing him, won't you?' said Isobel, so depressed about it that she could have shed the tears pricking behind her eyes. But weeping was foreign to her, after so many years when permitting herself to give in would have meant the business declined.

'I will that,' her brother agreed cheerfully, but Isobel feared he didn't realise how much it mattered that her message wasn't forgotten.

Despite her concern for Carlos and a determination to continue to accept their relationship as it was, she had some insight into how unsatisfactory it was becoming. It seemed it only remained alive through her own constant affection for Carlos, and messages relayed by others. Messages which revealed nothing of any consequence.

She had written to her lover several times since his stay in Heptonstall. He had replied twice, short letters which seemed stiffly formal, though perhaps through his limited command of English. And mail between Yorkshire and Jerez still took an age, especially when war intervened. In spite of her yearning to share his problems, she was beginning to wonder if writing to him served any good purpose.

Would it be better for her own quiet of mind if she ceased to hope for word that only came rarely? When she felt hurt like this she forgot the ease with which she had committed herself to such a restricted relationship.

On his way back, Henry was to meet up with William in London where they were extending their Queenhithe premises to accommodate wine vaults and more staff to administer them. They knew enough now about port and sherry to be able to conduct more of the business from London, although his brother seemed content as things were.

'I don't mind that much when I'm needed in Portugal,' William acknowledged. Whenever he went back to Oporto he recaptured the delight experienced the very first time that he absorbed the atmosphere of Fortescue's port lodge. He still loved to see and to smell the ranks of casks, emitting the powerful aroma of maturing wine. And he never let a harvest pass without journeying up the River Douro. His only regret was Phillida's refusal to return and accompany him there. Words couldn't express how thrilled he was by those steep, terraced hills, but no one could convince his wife that she should see them.

'Phillida has taken it hard,' he'd admitted to his brother when offering his own congratulations on the child Catalina was expecting. I wish to God she'd try to fill her life with some different interest, he thought repeatedly. It couldn't be good to divide her time between sitting spinning yarn while she thought too hard and long, and sitting transfixed in that strange octagonal chapel. It seemed, though, that nothing but a child would alleviate Phillie's yearning.

When the news finally arrived that at long last his wife would soon bear him an infant, William could hardly believe it. Ecstatic and eager to celebrate, he hurried back to Yorkshire. But immediately he was alarmed. Phillie was so evidently over-anxious that he was afraid she might even induce a stillbirth. Instead of the elation he'd anticipated, she'd grown obsessive, heavy in spirit as well as in body,

197

scarcely moving from her chair and consequently unhealthily pale. Every lingering trace of her former beauty was erased.

They were into 1808 and Catalina was at the house, driven yet again from Spain by the latest threat there from Napoleon's armies. When Will sympathised, though, Phillida cut him short.

'There's no need to trouble about war in Spain and Portugal, there's a remedy to hand. They only need to send Arthur Wellesley there. He's a *Wesley*, you know, that's the name he was born with.'

William suspected Phillida was in just the state to produce strange notions, supposing some connection between Wellesley and John and Charles Wesley. Not that he cared, so long as the man – if selected to rout the French – proved effective. It was four years now since Napoleon had declared himself Emperor and the French needed containing. In the Iberian Peninsula unease was growing. Will was troubled by the number of fellow English merchants who were not only sending their families to safety, but were also leaving themselves. Those remaining met at the Factory House to exchange word of Napoleon's latest position.

Inside the counting houses of Rua Nova dos Inglezes, the 'Change' of Oporto, current news was of companies being handed over to their Portuguese staff. So much so that this street of tall balconied buildings had hardly warranted its name since 1807. Even the royal family had departed for Brazil since Junot's march on Lisbon.

But Fortescue's meant as much to William as it did to his brother. Luke and Matthew had endowed them both with a powerful sense of responsibility by leaving them the company. Will wished he could keep a finger on every part of it. Despite their competent staff in London, he'd have enjoyed settling deals for port, and attending Mr Christie's auctions himself. But he was too conscientious to stay away from Portugal for long, and his next visit to the West Riding to inspect his new daughter ensured that he became far happier about his wife. He was delighted with the infant, and Phillie at last seemed utterly contented now that she was a mother. She'd even dismissed the agony of the actual birth.

Phillida had been greatly alarmed by the intensity of the pains wakening her in the night as a gale lashed snow against the windows. Her panicky gasping for breath had roused Catalina who'd come running from the adjacent chamber.

'Should it hurt so much?' Phillida demanded. 'I can't help thinking there's summat wrong . . .'

Catalina reassured her, and withheld her belief that the pains would become fiercer. For once, Phillida accepted that her sister-in-law understood more than she did. Whatever else, this Spanish woman had produced three children. After sympathising through the next bout Catalina left Phillie and went to waken her eldest son.

'Get dressed, Ignacio, as quickly as you can. Your Aunt Phillida needs her mother, I've explained you will fetch her.'

'Is it the baby at last?' the lad inquired wearily, already thoroughly bored by the infant which was two weeks late and had produced an infinite succession of panics.

'Let us hope so,' said his mother, smiling as her son cooperated. 'Just remember to wrap up warmly, it's snowing yet again.'

When Hilda Walshaw returned with him, she was no less anxious that this should really be the prelude to the babe's arrival. 'You'd better make sure you deliver this time, lass,' she told her daughter. 'I'm sick and tired of getting keyed up and then it coming to nowt.' Hilda had been staying in the house a fortnight ago, but after five days of Phillida's false alarms had gone back home.

'I'm not enjoying this, Mother,' came her tart reply, then her breath was caught by another spasm.

'You've nobody to blame but yourself,' Hilda continued, worry expressed in impatience. 'You've sat about fro' morning till night, how did you think that were going help the bairn into this world? You must be as stiff as an old board, and the child'll be that fast asleep it's none finding its way out.'

'Do you really think . . .?' Phillida began querulously, but her mother interrupted with a sigh.

'Nay, don't take no notice of me – I'm only wanting to get this over wi', same as you are.' Biting back any further reproaches, Hilda stayed at her daughter's bedside, reassuring and sympathising as the contractions quickened. She willed the birth to be easy and swift, and the baby itself to be completely normal.

Catalina and her children were dressed and moving about in the room below when Phillida staggered from the bed, startling her dozing mother. 'I'm bleeding, I can feel it,' she cried. 'There's summat up . . .'

Hilda glanced towards the puddle seeping into the floorboards. 'Nay, love, that's water – it allus happens.' She went to put her arms round Phillie. 'You haven't so long to wait now, just try to be brave.'

Brave, she thought, knowing her own daughter; you have it in you, but where's all your spirit?

Phillida still possessed the will that often made her intractable. When the pains grew rapid and agonising and went on and on throughout the difficult birth, she cried out, but clung to her determination. It was too late now for any more worrying. This child of hers would come into the world through *her* efforts! As she felt the head beginning to emerge, she gave a strange, wry laugh.

'Steady on now . . .' came her mother's voice, sounding far away.

Somewhere inside her head, beyond this infernal agony, Phillie continued laughing, exultantly. She'd show them now what she could do through this massive exertion. She wouldn't be different any longer, she had a bairn. And William would be proud of her.

'Jessica,' Phillida announced, firmly if huskily, when told the infant was a girl. While her mother tidied them both, she sleepily savoured her delight. Nothing would ever be the same again, thank God.

Holding the fragile bundle in her arms, she willed her husband to come home quickly to share this joy. And yet already she sensed that no matter where William might be in the future, there'd be no more of that dreadful discontent. There'd always be herself and Jessica, to understand one another.

*

Over in Spain, as well as struggling to run the business, Henry was also experiencing very real concern for his wife's family. He couldn't evacuate them all to safety in Yorkshire –indeed, he'd attempted to persuade Sēnora Escutia to go there, but without success. The younger ones, Marcos and Maruja, were in their late twenties now, both married with children of their own, but Carmen still rarely allowed more than a few days to elapse between her visits to them.

Carlos had been scornful of any suggestion that he might get away, and recently had grown secretive about his interests. So far as Henry knew, he was neither employed nor managing a business, and it was years now since he'd done much temporary work in the bodega. And yet he absented himself from both Seville and Jerez for considerable periods, and returned exhausted, his limp more noticeable than ever.

Whenever Henry was in touch with his family in Yorkshire, Isobel questioned him about Carlos, making him feel awkward. Intuition insisted he must reveal nothing to her of any question regarding the nature of his brother-in-law's activities. But when the dreaded invasion by Napoleon's armies came, Carmen revealed to Henry her suspicions about what was occupying Carlos. 'I may be an old woman, I am not a fool, and have I not watched this particular son of mine all his life, and seen him only content when he confronts danger. They stopped him facing *los toros*, that does not mean they destroyed his spirit.'

'You can't be certain that he's involved in any risk,' Henry began, trying to mollify her.

Carmen Escutia smiled as she interrupted. 'Carlos is happy – I see it in his eyes, in his entire manner. No amount of tiredness disguises that from me.' Her smile faded. 'And I am deeply afraid for him.'

If only in order to reassure his mother-in-law, Henry tackled Carlos on his next visit to the Escutia *casa*. He was refused an explanation, but that didn't preclude his wishing to find out more. Following his brother-in-law when he rode off at dawn didn't strike Henry as an appealing action, but he reckoned it was justified.

Clear of the undulating vineyards, they soon were into

wilder country, where steep escarpments overlooked broad plains. They reached the narrow streets of Arcos, lined with old houses and surmounted by an ancient church. The climb had been arduous and Henry saw in the distance that Carlos reined in his mount and paused awhile to rest. Henry was astonished by the magnificent view from the sheer cliff, with a meandering river far below.

But then the sound of a horse's hooves echoed back through the quiet streets. Henry caught him in the next small village where a handful of white painted buildings was gathered around a hostelry. Carlos met with roughly a dozen men who ceased their urgent conversation when Henry rode towards them. At first, his brother-in-law appeared annoyed, but as Henry reached his side, Carlos leaned back his head and laughed. '*Mi madre?*' he inquired.

Henry nodded. 'Your mother, yes. She was anxious for your safety. But I've not told her I was coming after you!'

Still grinning, Carlos informed him he had known he was being followed, but was less alarmed now he knew the identity of his pursuer.

'And what *are* you doing?' Henry asked.

'We'd show you if you weren't needed in Jerez. And if you weren't a man with many responsibilities.'

'Your task is dangerous then?' Henry wasn't surprised, but how could he simply ride home knowing as much?

'We are banding together to go into the mountains and drive back the French. We're not in that much real danger – we know the terrain far better than they do.'

The ride was long, far into the mountains and Henry, understanding little more of the rapid dialogue than what Carlos translated, often was more perturbed than his companions. Each time they stopped, however, to rest their mounts and to eat, the men appeared friendly enough and glad to have him with them.

They arrived at Grazelema while it was dark, and met up there with compatriots who had current news of where the enemy had been sighted. Taking up their positions in the narrow streets of the village built on a rocky ledge, they waited.

That night they slept fitfully in the open, in the cold of mountains where the Egyptian vulture swooped beneath the clouds.

Dawn was paling the eastern sky, increasing visibility to give their surroundings substance, when they heard an advance company of the French, hooves pounding through the stillness, up the steep incline from the wide valley.

'*Mire*,' said Carlos, 'look – our information was correct. They plan to take Grazelema. You will see how we stop them!'

The soft call to advance was breathed from one small group to the next. And then they were up into the saddle and off, riding three abreast and filling the street as they surged downhill, straight at the French.

Some of the Spaniards were armed, but fired over the heads of the enemy rather than into them. Dispersing and discouraging them had been their aim; the rapidity with which it was achieved left Henry grinning and breathless.

After moments of chaos, amid much snorting and whinnying, the French turned their horses and scattered, taking off down barely negotiable tracks to quit the area hastily. Pounding even more energetically, the hooves of their horses now receded, leaving Carlos and his band to quiet the inhabitants disturbed from sleep.

'I shall remain close to Grazelema until it is sure the French do not plan to return,' Carlos told Henry over breakfast. 'You would be welcome to stay, but I suspect that you've already been too long absent from Jerez.'

Reluctantly, Henry agreed. He had relished the opportunity to ally himself with these countrymen whom he'd adopted as his own. He'd loved the conspiracy and the brief confrontation with danger. But he must needs return to work and ease Carmen Escutia's anxiety about her son.

'You've made this damned awkward for me, haven't you?' he told Carlos, grinning. 'You've ensured it's impossible to tell her the truth of what you're occupied in.'

'You will think of something to reassure her,' Carlos asserted, shaking Henry by the hand and wishing him a safe journey.

It was only as the many towers, domes and spires of Jerez's churches appeared in the distance that Henry decided what he'd say.

Sitting in the elegantly tiled courtyard of the Escutia home, he managed a smile and hoped it wasn't overtly evasive.

'I have seen Carlos, you need trouble yourself no longer. He has work to occupy him, with friends some distance away, beyond Arcos.'

Perhaps because since being widowed Carmen had aged more rapidly than her years and now seemed an old lady, she was ready to accept that Carlos was safe and, almost as important, in steady employment.

'Maybe now, at last, I can cease to worry for him,' she said, and thanked Henry sincerely for giving her an easy mind.

He prayed nothing would occur to founder her hopes, and that he would guard his tongue so that none of the Escutia family should learn their brother's true occupation.

Returning to the bodega, he found Alberto Martinez staring wistfully up at the roof.

'Is something wrong?' Henry asked him.

The capataz grinned ruefully and shrugged. 'I was only wishing the storks would return. They bring fortunate times for the bodega.'

'We certainly need a bit of luck. Napoleon couldn't have chosen a worse place to fight, as far as Fortescue's is concerned.'

According to the last news he'd received before his journey into the mountains the situation in Portugal was even more alarming.

William had never felt more isolated. In the whole of Oporto and Vila Nova de Gaia, its twin across the river, so few British citizens remained that he only heard English from Portuguese members of their company. Except to sleep – which he did only badly – he rarely left their port lodge. But he couldn't abandon everything while their vineyards were decimated by fighting, and getting even one shipment of port out of the country required intense plotting and precise timing to coincide with the absence, however brief, of enemy vessels. For weeks now, he had been afraid. Local mobs surged through the streets, seeking and attacking anyone suspected of sympathising with the French, until no one knew whom they might trust.

As long ago as March, Marshal Soult had approached the city. The gallant resisting troops had looked down from the ramparts on to a mass of French soldiers, armed with bayonets. There was little hope of holding off the enemy, but the men defending Oporto went wild when they captured General Foy. Declared a great victory, this had all the city rejoicing, bells rang from every church and tower, rockets soared, until many citizens began to sing and to shout, running through the streets. Despite the element of hysteria, William had felt a thrill that prickled through the hairs at his nape.

The next morning, however, the French renewed their attack, leaving people wounded and dying in the streets. Will ran from his house to see Portuguese cavalrymen tearing downhill towards the river.

Heedless of the crowds of fleeing citizens, they charged relentlessly down the Rua Nova dos Inglezes; men and women were knocked aside, children and weaker folk fell under rattling hooves. Across the Douro, gunfire spurted from the Battery at Serra, attacking Soult's troops as they reached the quayside.

William watched, too appalled to move. The Portuguese cavalrymen were heading for the bridge of boats. Already packed with families rushing to safety, the bridge was too frail for additional weight. It began disintegrating beneath them as the troops attempted to cross. Hundreds of people were tossed into the river.

Galvanised into trying to assist folk out of the water, William ran to the quayside. Amid terrified cries from horses as well as people, and the frenzied lashing of those unable to swim, he managed to attract the attention of only three or four still rational enough to cooperate as he hauled them from the swirling Douro.

Across the river some of the French were rescuing citizens of Oporto. To one side, though, their fellow soldiers were slaughtering others as they staggered, spluttering, from the water. William shut his eyes, yearning to be transported to the West Riding, to calm and coherence.

For two months Oporto and its merchants existed with the French in daily evidence about them. Getting port out of the lodges and away to sea was impossible. The best William could do was prevent too much wine being appropriated by the enemy, and preserve the quality of their stocks in the lodge. He could hardly bear to think about Phillida and their much wanted child. Never in his life had he felt so far removed from everyone he loved. Exhausted, he couldn't permit too many emotions. One hint of weakness, and he'd bribe one of the few sea captains who reached the country to get him out of here. Yet in his heart he knew one thing: he'd never abandon Fortescue's Port to the will of Napoleon's men. The maturing wine had seeped into his being.

Another bridge of boats had been constructed to facilitate crossing from the city to Vila Nova de Gaia. Various rumours had prevailed: first that Sir Arthur Wellesley was on his way, then that his troops had been turned back by the French.

The first indication that the British *were* approaching came on the night of 11/12th May when Marshal Soult's French troops destroyed the bridge again and commanded that all craft on the river be wrecked or moored on the Oporto bank, and guarded.

Watching from Fortescue's entrance, William felt a tremor of anticipation which he instantly tried to quell. But he had lived through too many months of being thwarted and inactive. If there was to be a battle for this place that he'd grown to love, he could only pray for some means by which he might assist.

A rare smile, however tired, was curving his lips when Fernando Trancoso and his assistant came rushing to his side.

'Have you seen what they are about, Mr Bright? And we have three, maybe four, *barcos rabelos* on their way even now from the *quinta* upriver.'

'I don't think we need be too alarmed,' Will assured them. 'Our men know the Douro better than anyone, and they'll be alert to the French. Just in case of trouble, I shall remain at the lodge overnight . . .' He paused, grinning ruefully. 'Not that there's much chance of reaching t'other side tonight, short of swimming!'

His brief humour waned when there was no familiar sound of the oars of approaching wine barges. He'd grown anxious for their pipes of port, and more than anxious for his men whom, in common with everyone here, he regarded as friends.

In the slow hours long after midnight, when it seemed that all but the French soldiers slept, and he alone might be watching on behalf of the allies, Will heard a faint sound from the rear of the darkened warehouse. A shiver shot along his spine and the hair at the back of his head bristled.

'Mr Bright . . .'

His own name in a barely audible whisper brought immediate relief. This was their man in charge of river transport, his presence proof that at least one *barcos* had got through.

'I had to offload some way upriver, could not attempt to tie up here with full boats.'

'You did right, of course. All the men are safe, I hope?'

'Oh yes, sir. But the rest of the boats had to be left across the other side. Rowing them over would have attracted attention.'

'*You* have managed to get here, though . . .'

Will could hear the smile of satisfaction in his voice: 'Have I not worked all my life learning to know the Douro? If anyone can cross with scarcely any movement of oars, I am your man.'

After thanking him, William sent the man to his bed, yet still he could not rest. He walked quietly between the stacks of port casks towards his office. But after only minutes at his desk he was forced to move again through the lodge to the entrance overlooking the quay.

The quiet was not complete – he heard murmurs from the French guards across the river and the constant lapping of

207

water – yet it felt too intense. Unable to remain where he was, he secured their heavy doors and set out along the waterfront.

He was taking a risk, he knew, but anything was preferable to further hours of doing nothing, of waiting and not knowing. Was it wishful thinking, or was the darkness less impenetrable? And was there activity this side of the river around the Serra Convent?

Is that where Wellesley's stationed himself, he wondered; have his men made it to Vila Nova de Gaia? Will Napoleon's troops finally be driven back?

Waiting was chill out in the night air, but less alarming now with the strengthening of this uncanny certainty that the British were to hand. William made himself bearably comfortable in the angle of a wall and watched the horizon for the first glimmer of daylight.

He spotted Arthur Wellesley himself on the terrace of the convent as soon as the sky lightened sufficiently to make out a few military figures, and one holding a telescope to his eye. Minutes later Wellesley moved suddenly, sent men running swiftly yet silently under orders.

The voices Will heard approaching through the mist hanging over the river bank were scarcely louder than breath, but they were English. Aeons ago when Vila Nova de Gaia had seethed with British merchants, he'd not even have noticed anyone speaking in his own tongue. Today, elated, he hurried to greet them.

The men lunged from the shadows, seized him by both arms, and backed him up against the wall.

'What's your business at this hour?' one demanded roughly.

The other produced a pistol which Will felt pressing his ribs.

He told them his name, that he was in charge of Fortescue's, and by some miracle one of the fellows had a taste for their port.

'If that's who you are, you've guts enough to keep you here while the biggest part of shippers have long since fled.'

Their grasp on his arms loosened, though Will felt the

pistol still boring into him, and its handler peered through the gloom to judge his expression.

Eventually the weapon was withdrawn. The senior of the two soldiers nodded across to the far bank. 'Do you know anything about those barges moored over yonder?'

'I do an' all – they're ours.'

William gazed through dispersing mist towards where the *barcos rabelos* had been secured close in, with the overhang concealing them from the French guards above them on the bank.

The man looked at his companion, shrugged. 'Not much use to us, since the bridge has gone.' He turned to William. 'Unless you've some means of reaching the other side?'

'We've one other boat tied up on our waterfront, where Soult's men wouldn't spot it. I'll take you across, if that's what . . .'

'Are you skilled at manoeuvering one of those things?'

'There's others far better but I've sent them to their beds. I'm willing to have a go.'

'We've been collecting volunteers. We only needed a method of getting hold of the barges over there.'

'Then take them, and welcome. I'll show you to the one near our premises.'

William led them by a circuitous route, approaching the lodge through the cooperage to one side. After marching through to the front, he unlocked the main doors and the soldiers slipped through and towards the place that he indicated.

He had to resist the urge to stand watching which might have drawn attention to events. Tense with excitement and anxiety, he returned the way he had come to the narrow street to the rear where he strode along then took the next turning towards the river.

A curious assortment of men was hastening in his direction. A local barber whom he knew slightly, a priest and several who looked like peasants. William wondered how skilled they were in handling the awkward wine barges, but happen they'd do better than he might! And maybe without his mistrust of water.

Work had begun in their lodge and other premises along the quay. Voices breached the early morning quiet, and the noises of casks being shifted merged with the general sounds of carts passing and hooves in the network of roads behind them. Would such sounds really conceal from the French the activity down on the water? Would even the one *barco* make it to the other side in order to bring back the others? And even if all the barges reached Vila Nova de Gaia, for how long could the French be expected to remain oblivious to the sight and the sounds of British troops being ferried across the river?

William wasn't sorry that he had problems of his own to occupy him. A sea-going vessel had put in some few days ago, a rare event at present. The captain came with complaints that an earlier shipment of port from their lodge had arrived in England in poor condition.

'Barely drinkable' was how it was described in the letter from their clients in London.

'It's the delays at sea, with all these troubles, I'll warrant,' William remarked when he stood in Fernando Trancoso's tasting room.

'We shall have to add even more brandy,' said the elderly man who had returned as chief taster while younger men enlisted to fight.

'I'm afraid so. It's better we should invest more in the wine to preserve it than have it deteriorate. We'd have it left on our hands if any more inferior port reached London.'

They had difficulty making the new blend acceptable: the addition of too much brandy, and too soon, could arrest fermentation. Even so, William's ears often strained beyond the lodge, and he prayed he'd not hear gunfire directed towards the river. From time to time he was again compelled to make his way through to the doors overlooking the waterfront, to pause there and glance away to his right where the ungainly craft were being coaxed with surprisingly little fuss across to Oporto.

Could it really be that Soult's men were unaware of the British troops being transported? Or were the French merely waiting, preparing a trap on the other side of the Douro?

13

'They have done it, they have got there!'

Despite his age, Fernando Trancoso came literally running into the lodge, his eyes gleaming with thankful tears.

'The English! Six hundred of them have managed to cross to Oporto.'

No more than thirty at a time, they had filled each *barco rabelo* to be propelled across by the volunteer ferrymen.

'Out there you can hear the battle already,' he exclaimed, 'and the French are surrendering.'

'Nay, not by now surely?'

'Come and see for yourself.'

The taster was still so excited that Will had to hurry to keep pace as they strode down the aisle between casks. Leaving the lodge, they crossed to the edge of the quay. Fernando pointed energetically.

Shading his eyes, William focused on Oporto's steep slopes and the buildings crammed in about her streets. Even from this distance, he could see masses of white waving handkerchiefs, the flags signalling the French retreat.

News poured back to them throughout the afternoon. Wellesley had crossed the Douro after his officers and men. Soult's troops were leaving, hurtling away over the hills to escape the British.

'We'll close for the day, in celebration,' William decided. 'We'll never have more of a struggle than recently to keep the place going.' Everyone had earned a rest, and the opportunity to rejoice.

William also ordered that some samples of their best port be supplied to Sir Arthur Wellesley and his regiment – now ensconced in the Palace of the Carrancas. Perhaps Wellesley would then keep in mind that Fortescue's was a wine business to visit in happier circumstances!

Oporto rejoiced on into the next day whilst William studied ways of restoring Fortescue's trade, and looked forward to the return of other English merchants. The British Factory in the city – the association of Factors, or British Merchants – had become almost non-existent. And he recognised how deeply he missed this fraternity. He longed for its other members to return and work again in both Oporto and Vila Nova de Gaia.

First, though, as soon as he was confident that their company was recovering, he would book a passage to England. He ached to see his baby daughter and his wife. And he must persuade Phillida to join him here again! There had to be some way that the two different parts of his life could be made one. He would show her the Douro, and their vineyards upriver which were to be restored and properly cultivated once more. He'd make her understand what bound him to this place.

William's next visit to Yorkshire quickly assured him that all his wife had needed to fill her emptiness was a child of her own. And young Jessica was a bonnie bairn. Possessing her mother's glorious flaming hair and green eyes, she was an enchantress already, charming him by her ready smile almost as soon as he came through the familiar door. What delighted Will even more, though, was the way Phillida seemed restored. She hugged him and she beamed, convincing him immediately that she'd regained her old vivacity.

That first night in their bed she drew close, kissing and caressing so freely that he knew she'd overcome her depression. How beautiful she seemed again, now that the terrible sourness had dispersed. Throughout his stay, she laughed and even teased, challenging him with lustrous eyes which reminded him of years past – before his decision about joining Fortescue's.

They seemed so joyful, playing with their daughter and exchanging indulgent smiles when she went into a tantrum, that William began to understand Phillie's one remaining need for them to live as a proper family. 'You know I shall want to show Oporto to Jessica, don't you,' he said one evening while the baby, warm and ready for her cot, drowsed on his lap. 'I want you both to spend some time wi' me over there . . .'

Phillida stilled the protest that was second nature, smiled across at her husband. Hadn't she vowed, ever since her little girl was born, that she'd make some sacrifice? And if she couldn't go gladly with him, she would still go. 'Aye, we'll come, love,' she agreed. 'But not just yet, when our Jessica's a bit bigger.'

Halifax Piece Hall was bitterly cold in February, chilling Isobel until her marrow felt frozen. Even the numerous rooms where cloth was traded were so draughty that they seemed little better than the wide expanse open to the sky. She had coughed most of the way here on the wagon and much of the time since their arrival.

If Amos had noticed, it was only for long enough to reproach her with sharp eyes when her hacking interrupted his dealing. She was waiting for him now, shuddering beneath her cloak despite layers of good, warm petticoats.

'Nay, Isobel, you should have kept to your bed!' It was their old friend Roger Wheatley, pausing by the door and warming her now with his concern.

'Aye,' she agreed ruefully. 'Happen I'm getting too set in my ways – can't bear to have other folk taking over my job.'

'But that lad you've got is framing champion, isn't he?'

'He is an' all. It's me that's . . . Oh, take no notice, Roger.'

He wasn't dismissed that easily. For many a year now he'd been well aware that Isobel made too many sacrifices for Bright's. When she coughed again, he frowned deeply. 'If I see your father, I'll suggest you have the doctor call.'

Isobel grinned. Roger always seemed like an older brother to her, but Amos Bright wouldn't consider him close enough to be giving them advice! 'And do you think he'll thank you and agree?'

And what good would be the doctor? What ailed her was needing to get away, to Carlos. The intervening years since he'd first made love to her hadn't lessened her longing to be

213

with him. She did still dream of their being reunited. And though she suspected there was scarcely any hope, she couldn't surrender the belief that they had been too well attuned for their love to have ended.

'Have you had any word yet?' Roger asked, and Isobel started.

'Word . . .?' Did everyone know that Carlos never wrote to her now?

'About that new mill setting up on t'road to Bradford.'

'Oh – no, nowt no more since what you told us last week.'

'The time's coming when we'll have to do something, me and my uncle's lost nigh on a quarter of our trade. And it doesn't look as though you're doing so much today.'

'We have been, we've sold all t'cloth we brought with us. I'm only staying till Father reappears, then we're off home.'

'I hope so an' all; see you look after that cough!'

After Roger had left, Isobel shook her head at her own lack of logic. Why couldn't she learn to love somebody like Roger? Instead of eating her heart out over Carlos – a man who'd never marry!

Strangely, it was through visiting Phillida during the ensuing months that Isobel found some comfort. She'd been drawn to baby Jessica since the day that she was born, admiring her green eyes and flaming hair in a way that she'd never taken to Phillida's. And even as the child grew more wilful Isobel couldn't condemn spirit which so often reminded her of herself as a girl.

Isobel's evident liking for her daughter ensured a welcome every time she knocked on Phillie's door. Their unlikely friendship strengthened with each occasion that Isobel merely smiled over Jessica's misdeeds. For weren't some folk already beginning to find the child too precocious? Even William, after his first few visits, had voiced his disappointment that his daughter seemed so self-centred.

'I hope you're not giving her too much of her own way while I'm not here, love,' he'd said mildly, not wishing to provoke an argument for Phillida was still so agreeable and loving towards him.

His wife hesitated, smiled. 'Do you think I'd make a rod

for my own back? I daresay it's nowt no more than t'little lass being over-excited now – I've been telling her for ages you were coming home.'

William had wondered at first if his own overtiredness made him impatient with the child. Since the ending of the Peninsular War, Fortescue's had struggled to restore full production in Portugal and Spain. Both arms of the business were recovering now. Vineyards in the Douro and around Jerez, where vines had been trampled by the warring armies, were being replanted. Until they were established, he and Henry both had to scour the countryside for good yields of the right kinds of fruit. William would relish showing Phillie what he'd achieved, he couldn't believe he was letting months run into years before insisting on having her and Jessica out there with him.

He could introduce Phillida to friends within the British Association, and show her the Factory House. Last year its official opening had been marked by a ceremonial dinner. Held on 11th November, 1811, eleven members were waited upon by eleven servants who'd offered eleven wines to company the eleven courses. William had been thrilled.

Very shortly, during 1812, there'd be a grand ball in honour of the Prince of Orange. He would be so proud to have his wife accompany him. And, at last, they could extend her visit to include exploration of the whole city and up the Douro as far as the Fortescue *quintas*.

'I know we've only talked from time to time of you coming back to Portugal with me,' he began one night when Jessica, exhausted, had finally settled to sleep. 'I've been that busy getting trade on to its feet again, but I haven't forgotten what we've said. Now our Jessica's turned three, she'll withstand the journey so much better.' And I'll keep her in check, he thought.

Phillida listened, willing her frown under control, until William finished telling her about the ball. Dismally, she swallowed. Over the years since Jessica's birth she'd schooled herself to accept that only by visiting Oporto again would she satisfy her husband.

She had consoled herself that, this time, whenever he was

occupied at Fortescue's she'd have Jessica for company. Now, though, she was presented with this prospect of having someone strange mind her daughter, while she herself attended functions.

'A ball – do you mean there'll be dancing?' she asked, brittle-voiced with alarm.

'Aye, lass – it's nowt no more than a harmless way of celebrating things getting back to normal. And paying an ally some of the respect that he's due.'

'Respect? Happen so.' But this wasn't at all the way she'd pictured how it would be over there. Who would look after little Jessica while the ball was going on? Would they look after her properly? And she herself hadn't any idea how to dance. 'Ay, love – I don't know. That isn't my sort of place . . . all that wine drinking's bad enough, without getting folk dancing an' all.'

'I don't suppose that there'll be all that much time given over to dancing, any road, there'll be the banquet first, speeches . . .'

'Isn't it rather – wasteful? A lot o' folk that's eaten and drunk more than is good for them already, sitting down to tables piled high wi' stuff that'd keep whole families fed for days.'

'The ball will be only one evening. There'll be the rest of the time to enjoy. It'll be an experience for our Jessica . . .'

'One that she mightn't like.'

You didn't, he thought, he'd not forgotten the disaster of Phillida's only attempt at showing an interest in his life. Suddenly he realised he'd spoil everything for them all by insisting.

After William had returned, first to London for meetings with Henry and some of their clients and then to Portugal, Phillida relished her escape. Will had said he'd not ask her again. And she was happy here as she was; Jessica kept her occupied.

Catalina was cold; chilled through by the rain and winds buffeting the house. She moved from the window, sickened by the downpour that drove like a pale sheet across the moors towards them.

Phillida was out at her chapel. Her absence was somewhat offset by the presence of her daughter. Still everlastingly amenable, Catalina had continued on into 1812 telling Phillie that occasionally caring for one more child was no trouble.

The difficulty was created by the dainty girl's persistence in clinging to her own third child, Jorge. Idolising his older brother, Ignacio, Jorge had developed swiftly into a tough boy, the very last small person to tolerate a girl's fondness for him.

Thwarted in her determination to spend every possible hour with her cousin, Jessica's young life was a succession of tantrums. Whenever her mother was near the girl's consolation was a cosseting; when she was absent Jessica reacted against her Aunt Catalina's firmer hand.

Wearied by the girl's wailing which resisted Yolanda's attempt to play a game with her, Catalina appealed to Jorge's good nature.

'You should be pleased that your small cousin thinks so well of you, could you look at a book with her perhaps? It wouldn't be for very long, your Aunt Phillida will soon be home.'

'Jessica doesn't like my books, she never looks at them properly.'

Certainly, she quickly grew bored if even a fictional character drew attention away from herself! She'd no interest in books, even their illustrations. Catalina's own three, on the other hand, had pored over page after page since they were capable of treating a book properly. All three had learned to read at an early age and by fifth birthdays could converse in both English and Spanish.

Even now she was almost four years old, Jessica seemed to speak only when she wished, perhaps because of Phillida giving the child everything she desired, virtually *before* Jessica herself knew what she wanted. Catalina couldn't approve, but she did make allowances, remembering how long Phillida had waited for her firstborn.

Wryly, Catalina smiled and glanced around the room.

She'd never think of this place as home; even now that Phillida was more cordial it was only when Henry was here that she felt any part of it was *theirs*. But since, rightly she supposed, he would never relinquish his share of this house, she'd use it whenever circumstances prevented her living in Jerez.

She and the children would be returning there next month. For some while now she had marked off the days. How good it would be to feel the sun warming her bones again, but most of all to see her dear mother and brothers and sister.

Catalina wasn't alone in wanting the company of family. Phillida's parents were suggesting they see more of their granddaughter in their home. John Walshaw still wove cloth but didn't put in nearly so many hours in their upstairs room. Her mother had long since put away her spinning wheel. Hilda's hands were twisted and misshapen, making handling the yarn difficult. And she was content, most of the time, to brighten her remaining years with the regular walk to chapel. 'Why don't you come and stay in your old room for a while, Phillie?' she'd said. 'It's plenty big enough for you and little Jessica.'

Almost as soon as Phillida had moved out Henry arrived. He took Isobel aside.

'I'm worried about the house,' he told her. 'Will says Phillie is keeping an eye on it, but we can't be certain how often. There's clothes and possessions belonging to my family – as well as owt belonging to them three. It'll be getting thoroughly damp with all the rain we have round here and no fires lit, if nowt no worse than that happens like somebody breaking in!'

Isobel readily agreed to go over to Heptonstall occasionally, to light fires and see it had a thorough airing. 'It will make folk believe there's somebody around, an' all.' She had no fears about sleeping the night there.

Obliging Henry in this way suited her well. Her father was content to be left with Mrs Darwin the housekeeper who'd been persuaded to live in some years ago to give Isobel more time for the business. These days, Isobel could have worked a twenty-four day, and still have tasks unaccomplished. Not that all her efforts were directly concerned with her job as a clothier.

Since the day Samson Gaukroger invested his inheritance in a mill other factories, first producing yarn and then more recently woven cloth, had set up along the valleys of the West Riding. Not everyone had accepted this as progress, nor as inevitable. Men whose jobs were threatened by mechanisation were banding together. Most notably a fellow dubbed 'King Ludd' was organising folk to smash spinning frames, looms and other equipment, sometimes before they even reached the mills where they were to be installed. Isobel's involvement had begun through Roger Wheatley, one day at Halifax Piece Hall when he confided that he was joining a band of Luddites. 'These new mills hit us just as much as them that weave in their own homes.'

Initially, Isobel assisted with relaying information and organising parties of raiders. Recently, though, she'd persuaded Roger and his associates that they could use a woman who sat a horse with her ease.

She rode out to Heptonstall on a spring evening when the rain falling at intervals throughout the day had cleared.

She was thankful to get away from home. Amos was still alternating his drinking with promises of remaining sober. 'I lost your mother's respect, I'm not going to lose yours,' he would say, with a frequency that seemed almost as annoying as his inebriation. She would have been pleased to believe him – *if* anything in the past had provided relief from the worry that excessive alcohol would be the end of him. As things were, she was glad her escape was in a cause that could only help Bright's.

When the rain began again as she rode across Midgley Moor, Isobel dragged forward her hood to cover her hair, and struggled to hold her cloak together.

She was riding into the wind, the hood blew back around her neck, and her long brown hair became a mass of wet strands. Her cloak began billowing uselessly behind her, impeding progress as it was secured only at her throat.

Arriving at her old home, she put her mare in the stables then ran into the house, discarded boots and the sodden cloak and continued upstairs.

She would need to bring over some of her own clothing; meanwhile, she'd adopt someone else's. She wouldn't dare wear anything of Phillida's. And Catalina's gowns were too fine for an excursion with a gang of Luddites. But she found a coat of Henry's, pale buckskin breeches, and an old silk shirt. Another cupboard yielded his old tricorn hat and a long cloak surrendering to moths.

Dressing hastily, Isobel smiled as she stuffed the breeches inside a pair of William's boots, flung on the coat and seized Henry's cloak.

The deluge had eased when she crossed to the stables, but her horse resisted when Isobel mounted astride not side-saddle.

'Come on, come on, old love,' she urged. They were late already.

The men were gathered at the inn over towards Blackshaw Head, and swung round mistrustingly when she strode into their back room. No one recognised her in the thin light shed by their lantern.

'Nay, Isobel,' Roger Wheatley exclaimed at last. 'Are you trying to put wind up us!'

Shaking her head, she grinned. 'Sorry – and for being late. I got wet through riding to Heptonstall, had to find dry clothes.'

'You'll get yoursen noticed in stuff that old-fashioned,' Jacob, one of the older men, grumbled.

'It'll none matter,' Roger assured him. 'If folk start seeking a fellow dressed like that they'll be after someone as doesn't exist.'

'Could be useful,' Isobel suggested. 'While they're chasing me, you lot can make a break for it!'

'*If* we manage to get into yon mill,' another elderly man observed.

'If there's any way at all, we'll be in there,' Isobel asserted.

They had planned this night for weeks, since they'd caught the first whisper that yet another mill was taking in more machinery.

'Roger's got a fresh supply of staves,' they told her.

'Aye,' he added, 'and a blacksmith's hammer.' Knowing the tool he'd filched was used in modifying them machines tickled him.

When they rode out, Roger brought his horse alongside Isobel.

'Thought I'd have a quiet word. Some of t'lads are again' you coming with us.'

'Some of 'em allus have been. It hasn't stopped me yet.'

'It's just – be extra careful, eh? love? Don't take chances. I don't think the lads would be all that particular about looking after you, if we ran into trouble.'

Quietly, Isobel laughed. 'I've looked after myself sin' I were twelve years old. I'll not give over now. And I ride fast – faster than some of you lot if need be, specially dressed as I am.'

'Don't get a liking for danger, eh? You're a grand lass, Isobel.'

She heard in his tone the concern which she occasionally read in his behaviour towards her, and couldn't chide him for his anxiety. But she mustn't let his feelings for her develop. There was no time for emotions tonight. And for many a year she'd discouraged any man who appeared interested. She still couldn't disregard the love she'd shared with Carlos Escutia, though it seemed now to have flared between two entirely different people.

Through the darkness they could just distinguish trees beneath them on the steep-sided valley. The mill was virtually concealed, accessible by following a stream swift-flowing with rainwater. In single file they walked the horses to the mill yard, tethered them, and continued on foot towards the wall of the silent factory.

Somewhere close at hand an owl hooted. Isobel clamped her lips together, willing herself to utter no sound. She hadn't needed Roger Wheatley's reminder that most of the gang questioned her usefulness. She never came out like this

221

without being aware that she'd be obliged to prove herself over and over again before they'd really accept her. Suspecting she might never win that acceptance enhanced the thrill of the job that lay ahead.

Roger had overtaken the others and was first to begin testing windows. Swearing under his breath, he was shaking his head when they assembled quietly around him. 'Folk are getting too cautious now, that's trouble. There isn't one of 'em left open so much as a crack.'

'There'll be a loading door round t'other side,' someone suggested. And it was as he supposed. The sliver of moon shining down through the drizzle revealed a big door which looked to be only partly closed.

'That's twenty foot or more off t'ground,' old Jacob grumbled. 'We don't stand an earthly.'

'Oh, I don't know,' said Isobel, smiling to herself. She'd noted the last wagon unloaded before finishing time – standing empty where its driver had drawn it to one side. 'There's no weight there, a couple of our horses could have it in place in a minute or two.'

'And then what?' demanded Roger sceptically. 'You can't magic that there hoist down to take one of us up.'

'I can clamber on t'frame of yon wagon. There's a windowsill near enough on a level with its top. Once on that sill, anybody could reach that loading bay . . .' And she was thankful for the opportunity to show what she was worth as well as to advance their purpose. Only Roger would have prevented her, and Isobel was too determined to let him have the last word.

The others were glad of her making the attempt, the alternative was to abort their plans. If a lass were daft enough to reckon she was as tough as any man, she'd no one to blame but herself. And who else among them could be dispensed with if the worst happened?

Isobel swiftly scrambled up on to the wagon and began heaving herself up on to its frame. Not pausing to allow her nervousness to take hold, she reached out though the blackness towards the windowsill.

'You needn't bother to come any nearer,' a man's voice

222

cried, first startling but then annoying her. What right had one of the others to decide now that they weren't to proceed?

'Thought you'd be here afore the night was out,' the voice added.

Appalled, Isobel realised someone had waited, concealed, to catch them. And here she was – with a nigh on twenty foot drop below or one chance in a hundred of jumping and landing on a rigid bit of the wagon roof.

'Stuck are you? This way then,' he said, emerging at the doorway where thin moonlight showed her the hand extended in her direction.

It meant capture, could mean subsequent arrest . . . but below in the darkened yard she heard the gang assembling their horses, mounting . . .

The man's grasp was sure on her hand, his other fingers seized her wrist while she was pulled across the gap. Fear of missing her footing had evaporated; superseded by dread of her fate here.

As soon as she tried to walk inside the unlit mill, she stumbled into the cold iron of some machine. The grasp that had remained on her wrist appeared to tighten.

'Hold on a minute, lad. I'll lead t'way.'

They walked the length of the large room, went through a door, and afterwards clattered down stone steps. At their foot was a chill vestibule. The man released her to draw the bolts of a stout door.

Isobel couldn't believe how long he took nor that he didn't seize her again the instant the door was open. But she swiftly jumped the few steps and ran as she'd never run before until she was around the corner of the mill. All the way she prayed that Roger would, at least, have had the decency to leave her horse there. Yes, the mare whinnied at her approach, ready for flight as soon as Isobel drew herself into the saddle. Had the others waited some way on?

Tree branches snatched at her hair, tugging it from under the hat which, astonishingly, had remained crammed onto her head. The moon had disappeared as she relied on her instincts to take her back to the house at Heptonstall, but the shape of a horse and rider waiting on the skyline grew distinguishable through the blackness. It would be Roger who had dropped behind, letting the rest ride on.

'You see, they didn't hold me,' she panted, as he approached.

The man who turned as she walked the horse the last few uphill paces was a stranger.

'Our friends have ridden on,' he confirmed. 'I said I'd make sure you were all right.'

'I don't know you, do I?' But whilst wishing he was familiar Isobel couldn't help being thankful that someone was here.

'No, we haven't met up to now,' he agreed, smiling. 'And nobody let on that you're not the lad you appear to be.'

'My own clothes were soaked, that's all. These are my brother Henry's. I don't go in for disguises.'

'Maybe you should, our business is hardly a lady's – if you'd been caught wearing skirts, there's nobody'd forget you.'

'Happen you're right, I'd never thought. And this is t'first time we've been caught.'

'That's why I'm proud to join you all; Paul Copley's the name. I trust you'll permit me to be of service, and see you to your home.'

'I was feeling a bit nervous on my own.' It must be that scare at the mill, she wasn't easily frightened.

He was very tall beside her, and seemed as powerful as the huge horse he rode. When he'd doffed his hat introducing himself his thick hair had gleamed palely as clouds parted revealing the moon.

'You'll try again, no doubt, to smash the machines back yonder,' he remarked. 'Mind you let me know when, and I'll make myself useful. I'll show you my house as we go, you can leave a message with my housekeeper. No details mind, just your name and the time and place.'

'Oh, I haven't told you my name. It's Isobel.' For some reason she couldn't have identified, she withheld her surname.

'You came from Heptonstall way tonight. Is that where you live?'

'It's where I'm staying just now.'

Although she felt wary, to doubt Paul Copley's willingness to assist the cause was churlish. He appeared to know about their gang, most probably was acquainted with several of them.

'You know Roger Wheatley perhaps?' she suggested.

'Roger – aye. Known him for years, and most of his friends.'

Reassured, Isobel relaxed in relief that she'd evaded capture, and responded to a series of more personal questions.

'Do you have sisters?'

'Three brothers, two of them quite a bit older, and married.'

'And are they in the clothing trade?'

'Not any longer. They both ship wines, from Spain and Portugal.'

In the darkness, Paul nodded to himself. The Bright brothers.

'But you've remained loyal to your father's business.'

It wasn't a question. Isobel tried, and failed, to read his expression.

'And there's an attractive Spanish lady spends a deal of her life rearing her children in this harsh climate – your brother's wife?'

'Henry's, aye. Catalina's a lovely woman.'

'You're not married yourself?'

'I've enough on, running the business now Father's not so well.'

'And then there's this night-time occupation . . .'

They had reached her lane. Although strangely drawn towards the man she could hardly see, Isobel was too exhausted to linger. 'This is where I'm spending tonight. With my two sisters-in-law,' she added, not quite so foolish as to reveal that she'd be alone. 'My thanks for your company.'

'I'm only glad I was there.'

The light from the lamp she'd left in the window showed his strong features and eyes that appeared to be very dark blue. But no light was needed to reveal the most disturbing thing about him. Even while he was this distant from her, she sensed the latent power of the attraction that would draw any woman to him.

14

Paul was there three nights later when Isobel met up with Roger and the others in the back room of another remote inn. This time they were keeping well away from Heptonstall and Hebden Bridge, concentrating on a new spinning mill in the hills surrounding Halifax. The moment she saw him conversing easily with the rest of the gang, she felt relieved. She didn't have much time for anxiety, but since their encounter she had wondered if confiding had been unwise.

Now she smilingly returned his eager greeting, was glad to take the seat at his side.

'This time, you must admit it's a disguise,' he murmured, indicating her breeches and cloak, and the old hat worn previously.

Isobel acknowledged. 'You made me think. Happen I were daft wearing skirts.'

'With you being the only female following King Ludd . . .'

'Well, do you know any others?'

Paul was shaking his head when the outer door opened and the last member of their party strode in.

'There's nobody guarding yon place, I'll swear,' he announced. 'I've been twice round t'outside of the entire building.'

'That's good, Jacob. We'll away then.' Roger was in charge, issuing warnings along with instructions of who should ride together.

'You'd best come with me, Paul,' he said, and despatched Isobel with Jacob.

She was surprised by the degree of her own disappointment. Never since the relationship with Carlos had proved so fragile had she permitted herself to feel this exhilarated by a man. Ordinarily, she laughed off any advances. And no one learned how much her ready laugh concealed.

The mill was as deserted as Jacob claimed. Riding in pairs into the courtyard, they grinned from one to the other as they assembled: a dozen warriors true to the clothiers' cause.

The first tiny pane of glass shattered in one of the large windows. Swiftly, Roger and Paul worked to clear the shards then broke several adjacent panes. Once inside, they advanced towards the massive spinning frames. Producing implements from within their clothing, they surged over the machines, hacking repeatedly at each one until every frame was a useless mass of bent equipment.

That's for what you're doing to our trade! thought Isobel, her arm as strong as any of the men's as she set about the machinery with the hammer selected from her father's tools.

They had left the spinning factory and were heading back towards the town centre when one of the older men, a weaver, pointed to another darkened building.

'Have you heard about yon? Not content wi' spinning, they've bought in a lot of looms.'

'No, I've not heard,' said Roger quickly. They'd been lucky tonight, he wasn't tempting Fate. 'It's said they have armed guards.'

'You're not afeared of them, are you?' Paul inquired, glancing sideways as light from a nearby inn revealed the faces about him.

'I'm not seeking my own demise!' Roger retorted, 'nor will I sacrifice anybody else.' He had been shaken when Isobel was seized. He hadn't liked himself either, for instinctively taking flight and leaving her captive.

'We could have a look, though,' Jacob put in, 'cautious like . . .'

There were guards. Two men appeared from the shadows and fired the instant Roger led them near the cobbled mill yard. And there were dogs which were freed to tear, snarling, after their horses.

Paul was laughing when he rode up beside Isobel after they'd got away. 'We'll not risk attacking there, I dare say – till we're sure it's less well patrolled.'

Isobel grinned up at him, loving the way he seemed amused rather than perturbed by the whole incident.

'Does nowt frighten you?' she asked, recalling how undisturbed he'd been on that previous occasion, yet all her friends had galloped off.

'If one's cause is just, what is there to fear?'

'Being caught?' she suggested, but laughing in exhilaration.

Riding uphill past the Piece Hall, he nodded towards the massive structure. 'You'll be familiar with yon place, I reckon.'

'I am an' all – there's nowhere I like better. Happen that's why I go out like this, destroying them as'll put us out of business.'

'You're not afraid of delaying progress then?'

'You mustn't be either,' she retorted, still smiling. 'You laid into them spinning frames like t'rest on us. You haven't told me what you do, are you in t'cloth trade?'

'It's all I care about.'

'What, no wife and childer waiting for you at home then?'

'I was married once. My wife died in childbirth.'

'Ay, I am sorry.'

'Happen it's time someone jolted me out of my quiet routine.'

Each time after that when they rode out to deserted mills, Paul was at her side. She sensed his keen interest in her, and had no regrets. Wasn't it time she had a bit of excitement? She'd come alive for Carlos, but that had ended in heartache, and it wasn't going to stop her responding now. Having Paul among them added zest to her satisfaction when they wrecked another set of machines that were doing good men out of jobs. And conversing quietly as they rode away afterwards, she often forgot the danger of their being apprehended.

One night weeks later they'd been talking over their success at yet another mill when they lapsed into a silence that felt companionable. They continued on out of Halifax, only calling to the rest of the group as, one by one, they departed towards their own homes. Isobel was happy, though a little puzzled by the turmoil of her feelings. Paul's presence could be reassuring, yet at the same time he disturbed so many emotions.

Riding up the last steep mile to her home near the edge of the moors she realised the significance of Paul's still being beside her.

'You don't live this way,' she said. 'And I don't remember telling you where my home is either.'

He grinned. 'That's true. You led me to think it might be in Heptonstall, near your relatives. But I guessed that you're the sister of Henry Bright and William . . .'

'You know my older brothers! Fancy you not saying . . . Do you know our Charles, an' all? He's the youngster of the family, though you'd not think it to see him, these days.'

'I don't believe I do know Charles, he'd be much younger than us, I suppose . . .'

'He's nobbut a year less nor me, but I have to admit I've allus thought he were only a bit of a lad. Well, fancy you knowing our Henry – he's my favourite, you know. He always has been.'

'I suppose he's not at home?' Paul asked, his wish to be invited in so plain that she was delighted.

'Well, he wasn't t'other week when I stayed in Heptonstall again. He and Will own that house. But my father'd be glad to see you at any time. He doesn't allus get to the Piece Hall nowadays – he has the gout very bad.'

'He'd not be still up at this hour, though, surely?'

'He might, at that – why don't you come in?'

All her elation shrivelled as she opened the door.

Amos Bright was asleep, but not in his bed. Sprawled across the table top, a knotted hand outstretched towards the port bottle he'd overturned and his face in the remains of the supper Mrs Darwin had left him, he was snoring.

Mortified, Isobel turned and tried to prevent Paul entering. But nothing would have stopped him coming in. He'd already taken in the situation, and thought too well of Isobel to allow her to manage Amos on her own.

'I'm giving you a hand,' he asserted, disregarding her insistence that she could manage. He discarded his coat and strode towards her father.

'Come on, old fellow,' he urged quietly but firmly,

shaking him by the shoulder. 'We'll soon have you up them stairs . . .'

No sooner had he roused Amos sufficiently to ensure some small cooperation, than he was getting him to his feet and leaning him against the table edge whilst inserting his own arm beneath her father's.

'I'll take his other side,' Isobel began, but only to be interrupted.

'There's no need, love. Just light the way, if you will.'

Paul's strength astounded her. She'd recognised that he was tall but he seemed to experience no difficulty when he hauled the old man up and over his shoulder. Still refusing assistance, he carried him bodily up the stairs and along to the room which Isobel indicated.

Dreadfully embarrassed, she hastened to draw back the covers, her sole comfort the immaculate bed-linen in which their housekeeper took such pride.

'I'll loosen off his buttons,' Isobel said as soon as Paul had lain her father on the bed. 'I stopped trying to undress him long since. He only gets cantankerous if he isn't left to rest.'

Paul was waiting for her downstairs in the parlour. His pleasant face was concerned, the dark blue eyes more serious than she'd seen them.

'You'd better sit down,' she said quickly, 'I can't thank you enough for what you've done.'

There was more needing attention. The port that had streamed from the upturned bottle was soaking her best rug.

'Leave that for a minute.' Paul met her beside the table and checked her hand. His grasp on her fingers was strong and warm, seemed to stop her shuddering.

'Ay dear,' she murmured. 'I'd have given owt to avoid you seeing what my father's like.'

'Happen it's time that somebody shared the anxiety?'

'You talk as if I'm an only one, I've three brothers, don't forget . . .'

'But not *here*.'

'They have important positions to keep up.'

'And haven't you?'

'I'm used to Father, know what to do.'

231

'Experience forced upon you. You don't have to continue like this for the rest of your life, Isobel.'

'I've got to do what I can for him.'

Paul smiled slightly, drew her against him. 'I'd not have grown to love you so quickly if you were any different. Aye, lass. I do. And if you marry me, Isobel, I'll make your life easier.'

She was stunned by his proposal.

'There's room in my home for your father as well. Between us, we could maybe improve life for him, prevent his needing to resort quite so often to the bottle.'

'Don't tempt me,' she answered. 'You'd only regret it.'

'Not with you as my wife.' Paul was holding her closely as he said it.

'Oh, Paul,' she sighed, confused by the unfamiliar longing to accept his offer of care. Hadn't she always been the one to manage, to cope, to work. . . ? Even in her love for Carlos there had been a powerful urge to help *him* while he went through that difficult time.

His mouth prevented her saying more, and also prevented thoughts of the past. She felt awakened inside. She was past thirty, but hadn't lost the ability to respond to emotion. Eventually, alarmed by her own eagerness, Isobel attempted to draw away.

'You've not had time to think what you're suggesting,' she reminded him, but contrary to her own instinct. 'What possible benefit would there be for you in taking on both me and a father like mine?'

'I have responsibilities, an' all. There's my young Audrey, motherless for longer than she should be.'

'I didn't know.'

'And there's myself – wearied to death with existing alone. Happen it wouldn't be ideal, Isobel, but we could make this work for the good of all four of us. I'll not hope for your answer tonight, but don't forget your father might be glad to have a son-in-law who'd treat him with affection.'

Isobel marvelled. 'You'd better be on your way, Paul. You've a long ride ahead of you.' And if I don't see you out through that door there's no knowing where my tiredness and this longing might lead.

'Goodnight then, my love. Be safe . . .'

The tenderness in his lips made something stir within her heart. Too soon to be certain it was love, she couldn't deny that it was sincere affection.

'And you be safe as well, Paul.' Her kiss as they stood at the door was lingering.

Paul came again the following night, was introduced to her father whose aching head had convinced him (for twenty-four hours) that he'd foresake alcohol for ever. Their conversation grew convivial, even though Paul felt constrained by giving no hint that either he or Isobel were involved in obstructing the mechanisation going on in the factories taking over local valleys. Isobel let the men talk, glad that Paul knew so much about what was happening in the neighbourhood, and seemed to be acquainted with many of their business friends.

By the time Amos decided to take his troublesome head to its pillow, he was sufficiently impressed with Paul to draw Isobel aside.

'Yon's a personable young fellow, and seems inclined to consider me capable of having the occasional thought that's worthy of notice. Am I right in gathering that he's a widower?'

'With a little lass, aye.'

'You seem to be friendly enough wi' him already, has it occurred to you that you might do worse than encourage him?'

Isobel didn't reply. There was a difference between taking her father into account in her decisions and allowing him to suggest the direction they should take.

Amos, though, was hardly the most subtle of men; Paul had gleaned much of the converstion which had taken place at the foot of the staircase. When Isobel returned to the room, he was smiling in amusement.

'He's right, of course, you could do worse than marry me.'

'And remain in a perpetual state of embarrassment, by the sound of it! Wasn't it sufficient that you witnessed our situation last night?'

'You know it wasn't. I want you, Isobel – to give you a better life, as well as to sate the need to love you. There isn't one of us entirely responsible for the way we live. You're no more to blame for your father's condition than I am for being committed to rearing Audrey on my own.'

She was almost overlooking Audrey. 'I'd have to get to know her first, before I'd even think about becoming her stepmother.'

'Naturally. Any other way would be most unwise. But she's only a bairn, Isobel, you needn't worry that she'll not take to your kindness and instinctive concern.'

And there was his need as well. She couldn't remain impassive before the arms outstretched to draw her to him again. Their kisses grew deeper, more demanding, and his hands traced the outline of her waist then pressed at her lower spine. For so many years she had ignored her own need to be loved.

And suddenly his desire was voiced, in a tone scarcely recognisable for its emotion. 'Wed me tonight, Isobel, here.'

Gravely, she looked up into his eyes. 'You know I can't. And I'd not lie with you, Paul, till we were man and wife.'

'But you will make it soon, you'll not have me lingering on for your decision?'

Isobel *almost* concluded that allowing him to express the love developing between them would be simpler than arranging to marry. But there were memories to deter her, thoughts of Carlos and the way she'd been hurt when his love came to nothing.

Paul was smiling again, in command of himself. 'Forgive my urgency,' he said. 'I must make allowance for your innocence . . .'

'No,' Isobel interrupted swiftly. This was another thing that had bothered her. She'd been troubled that he'd learn, too late, that she wasn't the virgin he'd supposed. 'It's not that. There – there was someone, a very long time ago.'

'Was he – married already?' He had to know, yet felt she'd never have given herself in an adulterous relationship.

Isobel shook her head. 'No, he still isn't. But he's hundreds of miles away.' And had ceased writing to her.

'Do you still love him?'

'I don't believe so.' Hadn't she forbidden herself to think of him? If she married Paul it would be like surrendering Carlos – admitting their relationship had been just a bit of romantic fervour.

'Do you love me?'

'I think I'm learning to – quite quickly, when I consider how little I know about you.'

'And we are drawn together, aren't we, love?' he murmured, holding her against him once more.

Her laugh was light with a sudden unburdening. It would be so easy to let herself love this exciting man whose need of her aroused warmth as well as passion in a soul too long chilled by neglect.

'Oh, that's true enough! If I only heeded my senses. The trouble is there's common sense as well, and I've never dismissed that since I was a bit of a lass.'

'And I'll not urge you to dismiss it now. I want everything right between us, Isobel.'

Desire, though, would not permit him to leave her without renewing their embrace, promising how it would be if she agreed that they'd be married.

How can I not wed him? Isobel thought, as she lay restless on her bed. Her entire person had come alive, responding to Paul as strongly as she was drawn to his friendly personality.

Amos Bright had asked to meet Paul's parents: a request which wasn't fulfilled because of their absence at their home in London. But Isobel had been introduced to his young daughter Audrey, and immediately been bewitched. The child was a two-year-old enchantress, with eyes that replicated her father's. Her hair was but a shade or so darker than spun silver, straight and gleaming, so fine that its confining velvet band rarely stayed in place. Was it Paul's fumbling attempts to replace that ribbon which told Isobel that she would wed him? Could identifying love be that easy?

'We mustn't wait,' he'd whispered when she'd told him. 'There's no reason on this earth why we shouldn't marry soon.' He made his elation evident in his kisses.

'Aye, I think you're right,' Isobel said wryly.

'I'll see your father tomorrow, if I may. You'll not require his permission, I know, but that doesn't prevent my requesting it. As for the ceremony itself, if you want your brothers present, so be it. Even if that means delaying till Henry and William make the voyage to England.'

'I believe our Will and Henry are both in London at present. I'll write at once to Fortescue's in Queenhithe.' Her brother Charles would learn her news more quickly, she would visit his chambers during the next day.

Amos disappointed Isobel by rejecting their suggestion that he live with them.

'I'm staying in my own home,' he asserted.

'But it would be your home as well,' Paul assured him. 'The house is plenty big enough for you to have a bed-chamber with its own living room adjoining. We'd not trouble you, if you wished your independence.'

'And yet we'd be to hand if ever we were needed,' Isobel added.

Aye, thought her father, too damned close an' all. Paul would be watching him all the time, counting every drop he drank. Isobel was enough of a warder at times. 'Thank you,' he stated firmly, 'but I'll stay where I am.'

Initially, Isobel wondered if she might be obliged to reverse her decision. But Paul needed her no less than Amos, the same was true of young Audrey who regularly hurled her small person at her. And she herself needed them.

'I'll not let him make any difference to our plans,' she said at last. She couldn't spend all her life existing for her father. He'd still be well cared for by Mrs Darwin who would send for them if there should be some emergency.

Paul's ardent kisses made her ache for the day they'd be wed. She began to recognise that their life together promised her happiness.

The Luddite gang were riding out that night to a newly contructed mill, down a moorland track near her home. Isobel was disappointed when he said she must go there alone.

'I've no one to sit in the house with Audrey, you see.'

'What about that housekeeper of yours, Mrs Field?'

236

Just for a second Paul gazed at her, as though confounded. 'Oh – she's unwell, I'm afraid. It – wouldn't be wise to have her all over the child.'

And what's become of me, Isobel thought, only weeks after meeting him? Am I so changed already that I'm overlooking the need to master them that's replacing men with machines?

She kissed Paul goodnight and rode off to rendezvous with Roger Wheatley and the others. The factory was unguarded. Freshly delivered spinning frames and looms were displayed in their lantern light, beyond the door they had forced. The machines appeared to have been left there to await the men who would fit them.

'I can't believe they've been this incautious,' Roger murmured.

'Nor I,' another man whispered, a laugh deep in his throat.

The first hammer blow brought a yell from above them in the darkness. And a light, not their own, illuminated the group.

'The law's here an' all,' came the gruff shout from the mill master. 'You'll not get away this time.'

A hand clamped over Roger Wheatley's arm before he'd struck one blow with his hammer. The next man to him had the axe knocked from his fingers, then his wrist was seized and dragged round his back making him scream with pain.

'Drop your tools, and raise your arms over your 'eads,' someone commanded. 'There's more on us outside in t'mill yard, don't think to run for it.'

I'll not stand here and be captured, thought Isobel, not while there's a chance. She tossed her hammer towards the approaching officer's foot. And then she ran, her spine prickling with dread that she'd be stopped.

The warning that they'd be apprehended outside had been a bluff. But there were sufficient men inside the mill to hold the gang and still send someone after her.

The horses, though, had been freed and doubtless scared into bolting.

Only continuing to run could save her. Isobel began

scrambling up the coarse moorland. She'd be no use to Paul or anyone else if she was taken prisoner.

She was almost half-way up the hillside when she heard the commotion below in the direction of the mill. Her friends were being taken off to jail. If she saw them again, it wouldn't be for many a long month – unless she was captured as well, to stand trial with them.

Somehow, she managed to reach her home, and even got up early the following morning to attend Halifax Piece Hall. The fate of the group of Luddites was being discussed all around her, and with it the news that two of the gang had escaped. From the description, she gathered the other fortunate person was Jacob. She was very thankful that Paul had not been able to join them.

'You'd better come in,' she said to him, when Paul suddenly appeared with little Audrey at her father's house – come to see if she was all right. 'Please mind what you're saying here,' she whispered. 'Father knows nowt about last night.'

She sat in the wooden kitchen rocker with the child, while Paul went to join Amos on the settle and from there fixed Isobel with his affectionate gaze. Her father was saying how late they'd been returning from the cloth market, and suddenly enquired what exactly Paul's work was.

'I'm just starting something new, with having worked away until recently, you understand.'

'Oh, aye – what is it you're doing?'

Paul glanced away, hesitant, avoiding their eyes. 'The position was offered by a distant relative, couldn't afford to refuse it . . .'

Isobel knew before he'd told them that he was helping to manage a mill. She saw her father's frown, but was conscious that her own reaction was far more sickening. How could he live with the conflict inside himself? How had he gone about with the rest of them, smashing machines, when all the time he was working to make one of them wretched mills profitable!

—15—

Her father was reasonably well and Alfred Hanson had long since proved himself an able assistant. Why then had she experienced this strange unease ever since the mail coach had lurched along the road out of Halifax?

She was now aboard a vessel only an hour's sailing short of Cadiz, and still no more convinced that she'd been right to leave Yorkshire. No one, least of all Paul, had disputed her decision. She'd seemed almost on the point of collapse, through this great worry. At least, though, she had confronted her fiancé.

At first, she'd hardly known what to say to him when he'd visited and found her reclining on the Hepplewhite-style bar-back sofa which was the one good piece of furniture she'd persuaded Amos to purchase. And she must have looked exactly like one of the delicate ladies which she most definitely was *not*.

Paul had seemed prepared to believe her father's assumption that she was debilitated by some female malady. That was when she'd realised that as from that day there must be nothing but honesty between them. Or nothing at all.

Summoning strength from somewhere, Isobel rose. 'I'm not ill, Paul,' she announced. 'I need to talk to you, privately.'

Her father seemed the more put out of the two, though Paul's eyebrows arched slightly then settled. For once, Amos took a hint and began climbing the stairs.

'Which is the mill where you're working?' Isobel asked.

Before he'd finished telling her, she felt literally sick. 'And they do weaving as well as spinning! How do you equate that with the Luddite cause?'

'We can't always follow all our inclinations. I told you I have to work to support Audrey and myself.'

'Then you should never have joined us – you can't be on both sides, Paul.' He didn't answer. A faint smile curved his lips.

'It isn't a game,' Isobel snapped, recalling how elated he had appeared out with the gang. 'It's about men being robbed of their jobs!'

'Have I denied that?' he asked her calmly. 'It wasn't just for the excitement that I took up with the Luddites.'

'But you made a secret of where you work, kept it from me.'

Paul snorted. 'I hoped that when we'd established an understanding you'd be able to trust me.'

'Trust?'

'To use my own judgement. Evidently you can't. Since it seems there's no basis for our marriage, we'd best extricate ourselves from any commitment.'

'Paul . . .' she began, but he interrupted her.

'Take time to consider, Isobel. You're the one using this to divide us, if you decide you can believe in me you know where I live.'

It was Amos who had suggested that she might benefit from a short stay with one or other of her cousins; Isobel had realised that only Henry, still her favourite brother, might help her.

He met her off the ship, and was immediately all concern and warmth.

'Is it that wretched cough that's troubling you again, love?'

Trying to smile, Isobel shook her head. 'I simply needed to get away, to think . . . happen to seek your advice.'

She was a long time bringing herself to speak of Paul. Through three days and nights she tested the words within her own head. There was so little she could say without revealing that she and her friends were Luddites.

As perturbing as her misgivings about revealing too much, was this attachment to Paul which seemed to develop with each day. How *could* she dismiss him? From being an exciting friend he'd quickly grown into her potential life partner and now, almost against her will, rarely left her thoughts.

'I think I'm in love,' she confided, at last, but to Catalina rather than to Henry. 'I was on the point of sending you an invitation to our wedding when I made this awful discovery.'

'He's not married already?' Catalina asked anxiously, wondering how anything less could have drained all stamina from her sister-in-law.

Isobel shook her head. 'No – although he has been married previously. His wife is dead, there's a young daughter – Audrey. And she and I were getting along so well . . .'

'He's not ill, I trust?' Catalina pictured this unknown suitor sentenced by some terminal complaint. And then she wondered, increasingly appalled, if it were Isobel who was gravely ill. Certainly, she looked fragile enough to lend weight to that dreadful supposition.

'No – no. He's – it's the work he does. Helping to run one of them new factories. They go in for weaving as well as spinning. And they're doing a lot of t'old weavers and us clothiers out of work.'

Is that all, thought Catalina, but hadn't the heart to say it. 'You say he has responsibilities – a child?'

'Audrey, a little lass.'

'So his first priority must be providing for her . . .'

That was what Paul had said. Her unease shifted to questioning her own attitude. Was she too intolerant? Her pride was hurt because he'd not told her everything. Had this influenced her thinking worse of him?

Suspecting now that she might have over-reacted, Isobel couldn't succumb to Henry's and Catalina's concern for her. She spent two days around the bodega, savouring the sherry when it was extracted from butts of the latest blend, and renewing acquaintance with Alberto Martinez and other employees of Fortescue's. But she knew in her heart that it was only her way of delaying that question hovering over her future.

Uncertain of herself as much as anyone, and wondering why she'd come to Jerez hoping that she'd resolve something, Isobel left for Cadiz and the return voyage to England. Maybe she'd been a coward, she ought to have stayed at home to thrash out the problem with Paul.

Isobel was leaning on the ship's rail, gazing back towards the sunlit harbour at the same time as Carlos Escutia dismounted outside his sister Catalina's *casa*.

'Where is she then?' he inquired, smiling, as he strode through the door into the courtyard where Catalina was relaxing amid dark foliage that reflected in the gloss of brilliantly coloured tiling.

'Carlos!' she exclaimed, beaming, and then: '*No comprendo* . . .'

'Isobel, of course. Henry sent a message that she is here.'

Smiling ruefully, his sister explained that Isobel had left. He should have come more swiftly if he'd really wished to see her. Poor Isobel was too disturbed to settle anywhere for long.

Carlos was perturbed, and not least on his own behalf. What had become of his prized independence that he would rush here on Isobel's account? And what of his new-found efficiency if he could bungle the attempt to see her?

He forced a shrug, sank on to the chair adjacent to Catalina's, and prepared to steel himself against further questioning, and against asking questions.

But Catalina, already perplexed by her sister-in-law, decided Carlos was old enough to look after his own interests. If he inquired in more detail about Isobel, she would answer to the best of her knowledge, otherwise she'd let the matter alone. She knew there'd been something between the pair years ago, but not enough to prise Carlos from his bachelor status.

And he inquired no further. He hadn't changed so much that he'd let Catalina see that he wasn't indifferent to Henry's sister. After all, it had been for Isobel's good, surely, that he'd troubled to ride over here. For himself, life as it was provided sufficient interest, and women as well when he needed one in his bed.

He'd been called selfish often enough by *Madre* and by his siblings. He'd never wanted to explain that he still saw his solitary life as designed to *spare* others rather than dismiss them. The leg troubled him increasingly with age, a fact which he'd never admit; what had once troubled him more than the pain was the dread of a time when he'd be incapable of supporting himself. These days, he believed he'd found the solution.

Coming here had been a foolish whim, prompted by a sentiment which he didn't normally permit. He'd remain only long enough to prevent his sister accusing him of discourtesy, and then would take his unease to his own home.

Carlos couldn't feel sorry when he saw outlined against the night sky the familiar line of near-derelict buildings. He only regretted that he'd ever entertained the possibility of bringing Isobel here. Had the solitary life invoked some madness that he could have supposed she'd have seen anything but a house badly in need of repair and a succession of out-buildings which leaned crazily together for support? Would anyone, least of all someone reared in such different circumstances, have been able to visualise all that he planned here? To visualise his dreams?

'It's time we were realistic about this, and retrieved something from what circumstances have done to us.'

William was in the house in Heptonstall, brought here by his determination that his marriage would *not* sink while, by suppressing his pride, he might convince Phillida that he needed her.

He was afraid he could receive proof that she no longer needed him. The evidence suggested that she was content here, that all she really wished was to keep young Jessica to herself and revert to the life she'd known before their wedding. And he himself. . . ? William had never for one second intended to deceive, wouldn't have suspected that he had it in him to live a dual existence. If it hadn't been for Rosalind Parker. The daughter of a fellow port-shipper, she was the same age as himself, a woman of forty-three years who devoted her life to running her widowed father's household.

It was following the grand reopening of the Factory House in Oporto that she and William were reacquainted and suddenly this woman, who for years had been a pleasant female on the periphery of his circle, had grown into an animated friend. They met socially and they met alone, up the majestic Douro where she organised the household at the *quinta* adjacent to Fortescue's. In precious minutes obtained by compressing their work, they walked among the vines, elated by the splendour of their surroundings, no longer able to deny their elation in each other.

Who, except William himself, would fault him because the thrill he felt in at long last sharing the Douro was through this woman who was not his wife?

'I'm asking you again to accompany me, Phillida,' he said now, compelled to make a final attempt to set matters right. 'I told you ages since how important this grand ball is. I want my wife beside me, want to show you off to everyone I know.'

She still possessed the same bone-structure, returning happiness had resurrected most of her original beauty. He'd lavish whatever she required on a gown which would beat any that folk would find out in Portugal; make her feel more confident, and he'd take her up river; lay the ghost of other company by luxuriating in *hers*.

Phillida was confused by William coming all this way to ask her to reconsider. During the weeks since he'd first pressed her to agree she had been satisfied that she'd never have to uproot herself and Jessica. She didn't like upsetting Will, but was unable to explain how greatly visiting Oporto would upset *her*.

It wasn't only that she would feel out of place among folk who set such store by feasting and dancing, there was the edginess induced by keeping an eye on Jessica.

Dearly though she loved her daughter, even she couldn't deny that she was wilful, often downright naughty. Here, among family and friends Jessica's tantrums often made her feel disgraced, she'd not have them shown up before strangers. And whatever would Will have to say if coping with the child seemed beyond her!

'Ay, love – you go and enjoy yourself. We're all right as we are, and I know you're happy with the folk you know out there.'

'I'd be happier with you there. It's time we rediscovered each other, Phillida.'

244

'Jessica'd never give us any peace, any road. You know how she fusses round you.'

'You could leave her here, in familiar surroundings. With your mother perhaps. Or Isobel. There are several candidates.'

'That's just it – I couldn't leave her. She's at a difficult age.'

From what William could see, Jessica always would be difficult. But maybe a part, at least, of that was his fault. Hadn't his long absences denied her the discipline, and happen a little of the security, of having her father here?

Although his wife's excuses were less vehement than years ago, he read aright her deep-seated determination not to be shifted. William ceased arguing. Phillida, reluctant, would be worse than Phillida at home in Yorkshire.

Throughout the long journey south to London, he reflected that his wife seemed incapable of recognising that with every decision she was driving them apart. He was wearied to death; for the first time ever, would be glad if he never returned to Heptonstall. For this he felt guilty, but he wasn't the only one to blame.

Henry was in London, beaming when Will strode into the Queenhithe office, and suggesting that they dine together that evening. Loyalty to Phillida and intuition that he should keep silent about Rosalind made him hold his tongue about the situation. But later that evening, while Henry filled gaps in their mealtime conversation with reminders of his congenial life with Catalina, William began to realise he must act, or lose regular contact with young Jessica.

'You appear well-satisfied wi' life, Henry. I wish I could say the same. But then *my* wife and child have always been separated from me, haven't they? Stuck in Yorkshire.'

Puzzled by his brother's tone, Henry glanced across the table at him. 'I know. And we've all sympathised, but . . .'

'Sympathised?' William interrupted sharply. 'Nay, damn it, man, you've never lifted a finger to make things easier.'

'What could I have done?' Henry assumed that William was suggesting that his share of the house should have been surrendered. Though how that might have helped he could not imagine.

245

'Agreed to opening an office in the West Riding, that's what. You've always withheld your agreement, yet you were aware that it was a possibility long since, when we both joined Fortescue's.'

'Nay, Will. You know as well as I do that proposition wasn't viable. It'd cost far more nor it'd be worth.'

'You don't know that until you give it a try. And you've allus been too obstinate to even discuss it properly.'

'I certainly haven't given the matter serious thought for years.'

'Because it was me that wanted it, because it was my marriage that it could have saved.'

'I'm sorry but this is business. It's got nowt to do with arranging things to keep anybody happy.' His voice dropped. 'Not even Phillida.'

'We could go into it now, find out the cost of premises . . .'

Henry sighed. 'There's more to it than that, isn't there? The place would have to be staffed. Even if you elected to work from there permanently – and I doubt if that'd succeed – you'd need clerks.'

'I've considered all that. We could manage it, Henry, if you'd consent.'

'I'm afraid I can't.'

'Won't, you mean, won't!' Rising, William slammed the flat of both hands on the table, making plates and cutlery jump. People at the surrounding tables were staring, happen they'd been staring for the past few minutes. He didn't care; let 'em gawp.

'I meant precisely what I said, Will. We cannot throw money away on something that isn't essential. We're only just emerging from what repeated conflict has done to Portugal and Spain. You've got to give us a chance to get Fortescue's trade back on to a better footing.'

'Things are picking up . . .'

'Aye, thank God. But who's to say there'll be no more invasions? We've got to hang on afore lashing out on summat that doesn't matter.'

'It could matter to me, by being the one thing that could

prevent everything between me and Phillida finishing. And any time in t'future is going to be too late.'

William stalked away from the table and out into the London street. The following morning he re-booked his passage, ensuring that he sailed immediately for Portugal.

He'd seen the ballroom before, but never on so grand an occasion as the ball in honour of the Prince of Orange. The seven chandeliers glittered, illuminating exquisite panelled walls decorated in the style of Robert Adam. The musicians, already tuning their instruments in the gallery, enhanced the excitement. And even before William had thought to look for her, there Rosalind was, smiling as she glided towards him the length of the room which must be fifty feet or more. Her gown was fashionable, Grecian in style, simple yet dramatic in its immaculate draping of gleaming ivory silk. Here and there a touch of gold emphasised an elegant curve, so evocatively that he was compelled to discipline his gaze.

'She hasn't come then.'

'Ay, Rosalind, I wonder now how I ever hoped that she might. Or *why*,' he added firmly. He was past the stage of prevaricating. Phillida had made her decision. He'd no desire to pay her back, but nor could he remain resolutely indifferent to everyone else.

'It's good to see you here,' Rosalind said gently. And now her eyes had lit, rendering them translucent, making her radiant.

'I trust that you're not promised for too many dances? I'm no expert, I warn you, but I don't intend sitting out.'

The shake of her head made the short golden curls tremble, each hair gleaming beneath the flickering candles. 'I'm promised to no one,' she told him, and revealed in the darkening of her eyes the willingness to be associated with him.

They danced as soon as the orchestra commenced playing, caring no longer that their being together would be noticed, and only separated while William went to greet business friends. He had held Rosalind as closely as he dared

247

thoughout the evening and when it drew to a close he inquired, 'You'll not leave with your father. . . ?'

She smiled into his eyes, and shook her head. 'Since you're asking that I shouldn't.'

He offered to hire her a sedan chair, but she declined. Conversing quietly, they walked away from the Factory House uphill towards his home.

'I thought a glass of something perhaps?' Will suggested, and saw her smile to herself in the glow from lamps which shone either side of the door.

There seemed so little pressure to hasten indoors that they might have had the whole of life before them, to have been but twenty years old and both free to experience the future together – this new beginning.

His housekeeper had left more lamps alight in the entrance hall, and candles in alcoves on the stair.

They sipped brandy on the balcony of his room, with only the stars for witness and scarcely a word between them to dilute the incandescence of attraction. Suddenly William brought his chair closer to Rosalind's. The brandy was sampled on each others' lips. Her gown was cool beneath his fingers when he drew her against him, her arms became an exquisite pressure around his shoulders.

They rose to their feet, smiling into each other's eyes before William drew her close. Rosalind responded unreservedly to every kiss. Inside his room, he felt no remorse. The choice wasn't his, though he'd resolved that regrets would no longer colour his conduct with Rosalind. Her attitude throughout this evening had confirmed that she entirely reciprocated his emotions.

Her fingers shook slightly as he took the empty glass from them, were chilled despite the warmth of the Portuguese night. Inexperience made her the girl he might have loved years ago, and endeared her to him as he quietly divested her of the delicate gown.

Her skin gleamed, inviting his caress across her shoulders then towards the incline of her breast.

'I need you, Will,' she murmured, 'need you so very deeply.'

'Like this?' he asked, one hand tracing the line of her waist, smoothing the curve of a hip.

'And more . . .' Her gasp was scarcely more than a sigh. Words seemed drained from her lips just as thoughts were dwindling in her brain. From being composed, a practical woman, in one evening she'd learned to serve her eager heart.

'Whatever happens afterwards,' she said presently, 'I'm eternally glad that we are here now.'

He took her to the bed, lay holding her, until their urgency had him discarding his own clothing.

She was eager beneath him, each movement the echo of his own, the hands drawing him to her, sliding across his back to anchor on his spine. Her cry, when it came, was no louder than a breath.

Slowly, carefully, William took complete possession, giving himself until the strains of their love gathered pace in glorious elation. 'I love you, Rosalind,' he murmured into silken curls now moist, kissed her ear, and then again her lips.

'And I love you,' she responded.

They slept in each others' arms but only for a while before wakening again, and in the repeated giving of himself William was asserting a new loyalty, a new love which no other would displace.

'How did you expect me to trust you, Paul? I've always been straightforward with folk, I thought you were the same.' The words had tumbled out, despite Isobel's resolve, annoying her because she'd meant to handle this more coolly. Yet still she continued, 'You say you've been instructing lawyers who might obtain Roger and the others their freedom. If that's the case, how will you square that with your mill-owning cronies?'

They were at his house, standing awkwardly in the parlour because of her refusal to be seated. Isobel's heart was sore with trying to suppress emotions evoked just now by young Audrey's eager welcome.

'I don't know,' Paul admitted, surprising her, although maybe this honesty was the start of what she was seeking. 'All I do know is that it was something I had to attempt. I'd never have risked my own safety with the Luddites would I, if it weren't a cause I support. And as for having a manager's job . . . I was afraid to tell you, and incur your loathing.'

If I could have loathed you, Isobel thought, these past weeks would have been less hurtful. As it was, she still could only love him and pray she was right, believing there was something there to like.

'You haven't,' she said, 'and that's half the trouble. There isn't just right or wrong. But you know how I've hated these mills that are setting up, believed I hated everyone connected with them.'

'But here you are . . .' He had been so afraid she'd never come.

'Aye.' Her glance was rueful. It was her own judgement that she didn't entirely trust, these days.

'That position in the mill truly was the only work on offer. You know yourself how clothiers are struggling . . .'

The sincerity in his dark blue eyes made her think that she could understand how he might have been torn between a job that was offered him, and his opposition to mechanisation.

'If it'd alter the situation between us, I'd find something different at the first opportunity,' Paul added.

'Nay,' she said at last. 'That'd be proper daft. It's folk like me and my father that'll be finished afore t'mills. One of us has to stay in work, it'll be the one who has the better prospects.'

'You'll still wed me then, Isobel?'

'Aye, love – I will. I couldn't keep up my determination not to want you.' But that was enough of confession. She'd always been realistic. Life wasn't perfect, and nor were folk. She'd learn to live with Paul's commitment to the factory, and he'd have to accept her being a Luddite. She'd be careful, though, she'd never risk being imprisoned, or worse. Mill owners would continue to use force against them. She couldn't leave her father with no one at hand to care – and nor could she contemplate leaving Paul and young Audrey.

Suddenly, Isobel smiled. Now she'd made up her mind, she was going to see that everybody enjoyed this wedding! 'We'd best tell that little lass of yours that I'll want her to attend me. Do you think she can walk down the aisle without getting that excited she wets herself? I suppose Phillida will expect Jessica to be on show an' all – I daresay she'll behave herself for me.'

Paul was smiling back, and she was glad she'd pleased him. Coming so close to cancelling their plans had shown how much he meant to her.

Even the fact that they were to marry in winter didn't dull Isobel's happiness. And her family who travelled from abroad seemed to dismiss the cold. They were only thankful Napoleon's armies were fully occupied well out of the way, with the advance on Russia.

On the day, Amos drove their carriage himself. He'd never believed in wasting good wages on a coachman. Isobel could tell by the way he urged the horses to gallop that he wasn't any too happy, although she had to admit time was short. She'd kept him waiting while she tried to get her hair under control.

Conscious that she wasn't exactly a youthful bride, she'd thought a smart bonnet more suitable than indulging in lots of veiling and ribbons. Her dark hair, worn short ever since that grew fashionable, was freshly washed and seemed to have a life of its own. It had resisted several attempts before she secured the bonnet to her satisfaction. She tried to remain still in the lurching carriage, smoothing her gown, a pearly coloured silk and more closely draped than anything she'd ever worn.

Choosing Heptonstall church instead of the one near their home had been instinctive, and only inconvenienced the two of them. The rest of the family, so close at hand, were gathered inside when Amos halted outside the churchyard.

The first person Isobel saw was young Audrey, standing very quietly in her dainty muslin dress and rather intimidated by Jessica, now an assertive four-year-old. Not that Jessica was noticing – she was far more interested in staring from the porch away down the church. Jorge was home from Spain, and grown very tall and exciting.

251

Phillida had been keeping an eye on the two small attendants and set off down the aisle once she had handed them over. Isobel couldn't help noticing that Phillie still dressed well, despite William's absence. Being here on her own couldn't be all that easy.

Taking her father's arm, Isobel realised that he wasn't relying on his stick today, loved him for that, and concentrated on fitting her pace to his. She could see Paul now, tall and elegant, an imposing figure. When they reached his side, she smiled up at him, but still aware of her father and emotions he'd never admit. She was sorry Amos didn't want to make his home with them, but she'd not let that spoil this new life she was beginning.

The ceremony binding her to Paul passed more quickly than she'd have chosen and, concentrating on her responses, her feelings seemed to be constrained. But afterwards, returning through the church with all their folk smiling towards them, she felt Paul's hand tighten over her own, and suddenly was happy again.

Out in the open Audrey sought her father's other hand, and Isobel bent with a kiss and admired her pretty dress. Straightening up, she saw her other attendant, a real little beauty. Tall for her age, Jessica was wearing velvet the shade of sherry. The auburn hair inherited from her mother glinted in the wintry sunlight, and she was smiling all over her face.

Thank goodness she's in a good mood, thought Isobel, then noticed where Jessica's attention was focused. Her cousin Jorge was grinning and winking at her. Well away from Phillida's keen eye!

Catalina and Henry had congratulated them already, while witnessing their signatures, and were hanging back to make space for some of Paul's family. But the day was too cool for lingering outdoors, and soon they all were crossing the windswept churchyard.

'Your Jessica looks right grand!' Isobel exclaimed as Phillida walked beside her.

'Thanks, love.' Phillie smiled back. 'I must admit it does my heart good to see her like that, makes all t'hard work seem worthwhile.'

Isobel nodded and beamed. 'She's a credit to you.' And this occasion must make her sister-in-law even more conscious of the inadequacies of her own marriage.

But was it only on account of Will and and his wife that one phrase from the service seemed to stand out so starkly: 'For better or for worse'?

16

There had been several occasions when being married to a mill manager while she remained a clothier made Isobel uneasy. Not sufficiently uneasy, though, for her to surrender her interest in Bright's during these past three years. For a while, she told herself that when they had a family she would give up her job. Then she'd be justified in ending the work that she'd been so determined to begin all those years ago in 1790. And Father might not be sorry to sell the business. There had been no children of her own, though, and she'd grown to believe that she must be content with her step-daughter. She never really saw the lack of her own children as a great trouble. She was too busy to surrender to disappointment. Her father's gout quite often made him poorly, and while she kept Bright's running she couldn't ease up. Then there was Paul whose needs she'd never neglect, and Audrey was developing into an affectionate girl.

Only the other morning Isobel had been touched. The child seemed to understand if she was feeling unwell, and had brought her a cup of hot chocolate and, although she'd spilled more in the saucer than remained in the cup, the gesture warmed Isobel far more than any drink.

'It's to make you better, Mother,' Audrey had declared, sitting beside her on the sofa.

Grave young eyes had watched while Isobel drank the chocolate, then she had felt a firm little arm around her. 'Just you rest now, I'll look after you.'

The entire Bright family was together for the first time in many a year on the day that the Stoodley Pike monument was opened. Constructed as a result of a public subscription and commenced in 1814 to celebrate the surrender of Paris to the allies, the monument was completed soon after the battle of Waterloo brought peace with France. And despite increasingly indifferent health, Amos insisted on accompanying them all when they filled three carriages setting out to view the structure on the hillside not far from Todmorden.

'It's more than thirty-seven yards high,' Jessica informed William on the way from Heptonstall where her mother had put on a good dinner for everyone. Jessica was fond of sums and enjoyed impressing her father on his rare visits.

'Two feet and four inches more,' confirmed eleven-year-old Cousin Jorge, who was jealous of his Uncle William's capacity for winning Jessica's attention.

'You mind you tell me all you can see from the top of yon thing,' his grandfather told him. 'I shall expect a full account.'

Amos hadn't needed Isobel's advice against attempting the steps inside the monument. A straining heart and obligatory rests often cautioned that his staircase at home would one day have the better of him, but nothing would have kept him from this outing. Their Will's presence was enough to bring tears to his old eyes, which he laughed off as 't'effect of t'cold wind'.

For the first time recently, Amos thought of Eleanor, and how she'd have rejoiced to see their sons and daughter round them with their families. And no fratching between any on 'em. Though he wished Charles and his wife seemed more at ease with the rest of the family.

'What's wrong, Father, you're looking wistful?' Paul had left his own carriage and walked back to help as Phillida and Will struggled to get the old man's legs to cooperate.

'Nay, there's nowt wrong,' Amos assured him, grinning. He'd taken to Paul from the first. The lad couldn't help being born into a family whose brass was now tied up in mills. 'As a matter of fact, I were thinking about Isobel's mother. It's been a long time.'

Jorge, Jessica and Audrey ran on ahead, rushing to be the first to reach the top of the Pike. Watching, William was appalled. His daughter was pushing her way through a group of adults emerging from the monument. She'll feel the weight of my hand if she doesn't mind her manners, he resolved, yet knew in his heart that unless more severely provoked he'd do nothing.

Phillida had made it plain since his arrival that she was only tolerating his being here. She'd given him a bed in the back room which, had she but known it, had spared him a wealth of excuses. After long months of meeting covertly, he and Rosalind had finally braved whatever disapprobation they might face and set up house together back in Portugal. Today, Phillida was acting the adoring wife, for his father's benefit and maybe also for young Jessica. The act alternately pleased him and irritated, destroying his equilibrium with the constant swings of mood. But, if only for show, his wife was trying. She was walking alongside Catalina, talking as though they were affectionate sisters. William did wonder if Phillie might genuinely wish to make amends, to convince him of her desire for harmony. It was too late now, and he hoped not.

Henry caught him up, and gave a backward glance towards his wife and Phillida. 'I understand you've a fresh home in Oporto, these days, William.'

'You've heard then,' he said and waited, not without discomfort. They had avoided each other since Henry had steadfastly refused to go along with William's old desire to establish a local office of Fortescue's in Yorkshire. Using their staff as intermediaries hadn't furnished Will with clues as to how much Henry might say in front of Phillida and the whole family.

'About Rosalind Parker, aye. Can't say as I'm surprised.' Phillida had always tended towards rigidity. 'No, I shan't say owt. In fact, I thought you might be glad one of us could understand.'

William raised eyebrows in which grey was intermingled. 'To tell you t'truth, I'm surprised Phillida hasn't guessed. But I'd certainly prefer that Father shouldn't know.'

'He's aged fast this past twelve month.' Henry sighed pensively. 'It'd do him good if we could get him to come out to us in Spain. T'climate's more congenial . . . But I'm afraid we'll not shift him from t'West Riding.'

Before entering the monument, the adults congregated around Amos and Isobel who'd elected to wait with him until the others emerged.

'If you go round t'other side, you'll be shielded from this wind,' Henry advised. 'I'll be out again in no time, Isobel, then you can climb up to top.'

Charles and his wife offered to stay with the old man, but he was determined to appear self-sufficient. 'I don't need looking after, tha knows. You can all go together. I'm used to fending for myself.'

Only Isobel remained resolutely at his side, though she'd no reason then to suspect that she would always be thankful she'd done so.

Paul was to the rear of their party, approaching the entrance, she heard his pleasant voice greeting an elderly man who was emerging. 'Hallo, Mr Gaukroger, how're you keeping? And how's business?'

Samson Gaukroger shook Paul's extended hand, grasped his shoulder. Neither Isobel nor her father heard his reply, but his smile and the heartiness of his manner were eloquent enough.

'I'm right glad to hear you're doing so well,' added Paul, before hastening through the entrance into the monument after the others.

Samson Gaukroger was heading towards them next, surprise on seeing Amos evident in eighty-year-old eyes. 'By, but it's many a year sin' I saw thee!' he exclaimed. 'Aren't you going up to t'top?'

'Don't talk daft, man. How the heck can I? How long have I been a martyr to this 'ere gout?' Amos made no effort to be civil. How Gaukroger dared address him, after the way he'd ruined trade for good clothiers, he didn't know!

'Oh – aye. Of course. Still, it doesn't seem to keep you in t'house.'

'I never were one for giving in,' Amos announced.

Although admiring the spirit in his voice, Isobel was compelled to conceal a smile. But Gaukroger appeared happier to ignore her, and she'd not let him get away with that. 'You seem to know my husband,' she remarked, her voice barbed, if more in annoyance with Paul than with this old man.

'I do an' all. Allus said he'd get on. I'm glad that working away that time hasn't prevented him settling here again.'

257

It struck Isobel that her husband probably shared some of Gaukroger's characteristics; and that wasn't necessarily a recommendation. But a sudden sound from her father made her glance at him swiftly. Her concern intensified. He was tugging at his neckcloth as though it were throttling him. His cheeks looked sallow and his lips bluish.

'Are you all right, Father?' she inquired, wishing now that Samson Gaukroger would go. She was certain he was responsible for this change in Amos.

'Aye, there's nowt wrong with me,' he declared stubbornly and suddenly determined. 'And happen I will go up yon monument, after all.' He was seeing Gaukroger off with a steady glare.

Isobel guessed what he was about, and decided to comply. 'We'll say goodbye then, Mr Gaukroger. Come along, Father, give us your arm . . .' He no longer looked as if he was about to choke. Happen it wouldn't hurt to walk very steadily toward Stoodley Pike. Once inside the doorway, she'd see if he still needed warning.

Amos leaned against the wall just inside the structure. After a prolonged minute, gathering his breath, he grinned weakly at her. 'Thanks, lass. You must have known I'd not get no further nor this, but we'll not have Gaukroger knowing that, eh?'

Phillida was leading the way back down from the top, with Henry and Catalina immediately behind her, and Charles following.

'Come in here out of the wind, did you?' Henry inquired. Smiling towards Isobel, he continued: 'Go on up, love. The view's well worth it. I'll see Father comes to no harm.'

She could do nothing, remaining at his side, and he was recovering his breath now as well as some of his colour. She'd as much right as any of them to make the most of the outing – and Henry was right. As far as she could see on every side, the hills invited her to glory in their expanse. Purple-hazed moors ranged towards the horizon, contrasting with the varying greens of fields outlined by the drystone walls and the woods that clutched the lower slopes. In one direction lay

Lancashire, over to her right the road followed the Calder away towards Halifax.

The wind was keener than ever here, tugging tendrils of hair until they escaped the hat to which she was clinging, and thrashing her skirts against legs that were growing colder despite the sun overhead.

I could remain out here all day, she thought, away from them all. There felt to be more space than she'd encountered anywhere in the whole of her life. She had passed Paul on the way up, William and the children with him. The strange desire to refrain from rejoining any of her family gripped her so fiercely that she felt guilty.

But was she ever really herself, these days? Was even her work for Bright's given so ungrudgingly as in the past? Not that she would grumble; but what had become of the *resolution* she'd had as a youngster? What of the vision. . . ? Could this dissatisfaction be rooted in her own unspoken acceptance that the cloth trade as she knew it was doomed?

She glanced across to Heptonstall church, recalling her childhood spent in its shadow, and trying not to notice evidence that there were mills in the valleys about her. She couldn't halt developments within spinning and weaving, especially while her own husband was an important part of any such local progress, if progress it was. She experienced a brooding resentment towards Paul; another few minutes and she'd be convincing herself that her marriage was unsatisfactory . . . Isobel sighed, acknowledging privately she'd always believed she might have been happier with Carlos.

The sounds of a commotion somewhere near the foot of the monument brought her back to her responsibilities abruptly. That was Phillie's voice, and sounding particularly alarmed.

Clattering down the steps so hurriedly that she had to stop and retrieve one shoe, Isobel felt her heart rattling away inside her. But it was her father's heart that was causing concern, although he looked no worse than he had during the confrontation with Gaukroger.

'Whatever's wrong?' she cried, hurtling towards them.

Amos himself replied, reassuring her by being fit to speak

259

yet still appalling her with his words. 'What do you think, lass? You should never have let a chap like that come upsetting me. The sight of him were enough, then when he taunted me wi' not being able to climb up yon daft monument . . .' Amos was clawing at his neckcloth again, while his other hand pressed at his ribs through the opening of his coat.

Isobel tried to make him more comfortable.

Amos only shoved away her hands. 'Nay, tha's too late. I'm finished.'

'You'll be all right once we get a doctor to you. You'll come home with us, and we'll have you in bed directly.'

'You won't! By jove, but you won't. I'm going with Phillie and our Will. I spent the happiest years of my life in that house, that's where I'll end them.'

Gathering around them, the family were reassuring him, contradicting his assumption that he was dying; Amos ignored them indiscriminately, even snorting his disgust with Phillida whom he'd selected to accommodate him.

Despite her anxiety, Isobel couldn't avoid thinking that he'd never been much of a diplomat. But was it just recently that he'd ceased to be sufficiently tactful to look after his own interests?

Henry and William had fetched one of the carriages. Together, they carried the old man bodily from the wall where he'd been sitting.

'Thank you,' Amos muttered when he was installed. 'And don't you forget, Will, it's your house I'm going to.' He glanced up as Isobel led the others towards them. 'I'm none going wi' her and that husband of hers – I saw how he was siding wi' Gaukroger.'

Their father's health was creating such concern that they all seemed preoccupied. Even the youngsters were subdued as everyone piled into the carriages. Isobel was sickened, firstly by the old man's blaming her for letting Gaukroger near him, but also because she'd been glad to remain apart from the others at the top of Stoodley Pike. She felt the straining of her own loyalties.

★

No sooner had Amos been assisted into the house in Heptonstall than he declared himself recovered. William sent for the doctor, nevertheless, who pronounced his father remarkably well for a man of his years.

'Do you wish me to stay overnight?' Isobel asked Phillida.

'I don't think there's any need. There's more than enough of us here, while Henry and Catalina and the children are stopping wi' us.'

Eyebrows soared. Each of them reflected silently that the house belonged as much to Henry as to his brother.

'Well, at least we're not far away if you have to get a message to us,' said Isobel.

There could be no pretending that she wished to remain while her father was in his present mood. Being scared on his behalf was bad enough, but she'd been hurt by his belligerence.

'What had perturbed the old man this time?' Paul inquired as he assisted her up into their carriage again.

His 'this time' angered her. Was Paul's attitude changing, or had he previously disguised his impatience with Amos?

'As a matter of fact, you started it – by making a fuss of old Gaukroger. When he came over to us Father was seething.'

'I was merely being civil. Gaukroger's a family friend. It isn't only Brights who have family, you know.'

'Well, we've done it now, or you have! Father's allus slow to relent, like as not he'll always hold it against us.'

'Hold what, for heaven's sake? You're becoming as irrational as he is, Isobel. I've done nothing.'

Except being in with them that's ruining Bright's, she thought, and decided that *that* was best left unsaid.

When they arrived at home, Isobel resolved to say no more. She wasn't likely to change Paul.

'We'll allus have differences,' she observed as she went from room to room lighting lamps. 'We made up our minds that they'd not come between us.'

Although Paul agreed, the next few days were no easier. Amos did, indeed, seem to be so greatly weakened that he would be unlikely to outlive another winter. Isobel visited him whenever she could make the time, and always his greeting was frigid with disapproval.

261

She had the reason confirmed when Paul escorted her there.

'Sure you can spare the time from fraternising wi' mill owners?' his father-in-law snapped the moment Paul came in.

'My work's in a mill, isn't it?' said Paul gently. 'I'd always thought you were big enough to see it the way I do – that our jobs are very different, but both deserving of respect.'

Amos grunted. 'Of course, *you* would have to have t'last word – allus full of your fancy talk.'

When Paul would have replied, Isobel gave him a warning look.

Her father saw the glance and misinterpreted its meaning.

'Go on, the pair on you. You've only come here to gloat over me.'

'That's not true,' Isobel retorted. 'We came out of concern for you. Though, the way you carry on, I'm beginning to wonder why.'

Amos glowered at them, his grey eyes icy beneath their thick white brows. Nothing suited him, these days. He'd demanded to be brought here because he wanted to be in his old home, and to have nowt to do with Isobel and Paul. What he hadn't considered was Phillida, who'd always made such a fuss about the least little drop of drink.

After William, then also Henry and Catalina left Yorkshire again, there seemed no one to understand how her father's animosity disturbed Isobel.

Paul grew tired of listening. The day he decided to take action he said nothing to her, merely explaining that factory business would prevent his dining at home.

He arrived to see his father-in-law just as Phillida was clearing the table after their meal. Opening the door to Paul and his companion, her green eyes widened in amazement.

'You'll ask us in, naturally,' Paul prompted, then he stood back to let the older man precede him.

Amos was settling into his chair beside the hearth. When he saw who was visiting them, he struggled to his feet, rapped on the fender with his cane.

'Phillida,' he called, about to ask her to show them out.

Paul was too swift for him. 'Mr Gaukroger wishes to speak with you. I'm sure you'll not be so uncivil as to refuse to listen to him . . .'

'You're sure, are you?' his father-in-law retorted. 'That just goes to show you know nowt about me. I've said afore that I've nowt to say to Samson Gaukroger, you're a fool for bringing him here.'

'Isn't it time you let bygones . . .' Paul began, and got no further.

Amos spluttered, clutched at his throat, while his face turned an unhealthy bluish red.

'Now look what you've done,' Phillida accused them, converging with them at her father-in-law's side. 'If he passes away wi' this lot, I wonder who'll be to blame . . .'

'I'll fetch the doctor,' Paul volunteered, already striding towards the door.

Samson Gaukroger offered to come with him, but they parted in the road. Paul felt sorry for Gaukroger. He was an old man now, shouldn't have to endure the venom of the other old soul back there.

'I'm sorry,' Paul said. 'I only thought it might have worked.'

'As it could have, wi' some folk. Unfortunately, Amos Bright isn't one for admitting that producing cloth in factories is inevitable.'

Returning with the doctor, Paul discovered Amos comatose in his chair, his head propped against cushions while Phillida stroked a hand knotted with veins and misshapen by gout.

'It seems to me it's his heart,' the doctor pronounced gravely. 'If we leave him where he is, he'll be dashed uncomfortable if he survives. Yet carrying him up to his bed could be the finish of him.'

They moved him, nevertheless, with the doctor supporting the invalid's shoulders and instructing Paul who was taking his feet.

Being carried upstairs didn't kill Amos. He appeared rather better with pillows shaken by Phillida to support him, and additional blankets to warm the circulation back into limbs so pale they resembled wax.

'I'm going for Isobel,' Paul stated while the doctor was still present. 'We shan't be more than a few minutes.'

He read in Phillida's glance that she believed Isobel would only accelerate her father's demise, but if Amos was dying, he'd have his only daughter present. Whether he wished that nor not.

Clutching Paul's arm, for she was indeed inclined to believe that Amos had lived his span, Isobel emerged from their carriage but then she freed herself to run up to the front door.

'Hallo, Phillie,' she said grimly. 'Is it all right if I go up?'

Amos had been dozing but was awakened by her voice down below. Briefly, he was delighted, thinking of chatting with his daughter, having her company relieve this pain gnawing right through his ribs. But he remembered then whose husband had brought this trouble.

When Isobel entered the bedroom he was scowling, reminding her of a miserable, wrinkled child. Perhaps that was why she scolded him.

'You've given us all a proper fright again, I hope you understand that? There's no need for any of this, you know, it's only because you've worked yourself into a tantrum. Happen it's time we all stopped resisting progress . . .'

'*What?*' Amos demanded. 'Say that again and I'll knock some sense into you, sick though I am and old as you are. Nay, lass, it's them that's killing Bright's. It's fighting you should be, not giving in.'

'I have fought,' she said resignedly, suddenly feeling as old as the man in the bed, 'but I'm afraid them days are over.'

'You're too soft, you allus have been.' Her father choked on his words, coughed, and rallied. 'Each mill they set up is nailing into t'coffin of cloth businesses like ours. Nay, Isobel, you've let me down. Never . . . thought I'd . . . live to be so . . . disappointed in you.'

The final words emerged in a series of gasps. His head slumped sideways, the strange sound made by the breath at the back of his throat startled them.

Isobel felt Paul's hand on her shoulder. 'I think, love, it's time you said goodbye to your father.'

None of it seemed real; not the lifeless old man who merely resembled her father, not Paul's touch, nor her own strange numbness. Why couldn't she *feel*, why not sense that this was her father with whom she had worked since being a child of twelve, why did she merely feel so empty?

Grief came several days later, after the physical part of Amos Bright had been laid in Heptonstall churchyard. All his kin, and many old associates including Samson Gaukroger had attended the beautiful funeral. It was afterwards, while the family were sitting around the table in the house where they had grown up, that Isobel recognised the turmoil inside her as tears ripe for shedding.

'I'm off home now,' she murmured abruptly to Paul beside her and, leaving her step-daughter staring after her, ran from the room and out into the late afternoon drizzle.

Her father was dead. As long as he'd lived there'd been someone who cared that Bright's still kept going. Today, she felt bereft of her work, as well as of her remaining parent. What had it all been for? There'd been her early battle to make folk accept that she was capable within the business. And there had been struggles ever since, first while her father was floating himself in drink, then in attempting to stop the mill owners setting up with machinery. After that there'd been the unending effort to continue trading, while cheaper cloth was being offered everywhere. And as old weavers died off, new men rejected working ancient looms in upper rooms of wayside cottages.

Had she been misled – by her youthful dreams which, attaching her as they had to the Piece Hall in Halifax, had yoked her to a system already outliving its viability? Had what she'd believed to be the *vision*, compelling her to smash all that new-fangled machinery, been merely her own stubbornness? No less bigoted than her father's.

Even folk who hadn't really taken to Isobel had been unable to deny she possessed determination. But had she employed it in all the wrong ways, and merely to substantiate her own self-esteem?

Mrs Field their housekeeper was over in Todmorden, visiting an aunt. The house felt cheerless, depressing her even further. Her tears had dried on her cheeks in the wind as she walked down the hill, and now she couldn't weep again, though her heart felt as hard and uncomfortable inside her as a smoothing iron.

I won't let this get the better of me, Isobel resolved. This introspection was only a result of her grief. And of the words which her father had etched into her brain by making them his last.

Refusing to marry Paul might have stopped this division between mill folk and traditional clothiers disturbing her own hearth, she pondered. That meeting with Samson Gaukroger up by Stoodley Pike would have perturbed Amos less if his son-in-law hadn't greeted Gaukroger so warmly. But although her marriage to Paul was not as sound as it might be, she'd not wish away its benefits.

She was just longing for someone now, someone to understand her conflict, arms that would hold her. And for reassurance that her energies hadn't always been misplaced. It didn't help her when she had the strange feeling that it wasn't Paul who might provide this.

She was still cold with the emptiness of the house, still adjusting to bereavement – the memories to admit, the self-recrimination – when Paul eventually strode into their parlour. He swung Audrey down from his shoulder and set her on her feet then looked at his wife.

'Well, that's it . . . There's the house to be sold, some of the furniture'll fetch a decent price. We've decided Bright's will be sold, of course . . .'

'Will it?' Until his return, she'd been on the point of acknowledging that happen the time had come for one clothier, at least, to surrender to modern ways. Her family's automatic assumption that there was no other course stuck in her throat. 'I don't often make an issue over decisions that you've reached, do I?' she heard herself saying with a quiet disguising the violence of her disappointment. 'Maybe that's where I've been wrong. Bright's has nowt to do with you, it never has had. And not a great deal to do wi' them back

yonder. I was the one that had to keep it going through all
them years while father was drinking away the profits. I kept
it going through that, Paul, and I'll not sell at your say-so.
Nor on t'word of any of them that never lifted a finger.'

'They're your family, Isobel. They only want to do what's
best . . .'

'For whom?' she snorted. 'For me? They're just considering themselves. And as far as our Will and Henry are
concerned, that's how they've allus thought.'

'Just reflect how things will be, now there's no Amos to fall
back on. You'd never be free; if not out with that blessed
wagon, you'd be sitting up till all hours poring over ledgers.'

'There's worse things,' she said shortly. And wished with
all her heart she didn't have this premonition that she'd been
right, earlier. When she'd supposed it stubborn to continue
as a clothier.

17

'I used to admire my sister's spirit. I'm afraid nowadays I can only view it as stupidity.'

William was with Rosalind, sitting on their balcony in Oporto, watching the sun sinking beyond the city towards the Atlantic, while they sipped from glasses of the wine that was his livelihood.

'But she has managed for years, hasn't she, since you lost your father – and in a trade that's hardly a lady's province.' Although she'd never met Isobel, having been kept well away from William's family, Rosalind liked what she'd heard of her.

'She writes in her latest letter of her dread that some rift is developing between herself and Paul. And who's to wonder – with her toiling day long, and in work that competes with the mill he manages? She's a woman, isn't she, must possess some homemaking instincts! I'll maybe talk some sense into her while I'm there.' Though he'd scarcely find time for owt but his own problems. They were into 1826 and he was returning to Yorkshire soon to give his daughter in marriage.

Despite intense opposition from Phillida, Jessica was to wed her cousin Jorge. William doubted that his wife would have readily approved any man for her daughter, but no choice could have been worse than a son of Catalina.

He could see Phillie now, as she'd been during his latest visit, on the Sunday that Jessica had declared her intention. William already felt uneasy in that house on the hill at Heptonstall. When Phillida stormed in from the chapel she could hardly contain her vexation.

'You'll have to speak to her,' she began immediately. 'I won't have this! If the girl remains a spinster till the day she dies, I'll not watch her throwing herself away on *him*.'

'Do I take it that Jessica's announced her desire to marry?'

'Aye, and if you were a proper father to her things would never have reached this stage. You'd have been here to put a stop to it.'

'Who is this young fellow that you've taken such exception to?'

'Jorge.'

'George? George who. . . ?'

'Jorge, of course. Your own brother's lad. *That half-Spanish . . .*'

'Oh.' William was surprised, but not displeased. 'He *is* a Bright, Phillida. I'm not ashamed of our stock, and you shouldn't . . .'

'Don't tell me what I should or should not think. You're no judge. Else why would you spend t'best part of your life away from home?'

'My work is there. And you could both have lived with me.' He saw her expression darken. 'I know – you tried.' *Once* had proved nothing.

'I couldn't help not liking Oporto. And you have been away so much. Now Jessica's that out of control she'll marry against our wishes.'

'I haven't said that *I* don't approve of young Jorge.'

'Are you refusing to support me? You can't really want him wed to our daughter?'

'He seems to me to be a personable young man.'

Phillida snorted. 'You would say that. I've tried to discourage them for years. I've got eyes, and I'm not daft. I've seen this coming. You should have watched what they were about, prevented it.'

'And have them flee to Gretna? Jessica's fully capable of that.'

'Precisely,' Phillida snapped. 'That's the very reason I'm so vexed. They've connived to keep this to themselves until there's nowt we can do to stop that wedding. I blame that dreadful scandal last March. When that Ellen Turner caused such a commotion.'

'Commotion?'

'You'll not have heard, of course. Only a schoolgirl she

was, when she went dashing to Gretna Green with Edward Gibbon Wakefield.'

'But surely . . .'

'I thought at the time it was nobbut a bit of nonsense when Jessica kept on about how romantic it was.'

From the look in his grey eyes, Will was blaming *her*. How dared he come back here, after all these years, and find fault with her.

Phillida breathed deeply. A pulse vibrated in her head which felt as though a steel band compressed it.

'I felt so sure that I'd put them off marrying . . .' she gasped. Her voice, sounding so feeble, disgusted her. Hadn't she considered, all along, that she was a match for two headstrong youngsters. That she'd keep them apart, without help from William.

'You did know then that something was going on?' William frowned, willing himself not to state that she'd only herself to blame.

'And so did you – even when she was a little lass Jessica was partial to young Jorge.' And Phillida was most distressed by learning their daughter's plans from the minister.

'Our Jessica's done this on purpose, I'll warrant. Waiting to have us told until she was out of t'road staying with your Charles. *Told*, mind you, and her so young they've got to have our permission.'

He could only trust to his determination that the ceremony itself would be unmarred by dissent to get them through the day. He was thankful Charles would be present. He himself and Henry would be too heavily involved to induce a cheerful atmosphere.

Charles had grown rather apart from the rest of the Brights, despite being so close in age to Isobel. But her absorption with the cloth trade had precluded much socialising, even within the family. And their youngest brother appeared to have channelled everything into being a lawyer. Once a garrulous youth, he seemed to hold his tongue except for speeches in support of his clients. But if the family rarely saw him, Charles was to hand should he be needed. William hadn't seen him since their father's funeral. They corresponded once or twice in every year, although because of such

270

letters being addressed to Phillida, as well as himself, in Heptonstall it was often weeks afterwards that he saw them.

Returning to the present, William glanced towards Rosalind and said softly, 'There'll be nothing to tie me to Phillida once our Jessica's gone.'

She said nothing. She had schooled herself for fourteen years now to accept the joy they shared, and to hope for no more than that their joint existence here might continue. If it should come about that William declared their relationship openly, she would be supremely happy. But she'd not tempt the fates by seeking to change their situation.

The blue-mauve blossom of the jacarandas resembled a coloured mist swirling about their house in Jerez as Henry walked with his younger son in its gardens. It was scarcely daylight yet, he was anxious to get to the bodega, but he must first speak seriously with Jorge.

'You know the difference, I trust, between the love you profess to feel and desire that plagues without ceasing because the girl isn't for taking?'

'Oh yes, Father. Jessica's my cousin, remember, I know her very thoroughly.'

'I could hardly forget that fact,' said Henry dryly. Only last night, Catalina had again voiced doubts about such close relations marrying. He wasn't certain if her Church forbade such a union, had resolutely *not* asked her, but there appeared to be no chapel ruling to prevent it.

'You are certain then that you'll still be in love when passion wanes, as it eventually will, and you're no longer so obsessed with bedding her?'

'Did you grow tired of Mother, did you exhaust your love when you sated this "passion" you keep mentioning?'

His father resisted the impulse to cuff Jorge about the ears, and went on, 'You're prepared for the differences, I hope, Jorge. Jessica's grounded in her Methodist faith . . .'

'. . . And I've been reared a Roman Catholic. Surely, Father, you're the last to question if mixed marriages can be made to work.'

271

All the way in the carriage as he headed towards the bodega Henry continued to muse on their youngest child's future. He freely admitted to hardly knowing the girl herself, these days. He had ceased noticing more than that she increasingly resembled her mother. She was a beautiful creature, he'd not been so indifferent that he was oblivious to that. But the wilfulness created by Phillida's everlasting indulgence of the girl made him exasperated with her. Would she make Jorge contented, *could* she do so?

Perhaps I'm being prejudiced because Jessica's mother failed to hold on to our Will? he wondered wryly. Prejudging offspring by their parents' shortcomings was neither fair nor justified.

The sun was hot now, reflecting back from the white walls of the bodega, reminding him that next month when they were into June the heat would grow unendurable. He was planning to remain in London following the trip to Yorkshire for the wedding. Catalina had intended staying with him, but her mother's health was causing concern and might result in his wife's early return to Spain.

They had been fortunate that Carmen Escutia, although around eighty years old now, had until recently been remarkably well. After overcoming the immediate grief of her bereavement she had endured widowhood and given no one reason to suppose she was unduly miserable.

He wished his own mother could have adapted to the changes life had brought for her, felt certain that if she'd given her mind to it she might have been alive even today. And as for his father . . . Henry sighed. Well, at least, none of them appeared to have inherited his fondness for the bottle. And that's just as well, he reflected. If either he or William had been inclined to overindulgence they'd have been six foot under, long ago.

Rebuilding the business after both Portugal and Spain were ravaged by war hadn't been easy, but both he and Will had found it satisfying. Luckily they worked sufficiently well together, neither having too much say in the other's territory, except for their one major disagreement . . . The carefulness inherent in most Yorkshire folk had meant that he'd continued to prevent their spending capital on the West Riding offices which had, initially, seemed so tempting. In all the intervening years, he'd never got William to admit that he'd been proved right to be so cautious. But he could live with Will's obstinacy. With his resentment too, if need be.

Henry wished, occasionally, that Luke and Matthew Fortescue could have lived to see that the company which they had initiated still survived, and that it was now extending. They competed well with regard to both port and sherry.

Here in Spain, despite the revolution which resurged repeatedly to generate commercial and civil chaos, life was agreeable as well as prosperous. Relations with other sherry merchants continued in that strange combination of intense competitiveness and fellow feeling. And within their own company he was gratified by the involvement of his children. Ignacio was studying all aspects of production and was being trained by Alberto Martinez as their next capataz.

Catalina had returned to Fortescue's and was involved, in the main, on the financial side; the knowledge that she had a finger on this aspect of the business freed Henry to deal with other matters. In good years as well as bad, there were crises with the harvest. As word spread more easily about the country and beyond it, labourers gathering the grapes were less readily satisfied. The inevitable unrest was sometimes settled in the vineyards by his managers, but quite often it was only Henry himself who negotiated, and he who ultimately sanctioned an increase in the wages paid. Physically, he now found such problems taxing, he was after all in his middle fifties. Yet he'd never lost his enthusiasm for the life he'd chosen.

For the first time that he could recall in recent years, William had a smile on his lips and in his head when he climbed the hill towards the house. All the way from London in the mail coach, he'd been weighing the prospects for Jessica's future, and had concluded that *he* could help by instilling the right mood of gladness.

He was delighted that young Jorge would become his son-in-law, why shouldn't he show them this? And maybe confound the doubts of others! He would tell Jessica he was pleased, encourage her to prove all misgivings unfounded. He'd have a quiet talk with her, would put it to her that she was the person to prove to folk that this decision was the right one.

The shrieking met him before he'd left the lane for the last few yards of track to their door. Phillida's voice was the more strident, but Jessica's no less assertive. Without attempting to learn what they were saying, he resisted the growing impulse to stride right past, away up the hill, and hastened to the door.

'You'll not wed him, I say,' Phillida was shouting, so immersed in their quarrel that she was oblivious to her husband's arrival.

Jessica saw her father, and used his presence. 'There's only you says anything wrong against Jorge, Mother. And I no longer care! Father has nothing against him. Stay away, if you must, but I'll keep away from this house afterwards.'

'What's all this about then?' asked Will, though he knew well enough what caused the continuing battle between mother and daughter.

'See if you can talk sense to her,' Phillida snapped. 'She's that besotted she can't see she's throwing herself away.'

The absence of any greeting for himself stung, despite the years of indifference between them. Only his daughter seemed to sense this.

'Hallo, Father . . .' Jessica paused, gave him a hug, but the touch of her lips on his cheek was cool, absorbed as she was in the conflict.

'I've told her time and again that she'll rue the day she takes Jorge. Their ways are not ours . . .'

Thank goodness, thought William. Or Jorge'd have a loveless life ahead of him.

'They're brought up different, he'll not have any understanding of how our Jessica should be looked after,' Phillida concluded.

'And he's Catalina's son,' Jessica stated quietly, but with

all her bitterness towards her mother in her exquisite green eyes.

'You'll neither of you win, can't you see that?' Will interrupted, hanging his coat on the hook behind the door. 'You're driving your words like a hatchet into a relationship you both rely on. You, Jessica, should respect your mother's opinion. She is acting for your good, and from her feeling that nothing will ever be *too* good for you.'

Jessica's look conveyed that she didn't believe this. But he had silenced her. Phillida was near to tears, shaking with fury.

'I will speak with you later, Phillida.' Swallowing his sigh, he glanced from one to the other. 'Meanwhile, you'll keep peace in this house, or I'll be out of it by nightfall. And I'd not return. You'd better think on, or there'll be no one to give the bride in marriage.'

It was some while later when William eventually tackled his wife: 'Is there something I've not learned, that you've taken against young Jorge with such ferocity?' he inquired, sitting in his old chair near the hearth.

Phillida was busying herself with needle and thread, steadying fingers that still shook as she inserted tiny stitches in Jessica's wedding finery.

'No, nothing new, not as I've heard. It is, like she said, a matter of who he is. I'm only surprised that you don't see it the same way.'

What fresh remark could he make? They had covered this ground. And with Jorge himself not here to speak up, it all appeared grossly unfair.

'He's a decent young fellow, not given to any kind of overindulgence, a willing worker.' And *he* smiles now and again, will introduce some light into our lass's life, he added silently. 'Ay, Phillida, where's your sense? You'd achieve nowt, any road, if you could stop it. You'd only antagonise our Jessica, drive her away. We could still force them towards Gretna Green.'

'But . . .'

Her weary eyes shone with unshed tears, the lines developing over her face seemed more deeply etched.

William felt intense compassion for her, yet at the same time longed to shake her until he imbued more sense.

'Haven't you thought, lass, that she'd never stop here if you got her to give him up? Where'd she be then – on her own wi' nobody to look after her?'

The following morning the more congenial atmosphere suggested that his warning might have found its home. Although resignation, rather than anticipation, predominated in Phillida's manner, she'd ceased suggesting the ceremony be cancelled.

William was satisfied when Jorge and his family arrived later in the day and Phillida appeared to welcome them.

This calm, however insubstantial, lasted until they were gathered in the octagonal chapel when Jessica, at his side, was so radiant that he, for one, could scarcely contain emotion.

Her mother, as well, looked so magnificent that Will noticed the beauty originally enrapturing him. Phillida had chosen a most flattering gown. Its skirt resembled a trumpet, being full and arranged so that it widened towards the hem. The sleeves also were voluminous, but it was the shade that most attracted him; a gold colour which gleamed when she moved and enhanced the still-brilliant auburn of her hair.

Willing away a sigh for the love that they had lost, he placed his daughter's hand in his crooked arm for their walk towards her bridegroom.

The unfamiliarity of the chapel ruffled William's composure, making him long for the nave of Heptonstall church and a ceremony he'd have appreciated.

Gathering afterwards at the house, family and friends appeared compressed into so little space that seeking out those whom he wished to greet provided difficulties. But Jessica and her Jorge beamed happiness from their glowing young faces, assuring everyone that all misgivings had been unfounded. Even Phillida appeared quite calm. Tomorrow he'd be setting out for Oporto.

'No, Will, not in there . . .'

Phillida had taken care to keep him downstairs on some pretext until Henry and Catalina and all their family were settled in their rooms after their exhausting day. Covertly watching for the first sign of William's heading upstairs, she'd contrived to be close at his side as he reached the first landing.

'We couldn't refuse them the beds they requested,' she continued. And she'd not provide any of that lot with proof that she and Will were finished.

Glad of the half-light, for he felt his eyes narrowing, William elected to give no sign that he would only reluctantly share her room. Phillida would learn soon enough that, despite her attractiveness today, he would withhold his response.

Following her into the master bedroom he observed the fresh décor, which presumably he'd at some time financed. The bed hangings were a delightful brocade, similar in shade to her gown which he'd privately admired in the chapel. The walls above the wooden dado were a delicate tone of peach, warm in the candles' glow, intended as welcoming.

'So, there's only you and me again, Will. We've weathered a few difficulties, I grant, but we've come together again. That's good.'

'Not "together" in every sense, Phillida,' he began. There was no point in misapprehensions. 'There's been too much awry between us for any instant reconciliation.'

'I can't agree.'

She was removing her gown already, each movement from one button to the next precise and deliberate. It occurred to him that her plans were just as precise. If she had her way he'd be into that bed and coupling with her as though there'd been no intervening years. And no Rosalind.

'And I'll not have any of t'rest of your family thinking we're no longer man and wife,' she continued, removing one layer of undergarments.

Slowly, his back to her, William began unfastening his own buttons. 'I don't mean to pass the night upright in a chair, that is for certain,' he assured her. 'But as for this being for the benefit of our Henry and so on, you're rather late with your pretence, Phillida. He's known for long enough that it's not here that I look for my comfort.'

'*I beg your pardon. . .?*'

The raising of her voice suddenly struck him as amusing. 'Careful, lass, you'll have them hear you.'

'I want them to hear! If what I think you're saying is the truth, I want you shamed by the whole world knowing.'

'Even them at t'chapel?' It was a mean reaction, but a natural one, though he'd not forgive himself later for seeming small-minded. 'You'd better think, Phillida, before you choose. You can have us continue to simulate marriage, or you can declare that I've abandoned you in favour of Rosalind Parker. She's the daughter of a fellow port shipper, keenly interested in the business. She also happens to care quite considerably about me.'

'I care. I'm your wife, confound it.'

'And confounded is precisely how I feel when contemplating this façade of a marriage. When have you supported me, Phillida, either by your presence or by your interest in anything I've achieved?' He paused, praying that he might hurt her as little as possible while he expressed conclusions reached over many years and with some considerable degree of pain. 'It's best we now recognise the true situation, and free each other – if only privately.'

'What's that supposed to mean?'

'That I'd spare you the embarrassment of public knowledge that our relationship is ended. And, naturally, I'll provide for your needs.'

Phillida bit back her direction as to where he might consign his money. She'd no desire to spin yarn day and night in order to exist here alone, while he consorted with this Parker woman. Already convinced that her life without Jessica was to be intolerably wearisome, she'd ensure she at least gained the wherewithal to provide some comfort.

'I trust that you will,' she responded, with all the dignity she could dredge from within. 'Well, you'll most likely plan to take what belongings you value when you depart first thing.' Inwardly weeping, she gathered up her clothes and walked from the room.

She might have always known that William was unhappy, just as she'd acknowledged secretly the enormity of her own disappointment in their marriage. It was her punishment, of course, for yielding to the sensual enticement which even today he exuded. The tragedy was that, if God could forgive her for this weakness, she'd not forgive Him for the dreadful outcome.

18

Isobel was sad to see Henry and Catalina leave the West Riding yet again, but had been sadder still when William had departed and no word of goodbye to anyone.

'I've thought for a long time as he and Phillida had a poor marriage,' she began whilst sitting with Paul over dinner.

'Whose isn't lacking?' he murmured dourly.

She frowned across the table. She could neither forget nor forgive his latest attempt at forcing her to sell Bright's in order to finance his bids at last month's auction in Todmorden. Glad enough that he was actually taking a day off from his precious mill, Isobel had set out with him in their carriage.

Auctions were of no interest to her and she hadn't inquired what items were up for offer. Initially, she was rather bored to discover that the Tolls upon local Turnpike Roads were up for letting.

'Why have you brought me here?' she whispered, as the room filled with business men and she looked around in vain for another woman.

Paul merely warned her to keep still and silent. 'You'd best not have them think you're bidding until there's a tollgate you've an interest in.'

Isobel snorted. The only interest was in each tollgate being put up at the amount of profit raised in the previous year. There was some disparity between the amounts. King Cross, Tuel-Lane and Longbottom, had altogether produced a mere £440, while Todmorden appeared to be worth an impressive £920.

She was staggered when Paul made a bid for the latter. If he possessed that kind of money, he'd kept the fact to himself, depriving her of the opportunity to find a better use for it! Her amazement turned rapidly to disbelief as he proceeded to outbid everyone else and was called upon to give the appropriate securities.

The next few minutes were so confused and utterly embarrassing that Isobel never recalled the details coherently. What had emerged from their urgent discussion was that he expected her to sell Bright's to raise the capital.

'I'll do no such thing,' she asserted, appalled by the stupidity of his attempting to coerce her by contriving this situation. 'And certainly not when there's been no prior discussion.'

'But you could interest yourself in keeping records of the tolls,' Paul was beginning when Isobel flung away from him and, pushing a way through the throng, headed for the door.

Out on the pavement, she had stood motionless, willing herself not to weep with annoyance. And then she'd walked on briskly, to the first carriage available for hire.

Paul had returned home irritated by being compelled to extract himself from the bid by admitting he lacked the necessary resources. But he had apologised to her. He'd even assured her that he hadn't understood the extent of her commitment to Bright's and would never again try persuading her to relinquish it.

The harm was done, though, leaving her convinced that it had been solely for the sake of gaining a homemaker that he'd asked for her hand. And was this less than she deserved? she asked herself wryly. Hadn't it really been liking rather than love on her part?

She was losing weight, she had been for some time. And it was months rather than weeks since they had made love. She missed the intimacy, any feeling that they were united. Somehow, she determined, they must improve the home atmosphere. 'Are you certain you couldn't learn to like some kind of work in your father's mill, Audrey?' Isobel inquired later that week, during a lull between examining materials for a new gown. 'It would please him more than anything in the world, you know.'

'More than your selling Bright's?' Audrey asked. There was no malice in her words, only the recognition that her step-mother would all but compel her to please him, whilst refraining from doing the one thing that *she* could which would achieve that end.

'Ay, love, it's time everybody stopped worriting about me and Bright's – it'll not be so long before selling's forced on me.'

'You'll be upset, won't you?' Audrey's eyes filled compassionately.

'It was grand, in the old days, taking stuff to t' Piece Hall. I was younger than you, you know, when I began going.'

'Why do you think I'd prefer to join you there?'

'You're a good lass, I couldn't wish for a better daughter.'

'What will you do, though, when it's all gone?'

Isobel only shook her head, unable to visualise, not wishing to make the attempt.

'There's that many changes going on, these days, no one can say, not for sure. All these mills springing up, new sources of power. Then look at these railway engines they're developing . . .'

'I've heard tell in the town that George Stephenson plans to visit Jerez, what do you think to that, eh?' Henry had come striding in, glowing with enthusiasm.

Catalina raised a dark eyebrow, although she was smiling. 'I thought we managed well enough getting our sherry to the vessels without a railway . . .'

Her husband laughed, 'Maybe we don't need one, but it could help Spain to modernise in this way. And, anyway, it'd do no harm for folk here to have such an inventive man in their midst for a while.'

'Are you saying we are a backward race?'

To laugh again would have been unfair, but her indignant expression did amuse him, and reminded him of the rather assertive woman 'he'd fallen in love with. When her dark eloquent eyes prompted him to enlighten her further about George Stephenson's proposed visit, Henry shook his head, but he'd been warmed by the thought that a British inventor was interested in making developments over here.

His wife had spent a few hours that day at the Escutia

house, he asked after her mother and was perturbed by Catalina's frown.

'I do not know, Henry – there appears to be no definable illness, yet she most certainly appears listless and unwell.'

'Happen a change would do her good – do you suppose she'd come to England with me next month?'

Catalina considered for a moment, but still seemed unsure. 'We could ask her. I'd have thought she was a little too old for long journeys, but I may be wrong.'

'It would mean you could come as well if you no longer had to remain here for her sake.'

'But we've only recently returned from Yorkshire. And I am not at all certain that Mother would relish staying with Phillida.'

'I can imagine. We could ask Isobel, though, I believe she would happily accommodate us.'

Carmen Escutia looked very grand, attired in the black she'd worn ever since her husband's death, but today in the very latest style. Her skirts were full, trumpet-shaped and rustling over wide petticoats, her sleeves were bell-shaped, of fine black lace. Her regal deportment and aristocratic features commanded respect wherever she strolled on deck, and won her admiration. She felt rejuvenated already, was enjoying the experience immensely.

'I cannot imagine why I have never travelled more widely in the past,' she confided to her son-in-law. 'I believe it suits my constitution.'

The entire voyage delighted her, any discomforts seemed only to be a challenge and, instead of sickening as Henry and Catalina had feared she might, when rough seas consigned others to their cabins, Carmen continued to explore the ship.

The captain had noticed her, of course, and consequently the three of them were frequently invited to dine at his table. Relishing yet another new experience, Señora Escutia regaled him with stories of her youth and more than a few episodes in recent Andalusian history.

Their journey by stage coach as far as London was less to

her taste, but she steeled herself to endure indifferent food in the coaching inns and resolved to make up for the journey's shortcomings when they eventually gained the capital.

London was dry and dusty and hot that September but to someone accustomed to the heat of southern Spain it felt agreeably warm. While Henry attended Fortescue's City office, Catalina and her mother hired carriages that took them from The Tower to Westminster or out to Hampton Court where they became absorbed in British history.

Most evenings, tired by the day's excursions, Carmen was content to dine quietly in their hotel before retiring; but they made one visit to Astley's Theatre. Catalina and her husband exchanged sympathetic smiles while Señora Escutia, exhausted already, pretended that her difficulty with the language wasn't reducing her to repeated dozing.

There could be no lapses into sleep once they arrived in the West Riding. Paul met them off the mail coach and drove them swiftly in his open landau away from Halifax, along the valley of the Calder and up the steep incline to his home near Heptonstall.

The wind was fresh and quite as strong as any which, at certain times of year, tore over the land around Cadiz. Carmen was chilled to her prominent bones, but she merely sat more erectly and smiled more determinedly at features of the landscape. And the wooded slopes, soaring from river banks, often to finish in craggy heights, certainly impressed her. The stone houses had a stout look which she found pleasing, and she won a grin from Paul by remarking that they should endure for some years.

'That's right, Señora Escutia, trust Yorkshire folk to build to last. We're careful with our money here, you know.'

'And that is as it should be,' she agreed. Although short of nothing, she'd learned from other widows that consideration of the future was essential.

The welcome Isobel had prepared banished every last suspicion of chill. A massive fire was blazing on the hearth and, though it was scarcely dusk, every candle in the chandelier was lit.

Isobel had thought her husband's new acquisition

ostentatious for a home that was only moderately large, but today she was glad of its light, and of its evident signs of their material success. She'd always known that Catalina's family were quite well off. Although delighted to have Carmen Escutia here, she herself was always too busy to have done much entertaining.

From the moment of being shown to her room, however, their guest smiled delightedly and approved everything. And she asked Isobel to refrain from drawing the curtains until she'd admired the view. 'You live in beautiful countryside, Isobel.'

'And I'll take you on my favourite walks, if I may.'

'I hope that you will. What I would most like, though, would be to accompany you while you work. I have heard for so many years about your marketing of cloth . . .'

Isobel was astonished. 'Oh, but . . . I'd love to show you, but – well, we go in the wagon, you understand, it's most uncomfortable.'

Carmen's laugh was sharp, her near-black eyes glinted. 'One advantage of age, Isobel, is that one ceases to worry too greatly concerning the consequences of a little discomfort. I shall look forward to joining you.'

Isobel had instructed Alfred Hanson and Joseph, the lad they employed, to fill the front of the wagon with rugs and cushions. All the cloth pieces were stacked with even more than usual care in order to prevent their falling with the jolting of the wagon.

The morning was dry, at least, and the wind had dropped when they set out. Providing that the weather didn't change as sharply as it had all those years ago on this same journey, they should be passably comfortable.

'The cloth in which you deal is, I believe, all woven in the homes of your artisans?' Señora Escutia began as they trundled down the hill to join the main route from Lancashire.

'Yes, that's right, every yard of it. Did Catalina tell you?'

The older woman nodded. 'I was asking her to explain the difference between the cloth your husband's factory produces and your own.'

'And did she tell you they use big machines in the factories?'

'Which, I gather, have cut down on manpower.'

'They have an' all.' Isobel hesitated for a moment, then began telling her about the gang she had joined. 'I think, on the whole, the Luddites might have saved themselves the trouble. The mills ended up full of machines just the same in the end.'

'But you had to try – you cared so deeply to preserve the old ways.'

Her ready understanding made Isobel smile, warmed her still further towards this elegant Spanish lady whose dark eyes reminded her of Carlos.

The sun was reaching them now it had risen over the surrounding hills. Alfred Hanson removed his hat, grinned at the lad beside him as he doffed his own.

'Alfred has been invaluable to me,' Isobel explained quietly. 'He's turned out that well! He was nobbut a bit of a lad when we took him on.'

'And now he's educating this new young man in the business?'

'That's right. I just wish I believed Bright's would last long enough to give him a steady job.'

'That sounds ominous, Isobel . . .'

'The competition from factory-produced cloth is so unfair. They can weave that much faster, and they don't have to traipse all over t'West Riding collecting up the pieces either. Then there's Paul. I'd have sold out long since, if I listened to him.'

Half regretting her frankness, Isobel ceased her comments on the clothiers' business and remarked instead on the small stone-housed communities they were passing. She felt guilty about not honouring the essence of all her marriage vows, but she was a person in her own right, should perhaps have some entitlement to her own will. And with his mother beside her how could she not remember Carlos? What kind of life would she have had with him. . . ?

By the time they halted at King Cross to pay their turnpike toll, Isobel was putting misgivings behind her.

286

And soon they were arriving at the Piece Hall itself. With a tiny exclamation, Carmen Escutia gazed up and around at the tiers of small rooms, the colonnades of sand coloured stone, glowing in the autumn sunlight.

'How magnificent! It does not surprise me that you like this.'

'When I was little I used to imagine it as a palace – daft, I suppose, really.'

'But no – I can visualise elegant carriages drawn by beautiful horses, and exquisitely dressed people gathering here.'

'That's just how I used to see it!'

Although much of the conversation was too swift for her to grasp all the details of the actual dealing, Carmen relished the thrust of keen buying and selling. 'I am greatly impressed with the vitality of business here,' she told Isobel.

'Oh, we still drive a good bargain. But you would have loved it when I began coming with Father. There was a lot more going on.'

Carmen Escutia's entire visit was hugely successful. When she eventually departed with Henry and her daughter she had lost the jaded air which had caused them to worry.

'You will come to Spain again, you must,' they entreated Isobel.

She promised eagerly enough, although she sensed that she would prefer to go there without Paul. She couldn't know that it would be only after being almost destroyed by events that she would carry out the intention to visit them.

Isobel soon had more to trouble her than her husband's shortcomings. One morning four weeks later she prepared as usual for her journey to the Piece Hall. She sensed something amiss as soon as Alfred Hanson and young Joseph, the lad they employed, arrived with the laden wagon. All day long she was aware that the two were ill-at-ease with her.

After all the cloth was sold Alfred requested a private word. Isobel led him up to one of the many rooms used by merchants.

'What's on your mind?' It seemed apparent that he wouldn't find words to explain without some prompting.

287

'Ay, Mrs Copley, I don't know where to begin to tell you. I feel that bad about this, we both do, but we haven't really much choice.'

Isobel had a sudden premonition that he was leaving Bright's, but could hardly say anything until he confirmed or denied it. She faced him, and waited again.

'He's offered us that much more to go work for him, we can't neither on us countenance not going.'

She remained determinedly calm. 'I see. And when are you leaving? Where are you going, into one of t'mills, I suppose?'

'Carrying for them. I'll be virtually my own boss. I'll have a free hand, so long as stuff is delivered to time, yet without financial worries. Wagon and t'horses will belong to the boss.'

'Well, Alfred I'll be sorry to see you both go. You in particular when you've been with us so long. You haven't said where you'll be working, somewhere in Halifax?'

Alfred, looking more awkward than ever, shifted from one foot to the other, 'That's worst part about t'job. I'm going to work for Mr Copley.'

'For – Paul. . . ?' Her voice sounded like someone else's, her throat felt so taut. She tried to clear it in order to speak with something resembling her normal confidence.

'Thank you for telling me,' she managed finally.

'It weren't easy, Mrs Copley.'

I should hope not either, thought Isobel, compelling her lips to shape a smile. 'Please tell young Joseph I want a word with him.'

'He'll not change his mind, I'm afraid. Neither of us will.'

'I wouldn't wish you to.' Isobel marshalled all the dignity she could. 'I'd not hold employees who didn't want to stay with Bright's.'

Confronting Paul that evening, Isobel was seething with fury. 'Alfred Hanson told me his news today,' she began, meeting him in the doorway of the parlour when he arrived home from the mill. 'And that you're taking Joseph, as well. You might have left me one of them. But I suppose you thought to so inconvenience me that I'd be compelled to sell out.'

Very briefly, for the moments it took to remove his outdoor coat and transfer it to the hook, he appeared perplexed. When he faced her again, his smile was bland. 'My dear Isobel, I'm sorry. But in business, as experience must have taught you, one cannot consider personal feelings.'

'Evidently not.' And anyway, feelings seemed low on Paul's list of attributes. 'But I would have considered the justice of one's actions might be a factor in dealing fairly.'

'It's a compliment to you, you know – that you've trained your men so well that others see their qualities.'

And a lot of consolation that is! she thought. But she said no more. Speaking out had eased her vexation, she wouldn't show Paul her alarm by provoking a full-scale quarrel.

I'll manage on my own, if only to confound him, Isobel thought. I'll cope somehow with heaving those great bolts of cloth around.

'There are plenty of men like Alfred seeking jobs now, with trade at the Piece Hall declining so much,' she announced.

'You're suggesting I ought to have sought labour elsewhere, are you?'

Making herself smile, Isobel shook her head. 'On the contrary. I shall be able to find someone, even though you were incapable of doing your own searching.'

For days they hardly acknowledged each other whenever they met about the house. Meals were the essence of discomfort, with poor Audrey trying, and failing utterly, to reconcile them.

Determined to carry on the business, Isobel took on a fellow who was seeking casual labour. He seemed shiftless and she suspected he wouldn't last, but he could handle horses. He survived two journeys to the Piece Hall before returning to Ireland. Without him, Isobel became exhausted by attempting to collect and market the cloth unaided. Setting out earlier than usual, she quite enjoyed driving the wagon from one cottage to the next, having an agreeable chat with her weavers and accepting help with loading their material. It was afterwards, at the Piece Hall, that the situation was well nigh impossible. Being unable to carry a range of materials with her, she was obliged to return repeatedly to pick up more from the wagon and that involved so much trekking that her legs grew unsteady with fatigue. Nevertheless this was what she did for weeks, heeding nothing but her will to continue.

In summer time it would have been difficult enough; they were into December now with fog and frost combining to make each journey more hazardous.

Returning home from market one evening to find that Paul's day had ended before her own, and he and Audrey were already consuming the meal prepared by their Mrs Field, she felt hurt that they couldn't have waited for her. Yet Paul only complained that she was neglecting them. And it was he – *her own husband* – who'd engineered this unhappy situation. But he wouldn't force her to give up.

The next visit to Halifax was in dazzling snow that turned the road's surface to glass beneath the hooves of her horses. The wagon swung from side to side as they slithered. Attempting to negotiate one of the many bends, the wagon lurched and overturned.

Still clutching the reins, Isobel hurtled between the shafts, landing awkwardly amid heavy, sliding hooves. Although she succeeded in preventing the horses bolting, their abrupt halt had shunted several bolts of cloth out into dirty roadside snow.

Getting herself up while avoiding agitated hooves, and without releasing the reins, seemed to take ages. And she was growing increasingly wet, miserable and cold.

Struggling to stay on her feet on the icy road, she began checking that the horses were uninjured. Even though they were unharmed, Isobel felt dejected as she retrieved the valuable bolts of cloth. Some were so badly stained that they would have to be cleaned and dried before offering for sale, but the rest must be taken to market, and she would do that *today*.

Although they suffered no further accidents, Isobel was utterly weary by the time she arrived in Halifax. Friends she encountered asked what had made her so miserable, but she told no one. Listlessly, she humped the cloth around, piece by piece, until each one that was fit for offering was sold.

She was late, of course, returning home that evening. Paul was yet again dining without her. Permitting her no opportunity for explaining, he left her in no doubt of his opinion.

'You're making a habit of failing to be here when I need you. Is there nothing I can say or do that'll convince you of my disapproval?'

'I am sorry you've been inconvenienced,' she said very quietly. 'I'm afraid I'm not very good at holding the horses when they run into trouble in icy conditions. The wagon overturned, naturally that caused a considerable delay.'

Without further explanation or discussion, she mustered her dignity and walked from the room.

19

Isobel felt numb with exhaustion, too drained to care very much that Paul was proving again that he could show remarkable unconcern. She rang for hot water, bathed her wounds, then changed her tattered gown for a clean one. She toyed with the notion of returning to the dining-room, but decided there were limits beyond which she need not endure.

Sitting by the bedroom fire with the meal which had been kept hot for her, she discovered that as her appetite was sated so her revulsion for Paul's behaviour returned and increased.

She wouldn't have minded his apparent indifference to her interests, and even her welfare, half so much if he hadn't deliberately coaxed away the workers on whom she'd relied. She still found it hard to believe that her own husband could have behaved so badly towards her.

Isobel would have been surprised if she could have known how Paul was suffering now. He had pushed away his half-full plate as soon as the door closed upon her. It was only after she had left that the full impact of his wife's words hit him. *The wagon had overturned.* Isobel might have been killed, she could have been seriously injured; hadn't she been limping?

Instinct told him to run up to their room, to ask how she was, to beg her to forgive him. But begging for anything was an unfamiliar experience, these days, and made him hesitate. The explanations should have come years ago, and should have involved his intense dislike of her continuing to work. As it was, month by month, year by year, the affection and respect between them had been eroding. He envied his friends and associates with womenfolk devoted to organising the household and caring for their needs. The fact that they themselves employed an efficient housekeeper and staff made no difference. He yearned to have Isobel's complete attention devoted to his wellbeing.

His scheme had failed. He now acknowledged that failure was what it deserved. Encouraging Alfred Hanson to leave Bright's and work for him had been easier than he'd expected. But then Hanson was an intelligent man, if lacking in formal education. After that brief introduction to factory work, his involvement in the cloth trade had kept him abreast of developments. Even someone with less sense might have gathered that a secure future would only be found by following mechanisation. And where he had gone the lad he was training was bound to come after.

It was Isobel who'd confounded him. *By being so determined*. He had thought she would see how impossible it was for a woman to run Bright's without the aid of at least one man, that within days she would be admitting that the time had come to sell out.

And now here they were – she barely surviving the hazards of the winter roads; and he himself faced with the realisation that it wasn't only by means of a tragic accident that he might lose her.

In recent years he had so longed to be free of the exasperation induced by her work that he'd even imagined he might be glad to be free of her. But now, before she arranged that very situation, he must end all their contention.

The opening of their bedroom door startled Isobel into sitting upright. She had been dozing, thankful to escape the uneasy thoughts which pursued her whenever she was fully conscious.

'Oh, it's you,' she said, no longer caring to conceal her growing mistrust.

'And come to apologise,' Paul responded swiftly. Once decided to try and make amends he'd not shirk the necessary unpleasantness. 'I should never have behaved so unfairly, encouraging Hanson and the lad to leave your employ.'

'That's right, Paul, you shouldn't. I've never expected favours of you, but nor did I expect subversion.'

'Shall you find it possible to forgive me?' He was at her side now, gazing down at her, his blue eyes grave.

'I don't know. You shouldn't ask me that tonight, while

293

I'm dredged of every ounce of strength and sore in bones which I didn't know existed.'

'Were you severely hurt?' he inquired, going down on one knee by the hearth and taking her hand.

'It feels like it! But if I'd broken any bones I would know it by now.' She paused, looking at him, seeing the way firelight traced golden strands in his pale hair. 'You've hurt me more,' she told him frankly. 'And I think you know that.'

'I do now. Is it too late, Isobel? I do wish to make amends, if you'll only show me how.'

'*Is* there a way? Even if you sent Alfred Hanson back to Bright's it would do no good. With the prospects you'll have painted for him at the mill, he's not going to settle for working in a declining business.'

'You admit it's declining then?' he said quickly, it wasn't in his nature to let her admission pass.

'If you seriously believe that I could remain unaware that the clothiers' trade is gradually going out of existence, you must take me for a fool.'

'Which you're not – I do know that, Isobel. Unless it's in not selling out while you may still raise something on the business.'

'I think we've probably passed that stage already.'

'What'll you do?'

'The only thing that I know how – keep going, until I know for sure that I must give up.'

'And I'll stop trying to oppose you.'

They sealed his promise in each other's arms that night, in love-making so intense that Isobel began to believe that Paul did, indeed, love her. And she. . . ? She wondered afterwards. Was it love she felt for Paul, or simply need? The need for a man to share this life which she had chosen while she was only a child.

Phillida's father died in the December of 1830, collapsing on the steps leading down from the room where he'd woven cloth for Bright's to sell since the time when he'd been taught by his own father.

Phillida naturally grieved for him, but privately acknowledged that he'd have hated to drag on in an existence dependent upon others. Isobel was alarmed by the loss of their best worker, an alarm that increased to panic when another weaver died a month afterwards. It was the coming of the end, but once she recognised it as such a strange quiet overtook her.

She kept the business going through into the summer, taking dwindling supplies of cloth to market in the Piece Hall, until the day one of the horses went lame. She left him not far from Halifax town centre, in a field owned by a fellow clothier who eked out his income by farming.

With only the one horse to haul the wagon, even though it was empty, the journey back to Heptonstall seemed interminable as she dwelled on the inevitable outcome.

Paul had seen her return and was in the hallway to meet her.

'What's wrong? Where's the other horse?' Ever since her accident with the wagon, he had dreaded that there might be another.

'I had to leave him in Halifax. He's gone lame. That's it, Paul. He's been a good horse, but he's too old to be expected to carry on, even if his leg does heal. And it's no good buying another, not when I know Bright's is nearly finished.'

The following few weeks were occupied with selling off the few remaining bolts of cloth, paying up the weavers who had worked so well in cooperation with her and her father, and disposing of the wagon. She brought the horses home to their old quarters, they had earned a comfortable retirement, even though seeing them idle in the nearby field was a constant reminder of her own inactivity.

'I could find you something to occupy you in the mill,' Paul suggested after a while, seeing how unsuited she was to an existence no longer geared to her business.

'No, thank you,' Isobel responded while wondering how he could know so little about her that he'd suppose she might work in one of the places which had insidiously destroyed her family's business.

For two years Isobel struggled to accept not having work

295

which might take her outside the house, and found her life unfulfilling. Her step-daughter married a neighbour who farmed sheep, began carrying a child almost immediately and was sick so frequently that Isobel took to spending much of her time with her until Audrey produced a healthy young boy.

William had been spending most of his time in London, with only occasional visits to Oporto. Whenever he returned there it was to Rosalind's wholehearted welcome, but always their reunion was tinged with sadness. Her father had grown feeble-minded and incontinent, necessitating her constant care. Compelled to move back into Ernest Parker's house, she couldn't find any means of relieving the problems created for William and herself. They would contrive time together whenever he was in Portugal, but always there were interruptions from the old man who, through no fault of his own, had become as demanding as a child.

They were into 1832; she and William had been lovers for many a year, yet it seemed they would never be permitted a life of their own. On every return from London he appeared older, less energetic and his hair was fast turning white.

He worried a lot about Fortescue's trade. Although the excellent vintage of 1820 had reinforced the recovery of the port business following the ravages of the Peninsular war, there had still been disquiet, even among its shippers.

Social distinctions seemed odious to Will. But they were made between old-established companies dealing in wine, and fish as well, who belonged to the British Association – and those trading more recently in other merchandise such as cloth.

Around 1825 complaints had been made that the Factory House wasn't made available to all English merchants in Oporto. The response from the British Association was that it was purely a club for gentlemen of the wine trade to which they might invite their friends. Rosalind's father and other original members had suffered for acquaintances on both sides until eventually newer port merchants were admitted.

More serious unrest was disturbing the city of Oporto which had become the site of Jacobinism and Freemasonry. Spreading through the country, revolt had resulted in the heir to the throne being dubbed 'the first citizen' while a Constitution and a parliament had been introduced. Back in 1828 Prince Miguel had rejected the Constitution and taken possession of the throne. His brother Pedro, a Constitutionalist, had been upheld by Oporto, but the following year fierce reaction commenced when the Miguelites moved in. And these days the inhabitants lived in daily fear as each side warred for control.

William had been appalled when Rosalind wrote that several important citizens had been sent to the gallows erected in the Praca Nova. He had been compelled to remain in London, attending to urgent matters when further news reached him that men, of the calibre of Charles Noble of Warre's, were imprisoned in Oporto for their sympathies. For months afterwards if a letter from Rosalind was delayed he feared that she had somehow become involved.

He liked Ernest Parker but couldn't help yearning for the time when she would be free to travel with him on each of his visits to England.

In the early March of 1832 William returned to Portugal, with the soaring spirits which always occurred as he contemplated the spring. In Yorkshire in his youth, he'd watched the snows vanishing from rugged moors and the first buds forming on oak trees, and had felt elated. Spring upriver and in Oporto was a delight, the prelude to the heat which he endured knowing it was vital to their vines.

These days, he even contemplated his eventual return to England with equanimity, finding – in the assurance that the seasons of the grape persisted – a kind of security.

Meeting fellow port shippers in the Rua Nova dos Inglezes – the Change of Oporto – William consulted his watch as he approached the granite exterior of the Factory House. It was a little after two in the afternoon. Greeted from ahead and to the side, he acknowledged acquaintances and paused to speak with friends. Despite the apparent informality of the outdoor setting, certain proprieties were rigorously observed. He'd learned, for instance, that 'talking shop' was only permissible during Factory House luncheons. And it would be considered over-inquisitive if he were to visit another owner's lodge.

Already pleased to be back, William's delight increased when word travelled from group to group, exciting them all. Dom Pedro had landed to the north, at Mindelo. With an army reputed to number over seven thousand men, he intended seizing the crown for his daughter. Maria da Gloria should supplant Pedro's brother Miguel who had ruled for over three years of oppression.

Suddenly, bells rang out, '*Viva* the Constitution!' was the cry taken up through surrounding streets. A youth came running from a nearby square, red-faced with elation, yelling that the public executioner had been shot.

More running feet were heard, from all around them, as Miguelites, many of them *fidalgos*, wealthy merchants and priests, began fleeing. Some English merchants who'd even been spat upon during the past few years joined in shouts of rejoicing.

The arrival of Dom Pedro's army proved to be a disappointment, in number far fewer than was expected, and a strange amalgam of Portuguese troops and mercenaries.

Oporto was surrounded. The Miguelites placed batteries at Vila Nova de Gaia, shelling the city itself which Dom Pedro was holding. The river was busy with the vessels of a British naval force, dispatched by Palmerston to ensure 'play was fair'.

Although English residents were not personally involved, cannon-balls damaged the staunch walls of their Factory House. And grape-shot bouncing off the pavements of the Rua Nova dos Inglezes convinced them the battle was serious.

Instead of returning to London, William remained. Most days he succeeded somehow in crossing to Fortescue's lodge on the Miguelist bank. Shipping wine out of Oporto again grew more than difficult. When it became evident that the seige would continue for months, he sympathised with the merchants who decided to sail home. Yet he would not leave, not while he was faced yet again with keeping them in business; and when quitting would be to abandon Rosalind.

William found it hard to credit they were still existing in these circumstances in 1833. Although few English shippers had been inflicted with real hardship or injury, he cared too much to ignore the suffering of those inhabitants of Oporto already deprived by poverty. People were dying of cholera, more still from starvation.

Now isolated to landward, the city was dependent upon the scarce supplies brought in by vessels which offloaded at the Douro bar. William made sure that Fortescue's joined with other British merchants and opened soup kitchens, although the ingredients available were often no more than water and rice. Leaving her father in their housekeeper's care, Rosalind worked there for several hours a day.

The work was no more cheering than tending the old man. So desperate were people that donkey meat was selling for a shilling per pound. Troops were reportedly kidnapping their officers' pets.

One day someone approached Rosalind and her companion as they tossed more rice into the steaming liquid. A clean enough individual, despite his well worn clothing, he beckoned her. His good English revealed him as educated. 'I have something that will give body to the soup you're doling out, plenty of flesh on it.'

He took her around the corner to a sack he'd deposited in an angle of the wall. Untying rough string, he showed her its contents. Sickened, Rosalind stared at the motionless form. Beneath his dense brown fur, the puppy still seemed to be warm.

That afternoon, instead of returning home, she found someone to row her across the river. When she reached Vila Nova de Gaia she began running, dodging between batteries that continued the persistent firing towards Oporto itself.

Breathless, Rosalind reached Fortescue's and asked the first person she met if she might speak with Mr Bright. She was conducted between stacks of port casks sending their aroma towards the lofty roof. William met her at the door of his office, consternation swiftly replacing his smile when he saw Rosalind's expression.

'Your father. . . ?' he inquired gravely, taking her arm to draw her inside and to a chair.

Wearily, she shook her head. 'No – he was no worse when I left this morning. It's just – oh, everything! Oporto. We were offered dog meat today, to serve with our soup. We refused it, of course. But where will it end, William, *when*. . . ?'

'I wish I knew.'

'Even people like ourselves are suffering hardship now.'

'I know. All of Trancoso's daughters have sold their long tresses. A hairdresser is buying lengths of human hair, it raises enough to feed their families another meal.'

'We shouldn't complain, I know, we ourselves aren't in nearly such a dire situation. But it's all so utterly depressing.'

'At least, we're able to sell some of the port that we're unable to ship at present. I'll swear the army makes it a mainstay.'

'I don't know how the Portuguese endure so uncomplainingly.'

'I think some believe Heaven is reproving their sins.'

Rosalind had needed to see William, not so much to confide her distress as to be assured that he was alive.

She never weighed him down with daily reminders of concern for his safety. But this anxiety on his behalf always gnawed into her while she prepared endless gallons of soup for the poor.

'He's my husband, I've every reason to get upset. I've every right to have news of how he is.'

Phillida faced Isobel across the parlour of the old family home, her back rigid and her green eyes brilliant again in her agitation.

Isobel brought word from Henry who'd struggled for months to maintain contact with his brother and their company in Vila Nova de Gaia. It was ages now since he'd first had word of the seige there and until today Isobel had

300

insisted that Phillida shouldn't be told. Recently, however, writing to her mother from her home in Spain, Jessica had let slip some reference to the trouble in Oporto and now Phillida had begun pestering for the truth, demanding to be kept advised of what was happening out there.

'I've not given Will up, not ever. That's why I do still care, nobody's going to keep me in the dark about what danger he's facing.'

'But don't you see, Phillie – it's that far away, any word we receive is stale before . . .'

'Do you think I don't know that! Nay, Isobel! But we shouldn't be snapping at each other. You're his only sister, after all.' Aye – and the one person who could best be relied on to keep her in touch.

Later, walking the floor of the master bedroom in the chill of early spring, she felt rigid and isolated. She and Will might have had differences, but she'd never really stopped loving him. Learning that he had a mistress, she had been angry and humiliated, had experienced the pain of blaming herself. That didn't mean that she'd relinquished the need to be a part of his life, that she'd ever relinquish it . . .

To no one, not even to herself, had she expressed her hope that they might, ultimately, be reunited. Only with the news that he was in physical danger was she compelled to recognise that such a hope had become the only real thing in her life.

'Let him just live, Lord,' she prayed out loud, tears coursing down the lines of her once-beautiful features, 'and I'll make no demands of him.'

Around three in the morning, she lit a fresh candle from the stub of its predecessor, drew a wrap about her and sat down to write.

Dear William,
I won't be false and pretend there's been no problems between us, but I hope you'll feel as I do that there's nowt so bad as the difficulties you're facing now.
As soon as I heard what things are like out there, I just wished I could rush to be with you. I know you'll take that with a pinch of

301

salt, being as how I've so often refused to make that voyage a second time. It's my punishment that I miss you and, the way things are, that's fast growing unbearable. I'd give all I can, if I could nobbut see you tomorrow, and know that you weren't harmed.

I wish to God there was some way I could get in touch with you, without having to endure this long wait that seems to go on forever, while I pray for word that you're still alive.

Each time I hear a step outside, or a knock on the door, I shall be filled with dread, until you let me know how you are. Please write to me, Will, relieve some of the agony of waiting here so far away, of worrying every minute of the day and night.

Your still loving wife,
Phillida.

She sent the letter to Henry, at present in Fortescue's London office, with the request that he forward it immediately. Nothing helped, though. Every hour seemed laden with this terrible apprehension, and although she had been alarmed out of her torpor and was taking care of the house and herself, nothing blotted out thoughts.

Her attendance at the familiar octagonal chapel ceased to be a matter of habit and became a fierce intensifying of her personal prayers that William be preserved. She took to reading newspapers, scouring them for reports of events in Portugal, then growing even more depressed with each fresh detail of conditions there.

Seeing the extent of her concern, Isobel attempted to reassure her, to encourage her to think of other matters. She spoke of Jessica and Jorge – and all that did was prompt further anguish for the man who had fathered the girl.

'I ought to have appreciated him more, for giving me the little lass I wanted so much. If I'm allowed to see him again I'll make it all up to him, I swear by Heaven that I will.'

To Phillida, each day felt to move labouringly from one minute to the next, yet its eve created alarm because yet another twenty-four hours had gone with no word to reassure her.

One day the newspapers carried an account of how the

inhabitants of Oporto were being starved into acceptance of the Miguelites' will. Phillida didn't understand what all the trouble was about, but she did understand being deprived of food. How on earth could William continue to exist, especially with no one there to look after him?

'They'd not let me into the country, I know, not wi' all this bother on,' she confided to Isobel, 'else I'd book a passage on t'first ship that'd take me.'

Her sister-in-law saw this as no more than an empty declaration which seemed to ease Phillida's own mind. To Phillie herself, though, it was the expression of a yearning greater than any she'd survived. She had thought the longing for an infant, so many years unfulfilled, had been appalling; the need to see William became far more searing.

He's dead, I know he is, she would believe in the night, visualising him with life extinguished from those beautiful grey eyes, his powerful frame inert. She would worry on, wondering how she would set about having his body brought home for burial, and how she could live afterwards with no hope of any sort to which she might cling.

News came, at last, but in a strange hand. Receiving the envelope from Portugal, she feared instantly that it contained news of his death. A low keening beginning in her throat, Phillida opened the letter.

William was safe. Thanking her for her concern, he hoped she would forgive him for not writing in person. Glancing to the end, Phillida was astounded to see the signature Rosalind Parker. No matter how hard she tried, she couldn't prevent the relief that her husband was still alive being outweighed by the shock that his mistress had been delegated to address her.

As time progressed, Phillida found her attitude towards William changing. Although concerned that he should survive throughout the protracted seige in Oporto, she was beginning to feel free of the strictures of their ill-assorted marriage.

'I might keep his name,' she asserted to Isobel one day, 'but I no longer consider myself his wife. Not that I've anyone else in mind,' she added very swiftly.

There was someone, though, who was helping Phillida to survive. Whilst she had been so depressed that she was even neglecting her chapel, her sister-in-law had visited the minister's house, and had found an unfamiliar face there.

'I am here but temporarily, to deputise during illness,' he had told Isobel, after introducing himself as the Reverend Percival Downey. He had called on Phillida soon afterwards, and had won immediate approval. His speciality was as a listener. Within an hour, he'd had most of Phillida's life story; within two he understood all the nuances of her daughter's absence in Spain and of her own separation from her husband.

Before he left her, Phillida was already looking forward to the next few weeks. She couldn't actually pray for the continuing indisposition of their regular minister, but she hoped that he would make quite certain not to return before he was fully recovered.

On the day in July when a final Miguelite attack on Oporto was defeated, hopes soared that quiet might be restored again to the city. That very evening Rosalind's father died quite calmly, and William decided to get Rosalind away.

'Let's go home to England,' he suggested. She was free now to leave the city. And he would no longer feel he was neglecting greater responsibilities if he gave some time to the British end of shipping their wine.

Before plans were completed for their voyage, one last attack by Miguel's men shattered everyone within the port trade. They blew up the Wine Company's store in Vila Nova de Gaia.

For a while it seemed that the fire could spread to other nearby lodges. William, in common with all wine shippers, watched aghast. Was it possible that these flames would devour everything they had always worked for, and at a time when they were just beginning to believe they had survived?

Explosions rose above the roar of flames and startled him, making him turn repeatedly to verify that the casks in his own lodge were still intact. He could feel for his fellow shippers in the company that had suffered without expecting to share their loss. The air was heavy, not only with smoke but with the odour of hot port, fast becoming so powerful that the sickness he felt in witnessing such violent destruction was increasing.

He felt torn: anchored here by the need to ensure that his own port lodge wasn't endangered, yet feeling impelled to rush to help men who'd dined at his side in the Factory House in the days before the seige.

For many hours assistance and attention were focused on the Wine Company's premises, until eventually the blaze was contained, largely by the efforts of the navy's Captain Glascock and his band of seamen and marines.

Although the loss could have been infinitely more serious, every man in the port business was appalled to see the river coloured by virtually 27,000 pipes of wine sent streaming to mingle with its waters.

'I shan't give him another thought, not now as I know the fighting's ended out there. He's chosen his life,' she added to Isobel. 'It weren't owt that I did.'

Feeling exonerated was important to Phillida, and not only because she wished to remain on good terms with her sister-in-law. She was grateful for Isobel's concern which had made the black times more endurable. She sensed as well that she was coming to care seriously for Percival Downey. He had proved himself most attentive; she admired his forceful preaching and she was proud to have him as a guest at her table. She knew he, too, hadn't much of a life at home. Caring for a mother who was a martyr to rheumatism had kept him a bachelor.

Isobel thankfully decreased her visits to Phillida, and was glad that their infrequency passed without comment.

'I'll swear she doesn't need me at all now she's got yon chap in tow,' she observed to Paul.

There'd been some improvement in her own marriage since she'd begun to feel more content to spend time in their home. So they were both able to enjoy the companionship of the other.

'We're thinking of extending again down at the mill,' Paul told her. 'We're introducing more spinning frames. I know it's always been summat you find hard to accept – but I know, an' all, that you're glad for me at heart because we are doing good trade.'

'Aye, I am,' she agreed. She hadn't worked for Bright's all those years without developing a strong appreciation of business acumen.

'I've stopped asking you to come and work down yonder with me,' Paul continued. 'But I do see a time in the future, not too far distant either, when we shall spend more of our days together. I'm seeing this lot installed and running proper, then I'm going to ease up a bit.'

Isobel smiled, pleased to contemplate the outings they might share in their landau. People went away for holidays to the sea, these days; she and Paul would be able to do so. She glanced at the clock, still relishing the prospect of a more relaxed future.

The wet, windy night was darkening the August sky as clouds hung low over the moorland horizon. She'd lit candles and lamps hours ago, afraid that Paul would strain his eyes with poring over all those figures.

'Shall we retire early?' she suggested. 'That lot out there is only fit for shutting out.'

Paul looked across at her, setting aside his pen as he did so, and agreed. 'If you wish. You go up, love . . .' He called her love more frequently now, a sure sign that they were finally establishing their marriage on a better footing. He added that he'd left some important papers in the carriage. 'I'll just go as far as t'coach house. Can't do with anything being mislaid.' He was too meticulous these days to rest easily if he didn't have everything ordered to his satisfaction.

The gale seemed fiercer than ever. From upstairs in their room she could see the trees swaying. With a shrug, she drew across the curtains. They needn't heed the weather. In here they were warm and dry, protected. What was more, if she were any judge, Paul meant them to forget the entire world – in the joy recently rediscovered together.

Isobel undressed rapidly, folding each garment before

finding her nightgown. She would wear the blue silk, Paul's favourite. She was taking it from the drawer when first the shot, then the scream startled her. A man's scream of agony, and instantly recognisable as her husband's.

Thrusting arms and head into the nightgown, Isobel ran for the door. Blind with horror, she sped along the landing and down the long staircase. As she opened the door, rain lashed across her face and soaked the thin blue material covering her. But around to the side, in the direction of the coach house, she could see two men, bending over a third lying awkwardly on the stone paving. She needed no one to tell her that this was Paul.

Her feet were near silent as she hastened through the deluge, but some other sound evidently reached the pair above the noise of the storm. Together, they rose, glanced towards each other and sprinted off, heading for the field pathway. In their urgency, both attempted to mount the stile at the same moment. The taller man was compelled to give way and Isobel heard his impatient cry as she knelt to examine Paul; she was too distressed to wonder why it sounded familiar.

There was blood mingling with the puddles of rain. Draining from a head wound, it was carrying life back into the earth. 'No, no,' she whispered, appalled. 'No!'

She said his name, pressed suddenly dry lips to his bloodied cheek, felt with her fingers for the pulse in his neck.

'Ay, Mrs Copley, whatever are you doing out . . . here?'

It was their housekeeper, and the serving maid close behind her, brought by Paul's screams. 'You'd best go inside, Madam, afore you catch your death . . .'

As if that mattered, now. It was *Paul* who was dead, she needed no medical man to pronounce him lifeless.

Instead of moving to let the others near him, she took Paul's head on her lap, cradled the sticky fair hair against her.

Dully, Isobel heard the housekeeper dispatching the girl to fetch help, but she herself had dropped into a dim half-world where nothing beyond this man really penetrated.

'It's too late, you know,' she said huskily. 'Too late . . .'

Some while afterwards the doctor gently released her hands which still were holding Paul, and assisted her to her feet. Weak from shock, she staggered, was grasped by him.

'Did you see what happened?' he asked as, supporting her firmly, he walked with her slowly towards the house.

Isobel shook her head, found she could hardly speak. 'I was in our room. Heard this terrible scream. But when I got here Paul was – was already dead.'

It seemed like hours that she sat, shaking with distress, after she'd been assisted into a dry gown and robe. She understood nothing of the course which must be taken on account of the law, only that everyone – the doctor included – was preoccupied with matters which seemed to her to have no relevance. Paul was dead, what could possibly have any significance now?

They had induced her to sip hot beverages and spirits as well, but nothing dulled the pain, nor would ever eradicate the memory.

'Did you hear a shot?' someone asked, some long while later when it was daylight.

'No, no. Nothing until his scream.'

'And you saw nobody, of course . . .'

'Oh, but I did. Two men, bending over him when I came round the corner of the house.'

'But it was dark . . .'

'I could make out their shapes. And I heard one of them speak.'

'Did he sound like a local fellow?'

'I think so, I . . .' Remembering hurt so much that she could hardly bear, but hadn't she, just for a brief moment, thought that she knew the voice?

Shaking her head miserably, Isobel sighed, closed her eyes.

The doctor intervened, suggesting they halt their questioning and allow her to rest. The person interrogating her through her increasing haze persisted none the less.

'Were you going to add something just then, madam?'

'Only – that I might have heard his voice before.'

'Where – where might you?' he spoke urgently now, pressing her.

All she wanted was to sleep, that was the only way she might escape the appalling truth of what had occurred.

'Please, madam, if you'd just try . . .'

'It was so long ago – somebody I might have known.'

Henry travelled from London to be with her. He'd fully intended arranging to take Isobel home to Catalina once the funeral was over, but had found her too ill with grief and shock. Phillida was staying at the house, attempting to organise the household, for Mrs Field and the rest of the staff were shaken out of their normal competence. Daily, meals were planned and served, to be neglected by both Isobel and her step-daughter who visited constantly.

Although not present when the shooting had happened, Audrey was just as shattered as Isobel. No one, not even her husband Tom, was able to console her.

When Paul's body was conveyed to the ancient church at Heptonstall they were surrounded by a large, caring congregation. Men from his mill and from other mills in the vicinity were joined by old weavers and other folk who had known Isobel and Bright's all their lives.

Isobel wished she'd had more opportunity for getting to know Paul's relations, but really was aware of no more than that a lot of people attended that day. Even putting names to the faces converging about her would have required an effort of will she no longer possessed.

'There's only one thing I care about now,' she told Henry late that evening. 'And that's finding who did it, and seeing that they're hung.'

Each day succeeded the one previous and Isobel grew no stronger, except in her resolve. Who, in all the years that she had known him, could have borne Paul a grudge so strong? She asked advice of her brother Charles, but his legal knowledge compelled him to warn her that the little she had seen and heard would be useless in a courtroom.

A week or more after Henry's return to London, she was

sitting alone by the window, gazing towards the moors. Barely conscious of her surroundings, she was dipping into the past, willing memory to identify the voice she'd heard that dreadful night.

Over and over again, it seemed that the man's brief cry had given her a moment of reassurance, even while Paul's blood was draining away. If she were to hear the voice again, she would know it instantly.

Phillida persuaded her to leave the house, an expedition which required a deal of encouragement. They walked as far as the crossroads, and down the valley a little way, turning back when they reached a wayside inn.

It was as they turned and began retracing their steps that Isobel remembered. Glancing back over her shoulder, she stared at the inn again. She had met them in the back room there: Paul and the others, old Jacob, the rest of their gang of Luddites. *And Roger Wheatley.*

She called on an old neighbour of his who confirmed that Roger had been released from jail; she then knew she had to confront him, no matter how long it took. What possible motive could he have had? she wondered, even more distressed when she recalled how long Roger had been a friend of her family. And who would believe her, when nothing more substantial than a sharp cry uttered in darkness supported her conjecture?

When Isobel showed no sign of beginning to recover from the shock, Phillida suggested that she go and stay with Henry in Jerez.

'I will, one day, there's too much here requiring my attention.'

Audrey was present as well, alarmed by Isobel's inability to follow her own grim resolution and begin picking up her life again. She urged her step-mother to get away, and added her assurance that she would cope with matters arising from her father's will.

It's not *that* that's bothering me, Isobel thought; she alone of all the family might unearth the truth behind Paul's murder. 'You're all being very kind and considerate,' she

310

told them. 'In a little while you'll understand more, will see why I can't go away just yet.'

She could only pray now that circumstances might provide assistance. No one she knew had more information. She had been asking around, compelling herself to visit old friends, to speak with them of times long past, of the early days of her acquaintance with Paul. She had learned only that Roger hadn't returned to his old home.

One sunlit morning Isobel set out alone on horseback for the Piece Hall in Halifax. The trees on the surrounding hills were lush with late summer foliage. Belle, the mare beneath her, was reliable and even tempered, yet all she felt was dread.

Deciding to visit the cloth hall had required enormous determination. This site of her former dreams and later of her success would seem only to mock her now. Reviving memories had pained her intensely already, and she sensed that heading in this direction would increase her anguish.

Pausing beside the turnpike when she reached King Cross, she thought how delighted she'd been to have Carmen Escutia with her, and of the elderly Spanish lady's interest in the Piece Hall. How long it seemed since she had seen Catalina's family, since she'd seen Catalina herself . . . Had she been a fool to reject Henry's invitation?

But until she found out who was responsible for Paul's death and what motive they'd had, she must remain in the West Riding. She owed him that.

There were far fewer clothiers conducting business in the huge Piece Hall. Although this was as she'd expected, Isobel was depressed by its continuing decline.

After she'd tethered her horse, though, and begun walking through the colonnade she met several people she knew. Being greeted made her feel more at home again, and it was with a lighter step that she headed towards the upper gallery.

She was passing a room whose door stood ajar when she heard his voice. It had taken her days to recall how she had known the man whose exclamation identified him on that dreadful night. Today, in less than a second, she was certain.

A quick glance through the dusty window convinced her beyond doubt.

Her own calm astonishing her, Isobel waited a few paces along from the door. I shall have to confront him, she resolved, and make him understand that I know he's responsible for the murder.

Roger Wheatley came out at last, stuffing a bagful of money into his pocket. He was about to stride along the gallery when he saw her. For what felt like a full minute their glances linked, and then he lowered his gaze, turned sharply, and ran for the stone steps.

Isobel followed, running down the steps, then along the colonnade, dodging around people talking in groups, startling others. But Roger was almost out of sight now. And being a tall man and extremely strong, even if she succeeded in catching up how could she apprehend him?

She would have to let him go for now, but at least she had seen him again. She would go to her brother Charles, ask him for guidance.

'I should do nothing, Isobel.'

Sitting behind the large desk in a room lined with bookcases of legal tomes, Charles was no longer her young brother, but a dour representative of the law.

'Nothing?' she was horrified. 'I can't just let them get away with it! Roger and some accomplice *killed my husband*.'

'Or so you believe. If you are right, they'll be brought to justice,' he told her, though he was well aware that many criminals evaded that.

'For Paul's sake, I've got to do something. It was an unforgivable killing, for no reason whatever.'

'You've no evidence, love. There's only your word that it was this Wheatley fellow who was involved, all you have is your own testimony that you recognised his voice.'

'I'll not rest till he's convicted.'

'You haven't thought that you might regret digging to learn the truth?'

'How do you mean?'

'There would be some motive; you might be better not knowing.'

'*Not*? What're you implying, Charles?'

'Did you never think at the time it was very neat the way those Luddites were captured? Didn't you read an account of their case when it reached the assizes?'

Isobel swallowed, trying to recover composure. Even after all this time she'd not have Charles learn that she'd been present when they were taken, a member of their gang.

'I never had much time for reading newspapers,' she said hastily.

'From statements made by Wheatley and some of the others, it was clear they suspected they'd been given away by one of their number.'

'You don't think. . . ? It couldn't have been Paul,' she asserted, and then clamped her lips together. If she said another word, the whole story would tumble out. He'd know that she as well as Paul had been there in that mill.

'I'll see you again, when I've found out more,' she said hastily, leaving hurriedly, before her brother warned her to take care.

Riding back to Heptonstall, Isobel tried to gather her troubled thoughts. It was then that she remembered. Paul *hadn't* been with the rest of them on that occasion. But surely he wouldn't have. . . ?

Rushing back to her came the memory of her husband's initial concealment of his job. He'd kept from her the fact that some relative had offered work in his new factory. She knew some mill owners had united, had they persuaded Paul to infiltrate the Luddites?

But that couldn't be true. Paul wasn't like that. He'd had faults, like most folk, but though they'd had their troubles their marriage had eventually become happy.

Further recollections began surfacing and Isobel sighed, grimly. On that very first night, after being seized, she'd marvelled at how easily she'd been allowed to get away – *to meet up with the stranger who was waiting*.

Isobel continued compelling herself to go out. She'd not find out where Roger Wheatley was living now by sitting indoors. And locate him she would – she needed to learn the truth about Paul as much as to prove the identity of his killers.

She walked around Heptonstall and rode down into the valley where there were signs of development along the banks of the Calder and the River Hebden. Water was greatly respected, these days, as a potential source of power, but she'd be a long while accepting such a mundane use of the river known in mediaeval times as *Aqua de Heoppe Dene*.

Finding no one in Halifax who could answer questions about Wheatley was driving her to explore her own area. It was around here, after all, where they had banded together all those years ago.

Isobel had approached Eddie Gaukroger, and had received a berating for her pains. Eddie possessed a longer memory than she'd given him credit, and soon told her what he'd do to the likes of Roger Wheatley, if he came across them.

'If some of them Luddites has survived to come out of jail, they'll wish they hadn't. T'first one I set eyes on'll see t'business end of my musket.'

She had learned nothing at the factory where Paul had given such conscientious service. A new mill master had been appointed; although he'd served under Paul, he nevertheless had little interest in her concerns. He knew no one called Wheatley, and disapproved of her wasting good working time.

Isobel was close to weeping with frustration. She'd hardly cried about her loss, but she felt now that she might burst if there wasn't some outlet. Losing Paul so suddenly had been terrible, wondering if he'd been a traitor to everything she'd believed in felt even worse. But sick of scouring her mind for some clue to where Wheatley might be concealed, she harnessed all her old determination.

'Nay, I'll not give up,' she would repeat aloud while the servants were out of earshot. 'And I'll not give in to weeping either, or I shan't be able to keep on searching.'

One day in November Isobel rode out on Belle while the wintry sunlight cast long shadows. She was wearied to death. Ever since losing Paul she'd been sleeping badly, and she had spent the morning with Phillida.

Both being on their own might give herself and her sister-in-law one thing in common, yet she swore that nothing else in temperament or otherwise provided any link. Even inquiring after Jessica invited a torrent of reproach for the absent daughter whose neglect of her mother would break anybody's heart.

'How long is it since she deigned to come back here even for a few days, just tell me that,' Phillie had snorted.

'No doubt they're busy, as always. Jorge's very involved now with Fortescue's, and he'd not want Jessica travelling alone. I'm sure she just doesn't think . . .'

'Time she learned then! You needn't go sticking up for her neither. It's all right for you. You've got Audrey to hand, *she* never neglects you, does she, and not even your own daughter.'

That was true enough, Isobel thought now, smiling as she turned Belle onto the road leading towards Todmorden. She'd always sensed that she and her step-daughter couldn't have been much closer: since losing Paul the lass had visited constantly. She'd also asked Isobel to stay with them at the farm.

Isobel had declined. She'd had a hard grounding in a family where generations discovered by degrees that their differences weren't confined to the years separating them. She treasured the relationship with Paul's daughter, and wouldn't have it jeopardised by changing things to accommodate her own unease.

And she needed to feel free to come and go at will, following intuition or inclination, as they prompted. If, like today, she ended up learning nothing, but becoming interested in what was going on locally, it was at least proof that she hadn't given up.

But was this the best she could do? Where was her spirit? Had it finally been hammered out of her?

She was older, of course – so much older that, these days, she no longer ran up the stairs. At times, getting up from a low chair required no small effort. And if limbs and joints were stiffening, what of her brain? Even before the shock of Paul's death! Where, too, was imagination?

Stifled long since, she reflected ruefully, when keeping

Bright's going had conflicted with dreams of the lady she one day might become, and with all the trappings of fancy clothes, and fine settings for grand occasions. Is there any way that I'm still the same person, she wondered.

She was nearing Mytholm where the swift-flowing Colden tumbles downhill to its confluence with the Calder. To her right she could see the newly-consecrated St James's church, and beyond it the steep road that emerges eventually over the tops not far short of Blackshaw Head.

Approaching St James's, Isobel felt impelled to go inside. Her churchgoing had dwindled during her marriage and she'd become a stranger in Heptonstall's church where as a girl she'd been a regular attender. Happen this had a lot to do with what was wrong with her.

She was tethering Belle to a tree beside the churchyard when some sound alerted her. Turning swiftly, she glimpsed a man flinging himself into the saddle before riding from the rear of Mytholm Hall. His manner suggested he'd good reason for quitting the area; his size, shape and the way he sat a horse told Isobel his identity.

'At last,' she gasped, struggling feverishly to loosen the reins which she'd just secured so carefully. Once mounted, she concentrated on scouring the hill above her for another glimpse of Roger Wheatley.

A distant flick of his riding crop, a brown gleam that was the flank of his horse, a flash of blue that was his coat. She had him in sight, but only just, and a grim ride ahead of her.

A little under half-way up the hillside Wheatley slackened his pace. His intention had been to distance himself from whatever he'd been about at Mytholm Hall, and he'd had no cause to notice her.

Shortening the distance between them, Isobel drew close enough to be assured that she'd correctly identified him. Encouraged, she tried to compel her mare to a sharper gallop. But the stir alerted Wheatley. She was so near to him that she could see when he dug cruel heels into the side of his stallion.

'Come on, come on,' she urged into her own horse's ear.

Struggling to oblige, Belle stumbled, bravely limped on, stumbled again.

'Oh, what have I done to you!' Distraught, Isobel patted the horse's steaming side, murmured soothingly, and dismounted.

Whatever the loss, she'd never harm her mare. Couldn't forgive herself now if she'd inadvertently hurt her. Thank heaven they were almost at the top of the hill.

And fortune was compensating for the mishap. She was just in time to see Roger Wheatley leading his mount to stables beside a stone cottage in the lee of a copse.

'I'll be back,' she murmured. 'I'll be back.'

But now she must ensure that her mare received attention. Fortunately, Wheatley's home was within walking distance, she needn't ride there another time.

The days were raw, winter was setting in. And each time Isobel visited the house where she had seen him the place was deserted. She always returned to Heptonstall exhausted by disappointment as much as exertion.

Charles had recently advised her against even attempting to speak with Roger Wheatley. If she was right about him, he had committed murder, mightn't hesitate to do so again. The warning hadn't prevented repeated excursions to watch that house.

'Why don't you use the carriage?' her sister-in-law suggested, when she met Isobel trudging towards the village one afternoon.

'I don't know, Phillie. I've not liked to since Paul died.' The landau was *his*, as was his coachman Hopwood, who now spent most of his time helping with jobs about the house and grounds.

'You're paying good brass to keep him there, you want to make use of the man and of yon carriage,' Phillida observed. 'I would.'

Isobel could believe that. What she could scarcely credit was her own unconcern about money being paid out to employ someone no longer required. Was her subconscious holding on to the man rather than accepting that Paul would never come home?

I won't get rid of Hopwood just before Christmas, she resolved, but afterwards I'll sell the carriage and suggest he finds other work.

Christmas was looming like a formidable boulder. Audrey and her husband had spoken of expecting that she would share their festivities but, whilst thanking them and agreeing, Isobel could feel no enthusiasm.

It wasn't that she and Paul had made a great deal of Christmas in the past; he'd usually brought documents home from the mill, and might have set them aside only for Christmas Day itself.

Catalina had written from Seville where she had preparations in hand for a family gathering in the Escutia home in the Barrio de Santa Cruz there. Both she and Henry would be delighted if Isobel would join them and prepare to stay on afterwards.

I'll come in the new year, Isobel promised. By then she would surely have caught Wheatley at his home.

20

On Christmas Eve Isobel set out one last time. There was snow underfoot and in the air, fine flakes that stung her cheeks as the wind whipped them towards her. But she soon didn't care at all about the weather, her first glimpse of the cottage near Mytholm showed smoke billowing from the chimney.

Roger opened the door to her knocking, recovered swiftly from his astonishment, and actually invited her inside.

'You found me then,' he observed wryly, and offered her a seat.

Ignoring the chair, Isobel nodded. 'I think you and I have unfinished business. If it weren't so, you'd not have run off that day at the Piece Hall.'

Grimly, he sighed. 'Paul brought death upon himself, you know,' he told her calmly. 'By conniving to trap us all. You knew, of course, what he was about?'

'I knew nothing of the kind!' Isobel exclaimed, badly shaken.

'Didn't you think it was significant the way we were all captured when you got away that night? Must have been more than coincidence.'

'I wasn't the only one, what about Jacob?'

'Because of his age, they were afeared he might die on them afore morning. But you, they let you run free . . .'

'You're not saying. . . ? You can't think Paul gave you away and bribed them not to take me!' Isobel was aghast. 'I swear I knew nowt about it.'

'Do you think I'll believe owt you say? You introduced him to us, in t'first place.'

'That I didn't! He was sitting among you all when I arrived, that night he first rode out with us.'

'Because you'd let him know the time and place, had told him to say he was a friend of yourn . . .'

Isobel swallowed. The details were irrelevant now. Whatever the true circumstances had been then, everything she had learned ever since suggested that Paul had lied, and lied repeatedly. To her.

'Two of our lads died in jail, did you know that? And it's not an experience that I'd suffer again. Shooting was too civilised after what he did.'

'There's no reason justifies taking life.'

He snorted. 'The mill owners were paying him, you know – a proper Judas he was. 'Cept that he weren't really betraying us, were he – he'd never been on our side. And you swallowed every word. And married him.'

Isobel stared steadily towards him. Roger wouldn't learn from her that Paul hadn't hesitated to employ a trick or two with his wife. Their marriage, in its final period, had not been bad; she reckoned that some compensation for the rest.

Wearily, he shook his head. 'I wish you hadn't come. I bear you no ill-will, Isobel. You should have kept away from here.'

She'd been too shattered by all she'd heard to have considered the danger she was in. Roger Wheatley had appeared so calm, almost like the man who'd befriended her years ago. Only now she realised he'd not let her get away to reach the constable, and have him arrested.

She knew already she was no match for his size. But his gun wasn't in evidence today. If she surprised him by leaving now, mid-conversation, she might make it to the copse outside.

'Any road, you're still trading, aren't you?' she said. 'I was glad you were managing to pick up the threads again when I saw you down at the Piece Hall. Who've you got weaving for you?'

Before he could answer, she'd done it, darted backwards for the door, found the catch and opened it.

'Isobel, no . . .' he yelled, and went to a cupboard near the hearth.

She was already hurtling towards the copse when the shot startled her. Snatching up her wide skirts, she continued running, but back towards the lane. Hearing the gunfire had convinced her she'd not have him trap her in among the trees.

Her own footprints in the snow covering were the only ones. She was likely to remain alone out here with him, and nobody within earshot to aid her.

Still Isobel ran on, not daring to look back, struggling up the incline towards the bend in the lane which might conceal her from him.

Snow had muffled the sound of hooves, denying her warning of the carriage blocking her way as it almost filled the road from one drystone wall to the other.

'Help me . . .' she cried. And recognised the coachman.

Charles was beside Hopwood. Springing down before the landau wheels stopped turning, he took hold of her and thrust her inside. 'You fool,' he snapped.

'It's Wheatley, and he's armed.'

'I heard,' he said grimly. 'So am I.'

Weak with relief, Isobel sank back into the carriage as Roger Wheatley came running towards them.

'Hold steady,' Charles cautioned Hopwood while he aimed.

The shot caught Wheatley's arm, sending his pistol to the ground.

'Leave it,' her brother commanded, and strode off to seize him. 'I'll see you in court,' he added, bundling him into the landau. 'If only for attacking my sister.'

Later that evening when the constable had borne Roger Wheatley away, Charles told her how he'd arrived at the house to insist that she spend Christmas with them.

'You should be grateful to your servants. Yon coachman especially. He'd watched all your comings and goings, concerned for your state of mind. That soon told me what you most likely were about. Our setting out in pursuit, you know.'

The following few days spent with Audrey and her husband felt unreal, suspended as they were between seeing Wheatley taken and his being brought before the magistrates.

321

Although she welcomed the quiet which might help her to recover, Isobel could think of nothing but the prospect of that courtroom and what it might reveal.

Phillida was there as well, teaching Audrey the basic principles of spinning, and pleased to spend time away from her own hearth. It was some while before Isobel emerged sufficiently from her preoccupation to notice how unusually cheerful her sister-in-law appeared. The reason eventually surfaced.

'You'd better let your brothers know afore long that I shan't be dwelling in that house of theirs much longer. I've got myself a position as housekeeper.'

'Have you, Phillie!' Isobel exclaimed. 'Ay, I am glad. It's best thing you could have done.'

'Aye, I reckon you're right,' Phillida agreed, a satisfied smile brightening her features. 'When it were put to me, I hadn't the heart to refuse. Not when Percival seemed that lost since his mother passed on, poor soul.'

Isobel's thankfulness that Phillida had finally organised some kind of future for herself was accompanied by a touch of secret amusement over the direction she was taking. But it was the only interlude in her own anxiety. For so long she had believed that locating Wheatley was all that was necessary. Now she realised that the truth would emerge in court, revealing before everyone her own involvement in the Luddite cause which had been illegal. Worst of all, though, was the prospect of having Paul's name blackened. Nobody, whatever their allegiance, would condone his deception. Had she been utterly misguided in her determination that her husband's murderers would face conviction?

Exhausted by stress, a part of her was longing to get away. She'd had to write to Henry and Catalina postponing her visit, but carefully not mentioning that being called as a witness would detain her in Yorkshire.

Catalina's eventual reply only added yet another worry.

You will do much better to delay, she wrote. *It is so quiet here while Henry and Jorge are away. With all the trouble there, Henry felt that he must go over to Oporto to give William assistance. He decided to take Jorge also, it being time that he received a grounding in the port aspect of the business.*

By waiting until they return here, you will have a far more agreeable stay; and so I look forward to seeing you at some date in the near future.

Isobel was alarmed. What could have happened in Oporto, what was this 'trouble'? Only after a time did she realise that at least the reference to William indicated that he was unharmed. She wished yet again that there were some means swifter than letters for contacting her family abroad.

Rain had poured for days from blackening skies which seemed more suited to England than to the mouth of the Douro. William heard from other merchants that upriver it was far worse, the rapids raged with the pressure of water. Snow that had fallen earlier on the mountains was melting, cascading down the terraces to swell the river.

The seriousness of the situation hit William when he awakened in the night. Even this far up the hill behind Oporto, distant cries and sounds of people hurrying reached him from near the Douro.

He ran downstairs, thrust his arms into a coat, opened the door. The road where they lived was steep, and exceptionally straight. He could see lanterns and other wavering lights somewhere about the quayside. As well as human consternation he detected the rush of water.

Returning indoors, he hastened upstairs to drag on pantaloons and shirt and find his boots. Rosalind awakened, he told her his fears and that he must investigate.

He passed people in the street, men and women with children complaining, roused from their beds to escape from their homes. Before he reached the waterfront he knew for certain the Douro was flooding.

Chill water was soon swirling about his ankles. At its brink he peered through the paling of early dawn. The flood carried splintered remains of *barcos rabelos*, garbage and household articles, broken wine barrels. The quay where he stood was stinking already from sewage.

As daylight increased Vila Nova de Gaia grew visible. William stared towards Fortescue's. Water was filling the roadway, swirling about the arches to something like two-fifths of the way up their frontage. He would have to find some way across, learn the extent of the destruction.

There was only one boat, the rush of water tugging it, stretching mooring ropes. Splashing and slithering, he staggered towards it. A small rowing craft, it had lost one oar already, was half-filled with water. But there was no other and the bridge was impassable.

The tiny craft sank lower as William stepped into its rocking hull, water swished over the crude seat. Saturated, he clamped numbed fingers over the oar. Driven by dread of what he'd find inside their lodge, William began paddling with that one oar against the current.

The small distance he made towards midstream was nothing to the yards he was being swept down river. He thought of the nearby harbour mouth, of the Atlantic beyond.

Happen he'd been a fool putting out into a river this swollen, but he couldn't have done nothing. He must cling on now, struggle. He wouldn't sacrifice Fortescue's – not when he'd spent the best part of his life learning the business! And although he felt he'd not endure another day's hardship, he hadn't brought them through all those years of war and then Oporto's seige, to surrender to this wretched water.

He was winning, at last – was closer to Vila Nova de Gaia than to Oporto. So long as he made it to that quayside, he'd get along there somehow, even through waist-high water. Trying to step from the boat turned it over, plunging him into the flood up to his smarting eyes. His old hatred of water returned. But he was only feet from a bollard used for mooring their barges. Will didn't know how to swim, but he managed a frenetic paddling.

Struggling across the Douro had depleted him. Trudging through several feet of water was so exhausting that only the familiarity of Fortescue's arches and doors prevented him going past.

Inside were some of the labourers whose job was stacking

the heavy pipes of port. And they were moving them now to the rear of the lodge then hauling them up above the level of the water.

'Thank God for that!' Will exclaimed, still gasping. 'I was afraid I might be t'only one that had seen what was happening.'

They had been watching the river since last evening. Some who had experienced previous floods hadn't needed instructions on how best to save the wine.

No one could tell him if the casks would have withstood the water, and what tests would prove that the port was uncontaminated and hadn't suffered by being disturbed. But for the moment such worries must go unanswered.

One of the men who lived nearby fetched William dry clothing and hot soup to warm him.

By the time the water began subsiding every dry space which could take a barrel had been utilised. The men started sweeping away the silt and William was planning a thorough cleaning.

If he'd had some means of contacting his brother he might have acted contrary to his inclinations and asked for assistance. His own workers would be stretched to the limits. And he needed to discuss how best to save what wine they could. This situation was bad enough, he had to prevent it becoming a catastrophe.

The Spanish newspapers carried the story of the flooding which aroused sympathy among all sherry shippers. Henry called Jorge into his office.

'We're going to Oporto by t'fastest means we can find. You'd best be ready with all you'll need for the journey and for a stay of at least a week. It's the whole company that's affected, I'll none leave our Will to struggle on his own with t'problems.'

Never had Henry received such a welcome from his brother. Differences they might have had in the past, but his arrival and bringing Jorge with him spoke of true concern.

Henry was shown the level that the flood water had reached and they both thanked God that there'd been no loss of life. William neglected to mention his own hazardous crossing of the Douro, but some of the workers told Henry the full story which had endeared him to them.

Although relieved to see Henry and Jorge, William was rather disturbed. He hadn't requested help, but they'd come very sharply! Did they suppose he was getting past running this place?

'I hope you won't take this amiss,' Henry began one day the following week. 'But I think it's time we considered making provision for t'future of Fortescue's. I'm willing to have our Jorge here spend time with you in Oporto – so's he can grasp the differences between producing port and sherry.'

William gave him a look, glanced towards Jorge whose expression revealed very little. The scheme made sense, of course. He and Henry were both getting on in years. If the time came that he had to hand over, he'd rather it was to a Bright. And Jorge was his son-in-law.

Very slowly, William began speaking. 'Aye, well – you're the nearest I'll ever have to a son of my own, Jorge. And I daresay you'll find your experience in Jerez will have stood you in good stead.'

Both Jorge and his father were beginning to smile, encouraging Will so that he spoke more positively. 'You've a good grounding in wine making, which is far more than either your father or me started off with. Do I take it you and our Jessica are willing to move to Oporto?'

Jorge nodded. 'She'll be delighted to be living near you.'

Neither William nor Henry were too certain about that. Jessica still seemed to form few strong attachments, even her relationship with her husband appeared self-centred. But she'd be happy to be in Oporto for a while, at least.

'I'm glad that's settled . . .'

'I'm glad that's settled . . .'

The brothers had spoken word for word in unison; they exchanged glances and laughed. For once in their lives they were in accord, the continuance of Fortescue's greater in importance than individual ambitions.

21

Arriving at the Assizes in York, Isobel thought it was going to be the worst day of her life. Seeing her husband lying shot had been devastating, today she was in for reliving all the circumstances. And she dreaded her own loyalties being misinterpreted during evidence which was bound to tell everyone what a deceiver Paul had been.

More than once she'd been tempted to forsake her determination to have Roger Wheatley tried. But even if she'd weakened Charles would have insisted they continue. When Wheatley was brought before the local magistrates she and her brother had been relieved that one Justice of the Peace there had been present originally when Wheatley and the others had been convicted as Luddites.

On first mention of suspicions that Roger and an accomplice had killed Paul for giving them away, the J.P. had snarled across the bench.

'You've not learned yet then, Wheatley, that nothing justifies your taking matters into your own hands!'

After that, ordering him brought before the Assize court had been only a formality. But Isobel had worried all along that her evidence might not be sufficient to prove anything. And Charles also had expressed doubts.

'If only you were a man – a gentleman's oath of suspicion can be enough to obtain a conviction.'

She couldn't have felt much more inadequate, and believing that Paul's dubious behaviour would be revealed outweighed her original intention of doing all this for *him*.

Wheatley's accomplice had been traced, though; and was standing trial with him. His name was James Marsden, Isobel didn't know him. It soon transpired that Roger Wheatley hadn't known him well enough for his own good either!

The jurymen entered and were sworn, and the court rose for the entry of the judge. Already overawed by the imposing atmosphere, Isobel felt increasingly uneasy.

The words were often long and unfamiliar, legal phrases combined to fog her brain and make her dread all the more the moment when she'd be obliged to witness against the two accused.

She would do so, of course, or she'd not have gone to these lengths, but Lord, how she longed to be spared the ordeal! Perturbed, and confused by Prosecuting Counsel's formal language, she noticed only that initially the charge was being made jointly, to both prisoners.

James Marsden sprang up, interrupted. 'It weren't me as fired. It were *his* duelling pistol. I've never handled arms.'

By the look he gave him, Wheatley betrayed himself. When the trial continued after Marsden was reproved for interrupting, it seemed to take a fresh direction. Isobel breathed more freely. The weapon which Charles had retrieved after Roger fired towards her had been identified as the one killing Paul.

Relieved of some tension, she now found following the case much easier. Just as Learned Counsel found it easy to heap the evidence against Roger Wheatley. He was the one who'd suffered imprisonment through the trap Paul had laid all those years ago for the Luddites. It was he, not Marsden, who had a motive for revenge.

Isobel almost felt sorry for Wheatley when the Counsel he'd paid to defend them both chose to concentrate on saving Marsden's neck.

And then suddenly Roger halted proceedings, startling them all, and making his guards close in to either side. Raising a hand as if to command that there be no interruptions, he stared straight towards Isobel.

'I change my plea – I'm guilty as charged. I don't regret removing the scum who'd betrayed us. But I do sincerely regret the suffering I've caused his family. And I never meant to hurt Mrs Copley when I fired, only to scare her.'

Isobel sank back, so shaken that she didn't immediately realise how this altered everything. The entire courtroom was astir, jurymen gazed from one to the other, lawyers consulted with their underlings, until finally they were called to order.

Even by the time that the jury had reached their verdict and Roger Wheatley was sentenced to be deported, she could still scarcely believe that she hadn't been required as a witness.

She wanted to thank Roger for his flash of consideration, but of course wasn't permitted to speak with him. She could only feel thankful that his sentence was deportation, not death. His accomplice would be going with him, though for a shorter period.

They were told the men had been transferred from the prison hulk to the ship sailing for Australia one week before she left for Jerez. And now the coast of Spain was in sight. Ignacio had been an ideal companion throughout the voyage. Attentive to his aunt, yet never stifling her with overt fussing. Isobel had needed to think. Though the trial had been brief, it had resurrected too many incidents where Paul had proved what a schemer he was, even with her.

Memory had revived regrets about her parents, as well: would she ever rest easy about the moment of her father's death? How was it that she'd never completely accepted her mother's?

Somehow, she must learn to let all three of them rest. She'd forgive Paul, if she couldn't quite forget. He'd been a willing provider, even too eager to have her depend on him financially. And without him she'd have lacked the share she had in Audrey.

Her step-daughter was a good wife and mother. And was prepared to include Isobel in her life. She felt surrounded by folk who cared. Catalina and Henry had done better than sending for her, hadn't they, despatching their eldest son to escort her all the way from Yorkshire.

Ignacio was a splendid man, much like his uncle Carlos, in ways as well as appearance. So handsome he was as close as any man to being beautiful, he was intelligent and amusing. He also possessed his father's interest in producing sherry.

Isobel smiled as he approached her now, striding towards the sheltered corner where she was sitting on deck.

'We shall be in Cadiz within the hour. All our belongings are to hand in my cabin, and I've organised assistance as we go ashore.'

'Thank you very much. What would I have done without you, Ignacio?'

Her nephew laughed, teased in her own dialect. 'Nay, Aunt Isobel, don't talk daft – you'll none have me believing you can't look after yoursen.'

She laughed with him as she rose. 'And when did you learn to talk proper English? All those years ago, growing up in t'West Riding?'

'Happen you'll tell me to have more respect . . .'

'Respect's for old folk,' Isobel exclaimed automatically as they walked together to the ship's rail. But then she sighed as she paused to reflect. For long enough now, she had been feeling old – drained by events and maybe needing something to stimulate her into keeping active far beyond fifty-five.

'You don't forget respect in a family headed by Grandmother Escutia!' Ignacio exclaimed.

'She's always been good to me, though. All your family have, especially your mother.'

'*Si, mi madre* is . . . in Grandmother's mould, yet far more flexible.'

Cadiz was gleaming in the sunlight as their vessel began sailing towards the harbour. But it wasn't the glare of pale buildings which brought the stinging to Isobel's eyes.

'It was fair grand of you to come and fetch me, I'll not forget.' she said, beaming at Ignacio, willing herself not to turn emotional.

Where had her independence gone, and where her planning of her own future?

Catalina was as elegant as ever, waiting beside the carriage on the quayside, then welcoming them both, lingering with her arms about Isobel until Ignacio shifted impatiently.

'Do you not think we should be on our way, *Madre*?'

'The young are so intolerant, do you not think?' Catalina

observed, but smiling affectionately in Ignacio's direction. 'We will speak later,' she assured Isobel. 'You know how deeply concerned we all are for you ever since Paul's tragic death.'

'I know.'

She hadn't thought she'd feel other than strange in Spain, it was such a long time since her last visit. But the sight of the undulating vineyards around Jerez and all its towers and domes sent excitement coursing through her veins. Briefly, she might have been the young girl who'd arrived for that long ago wedding.

'How's Henry – well, I hope?'

'He keeps reasonably active. He has some trouble from painful joints, but "There's nowt ails me" is his favourite saying.'

'Happen he's not so bad then.'

The bright Spanish light, though, revealed something unnoticed in England. When he came out to greet them at the *casa*, she saw that Henry's face, tanned by long years of intense sun, had been dried as well, bestowing a tracery of lines.

'You look better than I expected,' he remarked, hugging her.

Isobel grinned back at him. 'If I didn't already feel at home, that would ensure I did.'

'Nay, love – you know what I mean.'

'Aye, I do. You've all felt for me, in recent months, I know that. You must have wondered what sort of a state I'd be in.' She paused, glancing over her shoulder for Ignacio, but he was unloading baggage and carrying it through the courtyard into the house. 'Yon eldest of yours has looked after me a treat.'

'You'll not be needing a regular dosage of our best sherry then, for the good of your health? And Will handed over a pipe of a very fine port.'

'How was William? And how serious the flood damage?'

'We managed to save most of our stock. And Will's all right. Like me, though, he's getting on. We're planning that our Jorge will go over there, learn that side of things.

Ignacio's had a lot of experience beside me here in Jerez, and puts it to good effect. Having Jessica around Oporto somewhere should be good for William.'

'But he is happy, isn't he, with Rosalind?'

'I dare say he's happier than ever he was with Phillida.'

'I saw Phillie the other week. Just before we sailed.'

'Has she altered at all?'

'For the better, at last.' Isobel told him how Phillida was keeping house for the minister she favoured. While her brother led the way through the shady courtyard and into the house, she asked after Yolanda then remarked that he'd reared a grand family.

'That's Catalina's doing – you know how often we were separated when they were growing up.'

'What have I done now?' his wife inquired cheerfully, tossing aside her gloves as she came indoors.

'It was a compliment, you needn't stand on your dignity,' Henry told her with a grin. 'Your sister-in-law's approving our young 'uns.'

'Isobel always was too generous,' Catalina said, but she hugged her again all the same. 'It is good to have you here.'

'It's good to see you all again. And I can never count on Henry reaching Yorkshire!'

'Each time I travel to London, I plan to journey that much further, but . . .'

'You have not the sense to know that visiting Isobel would justify any distance,' a voice interrupted from the doorway behind them.

No one had told her Carlos would be here. Astonishment anchored her to the rug covering the marble tiling of the floor.

'Hallo, Carlos,' she managed, and extended a hand which already was moist and seemed, ridiculously, inclined to tremble.

'*Hola, buenas tardes,*' he greeted her, grasped the hand, and kissed her fingers.

She hadn't expected him here, but that was no excuse. Why was she, *on the wrong side of fifty*, experiencing this incomprehensible attraction? How could she, when he'd been made a stranger by the years, and with her husband but a few months in the grave?

Carlos recovered the more swiftly; if, indeed, he needed to recover. No doubt he was totally indifferent to her by this time, especially after what life had done to both of them.

It was much later, after the family meal, that Henry told her how Carlos had insisted on dining with them that evening.

'He's still as independent as ever; as a rule, only calls on us when Catalina chides him about never visiting. And he's only a mile or two away now, over the other side of the city.'

'Here in Jerez?' Why should that seem so unlikely, except that since goodness knows when Carlos had gone his own way.

'He looks very prosperous,' Isobel remarked, not wishing to appear too curious about what Carlos was doing, but prompting for the answer.

Henry didn't oblige. 'And why shouldn't he appear that way? It's not only us Brights that have a head for business.'

'I know that,' she said very quickly, and steered their conversation elsewhere.

'How is Catalina's mother, these days, she must be a fair age . . .'

Discussing Henry's mother-in-law didn't stop Isobel thinking about Carlos. He seemed to have lost the sharpness induced years ago when injury prevented him continuing in the bull-ring. He did still limp, but surely not so pronouncedly? And whatever his work now it appeared to have restored enthusiasm for living.

On the following day when Catalina took her to sip sherry with her mother, Carmen Escutia revealed the cause of his revitalisation.

'You have seen Carlos, I believe? Do you know that he is living in the hills close to Jerez? He is happy at last, breeding our lovely Andalusian horses.'

'So that's what he's doing! I hadn't heard.'

'He did not tell you? I am surprised. We hear of nothing else.'

'I don't think we talked very much.' Isobel hadn't noticed

that last evening, had been too overwhelmed by his being there. She felt perturbed now – had she made him uneasy? Or simply put off by her awkwardness so quickly induced by the surprise of seeing him?

In many ways Carmen Escutia had changed hardly at all. She still relished everyone focusing on her; even though her conversation was largely concerned with people Isobel didn't recall, there could be no wandering of attention.

'*Mi madre* has always approved of you,' Catalina confided afterwards. Smiling a little as she encouraged the horses drawing the carriage to canter, she continued: 'You clinched that the time we stayed with you. But I believe the way you took over from your father and kept Bright's running ensured her high regard long before then.'

'I thought you Spaniards expected women to be home-makers?'

Her sister-in-law laughed. 'For our own, *si*. But though Mother applauded my resigning from Fortescue's to bring up a family, I think she wished also my success in business.'

'And you yourself. . . ?'

Again Catalina laughed. 'Initially, I was reluctant to relinquish my position. But that is over forty years ago. If it were now, I might more readily give up work.'

'You've always had a good marriage. And thanks to you, mainly.'

'It was not easy, especially in the early years, when war over here meant that I spent so much time in England.'

'Aye – Yorkshire must seem inhospitably cold to folk as aren't born there.'

'Not its inhabitants, though, they are most warm-hearted. Except . . .' Abruptly, Catalina was silent.

Carlos arrived during the next morning, surprising them all by stating that he was only remaining at the house for a moment.

'I have come for one reason only,' he stated, gazing rather solemnly towards Isobel. 'I would like to take you to my stables.'

Catalina loaned Isobel her mare then stood at the entrance of the house waving as they rode away up the hill.

'Do you mind if we call in at the bodega?' Isobel asked him. 'I promised Henry he could show me around today.'

'So long as you delay only to defer your arrangements.' He had considered lengthily before deciding to invite her over, would not tolerate anything that interfered with his plans.

Henry came out into the sunblaze before the bodega, stood shielding his eyes against the contrast between the light there and the dimness of the interior.

'Tomorrow will serve just as well,' he told her, 'or even the next day.'

He and Catalina had been anxious lest Isobel should grow bored in Jerez, or even depressed, he welcomed this intervention by Carlos. But he couldn't resist detaining his sister a moment longer.

'There's something I must show you, though, before you're on your way . . .'

Isobel began to protest that it should wait. 'All right, but . . .'

Smiling, Henry took her by the arm and walked her backwards until they both were able to gaze up at the red tiled roof. 'See that. . . ?'

While they watched one long-legged bird rose from the nest then settled again, its mate stretched wide-spanning wings. 'The storks have come home to us this year – that means good fortune, you know, for Fortescue's.'

'How long have you been raising horses then?' Isobel asked Carlos when, at last, they were riding out of the city.

'For several years now. I am surprised that you did not hear.' Except that, knowing his sister and her husband, they would be cautious about mentioning his name, never knowing exactly what it was that had occurred between Isobel and himself all those years ago.

'The mare you have there is one of mine, not one of my best, I fear; but she suited Catalina.'

Isobel grinned. 'She suits me, an' all. But then I've never thought of myself as much of a horsewoman.'

'That is strange, I believed . . .'

'I certainly put myself to shame just before Christmas.

335

Belle, my mare, went lame, all through my fault. I was after somebody, you see . . .'

'After. . . ?' Carlos was puzzled.

'Chasing. Did they tell you that Paul was killed – murdered?'

Gravely, he nodded. '*Si*. I was greatly troubled for you.'

'I was positive it were some of them that got put in prison for being Luddites. Paul gave 'em away, I'm afraid. Any road, I set off after one of 'em. But he was a far better rider. It was rough and terribly steep. Wheatley got away that day.'

'But later you got him, brought him to justice.'

'Who told you about that?'

'Henry perhaps, or my sister.'

'I suppose they told you as well how I first became involved?' She'd never been certain how much any of the family had known.

'Riding out, risking your lives to try and prevent factories using more machinery.'

'You must think we were proper daft.'

'On the contrary . . .' Pausing, Carlos sighed. 'I do not like to think that you were in danger, but I am compelled to admire your courage.'

Isobel was moved. She'd been so shaken by finding that Paul opposed everything she'd set out to do. Then when he'd been killed by folk who'd harboured a grudge that long, she'd doubted if the Luddite cause justified any of it. Hadn't she wondered sometimes if she'd been right to stand up for the traditional weavers, for Bright's?

'Nay, I only did what I thought was best at the time. You're the courageous one – what about t'way you set out to challenge the French over near Grazelema?'

'You have never mentioned that when we've met.'

'I hadn't heard about it then.' And when she'd been told she'd felt deeply concerned for what *might* have happened to him. But still she'd done nothing to show how thankful she was that he had survived. Had she always been this confused, this ineffectual, where Carlos was concerned? Had it been so easy to let life come between them? Was it too late to begin catching up?

'I vowed at the time to go back there, but I never have returned.' Impulsively, he glanced sideways. 'Would you like to accompany me?'

'Into the mountains? Aye – I think I would. Why not?'

Carlos laughed. At first, afraid that he was amused by her Yorkshire talk, Isobel gave him a look. She needn't have worried. His laugh was utterly delighted.

'I hope you don't mean today, though,' she added.

He grinned back at her. 'No – we must make preparations. It is quite some distance.'

'And our Henry would be disturbed if I just disappeared!'

She felt so different already here in Spain. So warmed by everyone's concern, restored by their peace and order.

They had reached the place which Carlos referred to as his stables. Coming upon it as the track rounded the foot of a low hill, she was confronted with its immense size without having opportunity to grasp that his interpretation of a 'stables' embraced far more than her own.

The land on which innumerable horses wandered, grazing, extended on all sides to the horizon. Some areas were fenced, providing security while horses were broken, and then there were blocks of actual stabling.

Adjacent to them was the *casa*, single-storeyed, white-painted in the Andalusian style, and formed of two wings constructed at right angles to each other. The budding stems of bougainvillaea softened the regular lines of the arched veran-dah, and in May the blue-mauve of his jacaranda trees beyond the house would cascade blossom towards the red tiled roofs.

'My word, but that's lovely! Did you have it specially built?'

Carlos smiled again. 'Rebuilt – it all was in ruins when I first came here. I am afraid nowhere else that I examined satisfied me.'

'I can believe that. If this is what you had in mind, there couldn't be anywhere else as nice.'

'I am gratified that you approve.'

He took the reins from her hand but when she made to dismount, he shook his head. 'We shall walk the horses around whilst I show you everything.'

337

Isobel soon understood the wisdom of that choice. Although the place had looked extensive, only by exploring it all could she begin to comprehend just how large it was. The equipment, too, was of the highest quality; you didn't need to know much about horses, tackle and stabling to understand that only the best would serve Carlos Escutia.

It was, though, the house which most impressed her.

'Do you really live here on your own?' she inquired as he led the way in through a tiled court fragrant with green-leafed plants.

'At present, yes,' Carlos replied tersely.

Isobel coloured, sensing that she had perhaps seemed over-inquisitive about his existence here.

'Unless you count a housekeeper, and a manservant,' he added.

Isobel still felt that he was keeping from her some detail of his intimate life.

The housekeeper appeared before the awkwardness grew prolonged, and led Isobel away to refresh herself before luncheon.

Carlos still seemed a little constrained when Isobel rejoined him, making her wish that she hadn't lost the ease of her youth when she'd felt so free in his company. But whatever had changed, wasn't she the one who'd altered everything by marrying?

He was an attentive host, though, and an interesting one. No dish arrived at their table overlooking the patio without his explaining its constituents. And any pauses were filled with his description of his life raising horses.

The wine they had drunk made her feel sleepy, suddenly so relaxed that it was impossible to credit that there'd so recently been any constraint between them. If this was the effect of wine, happen she could allow that her father might have needed its help. Briefly, she closed her eyes and opened them to find the other chair unoccupied.

The strains of a piano drifted to her from the next room, linked with this by glass doors. Glancing through the panes, she saw it was Carlos playing. The melody was new to her but pleasing, and drew away old cares. The second piece she recognised, smiling to herself.

Mendelssohn had revised parts of 'The Hebrides' overture, dissatisfied by his own interpretation of Fingal's Cave. This was his final version, completed a year or two ago, so evocative of the rocky coastline and its cave that a shiver traversed her spine.

She hadn't known Carlos was musically inclined, but then what did she know about him?

He had aged gracefully, she decided on the day they set out to ride into the mountains. He still sat a horse with all the flair of his youth, and the maturity sketching white streaks into hair that was nearer black than brown had also bestowed an enviable calm.

Several times during their journey, she wished she possessed the quiet spirit which, so evidently, reigned within him. Even when his mount stumbled in the steep streets of Arcos, casting a shoe and causing a delay, Carlos merely smiled.

Waiting for the shoeing to be completed, he took her to the rim of the precipice on which Arcos was constructed, continued to smile when Isobel remarked on the view.

'Your brother halted on this same spot – years ago, when pursuing me.'

'Henry pursued you?' she asked disbelievingly.

'You're the only one I've ever told. I believe *Madre* goaded him into doing so. She never could stand not knowing my intentions. Henry had a lot of courage, though, followed me right to our present destination in the mountains.'

'Is it very remote there?'

'You shall see,' he promised.

He would take good care of her, though, had sent someone ahead to arrange accommodation for them in a wayside village.

The food was plain but plentiful, the beds hard but welcome enough after hours in the saddle. Since before leaving Jerez, Carlos had discarded the last strands of unease with her. He talked a great deal, mostly about the expedition to this area in Napoleon's time, but occasionally of his life and his horses. Never once did he speak of Paul, of her life.

Grazelema was another village on a promontory, but with more barren countryside in its environs, more impressive mountains than any she'd seen in Spain so far. There were flowers, as well, just a springtime sprinkling, witness to the summer multitudes which would transform the slopes with their innumerable shades. The contrast between these few sturdy blooms and the rugged grandeur seemed symbolic of this interlude in her otherwise dour world.

On the homeward journey even Carlos appeared subdued, speaking less, and when he did converse it was on more sober subjects. As before, they slept a night in the plain little house. All Isobel could think of was their eventual parting. That would resemble another dying.

It was early when she awakened. The dawn was no more than a promise of light appearing as a thin band outlining the craggy mountain. Aware that sleep wouldn't return, she dressed and went out quietly so she wouldn't disturb their hosts.

Carlos was awake before her, startling her by being a dark shape which moved away from the blur of a group of bare trees.

'You're troubled,' he said, and drew her against him.

Minutes passed with neither speech between them nor any movement, until his kiss which traced her hairline.

Their lips met and held, an echo of arms that locked them closer in an embrace unmeasured by time.

She did not question his leading her indoors to his room, made no attempt to check his hands as they found her gown's fastening.

Together, they reached the simple bed, smiled half in amusement as it creaked with the weight of their bodies.

His touch was as she'd remembered, though less hasty, tuning her to supply their needs but with his urgency contained. Was it the mountain quiet made their loving so leisurely and complete, or was it a maturity that she'd never experienced with anyone?

340

Carlos was quieter still as they continued the ride to Jerez, and Isobel said little, afraid now that she had altered beyond recognition in his estimation. And she was saturated by dread; acutely aware that her stay in Andalusia was so transitory, that the real life awaited her in Yorkshire.

The evening sky had darkened to cobalt when they encouraged their tired horses the last mile towards his home.

Lanterns illuminated the area about the stables, lamps set by his housekeeper warmed their path to the open door and the windows to its side.

I feel as if I'm coming home, thought Isobel, and wished to God that she were.

The fault was her own. She'd always done the wrong thing where Carlos was concerned. It couldn't be any more right that she'd let him love her today than it was in that other lifetime. Sharing their physical need could feel wonderful and still be so wrong for them.

If only by her devotion to her father and to Bright's, she had starved their original relationship, denying Carlos the bridge back to her which might have straddled his determined independence. He couldn't be blamed for the aeons of non-communication. And she had chosen to marry Paul, she reflected yet again.

Carlos checked her with a firm hand as soon as they dismounted. Strong, dark eyes scoured her face.

'Horses,' he said, 'do you like them at all? You seem to have cared that your mare was injured. Could you learn to like them enough to – to – one day, when you're over your loss, to come out here to me?'

Isobel felt her grin developing. When she spoke it was all in a rush. 'I loved the packhorses first of all. Down at Halifax Piece Hall. I was nobbut a bit of a lass then, I couldn't accept that they had to be so overburdened.'

He was stroking her hair, holding her to him.

'You are a Yorkshirewoman, Isobel, you must consider that. Your home is there, could you bear to be uprooted?'

All she'd been thinking was that she couldn't bear to leave this place, to leave this man. 'It's not been a real home.

Happen I've never really had one since that time my mother left Father.'

He cleared his throat. He still held her, gentle fingers continued caressing her hair.

'If you need to go away, I will understand. You need time, anyway, to – to free yourself. I shall be here, Isobel, this is where I belong. And I shall be waiting.'

'I'll have to sell the house. And I shan't be sorry.' She'd made all the choices that had given her the life she'd had in the past. Suddenly, she recalled what her mother had said. *It won't be all roses, when the thorns prick remember nobody forced you into it.*

And now Carlos had released her. Though she'd return to Yorkshire, there would be nothing to hold her there, nothing to keep her from him.

It was high time she told him all she was feeling. Thank goodness advancing years made you see the sense in speaking up.

'Nothing will keep me away. I love you, Carlos, I always have. More than anyone. More than any.'

KAY STEPHENS
WEST RIDING

An absorbing saga of love and ambition in the Yorkshire hills

Rhona Hebden is the daughter of a mill owner in the West Riding of Yorkshire, a girl whose pretty heart-shaped face and tumble of auburn hair disguise a strength of will and character that surprises even herself. When she inherits shares in Bridge House Mill from her late father, she leaves her home in the familiar row of back-to-back houses in Halfield town and determines to break through the Depression years of the 1930s to make the knitting pattern and yarn business a going concern.

When civil engineer Wolf Richardson announces a plan to flood the beautiful Halfield valley in order to create a reservoir, Rhona's Yorkshire pride comes to the fore and she sets out to thwart his scheme. But Wolf is a hard man to win over and Rhona finds that she has more than met her match. Moreover, she realises that she is disturbingly attracted by his dark, brooding looks and fiery ambition. Then the war intervenes, bringing unpredictable tragedies, and Rhona is swept up by the effort to fight and survive. During a weekend leave, she hastily marries an old childhood friend, only to find herself longing once more for Wolf. Whilst battling against the heartbreaks of war, Rhona discovers that her greatest struggle is that of her own conflicting emotions and the desire to give up all for love.

Full of passion and ambition, WEST RIDING is an absorbing novel rich in emotion and infused with the spirit of the rugged Yorkshire countryside.

'A nicely crafted love story' *Yorkshire Evening Post*

FICTION/SAGA   0 7472 3330 6

EVELYN HOOD
—— THE ——
DAMASK DAYS

A captivating saga of Paisley weaving

Christian Knox is a girl who dreams – of a life beyond that of a Paisley housewife, of a world of learning beyond her Ladies' School, of possibilities her father dismisses as 'daft ideas'. But Christian is determined and when her father refuses to finance her education further she resolves to pay for it herself, by working as a tambourer, embroidering freelance for the local textile manufacturers.

Before long she's managing a group of tambouring women on behalf of Paisley's biggest weavers, and chief amongst her clients is Angus Fraser, a man old enough to be her father but wise enough to appreciate her talents. Plunged into the fascinating world of Scotland's fledgling textile industry Christian soon finds her combination of Lowland resolve and female flair begins to make its mark. And, in the shape of her greatest, most fought-for inspiration, the Paisley Shawl, it is a mark that will be remembered for generations to come . . .

'Reminds me of Catherine Cookson' *Glasgow Evening Times*

Also by Evelyn Hood (writing as Louise James) from Headline

Gold Round the Edges
'Bold and compassionate' *Liverpool Daily Post*

The Promise Box
'Can't put it down' *Glasgow Evening Times*

FICTION/SAGA   0 7472 3501 5

A selection of bestsellers
from Headline

FICTION

RINGS	Ruth Walker	£4.99 □
THERE IS A SEASON	Elizabeth Murphy	£4.99 □
THE COVENANT OF THE FLAME	David Morrell	£4.99 □
THE SUMMER OF THE DANES	Ellis Peters	£6.99 □
DIAMOND HARD	Andrew MacAllan	£4.99 □
FLOWERS IN THE BLOOD	Gay Courter	£4.99 □
A PRIDE OF SISTERS	Evelyn Hood	£4.99 □
A PROFESSIONAL WOMAN	Tessa Barclay	£4.99 □
ONE RAINY NIGHT	Richard Laymon	£4.99 □
SUMMER OF NIGHT	Dan Simmons	£4.99 □

NON-FICTION

MEMORIES OF GASCONY	Pierre Koffmann	£6.99 □
THE JOY OF SPORT		£4.99 □
THE UFO ENCYCLOPEDIA	John Spencer	£6.99 □

SCIENCE FICTION AND FANTASY

THE OTHER SINBAD	Craig Shaw Gardner	£4.50 □
OTHERSYDE	J Michael Straczynski	£4.99 □
THE BOY FROM THE BURREN	Sheila Gilluly	£4.99 □
FELIMID'S HOMECOMING: Bard V	Keith Taylor	£3.99 □

All Headline books are available at your local bookshop or newsagent, or can be ordered direct from the publisher. Just tick the titles you want and fill in the form below. Prices and availability subject to change without notice.

Headline Book Publishing PLC, Cash Sales Department, PO Box 11, Falmouth, Cornwall, TR10 9EN, England.

Please enclose a cheque or postal order to the value of the cover price and allow the following for postage and packing:
UK & BFPO: £1.00 for the first book, 50p for the second book and 30p for each additional book ordered up to a maximum charge of £3.00
OVERSEAS & EIRE: £2.00 for the first book, £1.00 for the second book and 50p for each additional book.

Name ....

Address ....

....

....